THE MIRACLES OF THE NAMIYA GENERAL STORE

KEIGO HIGASHINO

TRANSLATED BY SAM BETT

YEN ON

NEW YORK

THE MIRACLES OF THE NAMIYA GENERAL STORE

KEIGO HIGASHINO

Translation by Sam Bett
Cover art by CoMix Wave Films Inc.

©Keigo Higashino 2012, 2014
First published in Japan in 2016 by KADOKAWA CORPORATION, Tokyo.
English translation rights arranged with KADOKAWA CORPORATION, Tokyo through TUTTLE-MORI AGENCY, INC., Tokyo and CHANDLER CRAWFORD AGENCY INC., Massachusetts.

English translation © 2019 by Yen Press, LLC

Yen On
150 West 30th Street, 19th Floor
New York, NY 10001

Visit us at yenpress.com
facebook.com/yenpress
twitter.com/yenpress
yenpress.tumblr.com
instagram.com/yenpress

First Yen On Edition: September 2019

Yen On is an imprint of Yen Press, LLC.
The Yen On name and logo are trademarks of Yen Press, LLC.

Library of Congress Cataloging-in-Publication Data
Names: Higashino, Keigo, 1958- author. | Bett, Sam, 1986- translator.
Title: The miracles of the Namiya General Store / Keigo Higashino ; [translation by Sam Bett]
Other titles: Namiya zakkaten no kiseki. English
Description: New York, NY : Yen ON, [2019]
Identifiers: LCCN 2019023608 | ISBN 9781975382575 (hardcover) | ISBN 9781975382582 (ebook)
Classification: LCC PL852.I3625 N3613 2019 | DDC 895.63/6—dc23
LC record available at https://lccn.loc.gov/2019023608

ISBNs: 978-1-9753-8257-5 (hardcover)
       978-1-9753-8258-2 (ebook)

10 9 8 7 6 5 4 3 2 1

LSC-C

Printed in the United States of America

Table of Contents

Chapter 1

Answers in the Milk Crate

1

Shota was the one who suggested the "handy shack."

"A handy shack? What the hell are you talking about?" Atsuya towered over Shota, looking down at his petite frame and boyish face.

"It's handy. You know, convenient, the perfect place for us to lie low? I stumbled on it when I came by to scope things out. Had no idea we'd actually have to use it, though."

"Sorry, guys." Kohei shrank back, hunching his large body, and cast a longing look at the worn-out Toyota Crown parked beside them. "I didn't think the battery would die on us *here*, of all places. Not in my wildest dreams."

Atsuya sighed. "No use thinking about that now."

"Seriously, I don't know why. I mean, there weren't any warning signs when we were on the road. It's not like we left the lights on or anything."

"It was her time to go," Shota said dismissively. "You saw the mileage. Well over a hundred thousand miles. This thing's like a senile old woman. She was on her last legs when we found her, and the trip out here was more than she could take. We should have stolen a newer car if we were gonna steal at all. Just like I told you."

Kohei groaned, crossing his arms. "But new cars have all those alarms."

"Enough already." Atsuya waved him off. "Shota, is this abandoned house or whatever close by?"

Shota cocked his head to the side. "If we hustle, twenty minutes?"

"All right, let's get moving, then. Lead the way."

"I'm down, but what about the car? Are we okay just leaving it here?"

Atsuya looked around. They were in a monthly parking lot in the middle of a residential neighborhood. They'd found an empty spot to park, but the real permit holder was bound to call the cops as soon as they noticed it occupying their space.

"It's definitely not *okay*, but it's not like we can move it. You guys haven't touched anything, right? As long as we didn't leave any prints, there's no way they can trace us to the car."

"Meaning we're crossing our fingers."

"Like I just said, we don't have a choice."

"Just checking. Okay, follow me."

Shota bounced off ahead, leaving Atsuya no choice but to follow. The bag in his right hand weighed him down.

Kohei caught up with them. "Hey, Atsuya, what if we grabbed a cab? There's a busy street up ahead. I bet there'll be a bunch of them there."

Atsuya snorted. "If three shady dudes hail a cab in this part of town at this hour, the driver's gonna remember us. The second they release a sketch of us, we're done."

"You think the driver's even gonna get a good look at us?"

"What if he's a nosy one? What if he's one of those guys with a photographic memory?"

Kohei was silent for a few steps before conceding meekly. "Sorry."

"Drop it. Shut up and walk."

They continued to walk through the neighborhood, high above the rest of the town. It was past two in the morning. The houses were clustered together, all modeled after the same design. Almost all the lights were off, but they couldn't afford to let their guard down. If someone overheard them carrying on, they might call the cops about some seedy guys messing around in the middle of the night. Atsuya wanted the police to think they'd driven away from the scene—assuming the stolen Crown would go unnoticed for the time being.

The road started off on a gentle slope, but as they walked, the incline grew steeper, and the houses began to thin out.

"Hey, how far we going?" Kohei asked between ragged inhalations.

Shota told them it was only a little farther.

It wasn't much longer before he came to a halt in front of the only house in sight—a traditional Japanese home with a store on the ground floor. It was a decent size, and its living quarters were constructed out of wood.

The shutter was barely ten feet wide and pulled all the way down. Other than a mail slot, there wasn't anything else on it. Next to the house was a small storage shed. From the looks of it, it was once used as a garage.

"Is this the place?" Atsuya asked.

"Um." Shota squinted at the house and tilted his head. "I thought it was."

"*Was*? What the hell does that mean? Isn't this it?"

"Yeah, I think we're good. It's just that the last time I came, it felt different. Like, I could have sworn it was a little newer or something."

"You came during the day, right? That's probably why."

"Yeah. Maybe."

Atsuya took a flashlight from his bag and aimed it at the shutter. Above it was a sign. He strained his eyes and barely made out the part that read GENERAL STORE. There was more, but the characters were indecipherable.

"A general store? Who's gonna come all the way out here to shop?"

"Nobody," said Shota. "That's why they're out of business."

"Right. And? How do we get in?"

"There's a door out back. The lock's busted. This way."

Shota led them down a narrow passage between the house and the shed, no more than three feet wide. As he slipped through it, he looked up at the sky. The full moon was right overhead.

As promised, they reached a door. Fixed to the wall next to it was a small wooden box.

"What's this?" muttered Kohei.

"Seriously? You've never seen one of these before?" Atsuya asked. "It's a milk crate. For deliveries."

"Huh." Kohei stared at the box with fascination.

They opened the door and stepped inside. The place smelled stale and dusty, but it wasn't too bad. They were in a mudroom beside a banged-up washing machine flaked with rust—broken, no doubt.

On a stone block that led into the house, there was a single pair of grimy house slippers. The three of them tried their best to avoid contact with the slippers and stepped inside without removing their shoes.

They found themselves in a kitchen with hardwood floors. A sink and a gas stove had been installed by the windows, and on the adjoining wall was a two-door fridge. A table and chairs occupied the middle of the room.

Kohei opened the fridge. "Damn, there's nothing here."

"Obviously," Atsuya snapped. "What were you gonna do if there was? Chow down?"

"I'm just saying… It's empty."

The room next to it was floored with tatami mats, where the owners had left behind a dresser and a Buddhist altar. Square cushions were stacked in the corner. The room had a closet, but no one rushed to open it.

Just beyond that room was the store. Atsuya peered in through the doorway with his flashlight. The shelves were still stocked with stationery, kitchenware, and cleaning products, though in short supply.

"Bingo!" exclaimed Shota, rummaging through the drawers of the altar. "Candles. We've got us some light."

He lit a few of them with a lighter and set them up around the house until the place was bright enough for Atsuya to click his flashlight off.

"Whew!" Kohei plopped down cross-legged on the floor. "Now all we gotta do is stick it out till morning."

Atsuya pulled out his cellphone and checked the time. A little after half past two.

"Hey, look what I found." Shota yanked something out from the bottom drawer of the altar. It looked like an old weekly magazine.

"Gimme that." Atsuya took the magazine from Shota and dusted off the cover. A photograph of a young woman smiled back at him. He could have sworn he'd seen her face before.

Then it suddenly hit him: He'd seen her on TV, playing the role of a mother in a few different dramas. By now she had to be in her midsixties at least.

He checked the date on the cover: It was over forty years ago. When he read it aloud, his two friends went bug-eyed.

"Man, I wonder what things were like back then," said Shota.

Atsuya flipped through the pages. The content wasn't too different from a weekly magazine today. "'Supermarkets Ransacked for Toilet Paper and Detergent.' Huh. I think I heard about this somewhere."

"Oh yeah, I know about that," Kohei remarked. "That must've been during the oil crisis."

Atsuya flipped back to the table of contents, then jumped straight to the pin-up page, but it wasn't the type of centerfold he'd hoped for. No nude shots or idols. He snapped it shut.

"How long has it been since someone lived here?" He stuffed it back into the drawer and took another look around the room. "They've got merchandise out there on the shelves, and they left behind the big appliances. Seems like they moved out in a hurry."

"Fly-by-night," concluded Shota. "No question. Their customers stopped coming, but the debt kept pilin' up. One night, they packed their bags and split. Game over."

"Yeah, maybe."

"I'm hungry," Kohei whined. "I wonder if there's a convenience store around here."

"Even if there is," Atsuya told him with a hard glare, "you're not going. We're stuck here until morning. Go to sleep, and it'll be over quick."

Kohei hung his head and hugged his knees. "But I can't fall asleep when I'm this hungry."

"Yeah, and who wants to cozy up in this grimy mess?" asked Shota. "We could at least find something to sleep on."

"Hold on a sec." Atsuya got to his feet and stepped into the storefront with his flashlight. He walked up and down the aisles, beaming the light along the shelves, trying to find a roll of plastic or a tarp.

Eventually, he came across a tube of the paper used for shoji doors. Anything would be better than sleeping in the dust. Just as he reached out to grab it, something clinked behind him.

He spun around just in time to see a white object slide into a cardboard box set against the shutter. He flashed the light at it. It was an envelope.

His pulse started pounding in his ears. There was no way any mail was being dropped off at this abandoned house, especially at this hour. Meaning someone knew they were here—and had something to tell them.

Atsuya drew a deep breath and poked open the flap of the mail slot to have a look out front. He fully braced himself to find the place swarming with police cars, but to his surprise, it was dark out. No sign of anybody.

With some relief, he grabbed the envelope. The front was blank, but the back was signed *Moon Rabbit* in bubbly script.

He took the envelope with him to the tatami room. When he showed the others the strange signature, they went pale.

"What the hell is that?" asked Shota. "Please tell me that was here when we got here."

"Someone just pushed it through the mail slot. I saw it. Look at this envelope. Paper's new, right? If it'd been sitting around, it would have been covered in dust, just like everything else in here."

Kohei cowered, trying to make his husky frame as small as possible. "I bet it was the cops…"

"That's what I thought, too, but I dunno. They don't have the time to play games."

"Yeah," said Shota. "And they'd never sign a letter 'Moon Rabbit.'"

"Then who would?" Kohei frowned. His dark eyes were uneasy.

Atsuya scrutinized the envelope. He could feel how thick its contents were. If this was a letter, it had to be a long one. What could the sender possibly have to say?

"Yeah, nope," he concluded, shaking his head. "This can't be for us."

His friends regarded him with disbelief.

"Come on, think about it. How long has it been since we got here? I could understand a quick note, but writing this would take at least half an hour."

"Makes sense," said Shota, "when you put it that way. Except it might not be a letter."

"True." Atsuya looked over the envelope again. It was sealed tight. He squeezed at the glued paper with both thumbs.

"Hey! What are you doing?"

"Opening it. That'll set things straight real quick."

"But it's not for us," protested Kohei. "We can't just do that."

"Well, what else are we supposed to do? It's not addressed to anyone."

Atsuya tore open the seal. With his gloves still on, he shoved a finger in and pulled out a sheaf of papers, the pages crammed with handwriting in blue ink. It started, *Please excuse my sudden request.*

"What the…?"

Atsuya began reading, with Shota and Kohei following along over his shoulder.

It was a very peculiar letter indeed.

> *Please excuse my sudden request. For the purposes of this letter, I'll go by Moon Rabbit. I'm a woman, but I can't give you my real name. I hope you'll forgive me. I have my reasons.*
>
> *I'm an athlete, but I'd rather not give you the specifics. I hate to brag, but I rank highly in my field, and I'm in the running to represent Japan in the Olympics next year. If I told you the event, you'd be able to narrow things down, since there aren't that many of us. But I need to mention the Olympics or else I wouldn't be able to fully explain my predicament. I hope you'll understand.*
>
> *There's a man in my life. A man I love, who understands and supports me more than anyone else. He's my biggest fan, and he wants me to compete in the Olympics from the bottom of his heart. He's even gone so far as to say he'd be willing to make any sacrifice to see it happen. I can't even count the number of times he's helped me, both physically and psychologically. To be honest, he's the real reason I've been able to make it this far. I've pushed through my most grueling training sessions for him. In fact, I've started seeing the Olympics*

less as a personal goal and more as a way of showing my gratitude to him for everything he's done.

But then, we found ourselves in the middle of a nightmare. My boyfriend suddenly collapsed, and when the doctor told me his diagnosis, the entire room went black. He has cancer.

The doctor confessed to me that there was almost no chance of recovery and that he had six months to live. No one has told him what's happening, but I suspect he knows.

My boyfriend tells me not to pay him any mind but to stick with it, push ahead, and smash the competition. He's right. This is a really important time for me. I've already made plans for all kinds of training, both here and abroad. I need to go all out to get picked for the Olympics. I know this in my mind.

But there's another part of me, separate from my identity as an athlete, that wishes to be with him. That part of me wants to forget all about the training, stay by his side, and tend to his needs. To tell you the truth, I've brought up the idea of dropping out before, but he looked so dejected that just writing about it here makes me want to cry. He begged, "Don't say that. You have to make it to the Olympics. Don't take that away from me. I won't die until I get to see you there. That's my only wish." He made me promise to keep going.

I haven't told anyone the specifics of his illness. We're planning to get married once the games are over, but neither of our families knows yet.

I'm really at a loss for what to do. I've just been going through the motions. If I try to practice, I can't focus. I obviously don't perform well. I keep coming back to the idea that I may as well quit training altogether, but when I imagine the pain it will bring him, I know I could never go through with it.

As I was struggling on my own with these thoughts, I heard some rumors going around about the Namiya General Store. I know my chances are slim, but I'm writing on the off chance that you might be able to help me figure things out.

I've enclosed an envelope for your response. Please help me if you can.

—Moon Rabbit

2

Upon finishing the letter, the three guys looked at one another.

"What the hell?" The first to speak was Shota. "Why'd she chuck *this* in the mail slot?"

"She doesn't know what to do," offered Kohei. "Says so right there."

"I can read," Shota said. "What I wanna know is what would possess her to write a letter asking for advice to a general store? An abandoned store, at that."

"Don't look at me. I don't have the answers."

"I'm not asking you, just thinking out loud. I mean, come on, what the hell?"

Atsuya stayed out of their conversation as he peeked inside the envelope. There was a return envelope folded up inside, with *Moon Rabbit* written in black marker in place of an address.

"What's this all about?" he finally asked. "I don't think this is some elaborate joke. She's actually asking for help. For a pretty serious problem, too."

"She probably got the wrong store," Shota guessed. "I bet there's another one that gives out advice, and she mixed up their names. Yeah, that's my guess."

Atsuya grabbed the flashlight and stood up. "I'll go check."

He went out through the back door and around to the front of the store, where he lit up the dirty sign.

He squinted. The chipped paint made the characters hard to read, but he was fairly certain it said NAMIYA in front of the words GENERAL STORE.

Back inside, he told the others.

"Guess she was right." Shota shook his head. "But why would you expect a response from some deserted shop?"

"Maybe she got the wrong Namiya," postulated Kohei. "Maybe the right Namiya is somewhere else, but since the names are the same, she came here by mistake."

"No way. You can barely read that sign. She had to know what she was looking for. Hey, wait a second." Atsuya picked up the magazine again. "I feel like I just saw this somewhere."

"Saw what?" asked Shota.

"The name Namiya. I think it was somewhere in here."

"Huh?"

Atsuya flipped to the table of contents and skimmed the page. He found the spot in no time: "The General Store That Answers Your Woes."

"It's a pun," he said. "Namiya and *nayami*, the Japanese word for problems, woes, whatever."

He opened to the page.

This neighborhood store has developed a reputation for being fully stocked with answers to life's toughest questions.

If you come by the Namiya General Store in XX city after hours and slip a letter through the mail slot in their shutter, an answer will be waiting for you in the milk crate around back in the morning.

The owner, Yuji Namiya, a cheerful man of seventy-two, gave us the backstory:

"It started off as a joke with some neighborhood kids. They kept mispronouncing the store name, 'nayami, nayami,' as in 'problems, problems.' There's a line on my sign that says, 'Need to Place an Order? Inquire Within.' So these kids started coming by and asking, 'Hey, Gramps, can we inquire about some of our problems?' I said, "Sure. Ask me anything." And what do you know, they actually started coming by with questions.

"At first, they were fooling around. 'How can I get straight As without studying?' and other stuff like that. But when I took their questions seriously and tried coming up with actual solutions, the questions got more and more personal. 'How come Mom and Dad never stop fighting?' That sorta thing. For the sake of their privacy, I decided to have them drop their questions through the mail slot and pick up my answers in the milk bin. That's when adults started leaving letters, too. I don't know why anyone would want advice from some boring old geezer like me, but I do my best to think each problem through and come up with an appropriate solution."

When asked what kind of questions he gets the most, Namiya said romance is the most popular topic.

"But for me, they're the hardest ones to answer." Maybe that makes the whole process a problem of its own.

The article included a small photograph, an interior shot of the shop. A small old man was standing in the foreground.

"This magazine wasn't left behind on accident. They saved it 'cause they're in it. But—I'm surprised," Atsuya whispered. "A general store that gives advice? And people are still coming here with questions? I mean, it's been forty years." He looked at the letter from Moon Rabbit.

Shota picked up the pages. "She says she heard the rumors about the Namiya General Store. Sounds like she only found out recently. In which case, it's still a thing."

Atsuya crossed his arms. "Yeah, I guess so. Hard to believe."

"She must have heard about it from some old fart who's going senile," ventured Kohei. "Someone who has no idea what happened to the store but told this Moon Rabbit to come here for advice."

"Nah, no way. Even if that was the case, she'd realize something was up the second she saw the place. It's obvious the building has been abandoned for years."

"All right, then Moon Rabbit's the crazy one. All that worrying made her totally neurotic."

Atsuya shook his head. "I don't think this was written by some nutjob."

"Okay, fine. Let's hear your theory, then."

"That's what I'm *trying* to figure out, okay?"

"Or maybe," Shota suddenly said, "it's still happening."

Atsuya looked at him. "What is?"

"This whole advice thing. Here."

"Here? Explain."

"Meaning someone's still answering letters, even if no one lives here anymore. The old man could live somewhere else. Maybe he comes by every now and then to pick up letters and leave his answers in the box. Then it'd all make sense."

"Logically, sure. But you're assuming this old guy's still alive. He'd have to be at least a hundred and ten by now."

"Maybe he's passed down the business."

"Still no sign that anyone's been coming by."

"That's because they don't need to come inside. They can pick up the letters by lifting the shutter."

Shota's theory was plausible. The three guys trudged out into the storefront to investigate. The shutter was welded shut from the inside, impossible to open up.

"Shit," cursed Shota. "How the hell is this happening?"

They returned to the tatami room. Atsuya gave the letter from Moon Rabbit a closer read.

"What do we do?" Shota asked Atsuya.

"Eh, just don't worry about it. We're out of here first thing tomorrow anyway." Atsuya put the letter back in its envelope and dropped it onto the tatami floor.

For a moment, it was quiet. They could hear the wind whistling outside. The candlelight ducked and shivered.

"Well, what's *she* gonna do?" Kohei whispered suddenly.

"About what?" asked Atsuya.

"You know, the Olympics. Is she gonna quit or what?"

"Who knows." He shook his head.

"She can't do that," said Shota. "Right? I mean, her boyfriend's dream is to see her in the games."

"But the man she loves is gonna die," argued Kohei, in a harder voice than usual. "How's she supposed to practice at a time like this? It's better for them to be together. I'm sure that's what her boyfriend really wants."

"I'm not so sure. He's fighting to stay alive so he can see her perform at her peak. Even if he doesn't make it past that day. If she just up and quits, he'll lose his reason to live."

"But look, it says right here she can't keep her head straight. How's she gonna make it to the Olympics? She can't make his wish come true *because* they're apart. It's a lose-lose situation, I'd say."

"That's why she has to practice like she's the one running out of time. There's no time for getting worried. For both of their sakes, she's got no choice but to train like crazy and land that spot on the Olympic team."

"I dunno," Kohei said with a grimace. "I could never do that."

"Nobody's asking you. We're talking about Moon Rabbit."

"Yeah, but I can't tell someone to do something I wouldn't do myself. What about you, Shota? Could you do that?"

Kohei's question disarmed Shota. Instead of answering, he made a sulky face at Atsuya and asked, "What about you?"

Atsuya looked them each square in the eye. "Why the hell are you two taking this seriously? None of this is our problem to worry about."

"So what do we do about the letter?" asked Kohei.

"*Do?* There's nothing left to do."

"But we need to say something. We can't just leave it."

"What?" Atsuya glared back at Kohei's big round face. "You planning to write something?"

Kohei nodded. "I think we should," he said. "We opened it without permission, after all."

"Listen to yourself. No one's living here. It's their own fault for leaving a letter at an abandoned shack. Of course no one's gonna respond. Right, Shota?"

Shota stroked his chin. "I guess when you put it that way."

"Right? Forget about it. Don't waste your time."

Atsuya disappeared out front and came back with a few rolls of paper. He divvied them up.

"Here, you can sleep on this."

"Thanks," Shota murmured.

"I appreciate it," said Kohei.

Atsuya rolled out his tube and laid himself down gingerly. He closed his eyes and tried to fall asleep, but he noticed that the other two hadn't stirred at all. He opened his eyes and raised his head.

Shota and Kohei were sitting cross-legged, hugging their bolts of paper.

"Maybe he could go, too," whispered Kohei.

"Who could?" asked Shota.

"Her boyfriend. The guy who's sick. He can stay at the dormitory or wherever she's staying. That way they can be together all the time, and she can practice and play in her events."

"That won't work. This guy's really sick. He's only got six months to live."

"Doesn't say anywhere that he can't walk. You never know. If he could use a wheelchair, why couldn't he go, too?"

"If he could do any of that, she wouldn't need advice. I bet he's bedridden, or can't move at all."

"You think?"

"Probably."

"Yo!" Atsuya yelled. "How long are you two gonna keep that shit up? I said drop it."

The pair shut their mouths and hung their heads for a brief moment.

Shota's head shot back up. "I know what you're saying, Atsuya, but I can't just let it go. Ms. Rabbit seems real worried. I want to do something to help."

Atsuya snorted and sat all the way up. "You? Do something? Gimme a break. What could any of us possibly do? No money, no education, no connections. The most we can ever hope to be is small-time crooks, breaking into some abandoned houses and shit, and we can't even do that right. Just when we steal stuff with value for once, our getaway car breaks down, and we end up sleeping in this pigpen. Who the hell are we to give other people any kind of advice?"

Atsuya's diatribe made Shota look down again.

"Just go to bed," Atsuya said. "In the morning, the streets will be stuffed with commuters. We'll blend into the crowd and make our getaway." With that, he lay back down.

Shota finally began unrolling his tube of paper, but his fingers moved at a crawl.

"Hey," said Kohei hesitantly. "Want to write something? Anything."

"Write what?" asked Shota.

"Geez, what do you think? A reply. We can't just leave things hanging."

"You're an idiot," Atsuya snapped. "Why are you still hung up on this?"

"Anything's better than nothing, I think. I'm sure she'll be grateful to have someone listen. Who wouldn't be? I bet she's having a hard time because she can't confide in anyone. Even if we can't give her good advice, the least we can do is say we got her message and we're rooting for her."

"Fine," Atsuya spat. "Do whatever you want. Man, how stupid can you be?"

Kohei stood up. "Is there anything we can use?"

"I think I saw some stationery over there," Shota said.

The two of them went out front, puttered around for a while, and stepped back into the tatami room.

"Find anything?" Atsuya asked when they returned.

"Yeah," answered Kohei. "All the markers were dried up, but we found a pen that works. Some paper, too." Looking thrilled, he went into the kitchen, set the pen and paper on the table, and pulled up a seat. "Okay! What should we say?"

"Didn't you just say it? 'We got your message; we're rooting for you.' Write that."

"I dunno—isn't that a little blunt?"

Atsuya clicked his tongue. "Suit yourself."

"How about what you said earlier?" asked Shota. "The idea of getting her boyfriend to come with her."

"Weren't you the one who said she wouldn't need to ask us for advice if she could do that?"

"Yeah, but maybe we should check, just in case."

Kohei picked up the pen, but he looked over at Atsuya and Shota instead of writing. "What's the best way to start a letter?"

"Oh yeah, the salutation or whatever," said Shota. "You could say 'Dear Ms. Rabbit.' Or maybe 'Greetings, Ms. Rabbit.' Honestly, though, I don't think you really need to. She didn't say anything like that, right? Just pretend you're sending her a text."

"Like a text. Got it. Okay. 'We read your text'— I mean, er, letter, right? 'We…read…your…letter…'"

"You don't need to read it aloud," advised Shota.

Atsuya could make out every stroke Kohei executed with the pen. He was really bearing down.

A few minutes later, Kohei announced "Done" and brought the piece of paper to the tatami.

Shota had a look. "You've got some really ugly handwriting."

Atsuya glanced over from beside him. It really was a mess. Plus everything was in lowercase.

> *thanks for the letter. it sounds like things are tough. i can see why you would be upset. i was thinking you could bring your boyfriend with you when you go away? sorry i couldn't think of something better.*

"Good?" asked Kohei.

"Yeah, that's fine," Shota confirmed. "Right?"

"Whatever," Atsuya said.

Kohei neatly folded up their letter and slipped it into the return envelope that Moon Rabbit had prepared for them. "I'll go drop it in the bin," he announced and went out back.

Atsuya heaved a sigh. "What the hell is he thinking, giving advice to a person he's never even met? And you, Shota, why the hell are you going along with this?"

"Lay off. Why shouldn't we be able to do this once in a while?"

"'Once in a while'? What the hell does that mean?"

"When was the last time someone came to us looking for advice?

Oh, that's right, never. And it won't ever happen again. This is our first and only chance. We may as well take it, just this once."

Atsuya exhaled sharply through his nose. "Don't forget who you are."

Kohei came back. "The lid of the bin was shut super-tight. Whew! Must not have been used for a pretty long time."

"No shit. It's not like the milkman is gonna…" Atsuya cut himself off. "Hey, Kohei, where are your gloves?"

"My gloves? Right there." He pointed at the table.

"When did you take them off?"

"When I was writing the letter. I mean, with gloves on, it's really hard to—"

"You jackass." Atsuya stood up. "The paper's probably covered with your fingerprints."

"Fingerprints? What did I do wrong?"

Atsuya was ready to smack Kohei upside his clueless fat face. "Eventually, the cops are going to figure we were hiding out here. What happens if this 'Moon Rabbit' lady or whatever doesn't come to collect our response? When they process the fingerprints, you're done. They have your prints already, right? From that speeding ticket."

"Oh… You're right."

"That's why I've been telling you to leave this crap alone."

Atsuya snatched the flashlight and strode across the kitchen and out the back door.

The lid of the milk bin was shut tight. Super-tight, like Kohei had said, but he managed to yank it open.

He scanned around inside with the flashlight, but there was nothing there.

He poked his head inside the back door and yelled, "Hey, Kohei, where'd you put it?"

Kohei came over, pulling on his gloves. "What do you mean, where? In the bin."

"It's not there."

"Huh? No way."

"Maybe you thought you got it in there, but it slipped out."

"No way! I'm positive."

"Where'd it go, then?"

"Dunno." As Kohei cocked his head to the side, footsteps scrambled to the back door. Out came Shota.

"What?" Atsuya asked. "What's going on?"

"I heard something out front, so I went and checked, and underneath that little slot, I found this." Shota held out another envelope. His face was pale.

Atsuya held his breath. He clicked off the flashlight and tiptoed to the edge of the house. From the shadows, he peered at the street in front of the store.

But no one was there. Not now, and not a few minutes ago.

3

Thank you for your prompt reply. After I left my letter in your mail slot last night, I was sure I'd asked too much of you. I spent the whole day worrying that I was annoying you, so it's a relief to hear back.

Your suggestion makes sense. If I could, I'd love to bring my boyfriend with me. But in his condition, I'm afraid it isn't possible. The only reason he hasn't gotten worse is that he's being treated at the hospital.

With that in mind, you might ask, why not practice near the hospital? Unfortunately, there aren't any training facilities nearby. As it stands, I can only go see him on my days off, and it takes me hours each way.

But time still keeps passing, and I'll be leaving for my next training session soon. I went to see him today. He told me to work hard, and I nodded and said I would. What I really wanted to say was that I didn't want to go, I wanted to stay put, right here, but I held it in. I knew if I said that, it would only hurt him.

When I'm away, I wish there was some way I could see his face. Sometimes I daydream about having a TV phone. They always have them in manga.

But what good is that fantasy going to do me?

Mr. Namiya, thank you so much for listening to my problems. It has been a huge relief for me to put them in writing.

I think I need to figure them out on my own, but if you have any more advice, please let me know. And if you don't, please just write and say so. I don't want to be a nuisance.

In any case, I'll check the crate again tomorrow.

Thank you so much.

—Moon Rabbit

Shota was the last to read the letter. He looked up and blinked twice. "What's the deal?"

"No idea," said Atsuya. "What the hell is going on?"

"It's a response, right?" deduced Kohei. "From Ms. Rabbit."

Atsuya and Kohei both shot him a look.

"How did it get here, though?" they asked him at the same time.

"How? Huh…" Dumbfounded, Kohei scratched his head.

Atsuya jerked his thumb at the back door. "It was barely five minutes ago that you dropped the letter in that box. When I went to look, it was gone. Even if this Rabbit woman came and grabbed it in the meantime, she wouldn't have had time to write back. But we still got a second letter from her, like, instantly. This is way too weird."

"Yeah, weird. But it's a definitely a letter from Ms. Rabbit. Right? I mean, she responded directly to my advice."

Atsuya had no rebuttal. Kohei was right.

He snatched the letter from Shota and scanned it again. No one could have written this without reading Kohei's response.

"Shit, man," cried Shota, exasperated. "Is someone screwing with us?"

"Bingo." Atsuya jabbed a finger at Shota's chest. "This is some kind of prank."

He tossed aside the letter and threw open the door of a nearby closet. Inside was nothing but futons and cardboard boxes.

"Atsuya, what're you up to?" Shota asked.

"Checking to see who's hiding in here. They probably listened to our convo before Kohei started writing and got a head start on their response. Or maybe someone's bugged the place. You two, look over there."

"Wait a second. Who would even do that?"

"How should I know? It's gotta be someone who gets off on playing pranks on people who sneak into this dump." Atsuya lit up the inside of the altar with his flashlight.

Shota and Kohei sat still.

"Come on, help me look around."

Uneasy, Shota shook his head. "I dunno, man. I can't imagine why anyone would bother."

"Well, I can. What other explanation is there?"

"I guess," said Shota, still unconvinced. "But what about the letter disappearing from the crate?"

"That was some kind of illusion, like a magic trick."

"A magic trick?"

Kohei looked up as he reread the second letter. "Something seems kinda off about this lady."

"What?" asked Atsuya.

"Well, she says she wishes there was a 'TV phone.' I don't get it. Doesn't she have a cell phone or something? Or maybe she just can't video chat with him?"

"They probably won't let him use a cell phone in the hospital," Shota offered.

"But she said they have them in manga. Sounds like she has no idea that cell phones can make video calls."

"No way. Impossible. What world is she living in?"

"No, that's gotta be it," said Kohei. "Let's tell her." He headed for the table.

"Wait a sec. Are you writing back? This is just somebody screwing with us."

"But we don't know that for sure yet."

"Someone is definitely screwing with us. They're probably listening to us right now so they can start in on the next letter. Hold on—wait a second." A light bulb went off in Atsuya's head. "All right, Kohei, write her back. I thought of something."

"What is it this time?" asked Shota.

"Just wait. You'll see."

Kohei labored through the letter and put down the pen. "Done!" Shota had a look over Kohei's shoulder at the paper. Chicken scratches, as usual.

thank you for the second letter. here is some good news for you. some phones can make video calls. all carriers have at least one model. just make sure the hospital doesn't find out.

"How's that sound?" asked Kohei.

"That's fine," said Atsuya. "Whatever you want. Just put it in the envelope."

Moon Rabbit's second letter, like the first, contained a fresh envelope made out to herself. Kohei folded up his new response and slipped it inside.

"I'm going this time, too. Shota, you stay here." Atsuya grabbed the flashlight and headed for the back door.

Once they were outside, Atsuya watched to make sure Kohei put the letter in the wooden container.

"All right, Kohei, you hide somewhere and don't take your eyes off this."

"Got it. Where are you gonna be, Atsuya?"

"Out front. To get a good look at whoever comes by with the letter."

Atsuya went along the side of the house and peered out from the shadows into the street. Still no sign of anyone. But shortly after, he felt someone approaching him from behind and turned to find Shota.

"What are you doing? I told you to stay inside."

"See anyone?"

"Not yet. Why do you think I'm standing here?"

Shota looked distraught. His mouth was open.

"What the hell is wrong with you?"

Shota answered by holding up an envelope. "We got another one."

"What the hell is that?"

"What do you think?" He licked his lips. "Another letter."

4

Thank you once again for the response. I'm comforted by the fact that someone out there knows about my troubles.

I'm very sorry to say that the advice in your last letter went a little—well, actually, went completely over my head.

I'm afraid I'm not educated or cultured enough to comprehend the joke you've written to lift my spirits, though I'm ashamed to admit it.

My mother always told me that if you don't understand something, don't assume people owe you an explanation—try to figure it out yourself. I always try to solve problems on my own, but this time, I have to say I'm lost.

For starters, what's a cell phone?

From the spelling, I thought it might be a foreign word, but I couldn't track it down. If it's in English, I'm guessing it could be short for animal cells or maybe cellmate, but neither of those seems right. Maybe it's from another language?

Without knowing what a "cell phone" is, your precious advice is lost on me, like pearls before swine. I would be grateful if you would expand on this.

I know you must be very busy, and I'm sorry to be taking up your time this way.

—Moon Rabbit

The three guys sat down at the kitchen table. Shota arranged the three letters from Moon Rabbit in a tidy row.

"Let's recap," Shota said. "Kohei's letter disappeared again from the box. And even though he stayed hidden and watched it like a hawk, no one came even close to it. Atsuya was staked out in the front—same thing. Somehow, a third letter showed up in the mail slot. Anything wrong so far?"

"No," said Atsuya curtly. Kohei nodded in silence.

"Therefore," Shota concluded, pointer finger upright, "no one came near the house, but Kohei's letter disappeared, and a new letter from Ms. Rabbit arrived. We've inspected the milk bin and the shutter, but there's no trapdoor, no nothing. Where does that leave us?"

Atsuya leaned back in his chair and interlaced his fingers behind his head. "We don't know. Why else would we be discussing this?"

"Kohei?"

His round face shook back and forth. "No idea."

"Shota," Atsuya started, "are you onto something?"

Shota gazed down at the trio of letters. "Something strange is going on. This woman has no clue what a cell phone is. She thinks it's in a foreign language or something."

"Maybe she's messing with us."

"Maybe."

"Definitely. At this point, every person in Japan knows what a cell phone is."

Shota pointed at the first letter. "What about this? It mentions the Olympics—*next year.* But think about it. There's not gonna be an Olympics in the summer or the winter. It just happened in London."

Atsuya let out a small cry. "Oh!" To cover it up, he screwed up his face and rubbed a finger under his nose. "She just got mixed up, is all."

"You really think so? Hard to believe she'd make a mistake like that. This is the biggest event of her life. Between this and her not knowing you can video chat, things are more than just a little off."

"I agree… And?"

"There's one other thing." Shota lowered his voice to a whisper. "This is totally weird, but I noticed it a minute ago, when I was outside."

"Noticed what?"

Shota faltered for a moment, then spoke again. "Atsuya, look at your phone. What time is it?"

"My phone?" Atsuya pulled it from his pocket and checked the display. "Three forty AM."

"Right. So we've been in here over an hour."

"Okay. So what?"

"Yeah, well, follow me." Shota stood up and led them out the back door to the passage between the house and the garage. He looked up at the night sky. "When we got here, the moon was directly overhead."

"Yeah, I noticed, too. What about it?"

Shota stared into Atsuya's face. "That's weird, right? It's been over an hour, but the moon hasn't budged."

For a moment, Atsuya was completely lost, unable to grasp what Shota was hinting at. But when he understood, his heart pounded in his chest. His face went hot, and something shivered through his spine.

He pulled out his phone again. The display said 3:42 AM.

"What the hell is this? Why isn't the moon moving?"

"Maybe the moon doesn't move that much this time of year," proposed Kohei.

"No such season," scoffed Shota.

Atsuya looked from his phone to the night sky. He had no clue what was happening.

"What about this?" Shota started fiddling with his own phone. It looked as if he was dialing a number.

His face was tense. His eyes, blinking repeatedly, were completely focused.

"What's wrong? Who are you calling?"

Silent, Shota simply held out his phone so Atsuya could listen for himself. Atsuya held the phone to his ear and heard a woman's voice.

"The current time is two thirty-six AM."

The three of them went back inside.

"It's not the phone that's broken," Shota began. "This house is out of whack."

"Are you saying that something here is messing up the clocks on our phones?"

Shota didn't nod this time. "I don't think the clocks are messed up. They're working fine. It's just that they're not displaying the right time."

Atsuya frowned. "What would cause that?"

"There must be a rift in time inside and outside the house. Time isn't passing at a normal pace; it can feel like a really long time in here, but it's only like a second outside."

"What are you getting at?"

Shota looked over the letter again and back to Atsuya. "We're certain no one else has come near the house, but Kohei's letters disappeared, and letters from Ms. Rabbit keep showing up. This should be impossible. But think of it this way: What if someone *did* pick up Kohei's letter, read it, and came back with a response—but we weren't able to see her?"

"Unable to see her?" asked Atsuya. "Like what? An invisible woman?"

"Ah, okay," mused Kohei. "Like a ghost, right? Wait, are there ghosts here?" He cowered and looked around the room.

"Not invisible, and not a ghost. Whoever this is, they aren't of this world." Shota pointed to the third letter. "They belong to the past."

"The past?" spat Atsuya. "What the hell does that mean?"

"Here's how I see it. The mail slot and the milk crate are connected to the past. When someone leaves a letter at the store back then, it lands here in the present day. In the same way, when we leave a letter in the box, it winds up in the same place in their time. Don't ask me why this is happening, but when you put it all together, it checks out. Ms. Rabbit is sending us letters from a really long time ago."

Atsuya couldn't string a sentence together. He had no idea what to say. His brain refused to process any of this

"Can't be," he finally said. "There's no way."

"I'm with you. But there's no other explanation. If you think I'm wrong, try and think up something better. Something that explains everything."

Atsuya had nothing. What else could explain this?

"You just *had* to go and write back," he said, rounding on Kohei without much conviction. "That's what got us into this mess."

"Sorry…"

"Don't blame Kohei. Look, if I'm right about this, we're onto something huge. I mean, this would mean we're exchanging letters across time." Shota had a twinkle in his eye.

Atsuya didn't like the sound of that, but he didn't know what to do with himself.

"Come on." He stood up to leave. "Let's beat it."

The other two looked at him, surprised. Shota asked him why.

"Doesn't this rub you the wrong way? If this gets out of hand, we'll be in deep shit. Let's go. There's plenty of other places we can lie low. Plus, morning is never gonna come, no matter how much time passes in here. There's no use waiting it out if the clock stops working."

But his friends wouldn't agree. They sat silently, heads heavy.

"What's wrong now?" Atsuya shouted. "Say something, god damn it!"

Shota looked up. The light in his eyes was formidable. "I'm gonna stick around for a bit."

"What? Why?"

He shrugged. "I don't really know yet. All I know is we're involved with something incredible. Chances like this don't come by often— In fact, this might be my only shot. I don't want to waste it. You can go if you want to, Atsuya, but I'm staying."

"What are you planning to do here?"

Shota looked over the row of letters on the table. "For now, I'll write a few more letters. Communicating with someone from the past is, like, insane."

"Yeah, what he said," Kohei concurred. "And we have to help Ms. Rabbit figure out her problem."

Atsuya backed away, still facing them, and shook his head dramatically.

"You're crazy. What's gotten into you? What's so fun about being pen pals with somebody from way back when? Give it up. Drop it. What are you gonna do if this gets outta control? I don't want any part of it."

"I said you can go if you want to." Shota gave him a gentler look.

Atsuya huffed a huge sigh. He wanted to protest, but the words wouldn't come out of his mouth.

"Whatever. Don't say I didn't warn you."

He stomped back to the tatami room to grab his bag and barreled out through the back door, without even a glance at his friends. Outside, he looked up at the sky and the full moon. It had barely moved at all.

He pulled out his phone. Remembering that its clock would automatically synchronize, he let it catch up and looked at the OLED display. Not one minute had passed since they'd called and checked the time.

Alone now, Atsuya walked through the darkness of the sparsely lit street. The night air was cold, but his cheeks were flushed red, and he didn't care.

There's no way, he thought.

A mail slot and a milk bin sending and receiving letters across time? With some woman named Moon Rabbit?

Bullshit. Sure, the pieces fit together, but that didn't mean it was actually happening. There must be some mistake. Someone was screwing with them.

Even in the hypothetical case that Shota was onto something, it would be best to leave that otherworldly shit alone. Worst case, if something went wrong, nobody would come to save them. They had to have one another's backs. That was the only reason they'd made it this far. No good ever came from relying on anyone else. Especially someone from the past. There was nothing this woman could possibly do for them.

After a few minutes, he turned onto a wider street. There were cars, but they were few and far between. Up ahead, he saw the lights of a convenience store.

He remembered the pitiful way Kohei had whined about being hungry. If the other two stayed awake any longer, they were only going to get hungrier. What were they thinking? But then again, if time wouldn't pass, maybe they'd never get hungry.

He knew if he showed up in a store at this time of night, the clerk was bound to remember his face. And even if not, he'd be there on camera.

Forget those two, he thought. *They'll figure things out.*

Atsuya stopped out front. There was no one inside except for one guy working the night shift.

He sighed. "You damned softy."

He hid his bag behind the trash can and swung open the glass door.

Atsuya was in and out; all he did was buy some rice balls, a few pastries, and bottled drinks. The clerk was young, but he didn't so much as look up at Atsuya. Maybe they got his face on camera, but shopping at this hour wasn't enough to pique the interest of the police. What criminal would risk it? No one. Of course not. At least, that was what he tried to tell himself.

He snatched his bag from its hiding spot and went back up the road he'd just come down. His plan was just to give the guys the food and split. He wasn't trying to stick around that spooky house.

He was back in no time. As luck would have it, he didn't pass anyone on the way.

Atsuya gave the house a once-over, then examined the mail slot in the welded shutter. If he slipped a letter through the slot right now, what year would it be when it landed inside?

Ducking down the narrow alley between the house and the garage, he went around back. The door had been left open. Peering inside, he stepped over the threshold.

"Ah, Atsuya!" Kohei cried cheerfully. "You're back. After an hour, we started worrying you really left us."

"An hour?" Atsuya checked his phone. "It's only been like fifteen minutes. And I'm not back. I brought you provisions." He dropped the plastic bag on the table. "I don't know how long you're planning to stick around."

"Whoa!" Kohei's face lit up. He eagerly snatched a rice ball.

"If you guys stay here," Atsuya warned Shota, "you'll never see the morning."

"Yeah, we figured out a work-around."

"A work-around?"

"The back door was wide-open, right?"

"Yeah…"

"If you leave it open, time passes at the same rate, outside and inside. Kohei and I tried all kinds of stuff and figured out this works. That's why we're only off by an hour."

"The back door, huh…?" Atsuya stared out through it. "What the hell makes it work that way? What's up with this house?"

"I'm not sure, but now there's no reason for you not to stick around. We can stay here right through till morning."

"He's right," agreed Kohei. "Would be better to stick together."

"I bet you guys just want to keep writing to your weirdo pen pal."

"So what? If it bothers you, stay out of it. But we do want your advice on one small thing."

Atsuya peered suspiciously at Shota. "My advice?"

"After you left, we wrote our third letter. Then we got another back. Anyway, have a look."

Atsuya looked at Shota and Kohei, who were both giving him puppy-dog eyes.

"Fine, I'll read it, but nothing more," he cautioned. "What'd you guys say to her anyway?"

"Here's a draft of what we sent." Shota handed him a sheet of paper, a draft of the third letter they'd sent to Moon Rabbit.

This time Shota had written it out. The handwriting was easy to read and properly capitalized.

> *Don't worry about the cell phone thing. It doesn't matter.*
>
> *Please tell me a little more about you and your boyfriend. What are you good at? Do you share any interests? Have you been on any trips lately? Seen any movies? If you're into music, what songs have you been listening to?*
>
> *If you could tell me these things, I can tailor my advice. Thanks. (Please excuse the difference in handwriting. There's nothing to worry about.)*
>
> —Namiya General Store

"What gives? Why'd you ask all that?"

"Look, first things first—we need to pinpoint when Ms. Rabbit's writing from. As long as we're not sure, we're not gonna be on the same page with her."

"Why not just ask her, then? Like, 'Hey, yo, what year is it?'"

Shota seemed annoyed by Atsuya's question.

"Put yourself in her shoes. She has no idea what's really going on. If we ask that out of the blue, she's gonna think we're crazy."

Atsuya pouted his lower lip and scratched his cheek. He couldn't disagree. "All right, so what'd she say?"

Shota picked an envelope up off the table. "See for yourself."

Wondering what was such a big deal, Atsuya pulled out the letter and unfolded the pages.

> *Thank you for your ongoing advice. I have been looking into cell phones and asking friends, but I still haven't been able to figure it out. I'm really curious, but I'll take your word for it that it doesn't concern me and try to put it out of my mind. I'd be grateful if you'd tell me in the future.*
>
> *Of course. I'd be happy to tell you a little bit about the two of us.*
>
> *As I mentioned in my first letter, I'm an athlete. My boyfriend used to compete in the same sport. That's how we met. He was nominated for the Olympics once, too, but beyond that, we're just two normal people. We both like going to the movies. This year, we saw Superman, oh, and Rocky II. We also saw Alien. He said he enjoyed it, but it really wasn't my cup of tea.*
>
> *We both listen to a lot of music, too. Let's see—lately, I've been listening to Godiego and Southern All Stars. Isn't "Ellie, My Love [Itoshi no Ellie]" just great?*
>
> *It lifts my spirits to write this all out and remember the good old days, you know, before he got sick. Maybe that was your intention. Either way, I can say for sure that this exchange of notes (if you'll excuse the expression) is giving me strength. Please write again tomorrow if you can.*
>
> —*Moon Rabbit*

Atsuya finished reading and mumbled, "Huh. Okay. *Alien?* 'Ellie, My Love'? That pretty much nails down the era. Right around when our parents were our age."

Shota nodded. "I just looked it up on my phone. Well, not just now. There's no service in here. You gotta go outside to use it. Anyway, all three movies were released in Japan in 1979. Same goes for 'Ellie, My Love.'"

Atsuya shrugged. "That settles it. It's 1979."

"Right. Which means the Olympic games Ms. Rabbit is trying to attend would be in 1980."

"Yeah. So what?"

Shota gave Atsuya a look, as if peering into the hidden reaches of his soul.

"What's up?" he asked. "Is there something on my face?"

"You really don't know? I mean, I figured Kohei wouldn't, but not you, too."

"What is it? Just tell me."

Shota took a deep breath and told him. "In 1980, the Olympics were in Moscow. Those were the games Japan decided to boycott."

5

Of course, Atsuya knew about the boycott. He may not have known it was 1980, but that didn't matter.

That would have been during the height of the Cold War. Things came to a head when the Soviet Union invaded Afghanistan, and the United States responded by announcing its withdrawal from the Olympic games, urging the rest of the Western world to follow suit. Japan held off until the last minute but finally caved to join them in protest.

At least, that's what Shota had said, after he'd consulted his phone. Atsuya had never heard the events outlined in such detail.

"Doesn't this solve Moon Rabbit's problem, then? If Japan isn't going to the Olympics next year, she may as well forget about the competition and spend all her time caring for her lover. Why not say that?"

Atsuya's proposal rang wrong to Shota.

"Even if we told her, there's no way she'd believe us. I mean, I read that the Olympic athletes in Japan all thought they were going to compete up until the boycott was officially announced to the public."

"If we tell her we're from the future…" Atsuya trailed off. His face went sour. "Never mind."

"She's gonna think this whole thing's a joke."

Atsuya clicked his tongue and banged the table with his fist.

"Um, guys?" Kohei ventured to speak for the first time in a while. "Do we have to say why?"

Atsuya and Shota both looked at him.

"Um, I mean," he said, scratching his head. "Why give the actual reason? Can't we just say we think she should quit training so hard so she can take care of her boyfriend? Or is this just some dumb idea?"

Atsuya met Shota's eyes. It was hard to tell who nodded first.

"No, that's good," Shota assured him.

"Not dumb at all. That's the answer. She's asking for advice because she's unsure of what to do. She's clutching at straws. There's no reason to go into the reasons behind it. Tell her straight up that if she loves him, she has to stay beside him till the very end. I'm sure that's what he really wants deep down."

Shota picked up the pen and scribbled down a few lines. "How's this?"

He'd basically written down what Atsuya had just said.

"Looks good to me."

"Great."

Shota took the letter out through the back door. It closed behind him. They could hear him lift open the lid of the milk bin and let it fall shut with a thud.

A moment later, something flapped into the box.

Atsuya went out front to look. In the box against the shutter, he found another letter.

> *Thanks so much for writing.*
>
> *To be perfectly honest, I was not expecting to receive such a cut-and-dried response. Not that I expected your advice to be vague, exactly, but I thought it would be more open-ended, you know, and force me to make the final call. But I suppose you don't leave things half-done. That's why everyone comes to you with their worries and trusts you with their deepest secrets.*
>
> *"If you love him, stay beside him to the end."*
>
> *This sentence truly struck home with me. I know this is right. There's nothing to debate.*
>
> *But I'm afraid the "That's what he really wants deep down" part isn't totally accurate.*
>
> *When I called him today, I was planning, as you advised me, to say I wanted to pull out of the running. But as if he knew my next move, he spoke first and told me that if I had the time to call him, I should spend it training, period. He said it was good to hear my voice, but it pained him knowing that as we speak, my rivals were getting ahead of me.*
>
> *I'm conflicted. I'm scared that if I give up the Olympics, he'll be so devastated that his condition will worsen. As long as I can't guarantee that won't happen, I can't let myself go through with it.*
>
> *Maybe I'm just pathetic for feeling this way.*
>
> *—Moon Rabbit*

Atsuya finished the letter and looked up at the cobwebbed ceiling.

"I don't get it. What's wrong with her? If she's not going to follow our advice, why'd she ask for it in the first place?"

Shota sighed. "There's only so much we can do. She has no way of knowing her advice is coming from the future."

"If she called him, that means she isn't close enough to go and see him," Kohei surmised, focusing on the letter. "I feel bad for her."

"I'm pissed at this guy," Atsuya said. "I mean, try to understand what she's going through! The Olympics are like a field day blown out of proportion. It's only a game, right? How can he expect her to focus when her boyfriend is suffering? I don't care how sick he is. It's selfish of him to pressure her into this."

"The guy has it rough himself, though. He knows it's her dream to make it to the Olympics. I'm sure he'd feel real guilty if he forced her to back out. He's fighting his feelings back and putting up a tough-guy front for her, or maybe just taking his good intentions too far."

"That's the part that gets me. He's in love with the idea of fighting that battle against his own weakness."

"You think?"

"Definitely. A tragic heroine. Well, hero. He just wants to play the part."

"All right. How should we write back?" Shota pushed the pages aside to clear the table.

"Tell her she's gotta open this man's eyes. That's the first step. She's gotta tell him straight. It's only a game, and definitely no excuse to put your lover in a bind. The Olympics are just a fancier version of a field day. Not worth getting worked up over."

Shota, pen in hand, squinted back at Atsuya. "There's no way we can tell her to say that."

"Whatever. It's what she has to say."

"Don't be ridiculous. If it was that easy, her letter wouldn't sound so upset."

Atsuya scratched his head with both hands. "What a pain in the ass."

"What if she got someone else to say it?" Kohei jumped in again.

"Someone to say it for her?" asked Shota. "Who? She hasn't told anyone but us about his condition."

"About that," added Kohei. "What's with not telling their parents? If she told them, I'm sure they'd take her side."

Atsuya snapped his fingers. "You're right. Her parents, his parents, doesn't matter. She's gotta get it out there. If they knew what was going on, no one would ever tell her to stick with the Olympics. Throw that in there, Shota."

"Got it." He started writing.

> I understand why you're conflicted. But please trust me on this one. Consider it a done deal and just follow my advice.
>
> Simply put, your boyfriend is wrong.
>
> You have to remember that this whole thing is only a game. At the end of the day, the Olympics are just a bigger version of a field day. To be honest, it's stupid to waste your precious time together on it. You need to get him to understand this.
>
> If I could, I'd gladly tell him on your behalf. But unfortunately, I can't do that.
>
> What you need to do is tell your parents—or his. Once you break the news to them about his condition, they're sure to take your side.
>
> That's the only way. You've got to accept it. Drop out of the Olympics. No one will blame you for it. Just do it. You'll be glad you did.
>
> —*Namiya General Store*

Shota went out to drop the letter in the milk bin, then came back in through the back door. "We really put the screws on this time. That oughtta settle things."

"Kohei," Atsuya yelled out into the store. "Anything come yet?"

"Not yet!" he shouted back.

"No? Hmm. That's odd." Shota frowned. "All the other ones came right away. Maybe the back door wasn't closed enough." He got up to check.

"Wait, got it!" Kohei hollered from the shadows of the storefront and came back into the kitchen with the letter.

> It's Moon Rabbit. Remember me? I'm so sorry for taking a month to reply.
>
> I meant to write back right away, but I just started boot camp. I guess that's just an excuse. If I'm honest, I was torn about what to write.
>
> I was caught off guard by what you said about my boyfriend being wrong. You dare to call a spade a spade, even if the person in question is suffering from a terminal illness, and your response made me sit up straight. I feel like I can learn a thing or two from you.
>
> Maybe you're right about it just being a game, just the Olympics… No, I know you're right. It could be that we've gotten ourselves worked up over something that doesn't even matter.
>
> But I could never say that to him. I understand it doesn't matter to most people. But we share a history of training for it. We've worked as if our lives depended on it.
>
> You do have a point about telling our parents. It's something we should do. But not quite yet. His younger sister just had a baby, and his parents are still experiencing the newfound joy of being grandparents. He wants us to let them enjoy it a little longer, and I can understand why he would feel that way.
>
> During this boot camp, I've had the chance to call him a few times. When I tell him how hard I'm training, he gets so happy. There's no way he's faking it.

But maybe I should give up on the Olympics after all. Just quit the training and attend full-time to his needs. Maybe he needs that more than anything.

The more I think it over, the more confused I get.

—Moon Rabbit

Atsuya wanted to scream. This one made his blood boil.

"What the hell is she thinking? We tell her to quit, and she ships off to another boot camp. What's she gonna do if he dies while she's away?"

"If she skipped camp," reasoned Kohei, "she would never be able to face him."

"But what's the point of even going? What's this crap about 'the more I think, the more confused I get'? We've spelled it out for her. Why can't she listen?"

"It's her way of showing how much she cares," said Shota. "She doesn't want to be the one to kill his dreams."

"Well, they're not gonna come true. Either way, she's not going to the Olympics. Shit, man, how are we gonna get this through to her?" Atsuya impatiently bounced his knee up and down.

"What if she got an injury?" Kohei suggested. "If she had to drop out on account of an injury, he'd have to give it up."

"Hey, that's pretty good," Atsuya agreed.

"No way," protested Shota. "That still means she doesn't make his final wish come true. That's the thing Ms. Rabbit worries about the most."

Atsuya wrinkled his nose. "Would you shut up for once about this goddamned dream? That can't be the only thing he wants in life."

Shota's eyes opened wide, as if he had a breakthrough. "That's it! She's just gotta tell him that the Olympics isn't all there is to life. She needs to steer his will to dream toward something else. Like maybe…" He thought it over for a second. "Kids."

"What kids?"

"Their kids! We'll tell her to tell him she's pregnant. With his kid, of course. That way she'd have to back out of the Olympics. He'd lose one dream, but he can redirect his efforts to dreaming about becoming a father. It would give him something to live for."

Atsuya thought this through and liked it enough to clap his hands. "Shota, you know what? You're a genius. Let's do this. It's the perfect plan. Her boyfriend only has half a year to live. She can lie without him ever finding out."

"Okay!" Shota sat down at the table, ready to write again.

Atsuya felt as if this time, they'd be good. It wasn't clear when the boyfriend had been diagnosed, but judging from the letters, it probably wasn't too many months ago. He got the sense that their lives had been normal up to that point, meaning they were most definitely having sex. Even if they'd used protection, there was always the possibility of one getting through, and there were ways to talk around the details.

Much to their chagrin, the letter that fluttered through the mail slot did not sound so convinced.

> I've read through your letter. I was surprised by your idea. I would have never thought of that myself, but it struck a chord. Giving him something new to dream about is definitely one way to go about this. He'd never go so far as making me have an abortion for the sake of getting to the Olympics. He'd want me to have a healthy baby.
>
> But I'm afraid there are a few problems with this plan. The first is the timeline of the pregnancy. The last time we slept together must have been at least three months ago. At this point, it would raise questions if I suddenly announced I was pregnant. What am I supposed to do if he asks me to prove it?
>
> If he did believe me, I know he'd tell his parents. Of course, we'd

need to tell my parents, too. I'd imagine word would spread to all our relatives, and everyone would know. But there's no way I can tell them all that the baby is a lie. I'd have to explain why I would lie about it in the first place.

I'm not good at acting, and I'm an even worse liar. Everyone is going to get incredibly excited when they hear I'm pregnant, and I'm not sure if I'll be able to hold it all together. I'd need to fake a baby bump, since people would notice if my belly stayed flat, but I'm sure I can't pull that off, either.

There's another serious problem. If his condition progresses slower than anticipated, there's a chance he'll be alive on the due date of our fictional child. What then? If I don't give birth on schedule, he'll see the lie for what it is. It hurts me to imagine how disappointed he would be.

I think it's a wonderful idea, but I hope you understand why it won't work for me.

I'm so thankful for all the advice you've given me, Mr. Namiya. I got exactly what I needed, and I'm nothing but thankful. But I've realized that this is a problem I have to solve on my own. Don't worry about responding to this letter. I've taken so much of your time already.

—Moon Rabbit

"What is this crap?" Atsuya tossed aside the letter and stood. "We've stuck with her all the way, and in the homestretch, she tells us, 'No thanks, I'm good, I don't need another letter!' Makes you wonder if she ever even wanted our opinion to begin with. I mean, she pretty much ignored everything."

"She has a point," admitted Kohei. "It's hard keeping up an act."

"Shut up. How can you go easy on her when her boyfriend's on his deathbed? If you face death head-on, you can do anything." Atsuya sat down in front of the kitchen table.

"Do you want to write back to her yourself?" asked Shota. "The handwriting would change again."

"I just gotta lay it all out on the table now, or I'll go crazy."

"All right. Go ahead," said Shota, sitting across from him. "I'll write exactly what you say."

Dear Moon Rabbit,

Are you an idiot? No need to reply—I already know the answer's yes.

I've told you exactly what you need to do. Why didn't you just follow my lead, huh?

How many times do I have to spell it out? Forget the Olympics.

All this training? Trying to make it on the team? Yeah, it's all pointless.

You'll never make it. Quit now. It's a waste of time.

But the ultimate waste is worrying about what to do. If you have time to spare, go spend it with your boyfriend.

You think he'll cry if you drop out? Think his tears will make him sicker?

Quit screwing around. So what if you don't make it on the team? It doesn't matter. Trust me.

In case you didn't realize, there's a war going on. There's a bunch of countries in no position to be playing games. Japan can't turn a blind eye to this. You'll see soon enough.

You know what? It doesn't matter. Do what you like. Do whatever you want. Just be ready to regret it.

Oh, and on a final note: You're an idiot.

—Namiya General Store

6

Shota lit a new set of candles. Their eyes had adjusted to the dark, and a few flickering flames were enough to see all the way to the outer corners of the room.

"Still no mail," said Kohei. "This is the longest it's ever taken. Maybe she doesn't want to write to us anymore."

"I don't think she's writing back," said Shota, trailing off into a sigh. "She got her ass handed to her. She's either going to be butt-hurt or pissed. Either way, I can guarantee she won't feel like writing anymore."

"What the hell, man?" Atsuya glared at him. "You saying I'm the bad guy here?"

"No. I felt the same way as you did. I think it was good to write that. But now that you've said all you wanted to say, you can't complain if she doesn't write back."

"…Cool." Atsuya looked away.

"Makes you wonder what happened, doesn't it?" Kohei said aloud. "Like, did she keep on training or what? Did she get picked for the Olympic team? All that work, just for Japan to boycott the whole thing. She must have been devastated."

"If that's what happened, serves her right," Atsuya snapped. "She totally deserves it for ignoring us."

"What happened to the boyfriend?" Shota asked next. "How long did he live? Did he last to hear about the boycott?"

Atsuya was quiet. An awkward silence settled over the room.

"Hey, how long are we gonna do this for?" Kohei inquired. "The back door's still shut. Time's never going to pass."

"Yeah, but if we open it, we'll cut off our connection to the past. Even if Ms. Rabbit sent us a reply, it'd never arrive." Shota looked to Atsuya. "What should we do?"

Atsuya bit his lower lip and began cracking his knuckles. Once he'd cracked all five fingers on one hand, he looked at Kohei.

"Open the door."

"You sure?" asked Shota.

"What do we care? Forget about Little Miss Rabbit. She's nothing to us. Go on, Kohei."

Kohei stood just as a knocking sound came from the store.

The three guys froze. They looked at one another and then out into the shop.

Atsuya stood with great care and tiptoed toward the shop with Shota and Kohei tailing him close behind.

Again, the gentle knocking came on the shutter, the little *tap-tap-tap* of someone checking whether anyone was home. Atsuya stopped dead in his tracks and held his breath.

A letter fell through the mail slot.

> *Sorry to bother you. Does a Mr. Namiya still live at this address? If not, and someone else is reading this, please stop and burn this letter without reading any further. I don't have anything important to say, and you won't gain anything by reading it.*
>
> *The rest of this letter is intended for Mr. Namiya:*
>
> *It's Moon Rabbit. It's been so long since my last letter. I wonder if you remember me. We exchanged a series of letters toward the end of last year. It's hard to believe six months have passed. How have you been?*
>
> *I'm very thankful for all you did for me. For the rest of my life, I won't forget your kind advice. Each letter was so full of sincerity.*
>
> *There are two updates I'd like to share with you.*
>
> *The first is that Japan has decided to officially boycott the Olym-*

pics. I'm sure you're aware of this. I'd done my best to brace myself, but when they actually made the announcement, I was stunned. I already knew I wasn't going, but it tore me up inside to think of my friends who thought they were on their way.

Sports and politics… I thought they were totally different things, but in a conflict between nations, I guess it's hard to draw the line.

The second thing is about my boyfriend. He fought as long as he could, but a few months back, on February 15, he breathed his last. I was off that day and got to the hospital just before it happened. I held his hand tight and saw him off to the other side.

His last words: "Thank you for letting me dream."

He clung to his wish for me to play in the Olympics until the very end. I like to think that it gave him something to live for.

After that, I threw myself back into training. Sure, it was almost time for the Olympic team to be selected, but going all-out felt like the right way to pay homage to him.

I hinted at this earlier, but I wasn't selected to represent our country. I just wasn't good enough. But I had given it my all, and I have no regrets.

And even if I had been chosen, I wouldn't have actually gone to the Olympics. Regardless, I still wouldn't think I'd made a mistake.

It's thanks to you, Mr. Namiya, that I can think this way.

I'll confess that when I first wrote to you for advice, I was leaning pretty heavily toward giving up on the Olympics. A big part of me wanted to quit so I could stay beside the man I love and care for him until the end. But there was more to it than that.

For a while, I'd been facing a mental block. Every day, a new failure. I pushed and pushed but always fell short of my standards. I was painfully aware of my physical limitations. I was tired of competing with my rivals, and I was beginning to buckle under the constant pressure. I wanted to escape.

That was when we learned about the cancer.

I can't deny that I saw this as a way out of the brutal competition. When your true love is suffering from an incurable disease, you have to go and care for them. No one could blame me for my decision. And most importantly, I could forgive myself for doing it.

But he knew my weaknesses all too well. That's why he kept on telling me to never back out of the running, no matter what happened. Don't take away my dream, he said. He would never have said something so selfish before.

I became conflicted about what to do. The desire to care for my sick boyfriend, the desire to escape from the Olympics, the desire to make his dream come true—they all spun around my head into a big mess. I even lost sight of what I really wanted for myself.

When I was fed up with worrying alone, I wrote you my first letter. But I'm embarrassed to say that I wasn't entirely honest. I hid from you the fact that deep down, I was trying to run from the Olympics.

But, Mr. Namiya, you saw right through my attempts to deceive you, didn't you?

After we went back and forth a few times, you cut the crap and said, "If you love him, stay beside him to the end." When I read over that line, those words hit me like a hammer to the brain. My intentions weren't that pure at all. I was indulging petty, ugly, insincere thoughts to worm my way out of my responsibilities.

You followed up with more crystal-clear advice.

"This whole thing is only a game."

"The Olympics are just a bigger version of a field day."

"The ultimate waste is worrying about what to do. If you have time to spare, go spend it with your boyfriend."

Honestly, I was perplexed. What made you so confident in your convictions? Then it hit me: You were testing me!

If you told me to give up on the Olympics and I did exactly that, it would mean I wouldn't have made the team anyway. In that case, it would be best for me to quit and spend all my time with my boyfriend. But if I couldn't bring myself to quit, no matter how many times you insisted, it would prove how much the Olympics meant to me.

It was like I was suddenly myself again.

I've always been deeply connected to the Olympics. I'd dreamed about the games since I was little. I couldn't just toss it aside.

I told my boyfriend how I felt.

"I love you more than anyone," I said to him, "and I want us to be together as long as we can. If quitting would make life better for you in any way, I'd do it in a heartbeat. But as long as it won't, I don't want to give up on my dreams. This is what made me who I am, and this is who you fell in love with. You'll never leave my thoughts when I'm out on the field, not even for a moment. Just let me chase my dreams."

He burst into tears right there in his hospital bed. "I can't tell you how long I've been waiting for you to say that. It's been so hard to see you suffering because of me. To me, dying is less painful than the idea of making the woman I love give up on her dreams. Even when we're far apart, I know our hearts are one. We have nothing to worry about. I want you to chase your dreams, no regrets."

From that day on, I threw myself headlong into my training without any misgivings. I'd finally realized that sitting beside someone's sickbed isn't the only way to care for them.

In a matter of weeks, he was gone. His last words—"Thank you for letting me dream"—and the contented look on his face were my two greatest rewards. I may not have made it to the Olympics, but I came away with something far more valuable than a gold medal.

Mr. Namiya, I'm so grateful to you. If we'd never corresponded, I would have forfeited a massive part of me and carried the weight of that loss for the rest of my life. I have nothing but the deepest respect and gratitude to you for your insight.

I'm afraid you may not live here anymore, but I hope this letter finds its way to you somehow.

—Moon Rabbit

Shota and Kohei were both speechless. Atsuya assumed they couldn't think of anything appropriate to say aloud. That was how it was for him, anyway.

This last letter from Moon Rabbit was wholly unexpected. She hadn't given up on the Olympics after all. She stuck it out until the end, even though she ultimately wasn't chosen for the team, and Japan had decided to forsake the games entirely. And yet, she harbored no regrets at all. According to her, she was actually happy for gaining something much more valuable than a gold medal.

She went so far as to say she believed it was all thanks to the Namiya General Store. She was convinced that Atsuya's letter, a rant penned in a fit of anger and frustration, had steered her in the right direction. It didn't seem as though she was writing out of scorn or irony. If she were, she wouldn't have been compelled to write so much.

A smile crept over Atsuya's face. This whole situation was so absurd. Little spasms in his chest gave way to snickering, which became an audible whimpering that broke into an uproarious cackle.

"Come on, isn't this hilarious? We tell her to forget the Olympics, and she just hears what she wants to hear. And because things worked out all right, she thanks us for our 'insight.' As if we had anything to do with it."

Shota's face relaxed. "Is that such a bad thing? Things worked out, didn't they?"

"Yeah, I mean, it was kinda fun," volunteered Kohei. "I've never had the chance to give anyone advice before. Whether it's a fluke or not, I'm glad she asked us for advice. Aren't you, Atsuya?"

Atsuya screwed up his face and scratched under his nose. "Well, I can't say I feel any worse."

"See? I knew it."

"I'm not as psyched as you two are. Okay? Come on, I've had enough of this. Let's open up that back door. Otherwise we'll literally be here forever."

Atsuya walked over to the back of the house. He had his hand on the knob, ready to turn it, when Shota yelled out at him, "Wait a sec!"

"What now?"

Shota didn't reply and made his way to the shop.

"What is it?" Atsuya asked Kohei, but he only cocked his head and shrugged.

Shota came back into the kitchen. He had a grim look on his face.

"What's going on?" Atsuya asked.

"We've got another one," said Shota, and he raised his hand to show him. "Looks like it's from someone else."

He was pinching a brown envelope between his fingers.

CHAPTER 2

MIDNIGHT BLUES

1

At the check-in desk for visitors sat a scrawny man, who looked well over sixty and who definitely hadn't been here last year. He had the demeanor of someone who'd worked his entire life at some administrative job, only to retire and start working at this one.

Katsuro was uneasy when he told the man his name.

"Katsuro who?" the man asked, just as he'd predicted.

"Katsuro Matsuoka. I'm here to play the concert. For charity."

"Charity?"

"For the Christmas show…"

"Ah yes, the assembly." The man finally put it together. "I'd heard we were going to have some kind of musical performance. I guess I was expecting a band. But it's just you, huh?"

"Ah, yeah. Sorry." Katsuro heard himself apologize.

"One moment please."

The man picked up the phone and dialed an extension. He exchanged a few words with the person on the line and told Katsuro, "Someone will be right with you."

A woman with glasses came down the hall to greet him. He remembered her face. She was in charge of the party last year. She seemed to remember him, too, and approached him with a genial smile.

"Welcome back. Thanks for coming."

"Thanks for having me again."

"Our pleasure."

She led him to a waiting room outfitted with a few chairs and a table.

"You'll have forty minutes onstage. Would you mind choosing the set list, like you did last year?"

"No problem. I'll mostly be playing Christmas music. Plus one or two originals."

"Interesting." She flashed him half a smile, as if trying to remember the originals he'd performed the year before.

There was still some time before he would need to get onstage, so Katsuro sat in the waiting room, where a bottle of tea and a paper cup were waiting on the table. He poured some for himself and took a few sips.

This marked his second visit to Marumitsuen, a children's home. It was a four-story structure of reinforced concrete, set in a grove halfway up a hillside. It had living quarters, a cafeteria, baths, and a variety of facilities for babies, eighteen-year-olds, and everyone in between. By now, Katsuro had been to plenty of these places. Marumitsuen was one of the larger homes.

He hoisted up his guitar, checking to see if it was properly tuned one last time, and sang a few notes. Things sounded all right. He could be better—or worse.

The woman with glasses came back and said it was time. Katsuro helped himself to one more cupful of cold tea before standing up.

The assembly was held in the gymnasium. The children sat up straight in a couple of rows of folding chairs. Most of them looked to be in elementary school. When Katsuro came before them, they gave him a polite round of applause, as instructed by the adults.

A microphone, a folding chair, and a music stand had been set up for Katsuro. He bowed to the crowd of kids and took a seat. "Hello, Marumitsuen!"

"Hello," the children replied in unison.

"This is my second time here. I had the privilege of performing on Christmas Eve last year, too. I guess coming every year makes me a bit like Santa Claus. Ah, but I didn't bring you any presents." A smattering of laughter. "Don't worry. I'd like to present you with some music, just like last time."

Katsuro strummed the opening chords to "Rudolph the Red-Nosed Reindeer" and started to sing. Everybody knew the song, and partway through, they began to sing along.

He went on to play all the classic Christmas songs and cracked a few jokes in between tunes. The kids appeared to be having fun. Before long, they started to clap. Some of them were even rocking out, in their own way.

But midway through the set, Katsuro became fixated on one of the kids: a girl seated in the second row, all the way to the left. If she was still in elementary school, she would have to be in one of the upper grades. Her eyes were staring off into space. She wasn't even remotely close to looking at Katsuro. The music didn't seem to interest her, and she most definitely wasn't moving her lips to partake in the sing-along.

Katsuro was drawn toward her forlorn expression, tinged with something that didn't belong on the face of a child. He felt the urge to make her look his way.

After he'd come to the conclusion that the standard, run-of-the-mill tunes were boring her, he tried playing the Yumi Matsutoya song "My Baby Santa Claus [*Koibito no Santa Claus*]" from *Take Me Out to the Snowland*, a blockbuster from the previous year. Strictly speaking, he was violating copyright laws by playing the song, but who was going to report him?

Most of the kids enjoyed his rendition, but she was still staring off into the rafters.

He tried playing a few songs he thought girls her age might like, but nothing hit. Maybe music didn't interest her in general. Katsuro had no choice but to cut his losses.

"All right, here's my last song. I always play this one to close. Thanks for listening."

Katsuro put down his guitar and pulled out his harmonica. He took a deep breath and closed his eyes to blow the notes to a song he'd played a thousand times. He didn't need sheet music for this one.

Its melody lasted about three and a half minutes. Over the course of that time, the gymnasium fell silent. Just before his lips left his instrument, Katsuro opened his eyes.

His heart skipped a beat in his chest.

The girl was staring into him. Her eyes were dead serious. For a moment, he panicked and almost forgot how to act his age.

When he was done with his set, Katsuro walked off, awash with more polite applause from the children. The woman with glasses pattered over and thanked him for a job well done.

He was going to ask about that girl, but he swallowed back his words. What reason could he possibly give for asking?

But as it turned out, he wound up speaking with her anyway, albeit not exactly how he expected.

After the assembly, the children gathered to have dinner in the cafeteria. Katsuro had been invited to attend, and while he was eating his meal, the girl suddenly approached him.

"What was that song?" she asked, meeting his gaze directly.

"Which one?"

"The last one. On the harmonica. I've never heard that song before."

He chuckled and nodded. "That's not surprising. It's an original."

"Original?"

"It's a song I wrote myself. Did you like it?"

The girl nodded eagerly. "I thought it was great. I wanna hear it again."

"Yeah? All right, you wait here."

He sauntered up to his room for the night, which had been

provided by the children's home, to grab his harmonica. Once he returned to the cafeteria, he led the girl out into the hall and played the song for her again. She listened to the notes of the harmonica and gazed at him intently.

"Does it have a name?"

"It's called 'Reborn.'"

"'Reborn'…," she whispered to herself and started to hum.

When Katsuro recognized the tune, he was floored. She was repeating the melody of his song perfectly.

"You've got it already?"

She smiled at him, finally. "I'm good at remembering songs."

"That's amazing." Katsuro looked her in the eye. The word *genius* flashed across his mind.

"Mr. Matsuoka, how come you haven't gone pro?"

"Pro, huh…? I dunno about that." Katsuro shook his head and attempted to hide the tremor rising in his heart.

"I'm sure that song would be a hit."

"Yeah?"

She nodded. "I like it."

Katsuro grinned. "Thanks. Me too."

"Seri, you out there?" A staff member poked her head into the hallway. "Can you come feed Tatsu?"

"Ah, okay." Seri bowed once to Katsuro and slipped back into the cafeteria.

He followed a little ways behind and saw that Seri had sat down next to a little boy, trying to get him to hold a spoon. The boy was slight in build, and his face was unexpressive.

The woman with glasses stood nearby. Katsuro casually asked her about the two children.

"They're siblings. They came to live with us last spring. Fled from an abusive home. Tatsu won't speak to anyone but his older sister."

"Huh."

As Katsuro watched Seri looking after her younger brother, he began to understand why she didn't care for the Christmas carols.

When dinner was over, Katsuro retired to his room. Sprawled out on his bed, he heard the raucous sound of children's voices through the windows. He sat up and looked outside to see the kids playing with sparklers. They didn't seem to mind the cold in the slightest.

He spotted Seri and Tatsu, who were watching the others from a distance.

How come you haven't gone pro...?

It'd been a long time since anyone had even bothered to ask him that—maybe ten years since he'd last tried laughing off the idea with some pathetic excuse. But his outlook was completely different then.

"I've let you down, Dad," he murmured through the window into the night sky. "I haven't even had the chance to fight that losing battle."

He thought back eight years into the past.

2

On one of the first days of July, Katsuro received the call about his grandmother's death. He was getting ready to open up shop when the call came from his younger sister, Emiko.

He'd known their grandmother wasn't doing well. Her liver and kidneys were failing, and he'd admitted to himself that she was on her way out, but he still hadn't mustered up the strength to go home to see her. He wasn't *not* worried about her. But he had his reasons for not going home.

"The *tsuya* ceremony's tomorrow, and the funeral's the day after. How soon can you be here?"

Katsuro propped his elbow on the counter and scratched his head with his free hand. "I gotta work, so I dunno. I'll have to ask the boss."

He heard Emiko inhale sharply through her teeth.

"Work? You're just helping out, right? Didn't you say he ran that place alone before you started? Taking off a day or two isn't going to put him out. I thought you took this job specifically so you could take time off whenever you needed to."

She had a point and a whip-crack memory. Emiko didn't mess around, and he knew he couldn't fool her with a little fast-talking, so Katsuro went quiet.

"We're gonna be in trouble if you don't come home," she said in a sharper voice this time. "Dad's not in good shape, either, and Mom's exhausted from taking care of Grandma. Grandma did a lot for you, you know. The least you could do is come to her funeral."

Katsuro sighed. "All right. I'll figure something out."

"Come as soon as you can. Tonight, ideally."

"That's not gonna happen."

"Fine, then tomorrow morning. Noon at the latest."

"I'll think about it."

"Think hard. You've always been able to do whatever you wanted."

He was about to ask what the hell she meant by that, but she'd already hung up on him.

Katsuro replaced the receiver and sat down on a stool. He gazed absentmindedly at a painting on the wall, which supposedly depicted some beach in Okinawa. His boss loved that island. Every inch of this tiny bar was decked out with something Okinawan.

He gazed off into the corner of the room, where an acoustic guitar leaned against a rattan chair. Both were reserved for Katsuro. Upon request, he'd sit in the chair and play. Sometimes customers would sing along, but most of the time, he'd sing solo. They'd make a big deal the first time they heard him. "Listen to this! I can't believe you're a self-taught musician!" Once in a while, someone would ask him why he hadn't tried going pro.

"Ah, come on," he'd demur, but in his gut, his every fiber screamed,

"That's all I've ever wanted!" That was the reason he'd dropped out of college, after all.

He'd fallen for music in middle school. In sixth grade, he'd gone over to a friend's house and seen his older brother's guitar in a stand. The friend had shown him how to hold it, and that was the first time he'd ever touched a guitar. His fingers had been clumsy at first, but he'd quickly picked up how to play the main riff of a simple rock song. He tried it over and over again, and when he finally nailed it, no words could describe his euphoria. It was nothing like blowing into some recorder in music class. An unspeakable thrill coursed through his veins.

A few days later, he had taken the plunge and said to his parents that he wanted one of his own. His dad ran a fish shop. Music had played no role in his life, and he reacted first with shock, and then with anger. He told his son to quit hanging around whatever friends had planted that idea in his head, apparently convinced playing the guitar automatically made you a neighborhood delinquent.

Katsuro persisted, making every promise he could think of: "I'll study hard and get into the best high school, and if I don't get in, I'll throw the guitar away and never play again."

His parents had been nonplussed. After all, Katsuro had never wanted anything so badly. His mother eventually warmed up to the idea, and at last, his father had caved. But they'd brought him to a pawn shop, not a music store. He'd have to put up with a used guitar for now.

"Gonna end up tossing it in the dump, anyway. You're not getting a pricey one," his dad had groused.

Katsuro had been thrilled just having a guitar. He couldn't care less where it had come from, and he'd carefully laid it next to him on his pillow that night. After that, he'd practiced nearly every day, referencing instruction booklets from the secondhand bookstore. To keep his promise to his parents, he studied for class just as hard. His grades skyrocketed. On the weekends, he spent the whole day locked up in his room strumming away, and his parents had no room to complain. Especially after he was accepted to the best high school in the area, true to his word.

When he'd entered school, the first thing he did was join the music club. With a few members from the student organization, Katsuro formed a three-piece band, who took every chance they got to perform. At first, they did only covers, but as time passed, they'd started to add original material with most of it written by Katsuro. He did the vocals, too, and his bandmates thought very highly of his music.

But in their third year, they disbanded. Everyone was focusing on cramming for their entrance exams. They'd promised one another that if all of them got into college, they would reunite, but that hadn't been how things played out. One of the members had flunked the test and wasn't able to get in anywhere. He'd eventually gotten accepted somewhere a year later, but no plan to get back together ever arose again.

Katsuro went to school in Tokyo to become an econ major. At first, he'd wanted to do something involving music, but he thought better of it, knowing his parents would be opposed, especially because he'd been expected to carry on the family store. This had been established from when Katsuro was very young, and his parents didn't seem to have even the slightest suspicion that he might choose to do otherwise. Even Katsuro had a vague idea that this would be how things turned out for him.

His college had all kinds of clubs related to music, and he'd joined one. But before long, he knew he'd made a mistake. The club had been more into playing around than playing music; nobody took it seriously. He'd tried to bring this up on a number of occasions, but the other guys acted like he was crazy.

"Get off your high horse, man. Music is supposed to be about having a good time."

"Yeah, what are you so uptight about? It's not like you're gonna make it big."

Unable to come up with an appropriate rebuttal, Katsuro quit the club for good. He knew it was pointless to argue. They were after different things in life.

After that, Katsuro hadn't tried to hit up any of the other clubs. He'd felt like it would just be easier to make music on his own, since being around unambitious people stressed him out.

That was around the time he'd started entering competitions for amateurs. He was used to being onstage from performing at all sorts of gigs in high school. The first few times, he'd gotten nowhere, but once he got the hang of it, he made it to the final round more often than not. These contests had their regular acts, and Katsuro became one of them.

The mentality of this group was infectious. For them, music was their sole passion. They were willing to sacrifice anything in the name of their own tunes.

I gotta try to do better than that, he told himself whenever he listened to them play.

Almost all his waking hours were poured into musical composition. Even when he was eating or sitting in the tub, his thoughts were occupied by the music he was writing in his head. This was when he'd stopped going to class, once and for all. He couldn't see a reason to attend, which resulted in his receiving no credits and failing out of all his courses.

His parents had no idea. After they'd sent their only son to Tokyo, they'd assumed he would graduate in four years and come back home. When Katsuro had called home to tell his mother he was dropping out, she'd wailed over the receiver. That was the summer when he was twenty-one. His father had come on the line and demanded to know what the hell Katsuro thought he was doing, loudly enough to leave his ears ringing.

Katsuro was going to pursue his music. There was no reason to keep going to college.

When his father heard his reasoning, he began to scream his head off. Katsuro just hung up.

That night, his parents showed up at his Tokyo apartment—his father livid, his mother pale. They talked in that teeny six-tatami-mat studio until dawn. His parents had said that if he was going to drop out, he would have to move back home and take over the fish shop. Katsuro refused to nod in agreement. He'd told them that if he did that, he'd regret it for the rest of his life. And he was gonna stay in Tokyo until he made it.

In the morning, his sleep-deprived parents went home on the first train. From the window of his apartment, Katsuro watched them walk away. From behind, they looked small and lonesome, and Katsuro had unconsciously clasped his hands in prayer.

Three years passed. By now, Katsuro should have been out of college. Instead, he found himself with little to show for himself. His days were still a looped reel of contests and practice, practice, practice. He'd placed in many of them, and he assumed that if he kept on competing, a talent scout would eventually discover him. But so far, no luck. He tried sending demo tapes to record companies, but nobody bothered to respond.

Just once, a frequent patron of the bar had introduced him to a music critic, a man with white permed hair, who had listened while Katsuro played two of his originals.

At this point, Katsuro had been thinking about making a go of it as a singer-songwriter. He'd felt confident about both songs.

"Hey," the critic said, "that's not bad. The melody is catchy, and your voice is strong. Good stuff."

Katsuro was ecstatic. His heart pounded, and he knew he was steps away from his debut.

The customer popped the question on Katsuro's behalf. "Think he has what it takes?"

He went tense all over. He couldn't dare look the critic in the eye.

The critic paused for a beat before letting out a groan. "I think you'd better quit while you're ahead."

Katsuro's head snapped up to look at him. "And why's that?"

"Look. This city is full of people who can sing at least as good as you. If your voice had something special, something unique about it, it might be a different story, but it doesn't."

The man cut right to the chase, and Katsuro had no response. This wasn't news to him.

"What about the songs?" his boss interjected. "They sound pretty good to me."

"They're good. For an amateur. But good's not good enough." The critic's voice was unforgiving. "They sound like songs that are already out there. They aren't fresh."

This was excruciating, and Katsuro's body went hot with resentment and self-pity.

So I don't have any talent, and I'll never make a living from my music. From that day forward, Katsuro had taken these fears as givens.

3

He wound up leaving his apartment the following afternoon, carrying a duffel and a garment bag. Inside the latter was a black suit he'd borrowed from his boss. Not knowing when he was coming back to Tokyo, he'd been tempted to bring along his guitar, but the thought of what his parents might say gave him pause. Instead, he stuffed his harmonica into a pocket of the duffel bag.

He boarded a train for Tokyo Station. At that time of day, the train was so empty he had a four-seater booth all to himself, so he wiggled out of his shoes and propped up his feet on the seat across from him. To get to his hometown from that station, he had to transfer and ride for two hours. He'd heard of some people who supposedly commuted all the way to Tokyo and back each day, but Katsuro couldn't fathom how anyone could do that on the daily.

His mind wandered back to when his boss had heard about his grandmother's passing and how he hadn't hesitated to give Katsuro the okay to go to the ceremony.

"It's a good chance for you to go back home and talk things over with your folks. About what comes next and all." It sounded like a reprimand. The implication was that maybe it was time he gave up on music.

Gazing out the windows of the train at the fields of farmland, he asked himself dimly if maybe they were right, if maybe he didn't have what it took. He was sure that when he got home, somebody would make a comment. He could hear his parents already. "Come on; wake up; quit dreaming; life isn't easy; wise up and come home; take over the shop; it's not like any proper company is going to hire you."

Katsuro shook his head. He needed to stop mulling over these depressing thoughts. He unzipped his duffel and pulled out his Walkman and headphones, two devices that had been on the market for a little over a year and changed the world for good. Katsuro could listen to music anywhere he went.

He pressed play and closed his eyes. A gorgeous mélange of digital sounds fed into his ears, a song by a group called Yellow Magic Orchestra. All the members were Japanese, but they'd first made a name for themselves overseas. As legend had it, when they opened for the Tubes at a show in Los Angeles, the whole crowd stood and wouldn't stop cheering.

Is this what it takes to have talent? He'd tried to block the idea from his mind, but this time, it slipped by and went straight for his heart.

The train finally arrived at the station closest to his house. Exiting the ticket lobby, he found himself surrounded by familiar sights. There was a main street that curved into the highway and was lined with shop after tiny shop. These businesses had no customers other than their regulars. Katsuro hadn't bothered to come home since dropping out of college, but the atmosphere of the town hadn't changed in the slightest.

He stopped at a narrow storefront, set between a florist and a greengrocer, that had its shutter partially closed. The sign above read UOMATSU, and in smaller text to the side, FRESH SEAFOOD and EVENT CATERING.

The shop was started by his grandfather. The first location was more spacious, but that building had burned to the ground during the war. He had reopened here when it was over.

Katsuro ducked under the half-closed shutter. The shop was dark. He squinted at the refrigerated display cases. No fish. This time of year, fresh seafood barely lasted in the fridge for a day. Whatever was left had probably been frozen. On the wall, a handwritten message announced: NOW SERVING GRILLED EEL.

The familiar stench of fish tugged at his heartstrings. He walked to the back of the shop, where there was a stone slab that led into the rest of the house. The sliding door was almost shut, but light leaked through the gap, and Katsuro could sense someone moving beyond it.

He took a deep breath and yelled inside. "I'm home."

The second that left his lips, he wished he'd said only "Hello?"

The door rolled open, and his sister, Emiko, stood there in a black dress. It had been a while since he had last seen her, and she was all grown up now. Emiko looked down at Katsuro and sighed.

"You made it. I thought you weren't coming."

"Why? I said I'd figure something out."

Katsuro kicked off his shoes and stepped up into the tiny living room. He looked around.

"Just you here? Where's Mom and Dad?"

"They've been at the funeral home all afternoon. I was supposed to go and help them, but I stayed behind because I thought it'd make things harder for all of us if you came home to an empty house."

Katsuro shrugged. "Oh."

"Don't tell me you're planning to go to the *tsuya* dressed like that."

He'd shown up in a T-shirt and jeans. "Course not. Wait a minute; I'll go change."

"Hurry up, okay?"

"I know." Katsuro lugged his bags upstairs.

The second floor had two modest tatami rooms, six mats and four and a half mats. The bigger one had been Katsuro's until he'd graduated high school.

When he opened the door, he was ticked off by what he saw.

The closed curtains made it dark, so he flicked the light switch on the wall. Under the white fluorescent lights, he found his old room untouched. The ancient pencil sharpener was still bolted to his writing desk, and the posters of his favorite idols were tacked up on the walls. On the bookshelf, guitar books shared space with his old dictionaries.

Sometime after moving to Tokyo, Katsuro had heard from his mother that Emiko wanted to use the room. Katsuro had said he didn't care. By then, he'd already set his heart on pursuing a musical career and had no intention of ever moving home again. The fact that his parents had left his room this way made Katsuro wonder if they were expecting him to come back. The thought of it made his spirit sink. He changed into his suit.

He and Emiko left the house together. It was cool for July, mercifully so. The *tsuya* ceremony was being held at the community center. It was a new facility, ten minutes on foot from the house.

When they stepped out into the neighborhood, Katsuro was disturbed by how much the landscape had changed. Emiko had said a lot of people had been moving here. *Guess even a town this small has its fair share of change*, he thought.

"So, Katsuro, how's everything going?" Emiko asked him as they walked.

He knew what she meant, but he tried to dodge the question. "How's *what* going?"

"You said you had big plans. It'd be great if you could make a living off your music, but do you think you can make it happen?"

"Obviously. If I didn't think so, I wouldn't be doing it." He felt a prick in his heart. He wasn't telling the whole truth.

"I just can't get my head around the idea that I grew up in the same house as a person who has *that* kind of potential. I know your music. I've seen you perform, and I think you put on a great show, but could you do that for a living? Going pro is a whole different ball game."

Katsuro screwed up his face. "Don't be cute. What do you know about any of this? You're clueless."

He thought she would tear into him for that, but her tone was temperate.

"You're right. I am clueless. I don't know the first thing about the business. That's why I'm asking you. Like, what's the plan? If you're really so confident, I'm sure you can be more specific about your vision for the future. A concrete destination, and the steps you'll take to get there. How long is it going to be before you can get by on music alone? It makes me worried to think you don't have a clue. I bet it's even worse for Mom and Dad."

His sister's logic made perfect sense, but Katsuro dismissed it with an ugly burst of laughter.

"If things always went according to plan, no one would ever struggle. Though it might be hard to understand for a certain someone who's going straight to the local bank after graduating from a women's college."

He was talking about Emiko. She wasn't graduating until next spring, but she already had a job lined up. He was certain that this time she'd lose her cool, but she sighed instead.

"Do you ever think about how you're going to help take care of our parents? They're old, Katsuro."

He was silent. The fact that their parents were getting old was something he didn't like to think about.

"Dad collapsed again last month. Another heart attack."

Katsuro stopped and looked at her. "You serious?"

"Dead serious." Emiko looked straight back at him. "It wasn't severe, but the timing sucked. Grandma had just taken a turn for the worse. It really gave us a scare."

"I had no idea."

"Dad didn't want Mom to tell you."

"Man…"

His father must have thought there was no use telling a thankless child. Katsuro had no argument against that. There was nothing left to say, so they started walking again. The rest of the way, Emiko didn't say anything, either.

4

The community center was built like a traditional Japanese house, one story but on a larger scale. Men and women in funeral clothes were moving hurriedly about the entrance.

Their mother, Kanako, was standing in the lobby and having a conversation with a man who was positively skeletal. Katsuro took his time approaching them.

When his mother saw him, he watched as she soundlessly mouthed "Well."

Katsuro was about to say, "I made it," but just before he did, he saw the face of the man standing beside her, and he lost the ability to form any more words.

It was his father, Takeo. So skinny Katsuro mistook him for a stranger.

Takeo gave him a long, hard look and opened his rigid line of a mouth. "How'd you wind up here? Who told you?" he asked, no filter.

"Emiko called me."

"Is that right?" Takeo glanced at Emiko, then back to Katsuro. "Didn't think you had time to spare on a thing like this."

Katsuro parsed this as shorthand for: "I thought you said you wouldn't show your face around here again until you made it big."

"If you're suggesting I go back to Tokyo, I can hop on the next train."

"Katsuro." His mother gave him a look of warning.

Takeo waved his hand dismissively. "I'm not saying that. Cut the shit, okay? I don't have time for it today." He hobbled off in haste.

The three of them watched Takeo take his leave, and then Kanako said, "You sure came a long way. I was worried you might not make it."

It was starting to look as though Emiko's phone call had been her idea.

"Emiko wouldn't let up. Whatever. Anyway, Dad's getting pretty skinny. I heard he fell again. Is he okay?"

His mother's shoulders slumped a little under Katsuro's question.

"He acts tough, but I can see he's losing strength. I mean, he's over sixty."

"He's that old?"

As the story went, Takeo was already thirty-six when he married Kanako. He'd been so preoccupied with rebuilding Uomatsu that he hadn't had time to find a bride, or at least, that's what Katsuro had heard over and over as a kid.

As the clock neared six PM, the scheduled start time for the *tsuya* ceremony, more family began to show. Takeo had a lot of siblings, and between them and their kids, they saw at least twenty people from his side of the family. It had been ten years or more since Katsuro had seen any of them.

An uncle three years younger than Takeo approached Katsuro and extended his hand for a handshake.

"Hey, Katsuro, looking great. Heard you're still up in Tokyo. What've you been up to?"

"Ah, um. Yeah, you know, this and that." He was ashamed by his vague answer.

"This and that? Don't tell me you were held back just to screw around."

Katsuro was startled at the revelation that his parents evidently hadn't told his relatives he'd left school. Kanako was nearby; she had to be listening, but she neither spoke nor looked their way.

Humiliation bubbled inside Katsuro. So his parents felt like they couldn't admit their son was an aspiring musician. But he'd also been unable to tell his uncle. Was he going to stand there, tongue-tied, just like his parents? *No way*, he thought. *Not me.*

He licked his lips and looked his uncle square in the face. "I dropped out."

"Huh?"

"College. I dropped out." From the corner of his eye, Katsuro noticed Kanako stiffening up all over, but he went on. "I'm trying to make it in the music industry."

"Mu-sic?" Given his uncle's face and stilted pronunciation, he seemed almost unfamiliar with the word.

But their conversation ended there, mercifully. The ceremony had formally begun. His uncle walked off, incredulous, and cornered some relative, probably to verify that what Katsuro had said was true.

Starting from the chanting of the sutras, the ceremony proceeded in customary fashion. Katsuro partook and burned a stick of incense. Up at the altar, the memorial photograph of his grandmother smiled gently. Katsuro had fond memories of his grandma looking after him when he was little. He was sure that if she were still alive, she'd be on his side.

When the ceremony was over, everyone moved to another room in the building, where sushi and beer were spread out on low tables. As he looked around, he noticed that family were the only ones who'd stayed behind. Grandma had been almost ninety, and everyone was only a little bit sad. It had been so long since everyone had gotten together. The reception turned out to be more like a warm reunion than anything else.

Amid the revelry, a voice screamed, "Enough! What happens in my house is none of your business." Katsuro didn't need to look to know that it was Takeo.

"Your house? Before you moved the shop, it was our old man's. Not sure if you recall, but I lived there, too." The person talking back to him was the uncle from earlier. Both of their faces were flushed red from the alcohol.

"The house Dad built was burned in the war. I built the house that's there now. You've got no reason or right to complain."

"Listen to this guy! Only reason you could reopen the shop was because of the name Uomatsu. Dad may have left it to you, but did ya think you could close down shop without consulting us? That store's his legacy."

"Who said I was closing? I'm not going anywhere."

"How long you think you can go on in the shape you're in? Look at you. I bet you can't carry a flat of tuna across the shop. What the hell are you thinking? Sending your only son to school in Tokyo? You don't need an education to sling fish."

"Oh, is that all the family trade is to you?"

Takeo stood up. The two men were on the verge of a scuffle, but everyone rushed in to break it up. His father finally took a seat.

"…Crazy old goat. What're you thinking?" the uncle muttered, settling down. He nursed his cup of sake. "How'd you let your only son quit school? To become a singer? Stupid."

"Shut it. I don't need your advice."

Seeing the heat rising between them, the aunts escorted the uncle to a different seat at the other side of the room.

The argument between the two men may have quelled, but the tension in the room could not be neutralized. One of the relatives stood and said they'd better be going. The rest followed suit.

"Don't feel like you have to stick around," Takeo told Kanako and Katsuro. "I'll wait for the incense to burn down."

"Are you sure?" she asked. "Don't push yourself."

"Don't treat me like I'm sick or something."

Katsuro exited the community center with Emiko and Kanako, but after they'd trudged toward home for a little a bit, he stopped in his tracks and turned around.

"Don't mind me. You two go on ahead."

"What's wrong?" asked Kanako. "Did you forget something?"

"Not exactly…," he stammered.

"Are you going to talk to Dad?" Emiko guessed.

He nodded. "Yeah, I was thinking I probably should."

"Yeah, okay. All right, let's go, Mom."

Kanako showed no sign of leaving. She cast her eyes down, as if deep in thought, and then raised her head to look at him.

"Your father isn't angry at you, Katsuro. He wants you to be happy."

"…You think so?"

"You saw him fighting with his brother."

"Yeah…"

Katsuro had understood the meaning behind their conversation. *Shut it. I don't need your advice.* The whole fight with his brother was a way of demonstrating that his son could make his own decisions. That was why Katsuro wanted to talk to him, to ask him about his true intentions.

"Your father wants you to live out your dreams. He doesn't want to get in your way. He doesn't want his poor health to force you to give up what matters most to you. If you're going to talk to him, that's fine, but keep that in mind."

"Okay. Got it."

Katsuro watched his sister and his mother walk off into the night, then turned and ran the other way.

This was a development he hadn't been expecting when he boarded the train at Tokyo Station. He'd been prepared to be chided by his parents and guilted by his relatives, but not for his parents to shield him from their accusations. He thought back to the moment three years prior when he watched his parents limp away from his apartment, the night they failed to persuade him. How had they come to this change of heart?

Almost all the lights were off inside the community center, except for the window in the very back. Skirting the main entrance, Katsuro tiptoed along the side of the building and went up to the window. A paper screen blocked most of what was inside, but it was slightly ajar. Through the gap, he peered inside.

The room wasn't the one decked out for the ceremony, but the space where the coffin had been set up for the funeral. Incense burned before the altar. At the front of the neat grid of chairs sat Takeo.

What was his father doing? Takeo stood up and went over to a bag by the far wall. He pulled out something slender wrapped in a white cloth.

He started to unravel it as he approached the casket, and the object beneath glinted in the light. In that instant, Katsuro knew what he was holding.

A knife. A knife with history. Katsuro had heard its story more times than he cared to count.

His grandfather had used this blade from the day he opened Uomatsu. It had been handed down to Takeo when the decision was made for him to take over the business. This was the knife Takeo had used when he learned and trained how to cut a fish.

Takeo draped the cloth over the casket and placed the knife there. He glanced at the photo of his mother and clasped his hands in prayer. It ate away at Katsuro's heart to watch this happening. He had a feeling he knew what Takeo was saying to his mother.

He was apologizing. For closing down the business his father had bequeathed to him. For failing to pass down the family blade.

Katsuro stepped away from the window. Without ever going through the main entrance, he left the community center behind.

5

Katsuro felt awful about his father's state. Never had he felt guilt from the bottom of his heart. He had to thank his father for setting him free.

Still, could he live with the way things were going?

His uncle was right. His father's health was getting pretty bad. *Who knows how long we would be able to keep the shop alive?* Even if Kanako took over, she'd need to take care of her husband, too. They might close any day now, with zero notice.

What then?

Emiko was starting work next spring as a teller at a local bank, which meant she could still live at home. But her salary would be nowhere near enough to look after both their parents.

What was Katsuro supposed to do? Give up on music and take over Uomatsu?

That was the most realistic option. But what would come of the dream he'd nurtured all these years? After all, Kanako had said Takeo didn't want to be the reason why Katsuro gave up his dreams.

Katsuro sighed. He looked around and stopped walking for a second.

He had no clue where he was. The new houses had messed with his sense of direction.

He jogged around, up one street, down another, and finally made it to an area he recognized. When he was little, there used to be an empty lot around here where he loved to play.

The road had a gradual uphill slope, and Katsuro took his time walking along. A little ways up, on the right side of the road, he saw a building he remembered from when he was a kid. A little store where he bought stuff like pencils and paper. He was sure this was it. The grubby sign said NAMIYA GENERAL STORE.

His memories of the store went beyond his purchases. The old man who ran it used to hear him out when things were bothering him and offer him advice. Looking back, none of the things he asked for help about were serious. *How can I win first place in the race at field day? How can I get more money on New Year's?* Nevertheless, Old Man Namiya took him seriously. For the New Year's question, he suggested, *Make a law where all the envelopes for New Year's money from your relatives have to be transparent.* His reasoning? *They'll need to put more in, to keep up appearances.*

He wondered how the old man was. Gazing at the shop, Katsuro felt as if he were looking back in time. The rusty shutter was pulled down, and no light bled from the windows of the rooms upstairs. He went around the side of the house to look at the garage. They used to do graffiti on the wall here. But the old man never scolded them. The most he said was "If you're going to draw on the walls, at least draw something good."

He was sorry to find no trace of what they'd drawn. It had been at least ten years by now. The marks had weathered away and disappeared.

Then it happened. Bicycle brakes screeched to a halt out front. Katsuro poked his head out from the alley to find a young woman getting off her bike.

She pulled something from the bag slung over her shoulder and slipped it into the mail slot in the shutter. As he watched her, he found himself breaking the silence with a quiet "What?"

Although he hadn't spoken very loudly, the silent night gave his words ample clearance to reverberate. The woman looked frightened and straddled her bike. She probably thought he was a pervert.

"Wait, hold on; it's not what you think! I wasn't doing anything." Katsuro stepped out into the street, waving his hands wildly. "I wasn't hiding; I was just having a look at this wall. I used to play here, as a kid."

The woman sat astride her bike, one foot on the pedals, ready to push off at any second. She stared at Katsuro, her eyes glazed with suspicion. Her long hair was tied up at her neck. She wore little makeup, but her features were well-defined. She was Katsuro's age, or maybe a little younger. Her muscular arms peeking out from the sleeves of her T-shirt suggested she was some kind of athlete.

"You saw me, didn't you?" she asked, her voice a bit husky.

Unsure of what she meant, Katsuro didn't speak.

She elaborated. "Didn't you see what I was doing, just a second ago?" Her tone was accusatory.

"It looked like you put something in the mail slot…"

The woman scowled and bit her lower lip, averting her gaze. But then she looked at Katsuro. "Please forget you saw any of this. Me included."

"But…"

The woman bid him good-bye and made to pedal off.

"Wait. Just one question." Katsuro dashed ahead and stopped in front of her. "The letter in that envelope… Were you asking for advice?"

The woman drew back and eyed Katsuro cautiously. "Who's asking?"

"A friend of the store. I used to get advice from the old man when I was little…"

"What's your name?"

Katsuro scrunched his eyebrows together. "Shouldn't you give your name before asking someone else's?"

Still straddling the bike, the woman sighed. "I'm afraid I can't. And the letter wasn't asking for advice. It was a thank-you."

"A thank-you?"

"About six months ago, I asked him for advice and got exactly what I needed. I wrote to say thanks for helping me figure things out."

"You asked him? You mean someone at this store? Don't tell me that old man still lives here." Katsuro looked at the woman and back at the decrepit house.

The girl shook her head. "I'm not sure he does, but when I left a letter last year, I came back the next day, went around back, and there it was in the milk crate."

An answer. That's right. Come by at night and drop a letter in the mail slot, and the next day, you'll find an answer in there.

"I wonder if he's still accepting letters."

"Yeah, who knows. It's been a while since I got my advice. I'm not even sure he'll get this. But I wrote it with that possibility in mind."

It seemed as though whatever Mr. Namiya had told her had been extremely influential.

"Um, is that all?" the woman asked. "If I'm not home soon, my family's going to wonder where I went."

"Oh, yeah. Sorry."

Katsuro stepped aside. The woman stepped down on the pedals with impressive force, and the bicycle glided away with growing speed. Before Katsuro could count to ten, she was gone.

He turned to look again at the old storefront. It seemed deserted. If letters were being answered from an abandoned house, the only explanation was that the place was haunted.

Katsuro huffed through his nose. What a load of crap. There was no way that was what was happening. He shook his head and walked away.

Back at home, he found Emiko in the living room alone. She said she couldn't sleep, so she was having a nightcap. On the tea table before her was a whiskey bottle and a glass. She'd really grown up overnight. Their mother was already in bed.

"Did you talk to Dad?"

"No, I wound up not going back. I just went for a walk."

"Where'd you go this time of night?"

"Around. Oh yeah. Do you remember that old store, the Namiya General Store?"

"Namiya? Yeah, I remember that place. It's kind of in a weird spot, right?"

"Think somebody still lives there?"

"What?" Emiko's voice had the curl of a question mark. "I highly doubt it. They closed down a while ago. I'm pretty sure the place is empty."

"Ha. I knew it."

"Knew what? What's going on?"

"No, never mind."

Emiko scowled at her brother.

"Hey, Katsuro. What's the plan? You going to abandon the family business?"

"Abandon? I don't like the sound of that."

"Well, that's what it is. If you don't take over the store, we'll have to close. That on its own wouldn't bother me, but what's going to happen to Mom and Dad? Don't tell me you're just going to abandon them, too."

"Shut up. I've got a plan."

"What kind of plan? I'd love to hear it."

"I said shut up."

Katsuro marched upstairs and threw himself in bed in his borrowed suit. A swarm of thoughts spun through his head, but the alcohol prevented him from stringing them together.

After a while, he slowly peeled himself out of bed and sat down at his childhood desk. In the drawer, he found a composition notebook and a ballpoint pen.

He opened up the notebook and began to write.

To the Namiya General Store…

6

The next day, the funeral went along without a hitch. Since the night before, little had changed in the expressions of those in attendance. Katsuro's relatives showed up early, but everyone acted a little restless around him. His uncle kept his distance.

Interspersed with his extended family were people from businesses on the same street as Uomatsu and people from the neighborhood association who caught his eye. Faces he had known for as long as he could remember.

He spotted a classmate. It took Katsuro a minute to place him, thanks to the suit he'd worn to the service, but when it clicked, he was certain. They were in the same class in middle school. His parents had a store near Uomatsu where they sold handmade seals.

Katsuro started to remember this guy's story. His father died when he was little, and his grandfather taught him how to carve. After graduating high school, he went straight to helping at the shop. He was at the funeral to represent the family business.

The classmate burned a stick of incense for the departed and came before Katsuro and his family. He bowed his head as a sign of respect. The gesture made him appear years older than Katsuro.

Following the funeral service, they took the body to the crematorium. After that, the family went back to the community center for the requisite seventh-day memorial rites. Finally, Takeo gave a brief address to all his relatives, bringing an end to the proceedings.

Katsuro and his family saw the others off and started packing up. There was a lot to carry. They opened the rear hatch of the shop's delivery van and loaded in the ceremonial altar and all the flowers. The rear seats were crowded with luggage.

Takeo slid into the driver's seat.

"Katsuro, you ride up front," said Kanako.

Katsuro shook his head.

"Nah. Ma, you should ride back with him. I'll walk."

Kanako gave him a look of disappointment. She seemed to think he didn't want to ride beside his father.

"I want to make a stop on my way home. I won't be long."

"Huh…"

Katsuro turned his back on his puzzled family and walked off. He didn't want to deal with any questions about where he was going.

He checked his watch. It was nearly six.

The night before, he'd sneaked out in the middle of the night and walked over to the Namiya General Store with a brown envelope in the pocket of his blue jeans. The lines of that white paper were packed with a detailed explanation of what was bothering him. Of course, he had written all of it himself.

Apart from withholding his real name, he had outlined his present circumstances without hiding anything and asked for advice on what to do. In short, he wanted to know if he should chase his dreams or scrap them and take over the family business.

In all honesty, the next morning when he'd woken up, he'd been embarrassed about what he'd done. He saw it for the stupid fantasy it was. There was no way anyone was living in that house. The girl who came by on the bike was probably crazy. And if she was, he was in a pickle. He didn't want anyone else reading that letter.

Then again, maybe she was serious, and it was all real, in some fantastical way. Maybe he would find an answer to his problems. Something that would help him steer his life in the right direction.

With uncertainty and anticipation, Katsuro climbed the hill and made it back to the timeworn facade of the store. It had been too dark the night before for him to notice that the shop's walls, once a creamy color, had lapsed into a filthy gray.

There was a narrow alley between the shop and the garage. That seemed like the only way to get around back.

Taking care not to dirty his clothes against the walls, Katsuro carefully scooted sideways to the end of the alley.

On the back wall was a door, and sure enough, stuck to the wall beside it, he found a wooden milk crate. Katsuro swallowed and pried open the hatch with his fingers. It was pretty tight, but he yanked it open.

Peering inside, he saw a brown envelope and picked it up to get a closer look. They had reused his envelope. The response was addressed, in black ballpoint pen, *Dear Floundering Artiste*.

His heart did a somersault. Someone must be living here. Katsuro stood in front of the back door and perked up his ears. He heard nothing from inside.

Or maybe they lived someplace else and came by every night to check for letters. It was plausible, but why would someone go to all the trouble?

Katsuro cocked his head and left the question and the shop behind. He didn't really care at that moment. The Namiya General Store probably had its own reasons. What mattered to him more right now was the contents of the letter.

Envelope in hand, Katsuro walked around the area, hoping to find a quiet place to open it.

He found a tiny park—just a swing set, slide, and sandbox. No one else around. He sat down on a bench by the fence. It took him several deep breaths to open the envelope. Inside was a single sheet of stationery. With his heart pounding wildly, he began to read.

Dear Floundering Artiste,

Thank you for sharing this shamelessly privileged complaint with me. That's what it is, though, isn't it? It must be nice to be the heir to a family business. You're set to take over the store with no effort on your part, complete with a long-standing customer base and a reputation you won't have to sweat over to build.

If you don't mind my asking, haven't you noticed there are people in the world who are struggling to find jobs?

If the answer is no, then congratulations. You must live in a wonderful time.

But that's not how the world is going to be in thirty years. It won't be all fun and games. Just having a job will be a blessing. There will come a day when simply graduating college will no longer guarantee employment. That day is coming. You can bet on it.

And look at you. You dropped out. Up and quit. You let your parents pay your way through college, which you were lucky enough to get into at all, and you threw it all away.

All in the name of music. You say you want to be a performer so badly that you're willing to scrap a family business and brave it alone, just you and your guitar. Well, well, look at you. Really, there isn't much of a point to even giving you advice. You may as well do whatever you want. People who live with their head in the clouds deserve to hit the ground every once in a while. Eh, but I guess since I've advertised that I give free advice, I have to give you some kind of response.

You want my real advice? Put down the guitar and start cutting fish. Your father is in rough shape. This is no time for some carefree soul-searching or whatever. You're never going to make a living off your music. The only people who can do that are musical geniuses. People with special abilities. Which is not the case for you. Stop day-dreaming like a real idiot and wake up.

—Namiya General Store

Katsuro's hands were shaking. Shaking with rage.

What the hell? he thought. *There's no need to rip me a new one.*

Give up music and take over the shop—very original. What else would the letter have said? It was the realistic, safe solution. But why did this person have to be so rude? Frankly, Katsuro was insulted.

He regretted even asking for advice. He balled up the letter and the envelope and shoved them in his pocket. If he could have found a trash can, he would have tossed them.

But there were no trash cans on his walk home, and he arrived with the letter in his pocket. Inside he found his parents and his sister setting up the ceremonial altar in front of the bigger family one.

"Where have you been?" asked Kanako. "You were gone a while."

"Yeah…," Katsuro said on his way upstairs.

He changed into fresh clothes and threw the crumpled letter

in the trash, but instantly, he reconsidered. He smoothed out the wrinkled paper on his desk and read over it again. It left him just as hopeless as the first time.

He knew he should let it go, but he couldn't resist the temptation. Whoever wrote this was terribly mistaken. They wrote about the fish shop as if it were some eminent long-running business and treated Katsuro like some pretty boy from a wealthy family.

The letter told him to wake up, but as far as Katsuro was concerned, he was staring into the jaws of reality. That was why he was struggling, but whoever wrote this letter didn't seem to realize that.

Katsuro sat down to write. He pulled out the notebook and the pen and took his time composing the following reply.

To the Namiya General Store,

Thank you for your letter. It surprised me, since I didn't know if I'd be getting a response.

That said, I found your advice very disappointing. To be honest, you don't even remotely understand my problem. I don't need you to tell me that taking on the family business is the safest thing to do.

But just because it's safe doesn't mean it's what's best for me in the long run.

Contrary to your assumption, our shop is nothing special. Just a narrow storefront on a boring street. And it's not making any of us rich. We're lucky if we have enough to cover our expenses. Taking over that kind of a business, it's not like I'd be set for life. Which is why, one could argue, I might as well take a long shot at some other way. As I mentioned, my mom and dad are on my side and want me to succeed. If I throw away my dreams now, I'll only disappoint them.

There's one other thing you're mistaken on. I view music as a profession, not a hobby, and aim to make a living by writing and performing my own songs. You seem to think I'm doing this for fun, that making art is some passing interest of mine. Which I assume is why you addressed me as a "floundering artiste" in your response. Please allow me to correct you: I'm trying to make an honest living as a working musician, not indulge some daydream.

I'm well aware that success in music demands a special kind of talent. But who are you to say I'm not talented? Have you even heard my songs? Please don't make assumptions. If you never give it a chance, you'll never know.

I look forward to hearing from you.

—Floundering <u>Musician</u>

7

"When are you going back to Tokyo?"

It was the day after the funeral. Katsuro was eating his lunch. His father had just stepped up from the shop, bandanna wrapped around his head, to ask him this.

As of that day, Uomatsu was open for business. Early that morning, Katsuro had watched from his window as Takeo drove off for the market.

"Not sure yet," Katsuro whispered.

"You're fine just kicking back out here? Is your so-called road to stardom so easy that you can just hang loose at home?"

"Who says I'm kicking back? I'm taking my time to think things over."

"What kind of things?"

"What do you care?"

"Three years ago, you were spitting fire. You can't stop now. You need to push for it, like your life depends on it."

"All right! I get it. You don't need to remind me." Katsuro dropped his chopsticks and stood up. Kanako watched them anxiously from the kitchen.

That night, Katsuro stepped out for a walk. It wasn't hard to guess he was making his way to the general store. The night before, he had gone by and dropped his second letter in the mail slot.

He opened the wooden crate to find his envelope recycled, like the day before. Whoever was answering these letters must be checking every day.

He took the letter to the same park and sat down on the bench to read it.

Dear Floundering Musician,

Big or small, a business is a business. It's all thanks to that fish shop that your parents saved enough to pay your way through college. If business is lagging, isn't it your job, as the heir, to figure out a way to pick things up?

You say your parents are on your side, but any decent parent is going to side with their kids, as long as their aspirations aren't illegal. You shouldn't take advantage of their kindness.

I'm not telling you to give up music. It's fine, but as a hobby.

To be honest, you don't have the talent for anything beyond that. While I haven't heard your songs, I can say that much for sure.

I mean, you've been at it three years now, with nothing to show for it, right? That's proof you lack the talent.

Take a look at the people who've made it big. It didn't take any of them long to be discovered. People with that special something won't go unnoticed. No one has noticed you. Face it.

You don't like being called an artiste, huh? Maybe your thinking is a little bit old-fashioned. In any case, do yourself a favor and choose the fish shop.

—Namiya General Store

Katsuro bit his lip. This response was just as vicious. Katsuro felt gored.

But this time, strangely enough, he didn't get angry. It was actually refreshing to hear someone write so crassly.

Katsuro read the letter again. A huge sigh came out of him.

He had to admit that a part of him agreed with what it said. The words were harsh, but they pointed at the truth. If you have that special something, someone is bound to notice. Katsuro had known this all along, but he'd denied it. He consoled himself with the idea that fate hadn't turned in his favor yet. But maybe if you had enough talent, you didn't need to wait around for fate.

No one had ever spelled this out for him so clearly. Your chosen path is a difficult one—that was the closest anyone had ever said. After all, they didn't want to take responsibility for their opinions. Whoever wrote this letter was a different story. They didn't waver or falter in the slightest.

But then again...who was this person? He reexamined the letter.

They really knew how to spit things out. Most people would try to phrase things in a more roundabout way, but these letters were anything but sensitive. Katsuro was sure they couldn't have been written by Old Man Namiya. That geezer would have taken a much gentler approach.

Whoever it was, Katsuro wanted to meet them. There were so many things a letter couldn't show you, couldn't say. He wanted to meet up in person and hear more.

That night, he slipped out again, as usual, with a letter in his jeans. His third letter to date.

He had done his best to think things through and came up with the following rebuttal.

To the Namiya General Store,

Thank you for the second letter.

To be honest, it came as a shock. I wasn't expecting such a harsh critique. I had convinced myself I had at least some talent. I held on to the dream that this would be enough, and someday I would finally make it.

But your straightforward advice has helped me sort things out.

I'm thinking I need to take stock of my situation. Now that I think back on it, I may have become too attached to the idea of chasing a dream. It's made me unable to realize when I should take a step back and stop.

With that said, and I'm embarrassed to even add this, I'm not sure I can give up on things quite yet. I want to take this music thing just a little further, if I can.

I think I've finally realized what my problem is.

I've known for ages exactly what I have to do, but I can't bear the thought of giving up my dreams. Even now, I'm not sure how I ever could. In a way, it's like unrequited love. I know we won't fall in love, but I can't seem to give up on the one that stole my heart.

These sentences aren't doing justice to the way I feel. Which is why I want to ask you if you would be willing to meet up, just once, *to discuss this face-to-face. On top of everything, I'm also curious to see what you're like in person.*

Just let me know what I need to do to meet you, and I'll see you then and there.

—*Floundering Musician*

The Namiya General Store loomed desolate as ever in the light of evening. Katsuro stepped up to the shutter and popped open the flap on the mail slot. He took the letter from his jeans and slipped it in halfway but hesitated to push it through.

He thought he could sense that someone was there in the space behind the shutter.

If he was correct, then that person would eventually pull the envelope the rest of the way through. He figured he would stick around to see what happened.

His watch said it was a little past eleven.

Katsuro reached into his other pocket and pulled out his harmonica. He took a deep breath, faced the mail slot, and began to play. He wanted whoever was inside to hear him.

Out of everything he'd ever written, it was the song he was most proud of. A song called "Reborn [*Saisei*]." He hadn't added lyrics yet; he couldn't find the right words. Whenever he played at shows, he always performed it on the harmonica. It was a ballad with an easy, comforting melody.

After playing through the chorus, Katsuro stopped and focused on the envelope stuck in the mail slot. Nothing had pulled on it or even tested it. There wasn't anybody in there. The letters probably weren't picked up till morning.

Katsuro pushed the envelope with his fingertip. It flapped through the slot and faintly slapped on the floor inside.

8

"Ka-tsu-ro, wake up!"

Someone was shaking him awake. When he opened his eyes, he saw Kanako kneeling over him; her face was close and pale.

Katsuro scowled and blinked repeatedly. "What the hell?" He groped around and found his wristwatch. It was a little after seven.

"It's bad. Your father collapsed at the fish market."

"What?" He sat up in bed, wide-awake now. "When?"

"Just now. We just got a call from the people there. He was transported to the hospital."

Katsuro jumped out of bed and grabbed the jeans draped over his chair.

He got himself ready and left the house with Kanako and Emiko. They taped a sign to the shutter of the shop: Due to unforeseen circumstances, we will be closed today.

A taxi brought them to the hospital, where a middle-aged man from the fish market was waiting. He seemed to have met Kanako before.

"He was carrying some boxes, and next thing I know, he seemed to be in a lot of pain," explained the man. "We called the ambulance right away…"

"I see. I'm so sorry to interrupt your work day. We appreciate you going to the trouble. We'll take over from here." Kanako politely sent him off with a thanks.

Takeo had already been treated, and they were asked to meet with the doctor in charge. Katsuro and Emiko went, too.

"He's overworked, plain and simple, which is why his heart's under a lot of strain. Any idea why? Has he been through any stressful circumstances recently?" The doctor, a dignified man with white hair and a handsome face, had a very soothing voice.

Kanako explained how he had just lost his mother. The doctor nodded sympathetically.

"That must have been hard on him, both physically and psychologically. I can't say anything right now about the condition of his heart, but he needs to be more careful. I recommend he schedule regular screenings."

"We'll make sure he does," assured Kanako.

The doctor said they could visit him, so they went immediately to his room. Takeo was lying down on a bed for ER patients. He saw them and made an unpleasant face.

"Isn't this a bit much? What's the big deal?" he complained in a show of bravado, but there was little fire behind it.

"I told you it was too soon to open up the shop again. You have to rest a few more days."

Takeo scowled at Kanako and shook his head. "You think we can afford that? I'm fine. If we close for even a day, where will our customers go? There are people who depend on me for a good piece of fish."

"But when you overdo it, it's too much for your body."

"That's what I'm saying. I didn't overdo anything. I'm fine."

"Don't be ridiculous, Dad," said Katsuro. "If you really think we can't afford to stay closed another day, I can help."

All three faces turned to him, eyes colored with disbelief.

Takeo broke the silence. "What the hell are you saying?" he spat. "You can't even clean a fish."

"That's not true. Remember how I used to help out every summer, up until high school?"

"That was hardly enough to prepare you to run a business."

"Yeah, but—" Katsuro held his tongue. Takeo had raised his hand from under the sheets, holding off his son from speaking any further.

"What about your music?"

"Well, I've been thinking maybe I need to give it up…"

"What did you just say to me?" Takeo's face sagged at the corners of his mouth. "No son of mine is going to run away from his problems."

"It's not like that. I just feel I would do more good if I took over the store."

Takeo clicked his tongue.

"Three years ago, you talked all high and mighty, only to come back down to this. Well, listen up and let me tell you straight. I won't let you take over the store."

Katsuro looked at his father with disbelief.

"Takeo," cautioned Kanako.

"Things would be different if your heart was set on selling fish. But I know it ain't. If you take over out of pity, you won't be able to run the shop the way you should. Mark my words. A few years down the line, you'll regret not doing music, and you'll start whining all over again."

"That isn't true."

"Sure it's true. I can see it now. When that day comes, you'll give yourself all kinds of excuses: 'Oh, my poor father fell,' 'I had no choice,' 'I had to sacrifice my art to save my family.' You'll take no responsibility. Everything will be someone else's fault."

"Takeo, you don't need to talk like—"

"You stay outta this. What do you say, boy? If you can prove me wrong, say something."

Katsuro pursed his lips and glared at Takeo. "Is worrying about my family such an awful thing?"

Takeo snorted at him.

"You can only say that kind of high-and-mighty bullshit when you've accomplished something. But what have you done with your music? Has it gotten you anything? No, it hasn't. If you want this dream so bad that you're willing to turn your back on your parents, we expect you to have something to show for it. You come home empty-handed and think you can take over my business? Thinking it's *just* some fish shop? Don't insult me."

After this voluble outburst, Takeo's face showed signs of pain. He grabbed his chest.

"Takeo!" yelled Kanako. "Emiko, get the doctor."

"Quit worrying. It's nothing. Hey, Katsuro, listen up." As he lay on his back, Takeo eyed Katsuro steadily. "Neither me nor the shop is in rough enough shape to need you to come running to the rescue. Stop trying to be a hero and go back to Tokyo. Be a fighter. Give it everything you've got. Even a losing battle is worth fighting. Go out and make your mark. And don't come home again until you do. Hear me?"

Katsuro stood in silence.

Takeo asked him again. "Do you understand?"

"I understand," he said in a low voice.

"I mean it. Swear on it, man-to-man."

Katsuro nodded deeply to show he meant it, too.

Once they were home from the hospital, Katsuro started packing immediately. Not just the things he'd brought from Tokyo, but everything in his room. It had been a while since the room had been tidied up. This felt a little like spring cleaning.

"Get rid of the desk and bed," he told Kanako as he was taking a short break to eat some lunch downstairs. "I won't need the bookcase, either, so you can toss that, too. I won't be using that room anymore."

"Mind if I use it, then?" asked Emiko, not missing a beat.

"Sure, I don't care."

"Whoo-hoo," she said, clapping her hands quietly.

"Katsuro, if this is about what your father said, you know you can come home whenever you like."

But Katsuro smiled wryly at his mother's love. "You heard him. He said we swore on it, man-to-man."

"I know, but—" But Kanako said no more.

Cleaning out the room took him the rest of the day. In the early evening, just before he finished, Kanako went to the hospital and brought home Takeo. Compared with that morning, Takeo's face looked alive again.

Dinner was a pot of sukiyaki, and Kanako had splurged on some premium cuts of beef. Emiko went giddy like a little kid, and Takeo was lamenting that he couldn't have a beer. He'd been told to hold off on smoking and drinking for a few days. It was the happiest Katsuro had seen his family this side of the funeral.

With dinner over, Katsuro got ready to depart. It was back again to Tokyo. Kanako suggested he spend another night, but Takeo reproached her, saying to let him do what he wanted to do.

"All right, I'm off," he told his parents and his sister, luggage in both hands.

"Be good," Kanako replied. Takeo said nothing.

He took a roundabout route to the station, for one last visit to the Namiya General Store. Maybe he'd find a response to last night's letter in the milk crate.

When he went and checked, he found an envelope waiting for him. As he slipped it into his pocket, he looked over the abandoned building. The grungy sign looked as if it wanted to tell him something.

He proceeded to the station and didn't read the letter until he was aboard the train.

> *Dear Floundering Musician,*
>
> *I've read your third letter.*
>
> *While I can't go into the details, meeting you in person is out of the question. Even if it weren't, it wouldn't be a good idea. Honestly, it would probably bum you out. You'd hate yourself for putting so much trust in a shmuck like me. Let's leave it at that.*

So here we are. You're finally thinking about giving up music.

But I get the feeling this is temporary. You'll have a go at it again. Maybe by the time you read this letter, you'll have already changed your mind.

I hate to disappoint you, but I can't really say if that's a good thing or a bad thing. But there's one thing I can say for sure.

Your efforts in music will never be in vain.

Your music will save lives. And the songs you create will absolutely live on.

Don't ask me how I know. Just trust me. I'm positive.

Hold on to this until the end. The very, very end.

That's all I can say.

—Namiya General Store

Katsuro scratched his neck.

What's up with this one? he asked himself. *It's strangely polite. None of the bullying of the other letters.*

The weirdest part was that he had been able to perceive that Katsuro was determined to have another go at it. Maybe this ability to see the truth of people's hearts was what had earned him the nickname in the first place.

Hold on to this until the end. The very, very end.

What was that supposed to mean?

Maybe it meant his dreams were going to come true someday. But how could he be so sure?

Katsuro put the letter back into its envelope and stuffed it in his duffel bag. Win or lose, he was ready to fight.

9

Katsuro passed by a music shop with racks outside stacked with blue-jacketed CDs. He picked one up, savoring the joy it brought him. Across the cover in big letters was the title—*REBORN*—and below it was the name of the musician: Katsuro Matsuoka.

Finally, he'd made it. Made it all the way. It had been a long journey.

Arriving back in Tokyo with newfound resolve, Katsuro had thrown himself harder than ever into making music. He entered every contest, sat for auditions, and sent tapes to record labels, and in between, he played on the streets more times than he could count.

Somehow that big break never came.

Time passed all too quickly. Before long, he began to lose direction.

That was when someone came up to him after a show and asked if he would consider playing for a charity concert at a children's home.

Not expecting it to get him anywhere, he figured what the hell.

When he showed up to perform, he found an audience of barely twenty kids. He was a bit confused but played anyway. His audience was just as confused as he was.

Then one of the kids began to clap along, and taking the cue, the others started to do the same. Pretty soon, Katsuro was getting into it. This was fun. It had been a long time since he had gotten so much joy out of singing.

From then on, he began touring facilities and homes all over Japan. He amassed a repertoire of over a thousand children's songs, and that was the closest he'd ever get to a big break.

But was that true? If so, what was this CD in his hands? It certainly looked like a big break to him. And after all, this was his favorite song.

He sang himself the opening melody of "Reborn," but for some stupid reason, he couldn't remember the lyrics. To his own song!

How did it go again? Katsuro opened a CD case and pinched out the jacket. He tried to find the lyrics, but his fingers couldn't flip the pages of the booklet. He couldn't pry it open. From inside the shop, a relentless din was pounding in his ears. What kind of music was this?

Katsuro opened his eyes. He hadn't the slightest idea where he was. An unknown ceiling, walls, and curtains. Eventually, he added it all up: He was inside one of the rooms at Marumitsuen.

A bell was clanging at full volume. Someone was screaming. A voice shouted, "Fire! Stay calm!"

Katsuro leaped out of bed. He grabbed his bag and his jacket and stepped into his shoes. Good thing he'd slept fully dressed. What about his guitar? Leave it. The decision was over in a second.

Outside his door, he was startled. The halls were smoked out.

A staff member with a handkerchief over his mouth was beckoning him. "This way. Exit this way."

Katsuro followed his instructions and went down the stairwell two steps at a time.

But he stopped short at the next floor down. Seri was standing in the hallway.

"Come on, get outta there!" he yelled.

Seri's eyes were bloodshot. Her cheeks were sticky with tears. "My brother... I can't find Tatsuyuki."

"Huh? Where'd he go?"

"I don't know. I think the rooftop, maybe. He goes up there when he can't sleep."

"The rooftop..." He struggled for a moment, but the rest of his motions were swift. "Take these and get outta here."

"What?"

He left her bug-eyed on the landing and shot back up the stairs.

In those few minutes, the smoke had thickened and congealed. Tears gobbed from his eyes. His throat stung. He could barely see, and it hurt to breathe. Most disturbingly, he couldn't see the flames. Where were they? What was burning?

This was getting serious. It would be dangerous to continue on. Should he run? Just when the thought crossed his mind, he heard a child crying.

"Hey! Where are you?"

Yelling filled his throat with smoke. He hacked out a cough and pushed ahead.

He heard something crumbling as the smoke cleared. A little boy was crouching at the top of the stairs. Definitely Seri's brother.

Katsuro made it to the boy and slung him over his shoulder. Together, they bounded down the stairs. At that moment, the whole ceiling came down with a crash. All they saw was fire. A sea of flames.

The boy wailed. Katsuro was beginning to panic.

But he couldn't stand still. Down was the only way out.

Hugging the boy to his shoulder, Katsuro ran through the flames. He lost sense of what was underfoot. He wasn't sure where he was going. Chunks of flaming debris tumbled around him. Pain tugged at his entire body. Breathing was no longer possible.

He was consumed at once by red light and empty blackness.

Someone called his name. But he couldn't reply or so much as twitch a muscle. He couldn't even tell if he was still inside his body.

His consciousness receded. Sleep followed him down.

Lines from a letter danced in the shadows of his mind.

Your efforts in music will never be in vain.

Your music will save lives. And the songs you create will absolutely live on.

Don't ask me how I know. Just trust me. I'm positive.

Hold on to this until the end. The very, very end.

That's all I can say.

*　　*　　*

Look at that. He was almost at the end. Just hold on, to the very, very end.

Maybe this is where I leave my mark, Dad. The losing battle was worth the fight.

10

Until this very moment, the packed arena had been alive with fanatic cheers. The three songs for the encore had been one crowd pleaser after another. That's how she planned them.

But this last song came from a different place. Her devoted fans knew what was coming next, and when she stood before the microphone, ten thousand people hushed in anticipation.

"This will be my last song. The one I always end on."

She was a genius, a rarity in any generation.

"This song was the reason I became an artist, but its significance goes even deeper. The man who wrote this song saved my brother, the only real family I have. He gave his life to save him. If we had never met, I wouldn't be who I am today. That's why I'll sing this song as long as I live. It's the only way I have to show my gratitude. Thanks for listening."

The opening chords of "Reborn" filled the arena.

CHAPTER 3

OVERNIGHT IN THE CIVIC

1

Outside the turnstiles, he checked his watch and saw the hands were showing half past eight. *That's odd,* he thought, and he spun around. As expected, the clock above the train schedule said eight forty-five. Takayuki Namiya scowled and clicked his tongue. *Damn watch, broke again.*

The watch had been a present from his father when he'd gotten into college. Lately, it had been running slow an awful lot. What would you expect, after twenty years? He'd been thinking it was time to replace it with a quartz crystal one. Those things used to cost as much as a new car, but recently, they'd gone way down in price.

He left the station and walked down the row of shops. It amazed him to see places open this time of night. From what he saw through the windows, they were doing decent business. Apparently, the influx of new residents had made locations by the station go up in demand.

You mean in this dead-end town? Takayuki found it hard to believe, but he didn't mind hearing that his hometown was coming back to life. Far from it. In fact, he only wished his family's shop was near the station, too.

He turned off from the shopping street into one of the side streets. Before long, he was surrounded by new buildings. Every time he dropped by, this place looked a little different. New homes were always under construction. There was supposedly a fair number of people who commuted into Tokyo from all the way out here, but even on express trains, it probably took at least two hours each way.

Takayuki couldn't imagine doing that every single day. He lived in the city with his wife and their son, almost ten. Their apartment wasn't spacious, but it had two bedrooms, a living room, a dining room, and a kitchen—it was enough.

But then again, as unreasonable as the commute itself might be, he could see the need to compromise on location. In life, things tended not to go as planned. If his problems could all be solved by extending his commute, he might just have to deal with it.

At the edge of the development, the road came to a T-shaped intersection. He turned right and kept walking, and the road sloped gradually uphill. Once he made it this far, he could get by with his eyes closed. His body knew where the road meandered. How many times had he been up and down this very street by the time he graduated high school?

Up ahead, he saw the little building on the right. The streetlights reached the sign, but its grubby letters were indecipherable. The shutter was pulled down.

Once he was closer, he stopped in his tracks to finally make out the words—NAMIYA GENERAL STORE.

A passage, maybe three feet wide, ran between the house and the storage shed beside it. Takayuki walked down the passage to the back door. In elementary school, he left his bike here.

Out back was a door into the kitchen, and right beside it hung a milk crate. It had been at least ten years since any milk had been delivered. When his mother died, they kept it going for a little while but eventually canceled. No one asked for the crate back.

Beside the milk bin was a button. If you pushed it, a buzzer rang inside. Used to, anyway. Not anymore.

Takayuki pulled the doorknob, and the door swung open. No resistance. Typical.

On the shoe rack was a familiar pair of house slippers and a ratty pair of leather shoes. They belonged to the same pair of feet.

"Hello, anyone here?" Takayuki called out in a deep voice, but no one answered. That didn't stop him. He took off his shoes and stepped into the kitchen. Beyond that was a tatami room. In front of that was the store.

In the tatami room, Yuji was sitting on his knees at a low table, dressed in a sweater and long underwear. He slowly turned to face Takayuki. Just his face. His reading glasses rested low on his nose.

"Oh, it's you."

"'Oh'? That's all you have to say? You can't leave the door open. How many times do I have to tell you? Lock it."

"Don't worry about it. If someone comes in, I'll know."

"You didn't know just now. You didn't hear me coming in."

"I heard something, but I was busy thinking. I didn't feel like answering you."

"More excuses." Takayuki placed a paper bag on the tea table and sat cross-legged on the floor. "Here, I brought some red-bean pastries from Kimuraya, Dad. Your favorite."

"Wow," said Yuji, eyes lighting up. "You really shouldn't have."

"Don't mention it."

Yuji grunted as he stood. He picked up the paper bag and turned to face the altar. Its doors were open. He placed the pastries on the stand inside, then rang the devotional bells twice and sat back down. Yuji may have been small and scrawny, but he had fantastic poise for a man of almost eighty.

"You eat dinner yet?" he asked Takayuki.

"I had a bowl of soba noodles after work. I was planning on staying the night."

"As long as you've told Fumiko."

"She's just as worried about you as I am. How're you feeling anyway?"

"Doing fine, thanks to you. No need to drag yourself all the way out here just to check on me."

"That's nice of you to say right after I spent two hours getting here."

"I'm only saying there's no cause for concern. By the way, I just got out of the bath. I left the tub full. It shouldn't have cooled down yet. Hop in whenever you like."

Yuji was preoccupied by some sheets of stationery spread over the table. An envelope sat beside them, *To Namiya General Store* written on the front.

"Did that just come tonight?"

"No, this one came last night, but I didn't notice until this morning."

"Shouldn't you have responded this morning, then?"

Responses to all letters to the Namiya General Store would be left in the milk crate by the next morning—that was Yuji's personal rule. It was why he woke up each day at five thirty AM.

"Not this time. They knew they were delivering this too late. They said so in their letter. Told me to take my time, the next day would be fine."

"Is that right?"

Takayuki had never gotten used to this. What business did the owner of a general store have giving people advice on their problems? Of course, he knew the backstory. It wasn't any secret; after all, some magazine had even done a feature on him. The number of letters spiked after that. There were some serious ones in there, but most of them were pranks. A fair share of these were blatant harassment. One night, Yuji received over thirty letters. All were obviously in the same hand, and their content was garbage. But Yuji replied even to these.

Takayuki had tried to stop him. "What the hell are you doing?" he'd asked. "They're clearly screwing with you. Don't be ridiculous. It's a waste of your time."

But the old man showed no sign of learning his lesson. He even treated his son with pity. "You don't have a clue, do you?"

"Don't have a clue about what?" spat Takayuki, but Yuji kept his cool.

"Harassment, pranks, it doesn't matter to me. I treat every letter that comes in as a cry for help. These people are no different from the rest of us. They have a hole in their hearts, and something vital is bleeding out. If you need proof, consider this: Everyone always comes by and checks to see if I wrote back. They stop and peek into the milk bin. They can't help but wonder what I had to say to them. Think about it. Even the one who sent me thirty letters of gibberish must have spent hours and hours writing. No one does that if they aren't hoping for some kind of response. So I respond, and I give those responses everything I've got. You can't ignore someone who speaks to you from the heart."

And Yuji did in fact reply to each and every one of those thirty letters. He finished his responses just in time to leave them in the milk crate in the morning. When he had a look inside before opening the store at eight, all thirty responses had been carried off. That was the end of that prank. Some time later, he received a piece of paper with just one line of writing: *I'm sorry. Thanks so much.* The handwriting matched the script on all thirty of the letters. Takayuki would never forget the proud look on his father's face when he showed the note to his son.

It occurred to Takayuki that this was what his father lived for. When Takayuki's mother passed away from heart disease ten years ago, Yuji had lost his verve. All his children had long since left home. For a bereft, aging man of almost seventy, the sudden shift to a solitary lifestyle was painful enough to sap his energy to live.

Takayuki had a sister, Yoriko, who was two years older. Since she lived with her husband at his parents' house, they really couldn't depend on her to help Yuji out. It was all on Takayuki, but he had his own young family to take care of. At the time, they were living in company housing. He had no space for Yuji.

Yuji must have understood the predicament his kids were in. Despite his flagging spirit, he made no moves to close the store, and Takayuki continued to depend on his father a little too much.

Then one day, Takayuki received an unexpected call from Yoriko.

"I'm stunned. It's like he's back to normal. Maybe even better than before Mom died. I'm so relieved. We should be good for a while now. Why don't you go up and see him? You'll be amazed."

It had been a long time since his sister had gone and seen their father. She was thrilled to see him like this.

"You know why Dad's feeling so good?"

Takayuki said he didn't know.

"Of course you don't—how would you? When I heard, I did a double take."

Finally, she told him what was going on: Their father had been posing as a life coach.

This didn't mean much to Takayuki. *What the hell's a life coach?* On his next day off, he took a trip back home. The scene at the house was truly unbelievable. A crowd had gathered at the Namiya General Store. Mostly kids, but some adults were there, too. They were looking at a wall inside the store. The wall was covered with taped-up sheets of paper. They were reading them and laughing.

Takayuki came closer and looked over the children's heads to read what was on the wall. The papers were sheets of stationery and notebook paper, and even a few tiny sheets from pocket-sized memo pads. In general, the subject matter was not serious:

> *Tell me how I can get an A+ on a test without studying or cheating or anything.*

The handwriting was obviously a kid's. The response was taped up below the letter. This was written in Yuji's handwriting, which Takayuki would have known anywhere.

> *Ask your teacher to test you on yourself. Since you're the topic of the test, whatever you say will be correct.*

What the hell is this? thought Takayuki. This wasn't advice. More like a wisecrack.

He looked over the rest of the taped-up letters, but every one of them was silly.

> *I want Santa to visit our house, but we don't have a chimney. What should I do?*

> *When the world turns into the Planet of the Apes, where can I learn Apanese?*

Yuji had responded earnestly to every question, and his responses were a big hit. Below the wall was a box with a slot cut in it. A sign read:

ADVICE FOR PROBLEMS:

ASK ME ANYTHING, ANYTHING AT ALL.

—NAMIYA GENERAL STORE

"Hey, you need to enjoy life somehow. It started off as a game with the neighborhood kids, but I played along, and things took off. People really seem to get a kick out of it. Some of them come from pretty far just to read these things. You really don't know what'll be a hit these days, but lately, the kids have been coming by with actual problems for a change, and I'm racking my brain to solve them. It's hard work."

Yuji laughed, a wry laugh that was full of life. Yoriko wasn't kidding: Their father was a different man compared with when he was mourning the loss of his wife.

This advice business buoyed Yuji's spirits, but as time went by, the questions grew more serious and somber. This made him uneasy about leaving the advice box in plain sight, so he switched over to the current system of mail slot in the shutter and milk crate out back. When goofy letters came, he still posted them, along with his response, on the wall.

Yuji, sitting on his heels at the table, crossed his arms. His pad of stationery was open, but he didn't reach for his pen. His lower lip was slightly pouted. Wrinkles appeared between his eyebrows.

"You're really giving that some thought," Takayuki noted. "Is it a hard one?"

Yuji nodded patiently. "It's a letter from a woman. The hardest kind."

In other words, romance.

Yuji's marriage had been arranged. Evidently, the pair knew nothing of each other until the day they married. *Asking someone from that generation for advice on love is misguided at best*, Takayuki thought.

"Just write anything. Who cares?"

"Excuse me? You think I could do that?" Yuji sounded perturbed.

Takayuki shrugged and stood up from the floor. "You got beer, right? I'll help myself."

He didn't get an answer out of Yuji, but he went to the fridge anyway. It was an early two-door model, one that had belonged to Yoriko's in-laws until they bought a new fridge two years back. Prior to that, he had been using a one-door fridge he bought in 1960, when Takayuki was in college.

Inside, Takayuki found two cold half-liter bottles. Yuji loved his beer and always kept the fridge stocked. He hadn't always cared for sweets. The buns from Kimuraya had only become his favorites in his sixties.

For now, Takayuki grabbed one of the two bottles and popped the cap. He took two glasses from the cupboard and brought them to the table.

"You drinking, too, right?"

"No, not now."

"Well, well. Everything okay?"

"I don't drink until I'm finished with the letters. I've told you that before."

Takayuki nodded and poured beer into his glass.

Yuji, deep in thought, turned his face on Takayuki. "The father has a wife and kids."

"Huh?" Takayuki vocalized. "What's that supposed to mean?"

Yuji held up the envelope. "The woman who wrote this. The father has a wife."

Takayuki didn't get it. He had another sip of beer and set down his glass.

"What's so odd about that? My dad had a wife and kids, too. She might be gone now, but the kids are still alive. Me, for example."

Yuji scowled and shook his head. He was getting pissed.

"This isn't about me. You're missing the point. I don't mean the woman's father—I mean the baby's."

"Baby? Whose?"

"That's what I'm saying." Yuji waved his hand impatiently. "The baby's in her belly. This woman's."

"What?" It took Takayuki another second. "Ah! Okay. So the woman's pregnant, and the man who got her pregnant has a wife and kids."

"Precisely. That's what I've been trying to tell you."

"Well, you could have made it clearer. Who wouldn't think that *father* meant her own dad?"

"That's what you call jumping to conclusions."

"Guess so." Takayuki tilted his head and reached for the glass.

"What do you think?" asked Yuji.

"About what?"

"About this, what else? This guy has a wife and kids, and this woman's carrying his baby. What should she do?"

Takayuki finally understood the problem. He had another sip and sighed impatiently.

"Girls these days have no principles. And they're stupid. Nothing good can come from fooling around with a married man. What the hell is she thinking?"

Yuji made a sour face and smacked the table.

"I'm not asking for a lecture on morality. She needs advice. What can she do?"

"Isn't it obvious? She has to get an abortion. What else is there to say to her?"

Yuji snorted and scratched behind his ear. "I shouldn't have even asked."

"Hey, what's that supposed to mean?"

Fed up, Yuji gritted his teeth and slapped the envelope against the back of his hand.

"'She has to get an abortion. What else is there to say to her?' —Leave it to you to say that. I think we can assume she's thought of that already. Can't you see her problems go beyond that?"

This harsh rebuke left Takayuki silent. He saw it now.

"Listen to me," Yuji started. "She's writing with the awareness that having an abortion is the right thing to do. She doesn't think he'll take responsibility, and she can see that raising this child on her own will make life harder for both of them. And yet, she can't rid herself of an urge to have her baby anyway. She can't bear the thought of an abortion. Do you see why?"

"I guess I don't. Do you, Dad?"

"Only because I read the letter. From what she says, this is her last chance."

"Her last? Why?"

"If she lets this baby go, she may never have another. She was married once before, but she couldn't get pregnant and went in for an examination. They told her that in her condition, she was going to have a hard time having a kid of her own. The doctor went so far as to say she'd better give up on having a baby. That was the beginning of the end for her marriage."

"Was she infertile?"

"What matters is that she sees this baby as her last chance. By now, I should think even you would understand why a simple response like 'She has to get an abortion' won't cut it."

Takayuki drained the last of the beer in his glass and reached for the bottle.

"I understand what you're saying, but don't you think she should reconsider? I feel sorry for the kid. Things are going to be tough."

"She says she's prepared for that."

"She says that now." Takayuki poured more beer and looked up at his father. "But if that's the case, she isn't asking for advice. If she can say that much, she's already decided. It won't matter what you say."

Yuji nodded. "Maybe."

"Maybe…?"

"There's something I've learned from years of reading people's letters. In most cases, they already have an answer to their problem. They're asking for advice because they want to see if other people think they're making the right decision. That's why a lot of people send me a response after reading my advice. Maybe they had a different solution in mind."

Takayuki took another sip and grimaced. "What a pain in the ass. I'm amazed you've kept this up for so many years."

"I'm helping people. What makes it a pain is what makes it worthwhile."

"You're a strange one, all right. But hey, doesn't that mean you don't need to overthink this one? Since it sounds like she wants to have this kid, why not tell her something like 'Good luck, hope it's healthy'?"

Yuji looked at his son as his mouth sagged at the corners. He shook his head.

"You just don't understand, do you? I know the letter hints that she wants to have the baby, but what matters here is the difference between what we feel and what we know. She might feel strongly that she wants to have the baby, while knowing she really has no choice but to let it go. She wrote in an attempt to harden her resolve. If that's the case, I can't just tell her 'Good luck with the pregnancy.' It would only make it tougher to decide."

Takayuki scratched his temple. His head hurt.

"If I were you, I'd say 'Figure it out.'"

"Lucky for you, no one is asking for your advice. I have to get inside her head. The key is somewhere in this letter." Yuji crossed his arms again.

Poor guy, thought Takayuki. Part of him felt bad for his old man, but he knew that these tough responses were the best ones for Yuji. This made it all the more difficult for Takayuki to say what he'd come to say. After all, he hadn't made the trip out here just to check on his aging parent.

"Hey, Dad, you have a second? I have something to ask you."

"In case you haven't noticed, I'm a little busy."

"It won't take long. You're not actually busy anyway; you're just stuck. Maybe if you think about something else for a while, you'll come back with a good idea."

Yuji must have reluctantly admitted he was right. He turned to his son with a sullen look. "What is it?"

Takayuki sat up straight. "Yoriko was telling me about the store. She said things are looking pretty bad."

"She gave you that garbage, too?" He scowled.

"She told me because she's worried. It's only natural. She's your daughter."

Years ago, Yoriko had worked for a tax adviser. She drew from her experience to take care of the store's tax returns. But this year, when she finished up the forms, she'd called up her brother.

"It's bad. We're not just in the red. We're crimson. It would look the same no matter who did the forms. There's no use hunting for loopholes. Even if I send it off, things are bad enough that we won't have to pay taxes on anything."

When Takayuki had asked if it was really that horrible, Yoriko had replied, "If we let Dad file himself, they'd probably make him sign up for welfare."

Takayuki turned toward his father.

"Hey, Dad, don't you think it's time you closed the store? People in the neighborhood are all shopping over by the station. Back before they built the station, the bus stop was enough to keep the business running, but not anymore. Let's call it quits."

Yuji looked tired. He stroked his chin. "Close the store, and then what?"

Takayuki took a breath. "You can come to our house."

Yuji's eyebrows jumped up. "What?"

Takayuki looked around the room. He saw the cracks in the walls.

"If you close the business, there's no use staying here. It's so far from everything. Come live with us. Fumiko has already given it the okay."

Yuji grunted. "You mean that tiny room of yours?"

"Actually, we're looking to move. We've been thinking of buying a house…"

Yuji's eyes went wide behind his reading glasses. "You? A house?"

"What's so funny about that? I'm almost forty. We've started looking into things. That's why your situation came up."

Yuji scowled and waved his hand. "You don't need to worry about me."

"Why not?"

"Because I can get by on my own somehow. I don't need to depend on you."

"You say that, but sometimes you need to call a spade a spade. You barely have an income. How would you survive?"

"That's enough, thanks. I told you—I'll get by somehow."

"Somehow? How—"

"I said *enough*." Yuji raised his voice. "I'm assuming you'll be commuting from here tomorrow morning. Quit your jabbering, take a bath, and go to bed. I'm busy. I've got work to do."

"Work? All you have to do is write that letter, right?"

Yuji glared at the paper. He had nothing more to say.

Takayuki sighed and stood up. "I'll take that bath now."

No reply.

The old stainless tub at the Namiya house was cramped. Takayuki had to hug his legs against his chest, like some kind of gymnastics exercise. Sitting in the bathwater, he gazed out through the window. There was a big pine tree beside the house, and he could make out some of the branches. This was a familiar view, one he'd known since he was a little boy.

Yuji was probably going to miss giving his advice far more than anything about the actual store. If he closed up shop and moved away, he knew the letters wouldn't follow him. People liked the current system. There was something fun about it. It was why so many people asked him for advice.

How could he take away his father's only joy in life?

He woke at six in the morning. His old windup alarm clock had come in handy. While changing in his room upstairs, he heard a noise outside his window. Parting the curtains, he peered down and saw a person walking away from the milk crate. A woman with long black hair and white clothes. He didn't see her face.

Takayuki left his room and went downstairs. Yuji was awake, too, in the kitchen, boiling water in a pot.

"Morning."

"Oh, you're up early." Yuji glanced at the clock on the wall. "Want some breakfast?"

"I'm good. I gotta get going. Hey, how'd that letter go?"

Yuji was pinching flakes of bonito from a canister. "It's done. It took me half the night."

"What'd you decide?"

"Can't say."

"Why not?"

"That's how it is. Those are the rules. It's called 'privacy.'"

Takayuki scratched his head. He was surprised his father knew that word. "Anyway, a woman was just looking in the crate."

"What? You mean you were watching her?"

"I mean, I happened to see her from the upstairs window."

"You don't think she noticed, do you?"

"I think you're fine."

"You think?"

"It's fine. It was just for a second."

Yuji pouted out his lower lip and shook his head. "You can't just look at these people. That's another rule. If they think they've been seen, they'll never come back for advice."

"Listen, I didn't look at her, okay? I saw her by accident."

"You go ages without showing your face only to pull a stunt like that," he muttered on. Yuji's soup stock smelled about ready. He spooned some up.

"I said I'm sorry," whispered Takayuki before he went into the bathroom.

Afterward, he brushed his teeth and washed his face and got himself ready. Yuji was making *tamagoyaki*, a type of Japanese omelet, in the kitchen. After years of living alone, he'd gotten pretty good at it.

"So no, then, for now," Takayuki confirmed to his father's back. "You know my door is always open."

Yuji was quiet. He hesitated to dignify the offer with a response.

"Okay, well, I'd better go."

"All right," Yuji said, barely aloud. He still had his back to Takayuki.

Takayuki stepped out through the back door. He checked the milk bin on his way.

Nothing.

What had his father written? He was a little curious—no, he was dying to know.

2

Takayuki worked in Shinjuku on the fifth floor of a building overlooking Yasukuni Street. His job entailed selling and leasing office equipment, and his customers were mostly from small- and medium-sized businesses. The young president of his company was adamant that they were "entering an era of the micro," an abbreviation for *microcomputer*. He said it would become the new standard to have one at every office in a few years. Takayuki had a background in the humanities and no idea what he would ever need his own computer for, but the president claimed its uses would be limitless.

"You guys will have to study up." Lately, this was the president's new favorite thing to say.

When Yoriko called him at the office, he was reading a chapter in *An Introduction to Microcomputers*. He hadn't understood a word of it and was just about ready to chuck it in the garbage.

"Sorry for calling you at work." She really sounded apologetic.

"It's fine. What's up? Is it about Dad?" Whenever his sister called, that was always his assumption.

He was right.

"Yeah. Yesterday, I went up again to see him, and the store was closed. Did he say anything about that?"

"Huh? No, he didn't mention it. What happened?"

"I asked him, but he said, 'Look, we can't be open every day.'"

"He's got a point."

"There's more to it than that. On my way back, I asked one of his neighbors, 'How's the store been doing?' and you know what they said? The shutter has been down all week."

Takayuki narrowed his eyes. "That's odd."

"Right? When I saw him, he didn't look so good. He was all skin and bones."

"He would tell us if he's sick."

"That's what I thought, too… But I don't know."

This got Takayuki's attention. Giving advice was what kept Yuji going. But to keep it up, it was essential for the business to be booming.

Two years had passed since he'd tried to get Yuji to shut the store down. Back then, his father wasn't sick at all and would never have closed shop, for even a day.

"All right. I'll stop by tonight on my way home."

"Would you mind? I feel like if you ask him, you'll get a different answer."

Takayuki wasn't quite so sure, but he told his sister he would "see and let her know" and hung up.

He left work on time and headed back to his hometown. On the way, he stopped at a payphone and called his wife. When he told her what was going on, she sounded worried, too.

He hadn't seen Yuji since New Year's, when he'd brought Fumiko and their son for a visit. Yuji had been looking good then. Six months had passed. What had happened in the interim?

It wasn't until a little after nine that he arrived. He stood in front of the Namiya General Store and took in the scene. There was nothing strange about the shutter being down that time of night, but the store felt void of life.

He went around back and tried the knob. *Oh, it's locked?* That was unusual. He pulled out his spare key. It had been ages since he'd used it.

He opened the door and went inside. The lights in the kitchen were off. He stepped up and walked over to the tatami room, where he found Yuji lying on a futon in the middle of the floor.

Yuji must have heard him coming in, as he turned over to face him. "What are you doing here?"

"What am I doing? Yoriko called me, and she sounded concerned. She said the shop's been closed for over a week."

"Yoriko. That girl can't seem to mind her own damn business."

"It's all our business. What the hell happened? You sick or something?"

"It's nothing serious," which meant there was something wrong.

"What is it?"

"I said it's nothing serious. I'm not in pain. Nothing's the matter. Got it?"

"Okay, then why close up the store? I'd like to know."

Yuji went quiet. Takayuki misread this as a sign of stubbornness, but when he saw his father's face, he started to realize what was going on. Yuji's brow was furrowed; his lips formed a hard line. His whole expression was full of anguish.

"Dad, what's the…?"

"Hey, Takayuki, you still got a room?"

"A what?"

"At your house. In Tokyo."

Ah, the room. He nodded. Last year, they had bought a house in Mitaka at the western end of the city. It was an older property, but they fixed it up before moving in. Naturally, Yuji had come to see it.

"I imagine you're using it for something by now."

Takayuki knew what his father was trying to say. He was surprised by this sudden change.

"No, it's free. It's set aside for you. It's the tatami room on the first floor. Didn't I show you? It's not big, but it gets good sun."

Yuji let out a heavy sigh and scratched the skin above his eyebrow.

"How's Fumiko feel about this? Is she really okay with it? You've finally got a place to yourselves, just you and the kid, and next thing you know, here's your old man barging in…"

"It's fine. We had this in mind when we picked it."

"…You did, huh?"

"You think you'd like to join us? We're ready when you are."

Without relaxing his expression, Yuji consented. "I'll take you up on that."

Takayuki felt a pressure on his chest. Here they were. The day had come. Still, he took great care not to show his emotion on his face.

"Anytime. Just out of curiosity, what happened? Last time I asked, you said you were never going to close. Are you feeling okay and everything?"

"That's not it. Don't kill yourself with worry. It's just, I don't know." Yuji paused. "I guess it's high time."

Takayuki nodded. "Yeah." He had nothing else to say.

A week later, Yuji left the shop behind. They rented a truck and moved him out without hiring extra help, taking only the essentials and leaving the rest in the store. They still weren't sure what to do with the building. It wasn't as if it would sell the first week on the market. For now, they would let it be.

On the way over to Mitaka, Southern All Stars' "Ellie, My Love" came on the radio of the truck. The song had been a huge hit ever since the single was released in March.

His wife, Fumiko, and their son gave a warm welcome to their new cohabitant, but Takayuki knew how they were feeling. Fumiko was definitely putting up a front, not to mention his son. She was just too prudent and kind to say anything. That was why he'd married her.

Yuji seemed to be enjoying his new lifestyle. He passed the time reading in his room or watching TV, taking the occasional walk. Above all, he seemed genuinely happy to be able to see his grandson every day.

But it couldn't last.

Not long after moving in, Yuji suddenly collapsed. He was in immense pain during the night, so they called an ambulance. Yuji complained to the doctor that his stomach was in unbearable pain. It unnerved Takayuki to hear this for the first time.

The next day, a doctor gave the family the diagnosis. He still had a few tests to run, but he said it looked like liver cancer.

"Late-stage cancer at that," the doctor said in an even tone, looking at them over his glasses. Takayuki asked if this meant they couldn't save him. The doctor calmly replied that it might be easiest to see things that way. Any kind of treatment would be futile.

It went without saying that Yuji wasn't party to this conversation. He was still under from the anesthesia.

They came to an agreement that the doctor wouldn't mention the actual name of the disease. He'd come up with a believable substitute.

As they listened to the news, Yoriko's face was streaked with tears. "I should have brought him to the hospital sooner," she said. She blamed herself for all of it. Takayuki was devastated. He'd thought his father had seemed less energetic than usual, but to hear he was battling cancer… This was beyond his wildest dreams.

With that began Yuji's arduous battle with the disease. Thankfully—if that was the right word—he wasn't in great pain. It was difficult to see him thinner with each successive visit, but up on the hospital bed, he was more or less his usual self.

After about a month, Takayuki stopped by on his way home from work and discovered Yuji sitting up and gazing out the window. It was a two-patient room, but the other bed was empty on this day.

"You seem like you're doin' well."

Yuji looked over to his son and laughed in spite of himself. "Most days, I'm at rock-bottom. But some days are better than others."

"Better is good. Hey, look what I brought." Takayuki set down a paper bag of red-bean pastries on the banquette.

Yuji cast his eyes on the paper bag and looked at his son. His face had changed.

"I have a favor to ask you."

"What kind?"

"Well," Yuji said, averting his glance. He was having a hard time saying it. When he finally did, it was not what Takayuki had been expecting.

"I want to go back to the shop," he said.

"What for? You can't expect to open up again, given the state you're in."

Yuji shook his head. "I don't even have the shelves stocked. What good would it do to open up? No, I'm fine with that. But I want to go back to that house."

"Why?"

Yuji shut his mouth, as if he wasn't sure whether to continue.

"Be reasonable, Dad. You're too weak to live alone. Someone's gotta be there to take care of you. I hope you can understand why that's not really possible."

Yuji scrunched his brows together and shook his head. "I don't need anyone to be there. I'll be fine on my own."

"No way. You can't expect me to leave my sick father on his own. Work with me here."

Yuji stared back at him with pleading eyes. "Just for one night."

"One night?"

"Just one night. I want one more night in that house. Alone."

"What's gotten into you?"

"It's no use saying any more. It'd be lost on you. Not just you—on anyone. You'd say I was crazy and refuse to help."

"How can you be so sure if you don't tell me?"

He tilted his head. "It's no use. You'll never believe me."

"Believe you? About what?"

But Yuji chose not to respond to his question.

"Come on, Takayuki," he urged, taking a different tone. "I know what the doctor has been saying. 'You're free to take him home. The treatment isn't working, so he might as well be comfortable.' He said that, right?"

It was Takayuki's turn to be quiet. Everything Yuji said was true. They'd been told he was beyond all hope. That he could die any day now.

"Help me out, Takayuki. This is what I want." He clasped his hands in front of him in prayer, begging his son.

Takayuki tightened up his face. "Don't do this to me."

"I don't have much time left. Don't say anything; don't ask me anything. Let me do as I please."

These words from his elderly father tugged at his heart. He didn't know where this was going, but he had a duty to fulfill his father's wishes.

Takayuki sighed. "When's good?"

"Sooner the better. How about tonight?"

"Tonight?" His eyes opened wide. "What's the rush?"

"I told you. Time is running out."

"But I need to let everybody know."

"There's no need. Don't tell Yoriko or anyone else in the family. You can tell the hospital we're running home for a bit. We'll go straight to the shop from here."

"What's this all about, Dad? Tell me why we're doing this."

He looked away. "If I say any more, you'll change your mind."

"I won't. I promise. Look, I'll bring you to the shop. Just tell me."

"You mean it? You swear you'll believe me?"

"I swear. Man-to-man."

"All right." Yuji nodded. "Here it goes."

3

Buckled in the passenger seat, Yuji barely spoke while they were driving, though he didn't seem to be asleep, either.

Three hours from the hospital, they entered familiar territory. Yuji began gazing nostalgically out the window into the night.

Fumiko was the only person Takayuki told about this escapade with Yuji. He couldn't drag his sick father onto the train; they had to use their car. And there was a strong possibility he wouldn't be coming home that night.

Up ahead, the Namiya General Store came into view. Takayuki rolled up to the shop in the Civic, which he'd bought last year, and parked. He yanked on the emergency brake and checked his watch. A little past eleven.

"All right, we're here."

Takayuki removed the key and made to get out of his seat, but Yuji reached over and barred his arm across his thighs.

"No, you go home."

"Wait, but—"

"How many times do I need to tell you? I'll be fine alone. I don't want anybody with me."

Takayuki turned away. He knew where his father was coming from. It made sense, as long as he believed what he'd said. But still.

"I'm sorry," said Yuji. "It's selfish of me when you've driven me all the way out here."

"Hey, that's fine; I don't care." Takayuki rubbed under his nose.

"So I guess I'll come back in the morning, then. I'll kill time somewhere nearby."

"You're not planning on sleeping in the car, are you? You'll catch a cold or worse."

Takayuki clucked.

"I don't wanna hear that from you. You're the sick one. Put yourself in my shoes. You think I can drop my dying father off at some abandoned house and go back home and sleep? Never mind the drive. I gotta come and get you in the morning. It'll be easier for me to wait in the car."

Yuji made a wretched face that exaggerated his wrinkles. "Sorry to put you out."

"You sure you're fine alone? If I come back to a dark house and trip over your dead body, I'm not going to be happy."

"I'll be all right. We haven't shut off the utilities. The lights should work." Yuji opened his door and lowered his feet to the pavement. It was a pitiful sight.

"Ah, that's right," he said and leaned back in. "I almost forgot the most important thing. I meant to give this to you." He was holding out an envelope.

"What's this?"

"Originally, I was going to leave it as my will, but I've already given you the lay of the land. You can read this now. It's actually better that way. Read it once I'm inside. Just give me your word that you'll do what we agreed, no matter what it says in there. If you can't do that, what I'm about to do is pointless."

Takayuki took the envelope. It was blank on the front and back, but it held some paper inside.

"Thanks for your help." Yuji got out of the car and walked off with the help of the cane the hospital had given him.

Takayuki couldn't cry out after him. He had the impulse but lacked the words. Without looking back even once, Yuji disappeared into the alley alongside the house.

For a while, Takayuki sat there in a daze. When he came to his senses, he checked inside the envelope sitting on his lap. Sure enough, there was a letter inside, but it contained the strangest message.

Dear Takayuki,

By the time you read this, I suppose I'll no longer be among the living. It's sad, but that's the way life is. And now that I'm gone, I suppose I no longer have a heart to feel that sadness.

I'm writing to ask a favor. That's the only reason why I've left you this letter. Something I need you to make sure you do for me, no matter what happens.

Simply put, I need you to make an announcement. Just before my thirty-third memorial service, I want you to circulate the following message. You use whatever way you see fit to tell the people of the world.

"On [write the date I died], from exactly midnight until daybreak, the advice box of the Namiya General Store will be reopening for one night only. We kindly ask that anyone who has ever asked for and received advice to give us your unfiltered opinion. How did it affect your life? Did you find it useful, or was it useless? Please leave your letters in the mail slot in the shutter, just like old times. We look forward to hearing from you."

I'm sure this sounds completely bonkers to you, but it matters a great deal to me. It may seem stupid, but please do this for me.

—Dad

Takayuki read through the letter twice and laughed dryly.

What would he have done if he had found this as his will with no further explanation? He knew exactly what: He probably would have just ignored it. He'd assume that his father's time had come, but not before he lost his mind. End of story. Even if he felt a sense of duty, he'd probably soon forget all about it. And even if he didn't forget it right away, there was no chance he would remember it thirty years later.

But after Yuji's uncanny explanation, he couldn't pretend to ignore it. His father had shared with him his innermost fears.

To start things off, Yuji had pulled out a newspaper clipping, pushing it toward his son and urging him to read it.

It was a news article from three months back. A story on the death of a woman from the next town over. It said that several people had witnessed a car drive off a coastal road into the harbor. The police and the fire department rushed to the scene, but the woman in the driver's seat was already dead by the time they arrived.

However, her one-year-old infant was recovered floating near the wreck. The baby was thought to have been with her and presumably thrown from the car just after impact. Miraculously, the child was unscathed.

The driver had been Midori Kawabe, age twenty-nine, unmarried. The car was borrowed from a friend on the understanding that Ms. Kawabe would be using it to drive her child to a doctor's appointment.

According to her neighbors, the deceased was unemployed and struggling to survive. She had outstanding payments on her rent and had been asked to vacate at the end of the month. Based on an absence of skid marks at the site, the police believed the likelihood of a murder-suicide was high and opened an investigation. The article ended there.

"What's this about?" Takayuki asked.

Yuji looked troubled. Wrinkles formed at the corners of his eyes.

"That's the woman. Pregnant with a married man. She asked me for advice. Remember? I'm almost sure it's her. The town's nearby, and the kid would be about one year old by now. It all adds up."

"No way," said Takayuki. "Wasn't it just a coincidence?"

"Hardly." Yuji shook his head. "The people who write in like to use pen names. Her name was 'Green River.' This woman's name was Midori Kawabe. *Midori*, the Japanese word for green. And her last name has the character for *river* in it. Does that sound like a coincidence? I sure as hell don't think so."

Takayuki didn't know what to say. It sounded like too much for a coincidence.

But there was more.

"It's not such a big deal whether this woman was the one who asked me for advice back then. What matters is whether I gave the right advice—not just that time, but all the countless times. Did my advice do any good at all? I put my heart and soul into those letters. Not once did I simply patch something together. Every one of them received my full attention. But did I actually help anybody? I have no idea. For all I know, some people wound up with nothing but misfortune, thanks to me. When it hit me, I completely lost my focus. I couldn't look at those letters without worrying about the consequences anymore. That's why I closed the store."

So that's what happened. Takayuki felt as if he finally understood. He'd been puzzled by Yuji's sudden change of heart after he'd been so steadfast about staying open.

"Moving in with you didn't help to get it off my mind. If I started wondering whether my advice had botched up someone's life, I couldn't sleep at night. When I fell, I couldn't help but think it was some kind of divine justice."

"Don't overthink things," Takayuki had told him. "Whatever advice you might have given, they made the final call. Even if things ended bad for some, you shouldn't feel responsible."

But Yuji had never been able to accept this rationale. He spent day after day brooding in the hospital. Then one night, he had started to have a strange recurring dream. There was only one thing it could have been about: the Namiya General Store.

"It's the middle of the night. Someone is slipping an envelope through the mail slot in the shutter. I'm watching this happen from somewhere, but I'm not sure where. It feels like I'm watching from overhead, or like I'm right in front of it. Anyway, I'm watching, but the thing is, I can tell it's happening in the future…decades from now. Don't ask me how I know that, but I'm positive."

This dream had come back almost every night until, finally, Yuji realized: This wasn't just a simple dream. It was a premonition.

"The people slipping these letters through the mail slot are the same people who sent me letters, who asked for and received advice from me. They're coming to tell me how their lives were changed. I want to go pick up those letters," Yuji had said.

"But how, if they haven't been written yet?"

"If I go to the store, I'll be able to retrieve them. I know it sounds insane, but I somehow know I can. That's why I need to make it there, no matter what."

Yuji's voice was adamant. He didn't look as if he was having a delusion, at least not to Takayuki.

This wasn't a story Takayuki could say he believed, but he had made a promise, and he had to heed his father's wishes.

4

When Takayuki came to, he was still cramped up in the Civic, and it was still dark. He turned on the interior lights and checked the time. A few minutes shy of five in the morning.

He'd parked on the street beside a little park. He cranked up the seat from its not-quite-horizontal incline back to normal, tried to crack his neck, and stepped out of the car.

After using the public bathroom in the park, he washed his face. He used to come here all the time to play. He had a look around, amazed at how small it actually was, and wondered how he could have played baseball in such a tiny space.

Back in the car, he started the engine, flicked on the headlights, and rolled off down the street. It was only a few hundred yards back to the house.

The sky began to take on color. By the time he parked in front of the store, he was able to make out the letters on the sign.

Takayuki left the car and went around back. He had his spare key with him, but he decided to knock.

After he'd waited a few dozen seconds, he heard a pattering sound behind the door.

The door unlocked. It opened, and there was Yuji, facing him. The look on his face was utter peace.

"I thought you might be ready soon," said Takayuki. His voice was ragged.

"Come, come in."

Takayuki stepped inside and shut the door snug behind him. Something about the air changed. He could feel it. As if they had been cut off from the outside world.

He took off his shoes and stepped up into the house. Though it'd been neglected for so many months, the interior was clean. He'd been prepared for it to be dustier.

"Wow, it's so clean. Even though it hasn't—"

"Been aired out" was what he was about to say. But he stopped short when he saw what was sitting on the kitchen table.

Rows and rows of envelopes. Dozens of them. All clean and white, almost all addressed to the Namiya General Store.

"Did these…all arrive last night?"

Yuji nodded and sat down in a chair. He scanned the rows of envelopes and looked up at Takayuki.

"It was just as I suspected. The second I sat down here, these letters came flapping through the mail slot. It's like they were waiting for me to come home."

Takayuki shook his head.

"After you went outside, I sat out front for a bit. I watched, but nobody came by. No one even passed the house."

"Well. Still, all these letters." Yuji uncurled his fingers. "Letters… from the future."

Takayuki grabbed a chair and sat down across from Yuji. "I don't believe it…"

"Didn't you believe me when I explained things to you?"

"No, I mean, yeah, sure."

Yuji laughed. "But deep down, you were skeptical. How about now? Or are you going to tell me you think I did this all myself?"

"I wasn't going to say that. I know you didn't have the time."

"It would take hours just to prepare all these envelopes, let alone write them all. And just in case you're wondering about the stationery, it's not anything we ever sold."

"I believe it. I've never seen anything like this in the store."

Takayuki was a bit uneasy. Could something like this actually happen outside the world of fairy tales? He thought for a minute that maybe it was all someone's idea of a clever joke or magic trick, but no one would go to all this trouble. Where was the fun in fooling an old man in his last days on earth?

Letters from the future—perhaps that was the only explanation. If what Yuji said was true, this was a miracle. Takayuki should have been ecstatic, but he kept his cool. He was still somewhat perplexed, but he was surprised he could keep himself together.

"So did you read them?"

"Yep," he said and picked up one of the envelopes. He pulled out the folded letter and handed it to Takayuki. "Have a look."

"You sure?"

"Sure, why not?"

Takayuki took the pages and unfolded them. The contents weren't written by hand, but in a typeface, printed on white paper.

"Whoa."

Yuji nodded. "At least half the letters are printed up like this. People in the future must all have personal printing machines for text."

This alone was strong enough evidence that these letters were from the future. Takayuki took a deep breath and started to read.

To the Namiya General Store,

Are you really opening up again? The post said it would be for just one night. What's the occasion? I debated what to do but figured hey, even if this is a trick, who cares? I'll write and see what happens.

I guess it's been almost forty years now since I wrote you with this question:

"Tell me how I can get an A+ on a test without studying or cheating or anything."

I know I was in grade school, but what a stupid thing to ask. But you gave me an amazing answer.

"Ask your teacher to test you on yourself. Since you're the topic of the test, whatever you say will be correct."

When I first read it, I thought you were messing with me. I just wanted to know how to get an A+ in real subjects, like literature or math.

Your response stuck with me. Through middle school and high school, I thought of it whenever I had a test. It made that much of an impression. It meant a lot to me that you would respond to my stupid question in such a thoughtful way.

But I didn't truly appreciate just how amazing your response was until I started teaching kids myself. That's right—I became a teacher.

From my first few days behind the podium, I was in trouble. The kids in my class wouldn't open up to me and wouldn't listen to what I said. They weren't getting along with one another, either. Nothing was working. They had no focus, and they wouldn't come together as a class. Aside from their friends, they couldn't have cared less who they were learning with.

I tried all kinds of things, like integrating sports and games into the lessons, or having the kids hold debates. None of them worked. No one was having fun.

Then one of the kids said, "I don't want to do any of this stuff; just teach me how to get good grades."

When I heard that, I knew what to do. I'd been reminded of a very important lesson of my own.

As you've probably guessed by now, I told them I was going to have them take a different sort of test, something we'd call the "Friend Quiz." They would be assigned a random classmate and answer all kinds of questions about them. We started with the basics, like their birthday, address, siblings, and their guardians' jobs, then went on to things like hobbies, talents, favorite celebrities. When they were done with the test, the "friend" would tell them the correct answers. Then, the students would all grade themselves.

At first, they were confused about what to do, but after two or three rounds, they got the hang of it. The only secret to scoring high on this test was to learn everything you could about your classmates.

My students were communicating with one another so effectively you'd think they were a different batch of kids.

For a newbie like me, this was a revelation. It gave me the confidence to stick with teaching. In fact, it's what's kept me teaching to this day.

All of this is thanks to you, Mr. Namiya. I've been wanting to thank you all these years, but I didn't know how to express my thanks. I'm so glad I finally had the chance.

Sincerely,
A + Akira

PS. I am assuming that this letter will be received by a family member on your behalf. I would be most appreciative if they would place it on your altar.

The second Takayuki looked up from the letter, Yuji asked him, "Well?"

"I mean, it's great." That's the least he could say. "I remember this question about how to ace a test without studying. It's so cool getting a letter from one of those kids."

"I'm amazed, too. And he's so appreciative. All I did was write a serious response to his jokey letter."

"But he's never forgotten."

"It seems like it. And not only that, he's run with it and made it into something new, adapted it to his circumstances. He says it's thanks to me, but things went the way they did because of all the effort he put in."

"But I think you really made him happy by seriously engaging with his little joke instead of ignoring it. That's why he still remembers."

"My response wasn't anything special." Yuji looked over the rows of letters. "Most of them are thanking me for how I helped them out. I appreciate it, but when I read them, I can't help but feel like my advice only worked because they put it into practice. If they hadn't had the resolve to do the work on their end, they wouldn't have gotten anywhere, no matter what I said."

Takayuki nodded. He agreed.

"It's good you got to see it, though, right? It proves you steered people in the right direction."

"That's one way to look at it." Yuji scratched his cheek. He picked up another envelope. "There's one more I'd like you to read."

"Why this one?"

"Read it. You'll know."

Takayuki took the envelope and pinched out the folded pieces of paper. The densely packed lines of the letter were handwritten in a neat script.

To the Namiya General Store,

I heard online that you were reopening just for tonight, and I couldn't pass up the chance to write this letter.

I actually only know about your advice indirectly through some stories. Someone I know wrote to you asking for advice. Before I say who that was, please allow me to explain how it is I made it here.

When I was young, I lived in a children's home. I have no idea when I arrived. My first memories are of being there with other children. I thought that was how everybody lived.

But when I started going to school, I wasn't so sure anymore. How come I had no parents? Why didn't I have a house?

One day, a caretaker told me how I had wound up in their care. She was the only one I trusted and confided in. She said when I was one year old, my mother was in a car accident and passed away. I never had a father. She said she would say more when I was older.

I was so confused. Why didn't I have a father? Time passed, but things didn't get any clearer.

Then in middle school, we were asked to do a report for social studies where we had to research events that took place the year we were born. I was looking through some newspapers that'd been scaled down at the library, and I stumbled across an article.

The article described how a car drove off the road into the harbor, and how the driver, Midori Kawabe, died in the crash. She had been driving with her one-year-old daughter, and from the lack of skid marks on the road, they thought there was a high chance of a murder-suicide.

I knew my mother's name, and I had once asked where she had been living when she died. This was her.

I was shocked, and not only to find that my mother's death was a suicide instead of an accident. It was also an act of murder. She had been trying to kill me, too. This was an enormous blow.

I left the library, but I didn't go back to the children's home. Please don't ask me where I went. I can't remember. All I could think about was how I should have died, and there was no reason for me to go on living. My own mother had wanted to murder me. Wasn't she supposed to be the one who loved me unconditionally? I was worthless, and I had no right to be alive.

I was taken into custody on the third day. They found me in a corner of this little amusement park on the roof of a department store. I have no idea why I was there. All I remember is having the thought that if I jumped from somewhere high, it would be easier to die.

They brought me to a hospital. I was so weak, and I had slash marks on my wrists. I was hugging a bag when they took me in, and inside they found a bloodstained razor blade.

For a while, I wouldn't speak to anyone. I couldn't even make eye contact. I was barely eating and got skinnier every day.

One day, I had a visitor—my best friend from the children's home. She was my age. Her little brother had a disability, and they had been sent to live with us because their parents were abusive. She was really good at singing, and I loved music. We became the best of friends.

With her there, I felt able to speak. We were chatting about nothing special, and out of nowhere, she said to me she had something very important to tell me. I got the sense the staff at the home had sent her. They probably knew I wouldn't have spoken with anyone else.

I told her I already knew everything and didn't want to hear it, but she shook her head aggressively and told me I only knew a piece of it, and I didn't know the real facts.

Like, for example, did I know how much my mother weighed when she died? I asked her how was I supposed to know that. She said she had weighed sixty-seven pounds. I was about to ask her how she knew, but I backtracked. Sixty-seven? That's it?

She nodded and went on.

When they found Midori's body, she was unbelievably skinny. The police investigated her apartment and found almost no food, except for some powdered milk. There was one jar of baby food in the fridge.

According to those who knew her, Midori couldn't get a job and had blown through all her savings. She was behind on her rent and was going to be evicted. This was enough to suggest that she killed herself and tried to kill her child, out of hopeless desperation.

But this didn't explain why her child had miraculously survived.

"In actuality," my friend explained, "it was no miracle at all." Before she went on, she had something she wanted me to read. She handed me a letter.

She said the letter had been found in my mother's bedroom, tucked away with my umbilical cord. All this time, it had been kept under lock and key by the staff at the home. They had talked it over and decided it was time for me to see it.

I looked at the envelope. It was addressed to "Ms. Green River."

I was hesitant but had to open it and see what was inside. It was carefully handwritten. For a second, I thought it might be written by my mother, but midway through, I realized it was written to her, not by her. My mother was "Ms. Green River."

The letter was offering her advice. Evidently, she had confided in this person in some way. From the letter, I gathered she had gotten pregnant by a man who already had a wife and kids, and she was torn up about whether to have the child or have an abortion.

It was disturbing to learn about the scandal behind my birth. It felt awful to know I was conceived under such immoral circumstances.

I screamed and cursed at my mother in front of my friend.

"Why did you even have me? You should have let me go so that I wouldn't have to be here suffering. You wouldn't have had to try and kill us both."

But my friend said I had it wrong and told me to keep reading.

Whoever wrote the letter said that the most important thing was whether her unborn child would wind up happy. It said, "Even having both your parents is no guarantee for a happy life, and unless you're prepared to push through every form of hardship for the sake of providing for your child, I would say you shouldn't have the baby. Even if the man was in the picture, I'd give you the same advice."

"Your mother had you," my friend said, "because she was prepared to do anything to make you happy. The fact that she held on to this letter was the ultimate proof. "That's why she couldn't have been trying to kill either of you."

She said the passenger-side window of the wrecked car had been all the way open. It had been raining that day since morning; there was no way they had been driving with the window down. Her mother must have opened it after the crash.

Which meant it wasn't a murder or a suicide. It was an accident. Midori Kawabe had barely been eating, and she must have gone into anemic shock from malnutrition while she was driving. She had borrowed the car, like she said, to bring her child to the doctor's office.

Midori blacked out and then came to when the car crashed into the water. Through the chaos, she opened up the window and freed her child from the vehicle, praying that would be enough to rescue her.

When they found her in the car, her seatbelt wasn't even unbuckled. The anemia must have dimmed her consciousness.

The rescued child weighed over twenty-two pounds. Midori had been feeding her enough.

My friend asked me what I thought of the whole story. Did I still wish I'd never been born?

I wasn't quite sure how to feel. I'd never met my mother in person. My anger was an abstraction. But trying to convert it into gratitude only made me more confused.

I told her I didn't think anything of it.

The car crash was her own fault, and it would never have happened if she hadn't been too broke to eat. Saving me was her responsibility as a parent. She was an idiot for not being able to save herself, too.

For that, my friend slapped me across the face.

She was crying and told me not to think of life that way. Had I already forgotten about the fire?

I didn't know what to say to that. She was referring to the fire that had happened three years earlier in the children's home on Christmas Eve. I was just as terrified as everyone else.

My friend's little brother was one step behind the rest of us and almost died. He wouldn't have made it if it weren't for this musician who had come for a performance. I can still remember what he looked like; his face was so kind. While everyone was scrambling to safety, he stopped and listened to my friend and ran back up the stairs to save her brother. Her brother made it out alive, but the man had third-degree burns all over. He died in the hospital.

She told me they would be grateful to this man for the rest of their lives and could only try to be worthy of his sacrifice. She asked me to remember how easily life can be taken away. She was sobbing as she begged me to see that, too.

I understood why the staff had sent her now. They knew there was no other person who could help me reconcile my feelings, who could teach me how to feel. And they were right. She convinced me, and I started crying, too. I could finally offer thankfulness to the mother I had never known.

From that day on, I never again told myself I wished I'd never been born. The road that brought me here today has been anything but easy, but I've persevered, conscious of this pain as a reminder of just how precious life is.

But I couldn't help but wonder about who had written to my mother. It was signed "Namiya General Store." Who was this person? What is a "general store"?

Only recently, I read on the Internet that you ran a general store—whatever that means—and gave advice to anyone who asked. I read about it on someone's blog. They were reminiscing about their experience with you. I wondered if there were other people out there, and when I looked, I found this post.

Mr. Namiya, I'm deeply grateful for the advice you gave my mother. I've wanted to find a way to tell you for so long. Thank you so much. I can finally say with confidence that I'm happy I was born.

—The daughter of Green River

PS. This friend of mine became a famous singer. She's a musical genius and one of the most celebrated artists in Japan. I'm working as her manager. She is also trying to pay someone back for their sacrifice.

5

Takayuki folded up the sheaf of pages and returned them to their envelope.

"That's great. Your advice hit the mark."

But Yuji shook his head.

"Like I said, what matters most is how much effort you put in. I was worried my advice could have ruined someone's life, but it seems like nothing a simple old man could have said was going to sway things either way. I got myself worked up for nothing."

Takayuki could see his father was at peace.

"These letters are a real gift, Dad. You gotta hang on to these."

Yuji looked pensive. "No, I want you to take them for me."

"What?"

"All of them. Keep them safe for me."

"You want me to keep them? Why?"

"Son, you know I don't have long to go. If I hold on to these and someone gets their hands on them, all hell would break loose. These letters are full of stories from the future."

Takayuki groaned. His father had a point. He was right, impossible as it may have sounded.

"How long should I hold on to them?"

This time, Yuji was the one who let out a low moan. "I guess until I'm gone."

"All right. How about I put them in your coffin? That way they'll be burned."

"Perfect." Yuji slapped his knee. "Let's go with that."

Takayuki nodded and looked back to the rows of letters. He couldn't believe these had come from people from the future.

"Dad," he asked, "what's this 'Internet' thing all about?"

"Ah, that." Yuji pointed a finger in the air. "That was bugging me, too. It comes up in a bunch of these. 'I saw your post on the Internet.' That and something they keep calling a cell phone."

"A cell phone? What the hell is that?"

"No clue. They made it sound like some kind of futuristic newspaper." Yuji narrowed his eyes and looked at Takayuki. "Did you read that letter I gave you in the car? It sounds like you circulated it pretty well."

"On an Internet, or a cell phone?"

"Looks that way."

Takayuki looked unenthusiastic. "I'm not so sure I want to get involved with that. Gives me the creeps."

"Don't worry about it. You'll figure it out. All right, let's get going."

Then it happened. They heard a faint sound out in the store. The sound of paper falling. Takayuki met eyes with Yuji.

"Sounds like there's another one," Yuji noted.

"A letter?"

"Yep," he nodded. "Go check."

"Okay." Takayuki went out into the store. They hadn't cleaned things out yet; the shelves were still partially stocked.

A cardboard box sat up against the shutter. He peeked inside and found a folded sheet of paper. It looked like stationery. He picked it up and took it back to the tatami room. "Must've been this."

Yuji unfolded the letter. A look of bewilderment came over his face.

"What's wrong?" asked Takayuki.

Lips pursed, Yuji showed the letter to his son.

"Whoa!" There was nothing written on the paper. "What's that supposed to mean?"

"I'm not sure."

"Think it's a prank?"

"Maybe. Still—" Yuji glared down at the paper. "I have a feeling that it isn't."

"What is it, then?"

Yuji put the letter on the tabletop and crossed his arms. "Might be from somebody who hasn't found a solution to their problem yet. Maybe they're still struggling with something and can't figure out what to say."

"But why send an empty sheet of paper?"

Yuji turned to Takayuki. "Excuse me, but would you mind waiting outside?"

Takayuki blinked. "What are you going to do?"

"I'm going to respond, I suppose."

"To that? There's nothing to respond to! What is there to say?"

"That's what I need to figure out."

"When? Now?"

"Don't let me keep you. You go on ahead."

Yuji sounded serious, and Takayuki gave in.

"All right, just hurry up."

"Uh-huh," replied Yuji. He was already lost in thought.

Takayuki walked down the alley to the car. It wasn't as bright outside as he expected. Strange. It felt like they'd been in that house for a while.

He got into the Civic and started to stretch out his neck, twisting it this way and that, when the sky started to visibly brighten, as if sped up.

Maybe time really did flow differently inside that house. He resolved to keep that little revelation from his sister and his wife. They wouldn't believe him anyway.

He sat in the car, yawning one yawn after another. A sound came from the direction of the house, and Yuji appeared at the end of the alley. He was hobbling along with his cane, in no particular hurry. Takayuki got out of the car and went around to the passenger-side door.

"Finished?"

"Yep."

"Well, where is it?"

"Where else? In the milk crate."

"Is that enough for them to get it?"

"They'll get it. I have a hunch."

Takayuki looked skeptical. It was as if his father were some other creature, not human.

Once they were both in the car, Takayuki asked him, "How'd you answer that blank letter anyway?"

Yuji shook his head. "I can't tell you. You know that."

Takayuki shrugged and turned the key.

Just as the car started to move, Yuji said, "Wait a second."

Takayuki slammed the brakes.

Yuji's eyes were locked on the store—his life and livelihood for decade upon decade. And this hadn't been your usual small business, either. It was hard to say good-bye.

"All right," he almost whispered. "Go ahead."

"Did you get what you needed?"

"I've done what I needed to do."

Yuji sat back and closed his eyes.

Takayuki started up the Civic.

6

It was a shame the letters on the sign were so dirty, but he snapped the shutter anyway. He tried a few more shots from different angles. He wasn't any good with cameras, and he couldn't know if any of them would turn out to be any good, but that didn't really matter. He wasn't going to show them to people anyway.

Gazing at the ancient building from across the street, Takayuki thought back to what had happened there a year ago. To the night he'd visited the store with Yuji.

It didn't feel like it was real. Sometimes he wondered if it had been a dream.

Had letters really come here from the future? The two of them had never spoken about that night.

But the ream of letters he'd put into his father's casket were cold, hard fact. His sister, Yoriko, had asked him about it. "What's with all the letters?" He didn't try to answer.

Yet, the way Yuji died was the strangest part. They had been told he could die any day now, but his life force seemed as if it were stretching on indefinitely, ever thinner without breaking, like the slimy strings of natto, or fermented soybeans. He rarely ate and most days barely woke up, but he lived around another year. It was as if time had slowed down inside his body.

Lost in thought, he came to his senses when he heard a voice.

"Um, excuse me?"

He turned to see a tall young woman dressed in exercise gear. She was standing in the street before him, holding up a bike. A gym bag was strapped down on the seat mounted over the back tire.

"Hi. How can I help you?"

Hesitant, the woman asked, "Do you happen to know a Mr. Namiya?"

"I'm his son. This used to be his shop."

She opened her mouth wide with surprise and blinked. "Oh, I see."

"Had you been to the shop?"

"Yes, I mean, not as a customer, unfortunately." She looked down at the street, hunched over in wordless apology.

Takayuki nodded, putting things together. "You came here for advice, then."

"I did," she said. "It made a huge difference in my life."

"I'm glad to hear that. How long ago was this?"

"Well, it must have been November of last year."

"Last November?"

"Is this store closed for good?" she asked, looking over at the shutter.

"Well, after my father passed away…"

She caught her breath in surprise, and her eyebrows drooped. "He did? When?"

"Last month."

"Oh, that's… I'm so sorry for your loss."

"Thank you." Takayuki nodded. He looked at the gym bag. "You an athlete?"

"I'm a fencer."

"Fencing! Wow." Takayuki was not expecting this.

"Most people aren't used to meeting fencers," she said with a chuckle and straddled her bike. "Sorry to have bothered you. Take care."

"Oh, okay. Thanks again."

Takayuki watched the woman disappear at the bottom of the street. A fencer. Not something you saw every day. More like once every four years in the Olympics. Even then, you saw only the highlights. But this year, Japan had boycotted Moscow, so he hadn't even seen it then.

The woman had said she got her letter last November, but she must have been confused. By then, Yuji was already laid up in the hospital.

Takayuki thought of something and walked across the street, down the alley alongside the house. He lifted the lid of the milk crate.

Nothing. Where had the letter Yuji wrote that strange night the year before gone? Did his response to the empty sheet of paper really make it to the future?

7

September 2012.

Shungo Namiya sat in front of the computer, at a loss. He probably shouldn't do this. If something went wrong and he made a mess, it was going to look really bad. He was on his family's laptop, which made it even worse. If the police traced it back, they'd have him in a second. The penalties for cybercrime were crazy, much worse than you'd expect.

But he didn't think Takayuki would have asked him to do anything wrong. Even at the very end, he hadn't been the least bit senile. When he asked Shungo to do the favor, his voice had been steady and clear.

Takayuki was his grandfather, who had passed away at the end of last year. Stomach cancer. Takayuki's own father had died of cancer, too. Maybe his whole family had cancer in their genes.

Before Takayuki had been moved into the hospital, he called Shungo to his room and asked him for a small favor, but it had to stay between the two of them.

"What is it?" Shungo asked. His curiosity got the better of him.

"You're getting pretty good with computers, right?"

"I guess you could say that." He was in the math club at his middle school. They used computers all the time.

Takayuki pulled out a sheet of paper. "Next September, I want you to take what's written here and put it on the Internet."

Shungo took the piece of paper and looked it over. This was so weird.

"Hey, what is this?"

Takayuki shook his head. "Don't worry about that. Just figure out a way to spread this to as many people as you can. You know how to do that, right?"

"Yeah, I mean, I guess so."

"Truth be told, I was supposed to do this myself. I promised."

"Promised who?"

"My father. Your great-grandfather."

"My grandpa's father..."

"But listen. I have to go to the hospital, you see. They don't know how long I'm going to live. That's why I'm asking for your help."

Shungo had no idea what to say. He'd gathered from hearing his parents talk that Takayuki didn't have much time.

"Okay," Shungo said.

Takayuki nodded over and over again. He was satisfied.

Before long, Takayuki left this earth. When Shungo attended the *tsuya* ceremony and funeral, he felt as if he could hear a voice coming from the coffin, saying "I'm counting on you, kid."

After that, the promise occupied the forefront of his mind. He wasn't sure what to do, but before he knew it, it was September.

Shungo read the paper on the desk beside him. It was the same sheet of paper Takayuki had given him.

> *On September 13, from exactly midnight until daybreak, the advice box of the Namiya General Store will be reopening for one night only. We kindly ask that anyone who has ever asked for and received advice to give us your unfiltered opinion. How did it affect your life? Did you find it useful, or was it useless? Please leave your letters in the mail slot in the shutter, just like old times. We look forward to hearing from you.*

Takayuki had given Shungo something else with the piece of paper: a photograph of the Namiya General Store, his great-grandfather's shop. Shungo had never been, but he'd been told the building was still there.

Takayuki had told him his family used to run a general store, but that was all he knew.

What was this about "advice"? And what did it mean by *reopening*?

He'd really better back out now. If he opened a Pandora's box, the undo button wouldn't save him.

Shungo turned off the computer, about to close the screen, but something caught his eye.

It was the wristwatch, set up in a display box on the corner of the desk. His grandpa Takayuki had left it to him as an heirloom. As the story goes, Takayuki's own father had given him the watch when he went off to college. By now, it was so old that it lost five minutes every day.

Shungo glared into his monitor. He saw his face reflected against its surface. His face, and the face of his grandfather. They overlapped and merged into one.

There was a promise he had to keep. Man-to-man.

Shungo turned on the computer.

Chapter 4

A Moment of Silence for the Beatles

1

Exiting the station and heading down the street of shops, Kosuke Waku felt an unsettling feeling creep across his chest. He was right. Just as he'd feared, hard times hadn't spared this town. There was a time when people had flocked here to settle down and turned the station and its neighboring shops into a hub of commerce, but that was in the 1970s. It was now forty years later. Times had changed. Out in the countryside, shuttered businesses marked the streets, and this old town was no exception.

He walked along, checking for things from his past. He thought he would remember almost nothing, but to his surprise, he recognized all kinds of places once he was actually there.

But it wasn't as if the town was completely unchanged. The fish shop his mother frequented had vanished from the street. What was it even called? That's right—Uomatsu. The owner had a deep-brown suntan. He was always calling enthusiastically out to passing customers: "Hey, missus, our oysters today are unbeatable. Do yourself a favor and buy a dozen; your husband will thank me later."

What happened to that guy? He thought he heard somewhere that his son was going to take over, but the memory was blurred. Maybe he had it mixed up with some other store.

Down the road, he figured he was close enough and turned right onto a side street, unsure if he would ever make it to where he was heading.

The street was poorly lit, but he walked on. There were street lights, but not all of them were on. After the big earthquake the previous year, Japan had imposed national restrictions on energy use. Having enough light to see your feet was now considered plenty.

The neighborhoods had been built up extensively since he was a kid. He faintly remembered hearing talk of the town's ambitious plans for development when he was in elementary school. He could still hear one of his classmates excitedly cheering "We're getting our own movie theater!"

Those plans could basically be considered a success to a certain extent. Eventually, the town made it to the Japanese asset price bubble, and for a time, it became a popular commuter town for those working in Tokyo.

The street he was on came to a T-shaped intersection. This was not unexpected. In fact, it was just as he remembered it. Kosuke turned right again.

A little farther, and the street started sloping gradually uphill. This, too, was how he remembered it. He was almost there—as long as what he'd read hadn't been bogus.

Kosuke walked up the hill, watching his footsteps. If he had watched the street instead, he would have known much sooner whether the store was still standing. But instead, he kept walking with his head down. Something made him scared to know before he got there. Even if what he'd read did turn out to be a lie, he wanted to hold on to hope until the last possible second.

He finally came to a halt. He knew he was close. He'd walked up and down this street a thousand times.

Kosuke looked up. He sucked in a huge breath of air and blew it out.

The store—the Namiya General Store—was still there. This shop had played a massive role in the course his life had taken.

He approached it slowly. The letters on the sign were grubbed up and indecipherable, and the shutter was rusted over, but the building was still standing. As if it had been waiting for Kosuke to arrive.

He checked his watch. It wasn't even eleven yet. He had come a bit too early.

Kosuke looked up and down the street. No one in sight. There was no way anybody lived here anymore. Could he really trust that story? After all, it was the Internet. Perhaps he should have been more skeptical.

But then again, what was there to gain by posing as the Namiya General Store? Only a handful of people would remember it by now.

He decided to hang around a little while longer, just to check it out. Besides, he still hadn't written his letter. Even if he wanted to be involved in this strange event, he wouldn't be able to without a letter.

Kosuke went back the way he came. Meandering through the neighborhoods, he made it to the street of shops. Most of them were closed for the night. He would have thought there would be a twenty-four-hour restaurant or someplace he could wait, but that didn't seem to be the case.

He did find a convenience store and went inside. He had some shopping to do. In the stationery section, he found what he needed and took it to the register. The cashier was a young guy.

"Any places open late around here?" Kosuke asked after he paid. "A pub or something?"

"There's a cluster of bars up the street, but I've never been to any of them," the cashier replied rather curtly.

"All right, thanks."

Sure enough, not far past the convenience store, he came upon a patch of bars and pubs. None of them seemed to be doing much business. He guessed they were the type of spot where local business owners might meet up for a drink after closing time.

One of the signs made Kosuke stop midstride: Bar Fab4. With a name like that, he had no choice but to investigate.

He opened the charcoal-colored door and peeked inside. Before him were two tables and, at the back, a counter with stools. On one stool sat a woman with a short bob, wearing a black sleeveless dress. No one else was there. She must have been the owner.

The woman looked at him, a bit surprised. "Here for a drink?"

She looked to be in her midforties. Her facial features were distinctly Japanese.

"As long as it's not too late."

The woman gave him a faint smile and stood up. "Of course not. We don't close until midnight."

"In that case, I'll have just one drink, thanks."

Kosuke stepped inside and took the stool at the very edge of the counter by the wall.

"No need to leave so much space," the woman laughed wryly. She handed him a hot towel to wipe his hands. "I don't think anyone else is coming out tonight."

"I'm fine, thanks. I have something I need to work on over a drink." He mopped his hands and face with it.

"Work? This late?"

"Yeah, work stuff," he mumbled vaguely. Explaining things would not have been easy.

She didn't probe him any further. "Well, don't let me bother you. Make yourself at home. What can I get you?"

"I guess I'll have a beer. You have anything dark?"

"Is Guinness okay?"

"Absolutely."

She crouched behind the counter. There must have been a fridge down there.

When she stood, she was holding a bottle of Guinness. She popped the cap and poured it into a tumbler for Kosuke. She knew her stuff, all right. At least a knuckle's worth of creamy foam floated on top.

Kosuke took a big gulp and wiped his mouth with the back of his hand. Its familiar bitter flavor filled his mouth. "Would you care for one yourself?"

"Why, thank you." The woman placed a tiny dish of nuts in front of Kosuke and took down a small glass. She poured herself some beer. "Cheers."

"Cheers," he replied.

He reached into his bag from the convenience store and took out a pen and a pad of paper.

The woman looked at him approvingly. "Are you writing someone a letter?"

"Basically."

She nodded, her suspicion confirmed, and moved to the other end of the bar. She seemed to be trying to give him space.

Kosuke had another sip of Guinness and had a look around the bar.

For a bar in a desolate town, this was not a down-home kind of place. The tables and chairs were simple yet refined, and the walls were decorated with posters and drawings. They were full of depictions of a well-known quartet of young men who had taken the whole world by storm well over forty years ago. One showed a yellow submarine drawn in psychedelic colors.

"Fab4" was a reference to "the Fab Four," a nickname for the Beatles.

"Is this place a Beatles bar?"

The woman shrugged agreeably. "That's our gimmick anyway."

"Huh." Kosuke had another look around and noticed a flat-screen on the wall. He wondered what Beatles content they would show on it. *A Hard Day's Night? HELP!?* Kosuke didn't think he'd discover some unknown cinematic treasures in a local spot like this.

"I'm guessing you were born too late to know them as a kid."

His question made her shrug again. "Don't be silly. When I was going into middle school, it had only been two years since they disbanded. They were at their peak. There were all kinds of events."

Kosuke looked at her face.

"This is nothing to ask a lady, but…"

She knew what he was trying to say and chuckled dryly. "I'm too old to let that bother me. But if you insist, let's just say I was born in the year of the pig."

"The pig. That means…" Kosuke blinked. "You're only two years younger than me?"

She sure didn't look over fifty.

"No—I thought you were the younger one."

She was obviously just saying that.

"That's crazy," muttered Kosuke.

The woman gave him her card. It said *Eriko Haraguchi*.

"You're not from around here. What brings you to town? You here for work?"

Kosuke choked. He couldn't think up a lie that fast.

"Not for work. More like a trip to my hometown, in a way. I used to live here. Forty some odd years ago."

"No kidding," Eriko said, eyes wide. "We must have run into each other somewhere."

"Maybe." Kosuke had a sip of beer. "By the way, where's the music?"

"Pshhh, what's wrong with me? Mind if I put on the usual?"

"Sure, whatever you'd like."

Eriko went up to the counter and pressed a few buttons. The first notes of a nostalgic song rang out across the decades from the speakers in the wall. The song was "Love Me Do."

Kosuke finished his first glass. He ordered another.

"Do you remember when the Beatles visited Japan?"

Eriko *hmm*ed and scrunched up her face.

"I feel like I saw it on TV, but that might be my imagination. It might have been one of those things where I heard my older brother talking about it with his friends, and now I feel like I was there."

Kosuke nodded. "That happens."

"How about you? Do you remember?"

"A little bit. I was young, too. But I'm certain I saw it with my own two eyes. It wasn't live, but I remember seeing footage of them driving down the Imperial Highway in a Cadillac after they got off their plane. It wasn't until much later that I found out it was a Cadillac, but I noticed that car. I also remember they had 'Mr. Moonlight' playing in the background."

"'Mr. Moonlight,'" she echoed. "That's not one of their originals."

"Right. But after they played it at their show in Tokyo, it was a huge hit. I mean, that's kinda why they got famous here. A lot of people think they wrote that song."

Realizing how passionate he must have sounded, Kosuke bit his tongue. It had been a long time since he'd had the chance to hash it out about the Beatles.

"Those were good times," Eriko said.

"Sure were." Kosuke emptied his glass, and she poured him another.

His thoughts flew more than forty years back in time.

2

When the Beatles came to Japan, Kosuke didn't exactly understand who they were. All he knew was that they were a group of four musicians from overseas. That's why he was so shocked to see his cousin crying in front of the TV set when the special broadcast of their arrival came on-screen. His cousin was in high school, but to the nine-year-old Kosuke, he was basically an adult. That was the day he learned that out there in the world were some truly amazing people. People so great that their mere arrival in Japan would make a grown man cry.

Three years later, his cousin died. It was sudden, a motorcycle accident. His aunt and uncle had been devastated, and they wished they'd never let him get his license. At the funeral, Kosuke heard them saying that if he hadn't been listening to that garbage, he never would have fallen in with the wrong crowd. By *garbage*, they meant the Beatles. "I'm going to throw those records in the trash where they belong," his aunt snapped.

"If you're throwing them out," said Kosuke, "I'll take them off your hands." He wanted to hear with his own ears who these Beatles were, to find out what it was that had made his cousin lose his mind that night three years ago. Kosuke was almost in middle school, just reaching the age when music really starts to take hold on a kid.

Some relative told his parents they'd better cut him off. "He'll go bad, just like his cousin." But his parents didn't listen or heed their advice.

"Listening to pop music won't make a boy lose his mind," said his father, Sadayuki. "Besides, Tetsuo wasn't a bad kid. Every high school boy has a bike these days." He dismissed the older relative's concerns with a laugh.

"That's right. Our boy's just fine," said Kosuke's mother, Kimiko.

Kosuke's parents were hip to the scene. They had a different take from your average set of parents, who seemed convinced that growing your hair long made you some kind of criminal.

His cousin had owned just about every Beatles record released in Japan to date, and the collection had Kosuke hooked. He had never heard anything like this. The first time he savored those melodies and experienced those rhythms, it lit up parts of him he hadn't known existed.

In the wake of the Fab Four's visit to Japan, a spate of new groups swept the country's music scene—bands of young men singing behind electric guitars. Kosuke knew these weren't Beatles imitators. They were imposters. Before long, the fad hiccuped and died.

When he started attending middle school, Kosuke realized that many of his classmates were Beatles fans. Sometimes he asked one to come over. When each new friend stepped into his room and got a load of his audio equipment, they always gasped. Every single time. And why wouldn't they? In their eyes, a solid-state amp and speaker system looked like something from the future. They weren't even used to seeing speakers in a kid's room. Back then, even well-off families had just one cabinet-style stereo in the living room, situated like a piece of furniture. Records were for listening together as a family.

"My dad's always saying 'Spare no expense for art,'" he'd tell them. "He says there's no point listening to music if you can't hear it right." Kosuke's friends would moan with envy.

He'd let them listen to the Beatles with his state-of-the art equipment. If the record was released in Japan, Kosuke had it. That alone was baffling to them.

"What the heck does your dad do?" they always asked when they came over.

"I'm not exactly sure, but I know he buys and sells stuff. It's like this. If you buy something for cheap and sell it for a lot, you make a profit, right? He has a whole company that does that."

"Wait, so he's the president?"

"I guess so," Kosuke said. It was hard not to sound proud of it.

But Kosuke knew he was blessed.

The house where they lived was high in the hills. A two-story Western building with a lawn out back where they held barbecues whenever the weather was fine. His dad was always inviting his employees over.

"Japan's been the office boy of the world for a long time," Sadayuki would often say to his subordinates, "and it's high time we do something about it. We need to be the ones to call the shots. To get there, we need to know the world. These other countries may be our competitors, but they're also potential allies. Remember that."

Just hearing his father's commanding baritone voice fanned up Kosuke's sense of pride. He believed everything his father said and thought there wasn't a more reliable man on earth.

Kosuke didn't have the slightest misgiving about his family being loaded. Plastic model kits, board games, records—if there was anything he wanted, his parents bought him piles of it. They even bought him things he didn't really want, like watches and expensive clothes.

His parents were living the life. Sadayuki boasted a golden wristwatch and smoked the finest cigars. He always seemed to have a new car. And Kimiko had her own image to maintain: She had the department stores send salesmen for house visits and ordered practically the entire catalog from front to back.

"Cheap things make for a cheap person" was her motto. "They don't just make you look cheap; they make your soul cheap. They suck away at your humanity. That's why you need to buy the best of the best."

Kimiko was also a devotee of beauty. There were times when she was assumed to be as much as ten years younger than the other women her age. When she showed up at the open house at Kosuke's school, his classmates were all stunned. He couldn't remember how many of them had told him, "Man, I wish my mom was as young as yours!"

The sky was the limit, and the sun was smiling on them. Or so it seemed.

But a time came when he felt the change. It was very slight at first. At the beginning of the 1970s, a dark cloud edged over the horizon.

In 1970, the World Expo in Osaka was the talk of Japan. An entire nation came together in palpable anticipation as it reached its climax.

Kosuke was entering his second year of middle school in April and dead set on trekking down to the Expo over his spring break. Going early gave him better bragging rights. His dad had already promised they were going.

On March 14, Expo '70 opened with outrageous fanfare. Kosuke watched it on TV. As the cathode-ray tube filled the screen with images of the opening ceremony, he felt that for all its garish color, there was very little substance. But it seemed like a fitting way to show the world that Japan had rebuilt its economy and returned as a contender on the global market. It was as his father always said—they were the ones who called the shots.

Except Sadayuki had stopped talking about their trip down to the Expo. One evening after dinner, Kosuke casually broached the topic. What his father said surprised him.

"Expo? Don't think so. I'm busy."

"Well, how about in May during Golden Week?"

His father didn't bother to answer. He was busy making faces at the business newspaper.

"Who cares about the Expo?" added his mother, off to the side. "It's just a bunch of countries showing off with a few dinky rides thrown in. Haven't you outgrown that kind of thing? I thought you were in middle school."

What was there to say to this? It wasn't as if Kosuke had a good reason for going. But he'd already gloated to his friends, and if he didn't go now, he was going to look like a real loser.

"It's time for you to focus on studying. You need to do well on your entrance exams for high school. The sooner you start prepping, the better. A year goes by quick. You don't have time to waste on expos."

Couldn't argue with that, either. Kosuke kept his mouth shut.

But this wasn't the only time he felt a disturbance in the air. From all angles, he could detect that his life was shifting; he just wasn't sure how.

Take his gym clothes, for instance. He was in the middle of a growth spurt, and they didn't fit him anymore. He was used to his parents buying him new clothes whenever he asked, but this time, Kimiko took a different approach.

"What, these are tight already? I just got you that last fall. Make it work a little longer. If I get you another set right now, you'll be asking for a bigger one next week."

As if he were doing something wrong by growing.

There were no more barbecues. His father's employees stopped coming by on days off, and his father stopped playing golf. The house became a battlefield of disagreements. Kosuke wasn't positive what Sadayuki and Kimiko were always arguing about, but he knew it had to do with money.

Sadayuki would make some pointed comment like "If only you took this more seriously," to which Kimiko would retort, "Maybe if you'd actually done your job, I wouldn't have to."

The Ford Thunderbird, his father's most recent favorite, disappeared from the garage. Sadayuki started to commute by train. Kimiko stopped shopping. And both of them were always irritated.

At the worst possible time, he got the news: The Beatles had disbanded. A British newspaper broke the story.

He swapped information with his friends. Back then, there was no Internet and certainly no Mixi, the Japanese social media platform that would become popular in the future. People had no choice but to listen to the paparazzi. "I saw this somewhere," "They said so on the radio," "I guess some foreign paper did a story"—if you amassed enough dubious material, the rumors somehow started sounding real.

No way, thought Kosuke. *Why'd this have to happen now?*

The various explanations for the breakup were hopelessly tangled. Some said it was because Paul McCartney's wife and Yoko Ono couldn't get along, but others blamed George Harrison for sabotaging their final project. There was no telling what was true from what was false.

"Here's one," said one of Kosuke's friends. "Did you guys know the Beatles really didn't want to come to Japan? Their label knew it meant big bucks and forced them into it. They were through with concerts and wanted to back out, but they had no choice. Gotta figure, they stopped playing concerts right after that."

Kosuke had heard this one before, but he didn't believe it. Or perhaps more accurately, he didn't want to believe it.

"Yeah, but I heard they put on an incredible show, and they looked like they were having a great time."

"They weren't. They weren't even planning to play a real set. They figured the crowd would be screaming so loud that no one would hear them playing, so they thought they could just come onstage and sing and play whatever, wouldn't matter. But the audience here was way quieter than they expected, and everyone could hear their performance perfectly fine, so partway through the set, they had to buckle down and do it right."

Kosuke shook his head. "I don't believe it."

"You can say that, but it doesn't change things. Listen, I don't want to believe it, either. But that's what happened. The Beatles are human, too. They thought Japan was just some little island, you know, basically the boonies. They figured they'd ham it up onstage and take the first plane back to England."

Kosuke shook his head. The broadcast of the Beatles arriving in Japan replayed in his mind's eye, along with the tear-streaked face of his cousin as he watched the screen. If what this friend had said was true, what was he to make of those tears?

That day, when he got home from school, he shut himself up in his room and binged on the Beatles, song after song. He could not accept that there would never be another one.

Time passed insufferably. Summer vacation made no difference to his mood. He was hung up on the Beatles. He heard that they were coming out with *Let It Be*, the movie, but there was nowhere for it to play in his town. According to rumors, if you saw the movie, you would get why they broke up. Wondering about what the movie was going to say was enough to keep Kosuke awake at night.

As his generation was being whipped around by the news, Kosuke was about to be backed into a corner by the hardest decision of his life.

One night, as he was listening to the Beatles, just like any other night, his bedroom door swung open. It was Kimiko. He was going to say she could have at least knocked first, but he couldn't speak. His mother's face was graver than he'd ever seen it.

"Can you come down to the living room? It's important."

Kosuke nodded and switched off his stereo. He had no idea what this was all about, but he had sensed something was coming, and it wasn't going to be good.

His father was sitting in an armchair with a glass of brandy. Expensive stuff. He'd brought it home on a trip abroad because it was tax-free.

When Kosuke sat down, his father began. What he said next turned Kosuke's world upside down.

"We're moving at the end of the month. Start getting your things together. Don't tell a soul."

Kosuke didn't get it. "What's happening?" he asked. "What's the hurry?"

Sadayuki was ready with an answer. "Son, I'm a businessman. And business is like war. It makes a big difference how much your enemies get from you. You follow me?"

He was always saying stuff like this. Kosuke nodded. Sadayuki went on.

"In war, sometimes you have to retreat. If you get killed, it's over anyway, get me?"

This time, Kosuke didn't nod. Maybe that happened in a real war, but did people actually get killed over business?

Unfazed, Sadayuki continued. "At the end of the month, we're going to retreat. This house? We're leaving it to the enemies. But that's okay. There's no reason to worry. All you need to do is keep quiet and follow our lead. You'll have to switch schools, but that won't be a problem. The timing is perfect with summer vacation and everything. With the first trimester done, it'll make it easier."

Kosuke was horrified. He had to start over, at a totally new school?

"It's really no big deal," his father said. "Kids have to switch schools all the time when their fathers change jobs. It's not unusual."

For the first time in Kosuke's life, his father's words left him uneasy. Uneasy about life itself.

The next day, Kosuke approached his mother as she was cooking in the kitchen.

"Is this a fly-by-night?"

Kimiko had been mixing up a stir-fry. Her hands froze. "Who said that to you?"

"No one. But based on what Dad said, that's what we're doing."

Kimiko sighed and stirred the pan again. "Don't repeat that to anyone."

He was hoping she would contradict him, but he had hoped in vain. The world went dark.

"Why do we have to do that? Are we broke or something?"

There was no response. Kimiko worked her hands in silence.

"What's happening? What about high school? Which school am I supposed to go to?"

Kimiko turned her neck, very slightly. "We'll figure that out once we get to where we're going."

"Where *are* we going? Where are we going to live?"

"*Enough*, Kosuke." His mother turned her back on him. "If you want to complain, save it for your father. This was his decision."

Kosuke didn't know what to do. He didn't know if he should be sad or angry.

For days on end, he barely left his room. All he did was listen to his Beatles records. Headphones on, volume at full blast, he could drown out the pain.

But this last remaining solace was soon taken away.

"We're getting rid of the stereo," his father announced one day.

Of course, Kosuke didn't let it go without a fight. "Like hell you are," he retorted. But Sadayuki wouldn't hear any of it.

"If we tried moving with that bulky thing, we'd barely make it out of town. I'll buy you a new one once we've made it to the next step. Until then, do without."

Kosuke exploded. "We're not moving—we're running away!"

Sadayuki glared at him. His look was fatal.

"One more peep out of you, and you'll be sorry, kid." He sounded like a member of the yakuza.

"Let's stop. Please. Why do we have to be so sneaky?"

"Shut up. Don't talk about things you don't understand."

"But—"

"They'll murder us." Sadayuki's eyes were bulging. "If they catch us hightailing it out of here, we'll each get a bullet in the head. You want that? We've got one shot at this, and we can't afford to let a single thing go wrong. If we blow it, the three of us will have to hang ourselves. We're this close to being completely screwed, Kosuke. That's why I need you to cooperate."

His father's eyes were bloodshot. Kosuke was nowhere close to speaking. Something was shaking loose inside him. His world was crumbling apart.

A few days later, some men he'd never seen before came by the house and carried away every piece of audio equipment in his room. One of the men handed Kimiko some cash. Sadayuki was nowhere in sight.

The room looked naked without the stereo. Kosuke felt his blood begin to boil. He wished he were dead. There wasn't anything to live for anymore.

Since he couldn't listen to the Beatles, there was no reason to stay home. Kosuke started taking long walks, but he never saw his friends. He felt that if he did, he'd wind up saying something about the escape. And if anyone came over, it would be difficult to hide that his stereo was missing.

He didn't have much money in his pocket. That ruled out the arcade, since he couldn't stay long anyway. Most of the time, his walks took him to the library. The big library in town was unusually sleepy, except for the private rooms, which were always crowded with students taking refuge in the air-conditioning. Most of them were in high school, or one year out, studying for college entrance exams. As he eyed them studying like crazy, he wondered if he'd ever have the chance.

He had put a lot of stock in what his parents said, especially Sadayuki. Up until this point, he had been proud to have him for a dad; he thought everything Sadayuki said was right. He'd honestly believed that if he followed in his father's footsteps, someday he would find himself just as successful.

But that wasn't how things played out. Kosuke had overheard enough of his parents' conversations to piece together the situation. Not only was his father a failed business tycoon, he was a pathetic coward. He was going to scramble off in the moonlight and leave his pile of debt for someone else to clean up.

Somehow he had bungled things so badly at the company that the damage was irreparable. Next month, the truth would come out. He hadn't said anything to his employees. His family's survival was his one concern.

What was Kosuke supposed to do? Was following his parents the only way? He thought their plan was shit, but he had no other choice.

At the library, he continued to browse their books on the Beatles, but his worries wouldn't go away. No book contained the answer.

3

The day of the escape was fast approaching, and there was nothing Kosuke could do. He had been told to pack his things, but he'd lost the will to act.

Then, one night as he was heading to the library, he noticed that the road was closed for construction, and it sent him on a detour.

The signs led him past a neighborhood store. There was a gaggle of kids outside looking up at something on the wall inside and laughing.

Kosuke approached the store to get a better look. Taped up all over the wall were what looked like letters.

> Q: How come when Gamera spins around he doesn't get dizzy?
> —Gamera's Friend
> A: I believe Gamera used to take ballet. Ballerinas don't get dizzy, no matter how fast they spin.
> —Namiya General Store

> Q: I'm trying to bat on one leg like Sadaharu Oh, but I'm not hitting any home runs.
> —Topple of the Eighth
> A: Practice hitting home runs on both legs before you try standing on just one. Or if two legs isn't working, grab another leg and try with three. Regardless, don't start off with an impossible goal.
> —Namiya General Store

Oh, this place, thought Kosuke. His friends had talked about this store. The guy who ran it gave advice on anything, no matter what the problem was. Only most of the time, people didn't ask serious questions. They were just playing with the old man. They wanted to see how he responded. He always came up with something good.

Looks dumb. Kid's stuff, he thought and walked away.

But then an idea struck him.

He rushed back home. His father was still at work, as usual, and his mother was out.

He went up to his room, sat at his desk, and pulled out some loose-leaf paper. Writing was not his strong suit, but he sweated over it for half an hour and came up with this:

> *My parents want to take me and run off into the night.*
>
> *They have a ridiculous amount of debt, and we can't repay it, so my dad's company is going under.*
>
> *We're supposed to leave town at the end of the month.*
>
> *They're saying I need to switch schools. I want to make them change their minds.*
>
> *They told me the collections man will hunt us down no matter how far we run. I'm scared that we will have to run forever.*
>
> *What should I do?*
>
> —Paul Lennon

He read over the letter several times, then folded the paper twice, slipped it in his back pocket, and left the house.

Retracing his steps, he found his way to the Namiya General Store. From a distance, across the street, it looked as though everyone was gone. The old man who ran the store was sitting out back, reading the paper. This was his chance.

Kosuke took a deep breath and walked up to the store. Earlier, he had figured out the system with the box. It was set up where the old man couldn't see it from his spot out back. *On purpose*, Kosuke thought.

He stepped inside. The old man was still reading his newspaper.

Kosuke pulled out the letter and walked over to the wall, pretending to have a closer look at the posted letters. The box was right in front of him. His heart was pounding in his chest. He was hesitant. Was this really okay?

He heard voices. Kids playing. Lots of them. *Crap. If they come in, there goes my chance.*

Here goes nothing. He dropped the letter in the box. It thwacked against the bottom, louder than he would have liked. Kosuke cringed.

The kids burst in, clamoring. "Hey, Mr. Namiya! Did you get me the Kitaro pencil case?" The kid who was shouting looked like a fifth grader.

"Sure did. I checked with a few of my suppliers and had them send me one. Is this the one?"

The kid wailed. "Wow! That's exactly the one they had in the magazine. Hold on, I'm gonna run home and get money. Be right back!"

"Sure, be safe."

Listening to this exchange behind him, Kosuke left the shop. It sounded as if this kid had put in a special order for a pencil case featuring a character from *GeGeGe no Kitaro*, a popular manga series.

Before walking off, Kosuke couldn't help but look back at the store again. The old man was looking right at him. The eye contact made Kosuke nervous; he averted his gaze and sped off down the road.

Almost instantly, he regretted what he'd done. He shouldn't have left the letter. The old man saw his face. The letter definitely made some noise when he dropped it in. When the old man opened the box to find the letter, he'd know right off the bat that it was Kosuke who had left it.

This worried him, but another part of him was fine with it. Point being, even if he had been seen, exposure was the goal. He wanted the old man to post the letter from "Paul Lennon" on his wall. He had no idea what kind of advice he would get, but he almost didn't care. What mattered was that other people saw the letter.

Rumors would begin to spread that a fly-by-night was planning to skip town. What would happen if the rumor spread as far as the people who lent his father money? They might guess that the writer's father was Sadayuki Waku. And he was certain they would act.

His hope was that his parents would hear the rumor first and give up on their plan.

That was Kosuke's gamble. An audacious bet. The best he could do as a middle schooler.

The next afternoon, Kosuke stepped out and went straight for the Namiya General Store. Luckily for him, the old man was nowhere in sight. Maybe he had gone to the bathroom. Kosuke scanned the letters pasted to the wall. There was only one piece of paper that hadn't been there yesterday. Except it wasn't a response, but an announcement.

Mr. Paul Lennon,

I received your letter asking for advice. You'll find a response in the milk crate around back, down the alley.

To all others:

The letter in the crate is meant only for Paul Lennon. Please leave it be. Opening or stealing someone else's mail is a crime. Thank you for your understanding.

—Namiya General Store

Kosuke was perplexed. The plan had backfired on him. His letter had not been posted. He'd swung for the fences, but instead of a home run, the game was canceled.

But what about this letter from the old man? He had to admit he was a bit curious. What kind of advice had he given?

Kosuke stepped outside, made sure the coast was clear, and slipped around into the narrow alley that led along the building. Around the corner, he found a door and, beside it, on the wall, a wooden milk bin.

Cautiously, he lifted up the lid. Inside were no bottles of milk, just a single envelope. He took it out and read the front: *Paul Lennon.*

Gripping the envelope a little too hard, he went back up the alley and poked his head out to check the street. Someone was coming up the hill; he ducked back in and waited till they passed. Once he was sure no one was there, he stepped into the street and ran.

Where to? The library. Except this time, he didn't go inside, but sat down on a bench in the park out front. He looked over the envelope again. The seal was glued shut, an extra precaution against any prying eyes. He tore the seal, making sure not to rip the letter.

Inside were several folded sheets of stationery, along with the letter Kosuke originally sent. He opened up the message. The lines were packed with neat script, written in black fountain pen.

Dear Paul Lennon,

Thank you for your letter. Frankly, it caught me off guard. This all started as a kind of game, with the neighborhood kids poking fun at my name. I told them I'd do my best to answer their life problems, and they started asking questions, most of them ridiculous. But your letter was serious, about a real-life, time-sensitive dilemma. I was sure you must have gotten the wrong idea. You must have heard my store was giving out advice and didn't know that it was just for fun. If that was the case, I felt like I had a duty to return your letter, at the very least, to tell you that you should ask someone else for better advice. That's why you'll find your letter tucked inside this envelope.

But then I figured simply sending back your letter without attempting to find a solution would be irresponsible on my part. Even if it was just an honest mistake, I felt I should give you the best advice I could muster, since you went out of your way to ask me for help.

So I started thinking about what you, Paul Lennon, might do in your predicament. These brains aren't what they used to be, but I've thought it through from every angle.

The best thing would be to get your parents to change their minds. I know several people who have had to run. I've never heard what happened to a single one of them, but my guess is they aren't living happy lives. Even if they found a way to settle down, they'll always be running away, just like you said. Running from creditors at first, and then whoever else is after them.

But maybe there's no use trying to convince your parents. I'm sure they came to this decision after a lot of contemplation. And they have all the vital facts about this entire situation that you might not. I'm sure you wouldn't have written to me if it were so easy to change their minds.

Which brings me to my question. How do you feel about your parents? Do you like them or hate them? Can you trust them, or have they made you lose your trust?

You may recall that your question to me wasn't what your family should do. It was what *you* should do. So before going any further, I'd like to know what your relationship with them is like.

As I said in the beginning, this is the first time I've had the occasion to answer a letter on a serious topic, and I'm afraid I'm not *quite prepared to give you a proper response. If this letter makes you lose your patience, we'll just have to leave it at that. But if you feel like having another go-round, please think my question over and give me your honest answer. I'll make sure I come up with something helpful.*

This time, there's no need to leave your letter in the box inside. I pull down the shutter at eight. If you can come by after that, you can slip your letter into the mail slot. I'll leave my response in the milk crate the next morning, as early as I can. Feel free to come by any time before we open or after we close. We open at eight thirty.

I'm sorry to disappoint you this time, but this is the best I can do for now.

—Namiya General Store

Kosuke tried to wrap his head around this. He read the letter one more time from the beginning in an attempt to digest it.

For starters, he understood why the old man hadn't posted his letter. All the other exchanges had essentially been jokes. Funny enough to draw crowds. But a letter like this was not meant to be shared.

The other thing was the old man could have easily rejected this serious letter, but instead he'd done his best to start a dialogue. This was a blessing for Kosuke. Having someone know about his circumstances made dealing with it a little easier, and he was glad he had written his letter.

But the old man hadn't exactly responded yet. He wanted Kosuke to answer a few questions first. Once he had these answers, he could come up with his advice.

That night, Kosuke sat down at his desk with another sheet of paper to write back.

How do you feel about your parents?

This was a tough one. How did he feel exactly?

Kosuke didn't really know. They had started to annoy him more since he started middle school, but he knew he didn't hate them. He just didn't like it when they got in his way or treated him like a kid.

But when they broke the news of the getaway plan, they had lost his blind faith in them. Forced to choose between love and hate, the best he could say was that he hated what they were doing to him right now. He couldn't trust them anymore. How was he supposed to believe that things would actually work out if he followed their lead?

Kosuke thought it over again and again, but this was the only answer that came to mind. *Oh well*, he thought and wrote it anyway. He folded up the letter and left the house. His mother asked him where he was going; he said a friend's house. As if her mind was occupied enough with harder questions, she didn't press the issue. Sadayuki wasn't home.

It was after eight. The shutter of the Namiya General Store was down when he arrived. He slipped the folded letter through the mail slot and ran off into the night.

The next morning, he woke just after seven. He hadn't really slept so well.

It seemed as though both his folks were still asleep. Kosuke tip-toed out of the house.

The shutter of the Namiya General Store was still down. He looked up and down the street to make sure no one was coming and went down the alley beside the store.

He lifted the lid of the milk crate. An envelope, just like yesterday. He checked what it said on the front, just in case, and got the hell out of there.

He didn't make it to the library. Along the way, he almost ran past a parked truck, then hid in its shadows to read through the response.

Dear Paul Lennon,

I think I now have a sense of what you're going through.

In your situation, it's no wonder you feel like you can no longer trust your parents. And it's only natural that this would make you start to resent them.

But I can't seem to bring myself to tell you to cut them out of your life and head in the direction that feels right for you.

My general opinion when it comes to families is that they should stick together at all costs, except when someone leaves home on a high note. It would destroy the very meaning of a family unit if everyone went their separate ways over fleeting feelings of anger or impatience.

In your letter, you told me that you hate what your parents are doing to you right now. I'd like you to try to see the hope in those last two words, right now. There must have been a time when you liked your parents and how they treated you, and there's a chance that as events unfold, you'll be able to repair your feelings toward them.

If that's the case, it would seem you don't really have another option.

There's nothing positive about fleeing from your circumstances. Ordinarily, I'd never recommend it. But since it seems there's no way out of it, I believe it would be best for you to go along with them.

I'm sure your parents have thought this through. They know they won't solve anything just by running away. They need to hide out for a while, wait for the right time, and work things out as they go.

It may take quite a long time to work things out entirely. There will be a fair amount of hardship down the line. But for that very reason, it's essential that your family stay together. I doubt your father would say so to your face, but you can bet he's ready to go through hell for you. Anything to save his family. It's up to you and your mother to support him in this fight.

The worst-case scenario would be for this event to destroy your family. That would be a total loss. I still can't say this getaway plan is the best thing for your family, but if it keeps you together and in the same boat, you have a fighting chance of getting back on course.

I'm not sure how old you are, but based on the level of your writing, I'm assuming you're in middle school or high school. Someday, it will be your job to look after your parents. To be ready for that day, you'll need to study hard and make a life for yourself. I hope nothing gets in the way of that.

Believe me. No matter how bad things are today, they'll be far better tomorrow.

—Namiya General Store

4

One of Kosuke's friends, a fellow fan of the Beatles, called when there was less than a week left of summer vacation. The same friend who had given him the dirt on their visit to Japan. This time, he called to ask if he could come over and listen to Beatles records like they used to do. Despite being a huge fan, he didn't own a single record. His family didn't have a record player. Whenever he'd wanted to listen to the Beatles in the past, he came over to Kosuke's.

"Sorry, I can't. We're renovating the house, so we can't get to the stereo."

Kosuke had had this excuse ready since the day they took the stereo away. He delivered the line flawlessly.

"Wait, you serious?" The friend hadn't seen this coming, and his voice filled with disappointment. "Man, I want to hear them so bad."

"Did something happen?"

His friend said yeah and paused suggestively. "I saw the movie. It opened today."

That's right. *Let It Be*. The movie.

"How was it?" Kosuke asked.

"It was eye-opening."

"How so?"

"Well, it set things straight for me, like why they broke up and everything."

"Does someone say why?"

"No, it's not like that. When they were filming it, no one was talking about disbanding yet, but you can sort of feel it, you know, in the air. Like, oh yeah, this is what was going on. It's hard to explain. If you see it, you'll know what I mean. I dunno."

"Cool."

The conversation wasn't going anywhere. They both hung up. Kosuke went back to his room. He flipped through his Beatles records and looked at every single cover. Between the ones he'd gotten from his cousin and the ones he'd bought himself, there were over fifty.

He didn't know how he could ever give these up. He tried to figure out a way to bring them wherever it was his family was going. His parents had both told him to pack light, but there was no way he would leave behind his records.

He'd decided he wouldn't think so hard about the getaway plan. Resisting wasn't going to change their minds, and they definitely wouldn't go ahead without dragging him along. Like the old man at the Namiya General Store said, his parents had thought this through. He just had to trust that someday they were going to work things out.

Anyway. What had made his friend so confident? What was seeing *Let It Be* going to teach him?

That night after dinner, Sadayuki finally explained the details of their escape. The plan was to load everything up the night of August 31 and slip into the night during the first minutes of September.

"The thirty-first is a Monday. I'll go to work. I'm already scheduled to take a week's vacation starting September first, so no one will be surprised when I don't show up the next day. By the next week, all kinds of notices and bills will have piled up. Everyone will know we ran away. We'll just have to lie low at the next spot for a while. But don't worry. We have enough cash on hand to live for a year or two. In the meantime, we'll figure out our next steps." Sadayuki's voice was full of confidence.

"What about school? Which school am I going to go to?"

Sadayuki glowered at the question. "I've given that some thought. It's not going to happen right away. In the meantime, you'll have to study on your own."

"You mean I'm not going to go to school?"

"That's not what I'm saying. You'll go, just not right away. Everyone needs to finish middle school. We'll get you in somewhere. No need for you to worry about it. I'll call your teacher and tell them we need to head overseas for a week for work and that you'll start the school year after that." Sadayuki brusquely informed him. His mood was turning sour.

"What about high school?" Kosuke wanted to ask, but he kept quiet. He knew exactly what his father would say. "I've got it covered; stop worrying." *Yeah, sounds about right.*

Was he really better off going with them? Indecision reared its head again. He knew he had only one option, but he couldn't picture himself going through with it.

Time passed anyway. Before he knew it, August 31 was nearly upon him. Kosuke was in his bedroom, going through his things, when the door swung open. Sadayuki was standing in the doorway.

"Have a minute?"

"I guess."

Sadayuki stepped into the room and sat down cross-legged next to Kosuke. "Everything packed up?"

"Basically. I figured I should bring all my textbooks with me."

"Right. You'll need them."

"And these are definitely coming, too." Kosuke pulled out a heavy cardboard box. All his Beatles records were inside.

Sadayuki looked into the box and frowned. "All that?"

"I packed as little other stuff as possible, to make room." Kosuke tried to sound resolute. "I'm bringing these with me."

Sadayuki nodded vaguely, looked around the room, and turned his eyes on Kosuke. "What do you think of your old man?"

"What do you mean?"

"Aren't you angry it had to come to this? You must think I'm a pretty lousy father."

"You're not lousy…," mumbled Kosuke. "I don't know what's going on. Honestly, I'm scared."

Sadayuki nodded. "That makes sense."

"Dad, are we really gonna be okay? Will things ever be back to normal?"

Sadayuki blinked a few times and said sure, they would be okay. "I can't say how or when, but someday I'll get things back to how they were. That's a promise."

"You mean it?"

"I mean it. My family is my number one priority. I'll do anything to keep you and your mother safe. I'm ready to put my life on the line. That's why—" Sadayuki looked straight into his son's eyes. "That's why we have to run."

Kosuke knew his father was being sincere. He'd never heard him talk this way before. It helped him take the words to heart.

"Okay, Dad."

"All right," Sadayuki said. He slapped his knees and stood. "What's your plan for tomorrow? You've still got a bit of summer vacation left. Don't you have some friends you want to see before we go?"

Kosuke shook his head. "I'm all set." He wanted to say there was no point, since he could never see them again anyway, but he held his tongue. "Is it okay if I go to Tokyo?"

"Tokyo? For what?"

"There's a movie I want to see. It's playing at the Subaru-za in Yurakucho."

"Does it have to be tomorrow?"

"How am I supposed to know if it'll be playing wherever we wind up?"

Sadayuki pouted his lip and nodded. "So that's how it is."

"Can I go?"

"You can, but come back early."

"I know."

Sadayuki said good night and left the room.

Kosuke looked through the box of records and pulled one out. It was one he bought that year. *Let It Be.* The faces of the four Beatles were in boxes, stacked into a square.

That night, he would think about nothing but the upcoming movie as he tried to fall asleep.

5

The next morning, Kosuke left home after breakfast. Kimiko disapproved, asking why he had to pick today of all days to see a movie, but Sadayuki did a good job mollifying her.

Kosuke had been to Tokyo a bunch of times before with friends, but this was his first visit alone.

At Tokyo Station, he switched to the Yamanote Line and got

off at Yurakucho. When he consulted the map inside the station, he realized the theater was close by.

There was a big crowd outside. Kosuke wondered if it was because it was the last day of summer vacation. He got in line and bought a ticket; he'd already checked the showtimes in the newspaper and planned accordingly before he came. He still had half an hour to kill before his show started. Now was his chance to have a quick look around the area. In all the other times he'd been to Tokyo, he'd never visited Yurakucho or Ginza.

Kosuke started walking. In minutes, he was astonished by what he saw.

He had no idea the city was so gigantic. He'd already been surprised by the number of people and the size of the buildings in Yurakucho, but Ginza was on another level. The endless rows of shops brimmed over with festivity; the streets were alive, as if something special was afoot. All the passersby looked sophisticated and successful. Other towns were perfectly content with the small pockets that mimicked this. They took pride in their fancy little shopping districts. But in this city, this was everywhere. Everywhere you went, it felt like a festival was taking place.

After a while, Kosuke realized he was seeing the logo for the Expo everywhere. The Expo. After all these months, it was still happening, down in Osaka. And from the looks of the sidewalks of Tokyo, the whole country was celebrating.

Kosuke felt like a minnow swept into the mouth of the ocean. There were places like this in the world, places where people celebrated life. But this was not his world to live in. He was born to live out his days between the banks of a thin, dim river. And starting the next day, he would sink to the bottom of it all.

He looked down and turned back the way he came. This was no place for him to be.

He got back to the movie theater just in time. He showed his ticket, went inside, and got a seat. There were plenty. It seemed as though lots of people had come alone.

The movie started, and the opening image was a closeup of the band's insignia: "THE BEATLES."

Kosuke's heart was thumping. This was it, the prelude to that legendary performance. He felt his temperature rising.

But that exalted feeling faded as the film progressed.

As he watched, Kosuke got a vague sense of how the film had happened. *Let It Be* was supposed to be a documentary, combining rehearsal footage with live performances. But these bits and pieces weren't filmed with this movie in mind. None of the Beatles looked remotely invested in making another film. It was more likely things had gotten so complicated that they couldn't legally refuse.

The half-hearted rehearsal was punctuated by exchanges among the members. These, too, were half-baked and hard to decipher. Kosuke's eyes raced along the subtitles, but he couldn't understand what anyone was getting at.

There was one thing he could tell for sure.

Their hearts weren't in it anymore.

It wasn't that they were fighting, or that anyone refused to play. The four of them were working through the task at hand. But they all knew they weren't creating anything meaningful.

In the end, they all went upstairs to the roof of the Apple building. Their instruments and amps had already been hauled up. Their entire staff was present. Everyone looked cold in the winter air. John Lennon was wearing a fur coat.

They started off with "Get Back."

It was soon clear that the show had not been formally announced. When passersby heard the Beatles singing live at a considerable volume from the rooftop, the area around the building was all astir. Police rushed to the scene.

The next songs were "Don't Let Me Down" and "I've Got a

Feeling." But the performance was dispassionate. This was to be their last show, but none of them appeared the least bit sentimental.

On that note, the movie ended.

Kosuke stayed seated long after the lights came on. He was in a haze. He didn't have the energy to stand. His stomach was heavy, as if he'd drunk a cup of molten lead.

What the hell was that? he thought. It was nothing close to what he had expected. They never had an actual argument, but when they did speak, they always seemed to talk past each other. The only things out of their lips were complaints, sarcasm, and the occasional stony laugh.

The rumor was that if you saw the movie, you would see why the Beatles split, but Kosuke never did. That was because the Beatles in the movie were effectively already over. He'd wanted to know how they got there in the first place.

On the train home, it occurred to him—maybe this is what a breakup is.

People don't drift apart for one specific reason. Well, you might be able to find a reason, but you could come up with one only after you made up your mind, a tired excuse tacked on after the fact. If their hearts were still in it and their bond was threatening to sever, you'd think one of them would step in and try to fix things. When no one does, you know the bond has already been broken. Which was why all four of them could look on from the shore as the Beatles sank right in front of them, without trying to save it.

Kosuke felt betrayed. It was as if something he treasured had been smashed. It was then that he decided.

At the station, he ducked into a phone booth and called his friend, the one who had called a week ago to tell him to see *Let It Be*.

His friend was home. When he heard his voice over the phone, Kosuke asked him to buy his records.

"What records?"

"My Beatles records. You said you wanted to collect them someday."

"That's true. Which ones are we talking about?"

"All of them. How'd you like to buy every Beatles record I own?"

"All of them?"

"How's ten thousand yen sound? If you tried to buy them one by one, you'd pay more than that, easy."

"I know that, but this is kind of sudden. I mean, we don't even have a stereo."

"All right, I'll ask someone else." Kosuke almost hung up.

He heard a harried voice yell "Wait!" from the receiver. "Let me think about it. I'll call you tomorrow. Deal?"

Kosuke pressed the receiver to his ear and shook his head. "Nope. Tomorrow's no good."

"Why?"

"Doesn't matter. I don't have time for this. If you're not gonna buy them right now, I'm hanging up."

"Wait. Wait just a second. Okay? Five minutes. Give me five minutes."

Kosuke sighed. "Fine. I'll call you back in five."

He hung up and stepped out of the phone booth. He looked up at the sky. The sun had begun its descent.

Kosuke wasn't exactly sure why he'd decided to sell all his records. He just had a feeling he couldn't listen to the Beatles anymore. Call it the end of an era.

It had been five minutes. Kosuke went back into the phone booth and called his friend.

"We're good," the friend exclaimed, almost delirious with excitement. "I talked to my parents. They'll give me the money, but I'm gonna have to buy the stereo myself. Should I come and get them now?"

"Yeah, I'll be here."

Things were in motion. All his records would soon be gone. His heart squeezed a little at the thought of it, but he shook his head to make the feeling go away. No big deal.

Back at home, he transferred the box of records into two paper bags to make them easier to carry. As he worked, he had a long look at the cover of every album. Each one held so many memories.

He stopped when he came to *Sgt. Pepper's Lonely Hearts Club Band*. The product of a period of musical experimentation for the Beatles. It had been described as a conceptual collage, as apt a description for the album as for its cover.

The four Beatles stood posed in colorful military regalia, accompanied by a tight brigade of cutouts of historical and pop-culture icons.

On the far right was a woman who looked like Marilyn Monroe, and beside her was a spot that had been filled in with black marker. When his cousin owned the record, he had taped a photo of his face there: a fanboy's attempt to make himself a physical part of the experience. Kosuke had torn the photo off, but the printed surface had peeled off with it. He tried to make the damage less conspicuous by coloring it black.

I'm sorry for selling your records. I didn't have a choice. He hoped his cousin would hear him up in heaven.

Kimiko saw Kosuke carrying the paper bags to the front door. "What's all that?" she asked.

He had nothing to hide and told her the truth. She nodded but didn't seem to care.

Before long, his friend was at the front door with a ten-thousand-yen bill in an envelope. In exchange, Kosuke set both bags of records at his feet.

"Whoa!" the friend cried out, poking through the bags. "Are you sure you're okay doing this? It took you forever to collect these."

Kosuke frowned and scratched his neck.

"It just hit me out of nowhere. I'm done with the Beatles. I saw the movie, you know."

"*Let It Be?*"

"Yeah."

"Ah." The look on his friend's face was half acceptance, half disbelief as he nodded.

He picked up the bags, and Kosuke held the door. "Thanks," he whispered and stepped outside. He looked back from a few steps through the yard. "All right, see you tomorrow."

Tomorrow? It took Kosuke a full second to comprehend. He had completely forgotten that the next day was the first day of the fall term.

Frantic now, he told his perplexed friend, "Sure, see you tomorrow, at school."

When he finally closed the door, he let out an enormous sigh. It was all he could do to keep from curling up into a ball right then and there.

6

Sadayuki came home a little after eight. It had been ages since he had stayed at work so late.

"I put the finishing touches on things at the office. I'd like to stall the manhunt for as long as possible." He loosened the knot of his tie. His shirt was translucent with sweat, clinging to his skin.

They ate dinner late. Their last meal together at that house was leftover curry from the night before. The fridge was already cleared out.

As they ate, Sadayuki and Kimiko spoke in low voices about their belongings. Valuables, clothes, the few essentials they would need, Kosuke's school materials… That was just about all they would bring, and the rest they'd leave behind. They'd gone through this tally several times before, talking over it again as a last precaution.

Kimiko brought up what Kosuke had done with the records.

"You sold them? All of them? Why?" Sadayuki sounded genuinely surprised.

"I dunno," said Kosuke, staring at his curry. "It's not like we have a way to play them."

"Wow. Sold them, huh? That's good. Sure helps lighten the load. How much you get?"

Kosuke paused for a beat too long, so Kimiko piped up. "Ten thousand yen."

"Ten thousand yen? That's it?" Sadayuki's tone changed entirely. "You little shithead. How many of those did you have? Most of them were LPs. If you went out and tried to buy those back again, you know how much it would cost? You probably couldn't do it with twenty, thirty thousand yen. And you got ten thousand? What were you thinking?"

"I wasn't trying to make money off them," Kosuke argued, head down. "Most of them were Tetsuo's anyway."

His father clicked his tongue loudly. "Don't give me that horseshit. When you sell anything, you need to haggle for more. Even if it's only pocket change. Don't expect to live the kind of life you've been living. You hear me?"

Kosuke looked up. He wanted to ask whose fault that was.

Sadayuki saw something different in his son's face and repeated himself. "Hear me?"

Kosuke didn't nod back and instead dropped his spoon into his bowl. "I'm done."

He left the table.

"Answer me, boy!"

"Shut up. I get it, okay?"

"What was that? You think you can speak to your father that way?"

"Sadayuki," warned Kimiko, "I think that's enough."

"No, it's not. Hey, what'd you do with that ten thousand yen?"

Kosuke glanced down at his father. Veins were bulging out of his temples.

"Whose money did you buy those with? That was your allowance. Whose hard-earned money does that allowance come from?"

"Stop it, Sadayuki. You're not going to take money from your son."

"Who's taking it? I'm just making sure he understands whose money that was."

"Enough," Kimiko cautioned. "Kosuke, go to your room and get your things."

Kosuke listened to his mother and left the living room. He went upstairs to his bedroom and threw himself in bed. The Beatles were staring at him from a poster on the wall. He sat up, tore it from its tacks, and reduced it to shreds.

The knock came about two hours later. Kimiko poked her head in and asked, "Done packing?"

"Mostly." Kosuke pointed to a single cardboard box and duffel bag beside his desk. This was all he had to his name. "Are we leaving?"

"Soon." Kimiko came into the room. "Sorry to put you through all this."

Kosuke didn't say anything. He couldn't think of anything *to* say.

"But I'm sure things are going to be okay. Hang in there, just a little longer."

"All right," he said quietly.

"Your father and I—well, your father especially—we're ready to do anything if it means giving you a good life. Even putting our lives on the line."

Kosuke bowed his head. *Bullshit*, he told himself. How could forcing your son to run away with you ever lead to a good life?

"Okay then, so come downstairs with your things in half an hour." Kimiko left.

Just like Ringo, thought Kosuke. In *Let It Be*, he thought Ringo was the only one trying to keep the Beatles afloat, but his efforts were a waste of energy.

At midnight on the dot, Kosuke and his family fled under the cover of night. Their getaway car was an old white cargo van Sadayuki had obtained for the event. They sat down in a row on the front bench seats. Sadayuki gripped the steering wheel. The back was stuffed with cardboard boxes and bags of all sorts.

Just before getting in, Kosuke had asked his father, "Where are we going?"

And his father had replied, "We'll know when we get there." This was the closest thing they had to a conversation. Once they were driving, they barely spoke.

Eventually, they made it to the highway. Kosuke had no idea where they were or where they were heading. All the highway signs were for places he had never heard of.

After about two hours on the road, Kimiko said she had to use the bathroom, and Sadayuki pulled into a rest area. Kosuke saw a sign saying they were in a place called Fujikawa.

The parking lot was almost empty this time of night, but Sadayuki parked the van in the corner of the lot. He was on edge, trying not to make them look conspicuous.

Kosuke went into the bathroom with his father. As he was washing his hands, Sadayuki came up beside him at the sink.

"You won't be getting an allowance for a while."

Kosuke looked at his father's reflection in the mirror.

"Should come as no surprise," Sadayuki continued. "Besides, you're rolling in it, with that ten-thousand-yen bill."

Again with the ten-thousand-yen bill. Kosuke was disgusted. It wasn't even that much money. And Kosuke was just a kid.

Sadayuki walked out without washing his hands.

Watching his father leave, Kosuke felt something break inside him. It must've been the last vestige of his desire to be with his parents. Their bond was severed. He was certain.

Kosuke left the bathroom and ran in the opposite direction from the parked van. He didn't understand the layout of the rest stop. All he knew was that he wanted to get as far as possible from his parents.

He ran for his life. His trajectory was random. Before he knew it, he was in another parking lot full of trucks parked in rows.

A man walked over to one and stepped up into the cab. It looked like he was about to drive off.

Kosuke rushed to the back of the truck and climbed up inside the canvas. He saw stacks of wooden boxes. It wasn't smelly, and there was space for him to hide.

The engine started. It was now or never. He slid himself against the decking.

The truck started off. Kosuke's heart was racing. His breathing was manic, no hope of slowing down.

Hugging his knees, he nestled his face between his legs and closed his eyes. He wanted to sleep. He'd sleep for now and think of what to do next when he woke up. But the seriousness of what he'd done, and his uncertainty of how he was going to survive, blocked any immediate relief.

It goes without saying that Kosuke was clueless about where the truck was going or what road they were on. The fact that it was dark out didn't help, but even in broad daylight, he wouldn't have been able to ascertain where they were from scenery alone.

He doubted he would be getting any sleep that night, but eventually, he dozed off. When he came to, the truck had stopped. Not at a traffic light, but at what must have been its destination.

Kosuke peeked out from the canvas to have a look around. He

was in some enormous parking lot. There were other trucks around him.

Making sure no one was around, he stepped down to the pavement. With his head lowered, he went straight for the exit. He was lucky there was no security. When he was out, he turned and looked at the sign at the entrance. Some kind of shipping facility. He was in Edogawa. Tokyo.

It was still pitch-dark out. No stores were open. Kosuke had no choice but to keep on walking. He didn't know where he was heading, but he kept on going anyway. He figured if he walked enough, he would wind up somewhere.

Day broke as he walked along. He started seeing bus stops on the sidewalk. When he read where the buses were going, it was as if the world had opened up before him. Destination: Tokyo Station. Perfect. If he kept on going, he'd get to Tokyo Station, too.

But what would he do from there? Go someplace else? Trains went in all directions from Tokyo Station. Which one would he choose? He pondered the question as he walked.

Taking short breaks in parks along the way, Kosuke forged ahead. Even though he knew better, he couldn't help thinking of his parents. What had they done after they realized he was gone? They had no way of finding him. But it wasn't as if they were going to report him missing. And they weren't going back to the house.

They probably just kept heading toward their next spot. Once things calmed down, they would maybe try to find him. But they couldn't come out in the open, and they weren't going to be able to use relatives or acquaintances to track him down. The feared taxman or whoever would have spread his nets in all those places.

He had no way of finding his parents, either. The pair were planning to lie low. They would never use their real names.

Which meant he would never see his parents. Ever again. The

thought burned dimly somewhere deep in his chest. But he had no regrets. Their hearts had grown apart. Once that happens, there's no trying to fix it. Sticking together would have been pointless. He'd learned that from the Beatles.

As time passed, the flow of traffic increased. The number of people walking with him on the sidewalk went up, too. There were kids on their way to school. Kosuke finally remembered: It was the first day of the fall term.

He kept walking in the same direction of the buses that drove past him. It was the first day of September, but the heat of summer lingered. His T-shirt was mucked with dirt and sweat.

He arrived at Tokyo Station a little after ten. Approaching the building on foot for the first time, he didn't realize right away that it was a train station. The grand brick building reminded him of some giant mansion out of medieval Europe.

Inside, Kosuke was awestruck by its size all over again. He wandered the halls, marveling at all the sights. He saw a sign for the bullet train.

He had always wanted to ride one. He thought this was the year he'd finally have his chance. It ran straight from Tokyo to Osaka, where the Expo was underway.

Posters for the Expo were slapped up everywhere he looked. They gave simple directions. Just take the bullet train to Shin-Osaka Station and a quick ride on the subway out to the pavilion.

He was going. In his wallet, he had fourteen thousand yen: the ten thousand yen was from the records, and the rest left over from New Year's.

So he'd go and see the Expo, and then what? He would figure it out once he got there. People from across Japan—across the world!— had gathered there to celebrate the latest innovations. In this carnival of opportunities, he was sure he could find some way of living on his own.

He lined up for the ticket counter and made sure he had enough. When he saw the fare to Shin-Osaka Station, he was relieved. It wasn't as high as he expected. There were two lines: Hikari and Kodama. He hesitated for a second but decided on Kodama. He was on a budget.

When he reached the counter, he asked the ticket agent for "one ticket to Shin-Osaka, please."

The agent scowled. "Student discount? I'll need your voucher and your school ID."

"Oh, I forgot it."

"All right, standard fare."

"Yes, please."

The man asked question after question. What time? Reserved seating? Or unreserved? Kosuke fumbled through his answers.

"Wait just a moment," said the man, and he disappeared out back. Kosuke counted his cash again. Once he had his ticket, he would buy himself a bento box for breakfast.

Then it happened. A hand landed hard on his shoulder.

"Excuse me."

He turned to face a man in a suit.

"What'd I do?"

"There's a few things I'd like to ask you. Would you mind following me please?" he said coercively.

"But I… My ticket…"

"It won't take long. I just need you to answer a few questions, and you'll be on your way. Let's go."

The man grabbed Kosuke's arm. His grip assured him that this was no voluntary chat.

The man brought him to what appeared to be his office. He had said it wouldn't take long, but Kosuke wound up detained there for hours. That was because he wouldn't answer the man's questions.

Not even the first one.

"What's your name and address?"

7

The man who had approached him at the ticket counter was a detective from the Juvenile Division of the Metropolitan Police Department. A lot of boys and girls tried to run away from home at the end of summer, and these detectives watched out for them at Tokyo Station in plainclothes. He had Kosuke the second he spotted him wandering anxiously around the station in his grubby T-shirt. He followed him to the ticket line, waited for his chance, and winked a signal to the ticket agent. It was no coincidence, then, that the man had disappeared out back.

The detective told Kosuke all of this in the hopes of getting him to finally say something. He had clearly underestimated how hard this was going to be. He expected Kosuke to give up his information, after which he'd go through the usual procedure of calling up his parents and his school, and wait with him for somebody to pick him up.

But Kosuke withheld his identity. If he peeped, he'd have to explain the entire escape.

Even after they'd moved him from an office in the train station to a conference room at the police station, Kosuke kept his mouth clamped shut. They brought him a rice ball and some cold barley tea, but he wouldn't touch it. He was starving but knew better than to scarf it down. If he did, he'd have to answer their questions.

"All right," the detective laughed. "Truce. It's about time you ate something." He left Kosuke in the room alone.

Kosuke stuffed the rice ball in his face. This was the first time he'd eaten since the leftover curry with his family the night before. It was just a ball of rice with a single pickled plum inside, but to Kosuke, the flavor was ambrosial.

Before long, the detective came back in. "You ready to talk?"

Kosuke looked at his hands.

"This kid is a nightmare," he sighed.

Someone else came in and discussed something with the detective. From the few words Kosuke was able to make out, it sounded like they were checking his description against missing persons lists across the country.

Kosuke was particularly worried about what his school would do. If they called every single middle school to look for him, his school would note that he was absent. Sadayuki had said he called and told them his son was out of the country with his family for a week, but hadn't they found that story a little fishy?

Night came, and Kosuke had a second meal in the conference room. Dinner was a rice bowl with tempura. It was damn good.

The detective was beat.

"Can you please just tell me your name?" he pleaded. Kosuke felt a little sorry for him.

"Hiroshi," he muttered.

The detective's face lit up. "Wait, what'd you say?"

"Hiroshi...Fujikawa."

The detective fumbled for his pen. "That's you, huh? What are the characters for that? Actually, you write it."

Kosuke took the pen and paper from the detective and wrote the characters for "Hiroshi Fujikawa."

It had occurred to him in passing that he would have to use a fake name. He took a Japanese character from the term *World Expo*, which could be pronounced "Hiroshi," and "Fujikawa" from the name of the rest stop.

"And your address?" the detective asked, but Kosuke shook his head.

He spent the night inside the conference room. They rolled in a cot and made it up with bedding. He wrapped himself in the blanket and slept straight through the night.

The next morning, the detective sat down across from Kosuke once again.

"It's time to make a decision. Either you tell me the truth about who you are, or you can head over to Juvenile Affairs. At this rate, we'll be stuck in here forever."

Kosuke wouldn't answer him. The detective was getting peeved and scratched his head.

"What the hell happened anyway? Where are your parents? Haven't they noticed that their son's gone missing?"

He stared into the surface of the tabletop.

"Ah well," the detective sputtered, all out of ideas. "Seems like you have a pretty good reason to keep quiet. And Hiroshi Fujikawa—we know that's not your real name. Is it?"

Kosuke glanced at the man and quickly looked down again. Upon realizing he was right, the detective let out a huge sigh.

Soon after, Kosuke was escorted to Juvenile Affairs. He was expecting something like a school building, but when he got there, he was surprised to find an old European mansion. When he asked, they told him it had actually been someone's residence once. Only now it was in awful disrepair with paint flaking from the walls and the floorboards buckling.

Kosuke spent about two months at this facility. Over the course of his stay, they had him meet with a lot of different people. Some were doctors, some psychiatrists. All of them were trying to get to the bottom of this "Hiroshi Fujikawa." But none of them could ever do it. What puzzled everyone the most was that not a single missing person profile fitting his description had been submitted. Not to any police department in Japan. Where were his parents? Wasn't anybody watching him? They all wound up at the same ragged nonconclusion.

The next place he lived was a children's home called Marumitsuen.

It was far outside Tokyo, but only about half an hour from where he used to live. At first, he worried that maybe they had figured him out, but the demeanor of the grown-ups there assured him they just happened to have space for him.

The four-story building was nestled in the hillside, surrounded by trees. The kids who lived there ranged from infants all the way to high school boys with unkempt stubble.

"If you don't want to tell us about your background, that's fine. But you need to give us a birthday. We can't send you to school until we know what grade you're supposed to be in." The person asking him was middle-aged, bespectacled.

Kosuke thought about this. His real birthday was February 26, 1957, but he thought it would be risky giving away his real age. Then again, he couldn't pretend to be much older. He had never even seen a textbook for third-year students in middle school.

The answer he gave was June 29, 1957.

June 29—the day the Beatles landed in Japan.

8

He polished off his second Guinness.

"Care for another?" Eriko asked. "Or would you prefer something a bit stronger?"

"Maybe, yeah." Kosuke scanned the liquor bottles lined up behind the bar. "I guess I'll have a Bunnahabhain, on the rocks."

Eriko nodded and took down a glass.

"I Feel Fine" was playing from the speakers. Kosuke drummed his fingers to the rhythm but caught himself and stopped.

He looked around the bar again. What was the deal with this

place? He couldn't believe that this was in his backwater hometown. There were other Beatles fans around him growing up, but he was proud to have been the resident maniac, their biggest fan.

Eriko broke ice into chunks with an ice pick. The way she worked the tool reminded him of when he used to carve wood with a chisel.

Life at the children's home wasn't so bad. He didn't have to worry about his next meal, and they sent him to school. His first year at the new school was a breeze, since he'd fibbed about his age and got to repeat a grade.

He went by Hiroshi Fujikawa, but everybody called him by his first name, which was unusual in Japan. There was a short period where he wasn't used to it, but soon he answered to it as if he'd been doing it his whole life.

He didn't have any friends. Or more precisely, he didn't make any. He was scared that if he got too close to anyone, he'd want to tell them who he really was. To keep this up, he had to isolate himself. Seeing him so reticent, few kids ever approached him, and a lot of them thought he was creepy. In fact, they found him too weird to bully, and he was always on his own.

He may have had no friends to play with, but he never felt especially lonely.

After moving in, he took up a new hobby: wood carving. He picked up fallen branches from the woods around the home and carved them into whatever took his fancy. At first, he was just killing time, but a few creations later, he was hooked. He made everything—animals, robots, superheroes, cars. The more complex, the better the challenge. He never worked off any plans; it was way more fun to make it up as he went along.

When a project was done, he gave it to one of the younger kids. At first, they didn't know how to respond, since Hiroshi mostly kept to himself, but when they held the carving in their hands, they smiled.

It was rare for these children to ever get a new toy. Soon the kids were putting in requests: "I want Moomin," "Hey, make me Kamen Rider." He looked forward to seeing these kids smile.

Kosuke's carving abilities were well-known among the staff. One day, he was called to the director's office and asked something completely unexpected: How would he like to do this for a living? The director knew someone who ran a wood-carving studio, and he was looking for a successor. If he moved in with the master and apprenticed there by day, Kosuke would be allowed to go to night school and get his high school diploma there.

He was almost done with middle school. Kosuke figured the staff was probably getting antsy about what to do about him.

As a matter of fact, they had just checked a very important item off their list. They wanted him to have a legal name. They had begged the family court to create a registry for him, and their plea had finally been granted.

This measure was generally reserved for abandoned children of a very young age; it was rare for a request to be accepted for someone as old as Kosuke. But it was more than that. There had never been another case where a person obstinately hid their background to the point that the police couldn't even suss it out. This was a unique request.

The people from the family court had come to meet him a few times. Like everyone else, they tried to get him to talk about his upbringing, his background, anything, but Kosuke assumed the exact same pose as always. He persisted through his silence.

"Maybe he's suffered some kind of trauma that erased his memory of his identity," they finally said. "Maybe he couldn't tell us even if he wanted to." That was the latest theory. Maybe those grown-ups had only picked it as a way of cleaning up the mess.

Just before graduating middle school, Kosuke's name was legally registered as "Hiroshi Fujikawa." And just after graduation, he left the children's home for Saitama, where he began to study woodworking as an apprentice.

9

Studying with the master wasn't easy. This man had the spirit of a typical craftsman: inflexible and stubborn. The first year, Kosuke was only allowed to tend to the tools, take stock of the materials, and clean the shop. After he had made it to his second year of night school, the master finally let him carve wood. But he could only carve whatever he was told, producing the same thing twenty or thirty times within a single day. He couldn't move on to another form until every rendering was identical. It wasn't what you'd call a dynamic job.

But the master was a good man who cared about Kosuke's future. He saw it as his personal mission to set him up as a working craftsman. Kosuke could tell this work wasn't just because he was cheap labor or because he was next in line to succeed the shop. The master's wife was just as kind.

When he graduated from high school, he started to work officially at the studio. In the beginning, he took on simple projects. As he got adjusted and the master placed more trust in him, his tasks became more complicated, but also more rewarding.

Those days were satisfying. The memory of fleeing town with his family had not escaped him, but he revisited that night less and less. He was now able to say he had made the right decision.

He was glad he hadn't stayed with his parents. Making a clean break was the right choice. If he had followed that old man's advice, where would he be?

This moment of peace was violated in December 1980. He heard the news on the TV.

John Lennon had been murdered.

The reel of his life replayed before Kosuke's eyes, starting with those vivid days when he first discovered the Beatles. There were sad and bitter memories, too, but even these were tinged with their nostalgia, as such things always were.

Had John Lennon ever regretted breaking up the Beatles? The question occupied his mind. Had he ever thought it was too soon?

Kosuke shook the thought away. There was no way. In the wake of the breakup, the four Beatles had launched careers as solo artists. This was possible only because the Beatles had broken free from whatever binding spell had held them together. Just as Kosuke had: He'd attained happiness only after he cut ties with his parents.

Their hearts had grown apart. Once that happens—he was certain—there's no fixing it.

Then in December, eight years later, he read a shocking article in the newspaper. There had been a fire at Marumitsuen. Not everyone had made it out alive.

The master told him to go and see how they were doing. Kosuke drove up in the shop van the next day, to show his support. He hadn't been back since the time he came to say a few words after graduating from night school.

Half the building was blackened and caved in. The children and the staff were hunkered down in the gymnasium of an elementary school nearby. The space was heated with kerosene heaters, but everyone looked cold.

The director was an old man by now, thrilled by Kosuke's visit, and perhaps a little baffled, too. This was the boy who wouldn't even share his name, now grown into a man, with tender feelings for his ill-fated childhood home.

"Tell me if there's anything I can do," Kosuke told the director.

"The thought alone means everything to us," he said.

On his way out, a voice behind him called out, "Is that you, Hiroshi?"

He turned and saw a young woman approaching him. Maybe in her midtwenties. She was wearing an expensive-looking fur coat.

"I knew it was you, Hiroshi. Hiroshi Fujikawa, right?" Her eyes were sparkling. "It's me, Harumi. Harumi Muto? Don't you remember me?"

Kosuke was sorry to say he didn't. The woman opened her handbag and pulled something out.

"How about this? I know you remember this."

"Whoa," he breathed.

She was holding a carved wooden puppy. He remembered making this. It was one of his carvings from when he was still living at the children's home.

He looked at her again and started to get the feeling he'd seen her face before. "Were you at Marumitsuen, too?"

She nodded. "You made this for me. When I was in fifth grade."

"I remember now. At least, I think so."

"Oh man, really? I never forgot you. This little guy is my favorite."

"Ah, well, I'm sorry."

The woman laughed. She returned the carved dog to her handbag and pulled out a business card for Kosuke. It said *Office Little Dog, Harumi Muto, CEO.* Kosuke gave her his card. Her face lit up with delight.

"A wood-carving studio... I knew you would go pro!"

Kosuke scratched his head. "My boss would say I'm only halfway there."

They sat down together on one of the benches outside the gymnasium. Harumi said she had come as soon as she could after hearing the terrible news. She mentioned offering the director her assistance.

"They did so much for me. I want to do something to give back."

"That's noble of you."

"Isn't that why you're here?"

"My boss told me to come." He looked down at her card. "You're running your own company, huh? What kind of company is it?"

"It's a small operation. We mainly put together events geared toward young people, produce ad campaigns, you know."

"Cool," mumbled Kosuke, just to have something to say. Whatever she did, he wasn't getting it. "That's impressive for your age."

"It's not like that. I was lucky; that's all."

"It takes more than luck. It takes ambition. I'm impressed by anyone who starts a company. It's so much easier to collect a paycheck."

Harumi thought it over.

"It's really just my personality. I'm not so good at taking orders. I could never keep a part-time job for very long. When I left Marumitsuen, I was struggling with what to do with my life. That's when someone gave me some advice. It was priceless, really. It gave my life direction."

"Someone, huh?"

"Well," she said hesitantly, "he runs a kind of general store."

"A general store?" Kosuke asked with confusion.

"It's just this little store, near my friend's house, but the owner would give you free advice, on any problem or worry. All you had to do was ask. I think someone did an article about it for a magazine. I had nothing to lose and tried it out, and he gave me the best advice ever. I'm who I am today because of him."

Kosuke was stunned. She had to mean the Namiya General Store. There couldn't be another general store like that around.

"I bet that sounds hard to believe, huh…?"

"No, not at all," he said, trying to act normal. "Sounds like an interesting place."

"Right? I wonder if it's still there."

"Well, I'm glad that work and everything is going well."

"Thanks. Well, to tell you the truth, I've been making a lot more from my side gig."

"What do you do?"

"Investing. Stocks, real estate, equity club memberships."

Kosuke nodded agreeably. He'd heard a lot about this lately. Real estate was skyrocketing, and the economy was riding high. It meant good business for a woodworker, too.

"Are you interested in stocks?"

Kosuke laughed at her and shook his head. "Not even a little."

"Really. That's probably for the best."

"Why's that?"

Harumi looked concerned. She took a breath and went on.

"Even if you're just dabbling in a little real estate, you should try to sell everything off before 1990. The Japanese economy is going to tank."

Bewildered, Kosuke gave her an interrogative look. She sounded all too confident about what she was saying.

"Sorry," Harumi laughed awkwardly. "That must have sounded pretty weird, huh? Forget I said anything." She looked at her watch and stood. "It was so good to see you after so long. I hope I see you around."

"Sure," said Kosuke, standing with her. "Take care."

They said their good-byes, and Kosuke went back to the van. He turned the key and started off but then hit the brakes.

The Namiya General Store, huh?

That place was on his mind now. Kosuke hadn't taken the old man's advice and thought he was better for it, but there were people out there, like Harumi, who had taken it and still felt they were indebted to him.

Whatever happened to that old store?

Kosuke hit the gas again. He had to force himself to do it, but at the last second, he turned the wheel and drove in the opposite direction from his way home. He wanted to check on the Namiya General Store. By now, it must have closed for business. He felt that if he could see so with his own two eyes, it would be a weight off his shoulders, somehow.

This was his first time back in his hometown in eighteen years. Hands on the wheel, he summoned his memories. He didn't think anyone would recognize him, but he took pains to avoid eye contact. A visit to his old house was not on the agenda.

The town had changed considerably. There were far more houses, and the roads had even been redone. Thanks to the economy.

But the Namiya General Store sat in the same spot with the same look. It was obviously in rough condition, and the characters on the sign were hard to read, but it was still the building he knew. It felt as though if you rolled up the rusted shutter, you'd still find the shelves well stocked.

Kosuke got out of the car and walked up to the storefront, wading through sadness and nostalgia. He thought back to the night when his worries about leaving town led him here with a letter for the mail slot.

Before he knew it, he had stepped into the alley and was walking around back. The milk bin was bolted to the wall. He lifted the lid. The bin was empty.

He let out a breath. *What am I doing here?* he asked himself. *Enough of this.*

At that moment, the door beside him opened. A middle-aged man was standing in the doorway.

He looked taken aback, too. Surely he wasn't expecting any visitors.

"Um, sorry," Kosuke said, letting the lid of the milk bin fall shut. "I'm not doing anything. I was just, uh…" No reasonable excuse would come to mind.

The man eyed Kosuke and the milk crate suspiciously. "Are you one of the advice people?"

Kosuke looked back in disbelief.

"You're one of the people who wrote to my old man, asking for advice. Right?"

Caught red-handed, Kosuke's jaw dropped. He nodded. "I am. Years ago."

The man looked relieved. "Of course you are. If you weren't, what would you be doing in the milk bin?"

"I'm really sorry. It's my first time in the area in years, and I felt like I had to come by and see."

The man waved his hand in front of his face. "No need to apologize. I'm his son. He passed away. Eight years ago."

"I'm sorry to hear that. So is the house…?"

"Nobody lives here anymore. I come by sometimes, to check on things."

"Do you have plans to tear it down?"

The man groaned. "We have to keep it standing. We're going to leave it up for now."

Kosuke wondered what the reasoning was, but he felt it would be rude to pry.

"Did you write one of the serious letters? The way you were looking in there tells me you asked him a real question, unlike some of those neighborhood punks."

Kosuke understood the reference.

"Yeah. I mean, it was serious to me."

The man nodded and looked at the wooden box.

"My dad was an odd duck. I always thought if he had the time to dispense all this advice, he should be devoting it to his business. But that's what kept him going. I think he was pretty satisfied, in the end, especially when people thanked him."

"Did people come by often?"

"Yeah, well, basically. They sent more letters. Years of giving advice, and he started getting worried about whether any of it was any good. But I think those thank-you notes put his mind at ease."

"So they wrote him to express their gratitude."

"Right." He steadied his gaze. "One person who got advice as a kid became a teacher and used that same advice to help his students. It worked great. Another came from the daughter of someone who got advice. Her mother was pregnant, with the child of a man who was already married with kids, and she was torn up about whether she should have the baby."

"The world is full of all kinds of worries, huh?"

"So true. I thought the same thing when I read through all those thank-yous. It's just one thing after another. My old man was a trouper just for keeping up. One day, there'd be a somber letter from a kid agonizing over whether to go with his parents when they split town to start over, and the next there'd be a kid who fell in love with their teacher, lamenting about what to do."

"Wait a second." Kosuke sliced through the air with his hand. "Someone asked for advice about skipping town with their parents?"

"They did," the man mused, but his eyes were asking "And what of it?"

"Did they send a thank-you letter, too?"

"Sure did. My dad told him he should stick with his parents, and he took his advice. He said things turned out great. Him and his parents worked out a way to have a happy life."

Kosuke knit his eyebrows together. "When was all this? When did your dad get the letter?"

The man gave him a look of trepidation. "It was right before he died. But there was a lot more to it than that. That's not when they wrote the thank-you."

"Meaning…?"

"To tell you the truth," the man started off, but he pursed his lips. "Crap," he muttered. "I shouldn't have said all that. It didn't make sense. I didn't mean anything by it."

This was strange. The man stepped out and turned the key to lock the door.

"I need to get going. Feel free to stick around, see what you need to see. Not like there's anything to see here."

He hunched over to shield himself from the cold and went up the alley without looking back. Once Kosuke saw that he was gone, he looked inside the milk bin one more time.

For an instant, the box warped out of shape. Or so it seemed.

10

Kosuke noticed "Yesterday" had come on. He finished off his whiskey and asked Eriko for another.

He looked down at the pad of paper on the counter. He had racked his brain to come up with the following letter:

To the Namiya General Store,

About forty years ago, I asked you for advice. I went by Paul Lennon. Perhaps you remember me.

My problem was that my parents were planning to leave town to escape their debt and wanted to take me with them, but I wasn't sure if I should go.

You told me that it isn't good for families to separate and that I should trust my parents and follow them.

I tried, at least at first, to do this. When we left the house behind, we were together.

But on the road, I reached a point where I knew I couldn't take it anymore. I lost faith in them—my dad, especially. I knew I couldn't trust them with the rest of my life. Our bond as a family had already been broken at the time.

I saw my chance and ran for it. I had no idea what life had in store for me. I just knew I couldn't go on any further with my parents.

I'll never know what happened to them. But personally, I think I made the right decision.

My life has had some twists and turns, but I've managed to find happiness. I'm at a point where I'm mentally and financially secure.

Which goes to say I made the right choice by not listening to your advice.

Just to be clear, I'm not writing out of spite. The post online said you wanted people's input on how your advice changed their lives. I thought you might want to hear from someone who turned it down.

My philosophy is that when things get heavy, you have to carry that weight yourself.

I realize there's a strong chance this letter will wind up in the hands of your family. I apologize for any disrespect. Feel free to dispose of it.

—Paul Lennon

A new glass of whiskey was on the counter. Kosuke took a sip.

He remembered a day in late 1988, when he met Old Man Namiya's son. Someone had asked the old man for advice about the exact same problem. Only difference was that they'd followed the advice and, by all accounts, wound up happy.

Strange coincidence, he thought. *Could there really have been another kid in that small town wrestling with the same problem?*

How exactly had that kid and his parents found their happiness? Based on his own experience, that outcome was impossible. Escape was not a choice; it was an imperative. Kosuke's parents had no other recourse, so they ran.

"Did you finish up your letter?"

"More or less."

"You don't see many handwritten letters anymore."

"Yeah, I guess you don't. It was kind of an impulse move."

It had happened that afternoon. He was looking something up online, and he came across a post on someone's blog. It was as if his eyes had tripped over the words *the Namiya General Store*, and he read the post in full:

> To all who requested advice from the Namiya General Store:
>
> On September 13, from exactly midnight until daybreak, the advice box of the Namiya General Store will be reopening for one night only. We kindly ask that anyone who has ever asked for and received advice to give us your unfiltered opinion. How did it affect your life? Did you find it useful, or was it useless? Please leave your letters in the mail slot in the shutter, just like old times. We look forward to hearing from you.

Goosebumps. Could this be true? It must've been someone's idea of a joke. But why would anyone joke about this?

He traced the post back to its source. There was a site called the Namiya General Store—One-Night Special. The site had been registered by someone going by "the Namiya Family." According to the post, this date was the thirty-third memorial service for the owner. They would be hosting a memorial service for him.

He couldn't get it off his mind. It was impossible to focus on his work.

He ate dinner at a local Japanese diner, the usual, and went home, but he was still restless. He decided to go out again. He hadn't even bothered to change out of his work clothes.

Since he lived alone, there was nobody to inform about where he was going.

Not sure what he was doing, he got on the train as if propelled by some invisible force.

Kosuke read through the letter he had written. He'd finally be able to tie up some of the loose threads in his life.

The song changed to "Paperback Writer." This was one of his old favorites. He glanced at the CD player and happened to see a record player off beside it.

"Do you play vinyl sometimes, too?"

"On occasion. When one of our regulars asks."

"Could I have a look at your collection? I won't ask you to play anything."

"Sure," she said and disappeared out back.

She returned with a few LPs.

"There's more where this came from, but they're upstairs." She lined the records up across the counter.

Kosuke picked one up. *Abbey Road*. It had been released ahead of *Let It Be*, but chronologically, it was the last record the Beatles ever recorded. The album cover of the four men crossing the street was legendary in its own right. Paul McCartney was mysteriously barefoot, contributing to the popular conspiracy theory that "Paul is dead."

"Man, this takes me back," he whispered and reached for another. *Magical Mystery Tour*. It had been released as a soundtrack to a movie of the same name, and he'd heard its plot was best summarized as "bonkers."

The third record he examined was *Sgt. Pepper's Lonely Hearts Club Band*. The unshakable ziggurat of rock and roll.

Kosuke fixated on a detail of the cover. A blond woman on the far right. He used to think she was Marilyn Monroe; it wasn't until he was older that he learned she was the British actress Diana Dors. Beside her was a black spot. The printing had been peeled away and filled in with a felt-tipped pen.

The blood in his veins coursed hot though his body. His heart was beating rapid-fire.

"Who, whose—" His voice was hoarse. He gulped and tried again. "Whose are these? Yours?"

She looked a little puzzled. "I'm looking after them now. They were my older brother's."

"Your brother's? How did you wind up with them?"

She exhaled. "He died two years ago. He's the reason I became a Beatles fan. He'd been a huge fan since we were little, and when we grew up, he was always saying how he wanted to open up a Beatles-themed bar. In his thirties, he quit his job and opened up this place."

"...Really. Was your brother sick?"

"He had cancer. In his chest." She patted her breast.

Kosuke looked at her business card. Eriko Haraguchi.

"Was his last name Haraguchi, too?"

"No, Haraguchi is my married name. I'm divorced, and on my own now. Changing names was a pain, so I just left it. My brother's last name is Maeda."

"Maeda, huh...?"

Maeda was the last name of the friend he sold the records to. Which meant the records lined up on the counter were his own. His lost collection.

He couldn't believe it, but it really wasn't so strange. When he thought about it, there were only a certain number of people in that town who would have opened up a bar devoted to the Beatles. When he saw the sign for Fab4, he should have anticipated that the bar would belong to somebody he used to know.

"Why do you ask?"

"No, it's nothing." Kosuke shook his head. "So you inherited these records?"

"Yeah, he left them to me, but they were actually from someone else. A previous owner."

"How do you mean?"

"Almost all of them he bought off a friend in middle school. A whole collection. His friend was an even bigger Beatles fan, but out of nowhere, he called him saying he wanted to sell them off. My brother was ecstatic, even though he thought it was kind of weird—" Eriko stopped herself and put her hand to her lips. "I'm sorry; I must be boring you."

"No, I'm interested." Kosuke sipped his whiskey. "Please go on. Did something happen to his friend?"

Eriko nodded.

"He didn't come back from summer vacation. As it turns out, his whole family had left town. I guess they had some egregious debt. Along the way, they must have realized there was no escape. Things ended horribly…"

"What happened?"

Eriko cast her gaze down. Her face grew somber. She looked up again slowly. "Two days after they left town, they committed suicide."

"They did? All of them? Who?"

"I mean, the whole family, all three of them. The father killed his wife and son, then killed himself."

Kosuke almost yelped, but he pushed it down with all his might. "How did he go about killing them? His…wife and all."

"I don't know the exact details, but they said he drugged them and dumped their bodies off a boat into the ocean."

"Why were they on a boat?"

"They stole a rowboat in the middle of the night and went out into the harbor. The father didn't take a high enough dose. When he washed up onshore alive, he hung himself."

"But did they find the other bodies, of his wife and kid?"

Eriko shrugged. "That, I don't know, but the father did leave a suicide note. That must have been enough for the authorities to determine that the other two were dead."

"Oh boy."

Kosuke finished off his whiskey and asked for another. His head was chaos. If his senses had not been dulled by alcohol, he may not have been able to hold himself together.

Even if they'd found another body, it would have to have been Kimiko's. If Sadayuki had written in his note that he had killed both his wife and his son, there was a low probability of the police suspecting otherwise, even if they never found the other body.

The question was: Why did Sadayuki do it?

Kosuke thought back to that fateful night forty-two years ago. The night he had absconded from the Fujikawa Rest Area, crouched among the boxes of a cargo truck.

He was sure that Sadayuki and Kimiko had been distraught when they realized he had disappeared. They could either forget about their son and proceed with the getaway as planned, or they could try to find him. Kosuke had imagined they'd chosen the first option. They had no way of finding him, even if they had wanted to.

But evidently, they'd chosen neither. Instead, they'd chosen suicide.

Another glass was sitting on the counter. He picked it up and shook it gently. Ice spun and tinkled in the whiskey.

It seemed Sadayuki had considered the option of a family suicide all along. Mind you, as a last resort. But there was no question Kosuke's actions had pushed him to it.

No, it couldn't have been just him. He and Kimiko must have talked it out and decided on it together.

But why go through the trouble of stealing a boat and drowning Kimiko?

There was only one reason for them to kill themselves: to make it seem as if their son was dead, too. The ocean is a big place. Sometimes bodies don't turn up.

In the throes of suicide, Kosuke's parents had been thinking of him. What would happen to their son if they died?

They probably couldn't imagine how he expected to get by on his own. But they must have reasoned he would need to scrap his name. They didn't want to stand in the way of his new identity and life.

And so they decided to wipe Kosuke Waku from the face of the earth.

The detective from the Juvenile Division of the Metropolitan Police Department, the case agents from Juvenile Affairs, and all the other grown-ups had tried to crack Kosuke's identity, but none of them could do it. Of course they couldn't. He was a ghost. All documents about a certain middle school student named Kosuke Waku had been wiped from the records. There was no trace of his former existence.

The words his mother said to him up in his room, just before they ran, crossed his mind: *Your father and I—well, your father especially—we're ready to do anything if it means giving you a good life. Even putting our lives on the line.*

She hadn't been lying. Kosuke was where he was today because they had been ready to make that sacrifice.

Kosuke shook his head and took another gulp of whiskey. No. He could have avoided all that pointless suffering if those people hadn't been his parents. He even had to give up his own name. He had gotten this far only by sheer will. That was all.

Nevertheless, the pangs of regret and remorse were growing in his heart.

When he'd run off, he'd left his parents with no other option. Kosuke had backed them into a corner. Why couldn't he have asked them one more time before they ran? Forget this whole plan and go back home. Start over, from scratch, as a family.

"Is something the matter?"

He looked up. Eriko's expression was concerned.

"Something really must be bothering you."

He shook his head. "It's nothing. Thanks."

He glanced over the stationery on the counter. As he read through what he'd written, a feeling of displeasure spread over his chest.

The letter felt worthless, a parade of self-satisfaction. No echo of gratitude for the old man's kind advice. *My philosophy is that when things get heavy, you have to carry that weight yourself.* What the hell was that? Who knows where he would actually be if it weren't for his tortured parents' sacrifice.

He ripped up the paper, tore it to shreds. Eriko gasped.

"Sorry. Listen, would you mind if I stuck around a little longer?"

"Of course not." She was smiling.

He took up his pen and looked down at the stationery.

Maybe the old man had been right after all. *If it keeps you together and in the same boat, you have a fighting chance of getting back on course.* That part of the letter came back to him. But Kosuke hadn't taken this advice. He'd bolted off alone, leaving the boat without a destination.

So what should he write?

That he ignored the advice and ran off from his parents, eventually driving them to suicide? Should he write the truth?

I can't do that, he thought. *It's the wrong thing to do.*

It was as yet unclear how far the story of the Waku family suicide had spread. But what if the news had made it to the old man? He just might have a hunch that the son was none other than Paul Lennon. He would have regretted telling the boy to follow his parents.

This evening, an event was being held for the old man's thirty-third memorial rites. Kosuke had a duty to offer a gesture to help him rest peacefully. It had said "unfiltered opinions" were welcome, but that didn't mean they wanted brutal honesty. The important thing was to express to them that the advice had been spot-on.

After thinking it over, Kosuke drafted a second letter. It started off almost the same as the first one.

To the Namiya General Store,

About forty years ago, I wrote to you for advice using the name Paul Lennon.

My question involved how my parents were planning to escape from town. I was torn about whether I should go with them. That letter was never posted on your wall. You said that was the first time someone had sent you a serious question.

You told me it's not good for a family to separate. You said that if it kept us together and in the same boat, we had a fighting chance of getting back on course.

I took your advice and went with them. I did what they asked me to do. It was the right decision.

I won't go into details, but my parents and I found a way to free ourselves from suffering. In the last few years, both of them passed away, but I think they each would have said they had a good life. I can say I'm blessed.

It's all thanks to you, Mr. Namiya. I just had to put pen to paper and thank you.

I suppose this letter will be read by someone in your family in your stead. I hope this is an acceptable contribution to your memorial service.

—Paul Lennon

After rereading the new letter a few times, Kosuke had a strange sensation. What he'd written was eerily similar to another thank-you letter, the one the old man's son said his father received from the boy who had the exact same problem.

It had to be a coincidence.

He folded up the sheets of stationery and stuffed them in an envelope. His watch said almost midnight.

"Can I ask you for a favor?" said Kosuke, standing up. "I'm going to go drop this letter off. I won't be long. Think I'll have time for one more round when I'm back?"

Eriko looked at Kosuke and the letter with some confusion, but her face broke into a smile, and she nodded. "Sure. That works."

"Thanks," said Kosuke. He took a ten-thousand-yen bill from his wallet and placed it on the counter as collateral to dissolve any suspicions about his leaving without paying.

He left the bar and walked into the night. The other establishments were all already closed.

He knew the way. In minutes, the Namiya General Store was up ahead. Kosuke stopped short. He saw a silhouette in front of the store.

Was she there for the same reason as him? Kosuke walked up to the shutter to see. There was a woman in her midthirties, standing in a suit. A Benz was parked in the street. In the passenger seat was a cardboard box filled with CDs from a certain female artist. Copies upon copies of the same CD. Maybe this woman and the artist were affiliated in some way.

The woman slipped something into the mail slot in the shutter and went over to her car. She noticed Kosuke and froze. Her face was flush with caution.

Kosuke held up the letter and pointed to the mail slot. She understood, and her face relaxed. She wordlessly acknowledged him with a simple bow and climbed into her Benz.

How many people were doing this tonight? The Namiya General Store must have touched the lives of more people than he realized.

Once the Benz had rolled off, Kosuke slipped his letter in the slot. He heard it flap down. A sound he hadn't heard in forty-two years.

It felt as if a chapter of his life had at last come to a close. Perhaps everything had finally been settled.

Back at Fab4, the flat-screen had been turned on. Eriko was fiddling with a remote behind the counter.

"What's up?" Kosuke asked.

"There's this video my brother loved. I was going to show you. They never released it officially, but I know it's somewhere on this bootleg."

"Hmm."

"What would you like to drink?"

"Right. I'll have another whiskey."

A glass of Bunnahabhain was placed in front of Kosuke. Just as he reached for the drink, the film started playing. He was about to take a sip, but he pulled the glass away from his lips. He knew what film this was.

"Is this…?"

Onscreen was the rooftop of the Apple building. Against the winter wind, the Beatles were playing again. This was the climax of the movie *Let It Be*.

He put down the glass and fixed his eyes on the screen. This was the film that had changed the course of his life. It had taught him just how tenuous the ties that bind us really are.

And yet—

The Beatles on the flat-screen were somehow different from what he remembered seeing in the theater. Back then, their hearts seemed scattered, and their performance refused to come together. But seeing them here, inside the bar, he got a different impression.

The Fab Four were rocking out. They were having a blast. Sure, they were breaking up, but playing together here reminded them of how it all began.

When Kosuke watched it in the movie theater, he'd seen them struggling, a projection of his own painful experience. He had stopped believing that anyone could stay together.

He grabbed his glass and gulped the whiskey down. Closing his eyes, he thought of his parents and prayed.

CHAPTER 5

PRAYERS FROM THE SKY ABOVE

1

Shota came back from the storefront. His face was not encouraging.

"Still nothing?"

He nodded and sighed. "I guess it was just the wind."

"That's all right," replied Atsuya. "No biggie."

"I wonder if he read our response," said Kohei.

"Why wouldn't he?" Shota responded. "The letter isn't in the milk crate. Who else would have taken it?"

"You've got a point. So why haven't we heard back?"

"Well," Shota began to say, but then he deferred to Atsuya.

"Who cares?" Atsuya said. "What are we supposed to do with him? It probably made zero sense to him. If another letter comes, it'll just be more trouble. What are you gonna do if he asks us to explain?"

The other two looked down.

"See? That'd be a pain in the ass. It's fine as it is."

"It's crazy, though," said Shota. "I mean, what a coincidence that Floundering Musician was that guy."

"I mean, yeah." Atsuya nodded. There was no way he could disagree.

Just after concluding their correspondence with Moon Rabbit, they had received a letter from a new person asking for advice. They were incensed by what they read. This guy's so-called problem was that he couldn't decide whether to take over the family fish shop or pursue his musical career. Sounded like a spoiled brat who was never going to be satisfied.

When they wrote back, they took potshots at him and called him out for being spoiled and told him to smell the roses. This was not at all what Floundering Musician had been expecting, and he shot them back an inflammatory rebuttal. The guys doubled down with some more invective, but something strange had happened when the next letter from the Flounder arrived.

The guys had been sitting out in the store, waiting for his response, when they physically saw the letter slip in through the mail slot—and stop halfway. But what really got them was what happened next.

Through the mail slot, they heard somebody playing the harmonica. It was a melody they knew well. A song called "Reborn."

This had been the breakthrough hit for the artist Seri Mizuhara, one with a famous backstory. And that backstory had a personal significance for the three guys in the store.

Seri Mizuhara was raised with her younger brother at a children's home, Marumitsuen. When she was in elementary school, the building caught fire on Christmas Eve. Her brother would never have made it out alive if it weren't for the man who saved him, an amateur musician hired to play a Christmas show. The man suffered third-degree burns all over his body and breathed his last at the hospital soon after.

"Reborn" was one of his originals. Seri sang his song for everyone to show her endless gratitude, and it had eventually launched her career as a singer.

These three had heard this story countless times since they were kids; after all, they were also raised at Marumitsuen. For the kids at the children's home, Seri Mizuhara was a source of pride and a ray of hope. They aspired to follow her example and find their own way to shine someday.

Which was why Atsuya, Shota, and Kohei were stunned to hear "Reborn" outside on the harmonica. When the song was over, someone pushed the letter through, and it thwapped through the slot.

The three guys asked one another what was going on. They had calculated by now that the people asking for advice were living in 1980. Seri Mizuhara would have been alive but still a kid. It would be years before she recorded "Reborn."

There was only one conclusion: "Reborn" had been written by the Floundering Musician. And he was the one who had saved Seri's younger brother.

The letter said he'd been thrown off by their advice but that this had given him a chance to take stock of his situation. He told "Mr. Namiya" that it would help him figure things out if he could meet him in person.

The guys were stuck. Should they tell Floundering Musician about what was going to happen to him? Could they really tell him, "Hey, buddy, listen up. In 1988, you're gonna play at a Christmas show at Marumitsuen, and the building is gonna catch fire, and you're going to die"?

"Let's tell him," Kohei suggested. "Then he won't have to die."

"But if he doesn't die," Shota reasoned, "her brother will die instead."

Kohei had no way of contesting that.

Atsuya made the final call: They weren't going to mention the fire.

"Even if we did, he probably wouldn't take it seriously. He'd think it was some creepster giving him a prophesy. It would turn him off, and he'd probably just forget about it. Plus, we already know about the fire and about Seri becoming a famous musician. Awful shit is going to happen, no matter what we write. All we can do is help him accept his fate."

Shota and Kohei were on board. But what exactly should they say?

"I want…to show him how thankful we are," Kohei began. "If it wasn't for him, Seri Mizuhara maybe would have never gotten famous, and we wouldn't have ever heard her singing 'Reborn.'"

Atsuya agreed, and Shota said, "Let's do it."

They worked together on what to write. The following is a snippet of their letter:

> *Your efforts in music will never be in vain.*
>
> *Your music will save lives. And the songs you create will absolutely live on.*
>
> *Don't ask me how I know. Just trust me. I'm positive.*
>
> *Hold on to this until the end. The very, very end.*
>
> *That's all I can say.*

They had left their letter in the milk crate and, a little later, gone back to check. The bin was empty. The Floundering Musician must have taken it away.

They were expecting a quick rebuttal. That's why the door was shut, why they'd been waiting all this time.

But no letter came. Up till now, it had taken no time at all for a response to show up in the mail slot. Maybe the Floundering Musician had read their letter and got what he needed.

"All right, let's open the door." Atsuya got up.

"Wait a sec." Kohei caught him by the leg of his jeans. "Just a few more minutes."

"For what?"

"You know." Kohei nervously licked his lips. "The back door. Let's leave it open just a little longer."

Atsuya sneered at him. "Why bother? I don't think Flounder is writing back."

"Yeah, I know. I'm done with him anyway."

"Okay. Then why?"

"Well, I was wondering if someone else might send a letter."

"What?" Atsuya snapped and looked down at him. "Listen to yourself. If we leave the back door shut, time will never pass in here. Get it?"

"I get it, I get it."

"Yeah? 'Cause if you did, you'd know we can't go pulling shit like that. We got in over our heads and had to muddle through, but now we're out. We're not goddamned advice columnists."

Atsuya kicked free from Kohei's hand and went out through the back.

He checked the time. A little after four. Two more hours to go.

The idea was to leave at six. The trains would be running by then.

He went back inside. Kohei looked dejected. Shota was toying with his cell phone.

Atsuya took a seat at the kitchen table. The candle on the tabletop was flickering. Must have been the air from the outside.

This sure is a weird house, he thought. He looked over the dingy walls. *What the hell was causing all this supernatural woo-woo? And why were we dragged into it?*

"I'm not sure if this makes sense," whispered Kohei, "but I feel like tonight, for the first time in my life, I've made a difference in someone else's life. Me, you know? An idiot like me made a difference."

Atsuya scowled. "That's why you wanna keep on doling out advice? It ain't gonna pay you squat."

"I'm not trying to get rich here. This is just the first time I've had a chance to seriously consider what someone else is going through, and maybe even help."

Atsuya clicked his tongue.

"And what good is it doing us, getting drunk on this idea of helping people? No one needs any advice from us. Ms. Olympics interpreted our letter in the most convenient way possible, and Flounder doesn't know what's good for him. I've been saying the same thing all along. We're losers. We got no business giving anyone advice."

"But even you were smiling when we got that last letter from Moon Rabbit."

"I wasn't pissed. But the exception proves the rule. We're in no position to offer people our opinion. We're—" He pointed to the bag heaped up in the corner. "We're good-for-nothing crooks."

Kohei looked hurt and hung his head. Atsuya saw his reaction and snorted.

At that moment, Shota let out a loud cry. "What the?"

Atsuya almost fell off his chair. "What's wrong now?"

"Wait, hold on." Shota held up his phone. "There's something on here about the Namiya General Store."

"On the Internet?" Atsuya raised his eyebrows. "Just someone writing about their memories or something, right?"

"That's what I expected, too, when I searched for it online. I figured someone must have posted something about it."

"Is that what you found? Some kind of memory-lane thing?"

"Not exactly." Shota showed Atsuya his phone. "See for yourself."

"Come on," he replied, but he took the phone and skimmed through the backlit screen. The header said "the Namiya General Store—One-Night Special." Once he read what followed, he knew why Shota had been startled. Atsuya himself felt his blood go hot.

> To all who requested advice from the Namiya General Store:
>
> On September 13, from exactly midnight until daybreak, the advice box of the Namiya General Store will be reopening for one night only. We kindly ask that anyone who has ever asked for and received advice to give us your unfiltered opinion. How did it affect your life? Did you find it useful, or was it useless? Please leave your letters in the mail slot in the shutter, just like old times. We look forward to hearing from you.

*   *   *

"What the hell is this?"

"No idea, but it says they're doing this because September 13 is the thirty-third memorial service for the old man. Someone in his family set this up."

"Wait, what?" Kohei hurried over. "What happened?"

Shota handed the phone to Kohei. "Hey, Atsuya. You know that's today."

Atsuya had realized, too. *On September 13, from exactly midnight until daybreak*—in other words, right now. They were in the thick of it.

"Wait, so they actually advertised that they'd be giving out advice again?" Kohei blinked repeatedly.

"That must be why all this weird stuff is happening. It has to be. Today is a special day. The present is communicating with the past."

Atsuya rubbed his face. The specifics were beyond him, but he sensed Shota's description was on point.

He looked at the back door, which was ajar. It was still black night.

"If the door's open, we lose connection with the past," said Shota. "There's still some time left before daylight. What should we do, Atsuya?"

"Do…?"

"We might be screwing things up, you know? What if the door should have been shut the entire night?" Kohei got up and shut the back door tight.

"What are you doing?! Open that."

Kohei turned around and shook his head. "It's gotta be closed."

"Why? If it's closed, time basically stops. You wanna be in here forever?" Atsuya had an idea. "Know what? Let's shut the door. Only let's shut it behind us. That solves everything. We won't be screwing things up anymore. Right?"

But neither of the other guys motioned to agree. They were crestfallen.

"Come on. You got something else to add?"

Finally, Shota spoke up. "I'm gonna stick around. You should go, Atsuya. You can wait outside or get a head start."

"I'm staying, too," chimed in Kohei.

Atsuya scratched his head. "Stay and do what?"

"It's not about what we're going to do," said Shota. "We just need to see this through. To see what else happens to this weird house."

"Do you understand anything about what's going on? In an hour, the sun's gonna come up. An hour out there is days on end in here. Are you telling me you're gonna sit through that with nothing to eat, nothing to drink? I don't think so."

Shota looked away. Maybe he knew that Atsuya was right.

"Give it up," said Atsuya. But Shota didn't reply.

Soon after, they heard the shutter rattle. Atsuya and Shota faced each other.

Kohei jogged out into the store. "It's just the wind again," Atsuya yelled after him. "It's just banging in the wind."

Eventually, Kohei loped his way back, empty-handed.

"Told you. Just the wind."

Kohei trudged back, but when he got closer to Atsuya and Shota, he dropped his act and reached behind him.

"Ta-daa!" He produced a white envelope. It must have been in his back pocket.

Atsuya was getting sick of this. Things were getting downright silly.

"This can be the last one, Atsuya," urged Shota, gesturing at the envelope. "We'll respond to this one and get out of here. Promise."

He sighed and sat down at the table. "Let's read it first. It might be something that's way too much for us."

Kohei carefully tore open the seal.

2

Hi, Mr. Namiya,

I'm writing because I'd like to ask you for advice about something.

I graduated from a vocational high school this year and started at a company in Tokyo in April. I didn't go to college because of some stuff happening at home. Basically, I wanted to start work as soon as possible.

But right after I started at the company, I started doubting that this was the right decision. This company only hires girls straight out of high school to do chores around the office. All I do each day is brew tea, make copies, and rewrite documents that the men at the company drafted in their crummy handwriting. Easy work. Anyone could do it. Even a middle schooler, or an elementary schooler who knew enough words. I never get that sense of satisfaction from a good day's work. I have a Class Two Bookkeeping license, but I never get to put my skills to use.

The company is under the impression that the only reason women take jobs is to land themselves husbands, and that once they find a suitable one, they'll marry him and quit. Since they only let us do simple tasks, they couldn't care less about our academic background. Let's just say the bar for that is pretty low. They want a steady turnover of women to give the men plenty to choose from. It's in their interest to pay the women almost nothing.

This isn't why I took this job. I want to be a financially independent woman. I'm not remotely interested in being some throwaway.

I was at a loss for what to do, but one day someone approached me on the street and asked me to work at their bar. It was a club in Shinjuku. The man was a scout for the nighttime entertainment industry, and he was hunting for new hostesses to charm customers at a hostess bar.

From what he told me, the conditions would be unbelievably good. A whole other level than my day job. Things sounded so good that I started thinking there had to be some kind of catch.

He asked me to come by to check it out and hang. I thought why not and went. I have to say, it was a culture shock.

I had associated the words club and hostess with a sort of shady atmosphere, but what I saw was a glamorous wonderland for adults. The girls were working the floor. Far from sitting around and looking pretty, they seemed to be strategizing, even teaming up, to please their customers to their utmost abilities. I wasn't sure I could handle this, but I felt like it was worth a try.

That's when I started working days at the company and nights at the club.

I used to just go home after work, but now I head to the club to work again. I'm actually nineteen, but I told them I'm twenty. The hours are tough on me physically, and handling the customers is harder than I thought, but it makes the day worthwhile. And financially, I'm far better off.

But after about two months, I started having doubts. Not about working as a hostess, but about staying at the company. Since there was little hope of ever doing more than busywork, there was no good reason to kill myself to stay there. Plus, if I quit and went full-time as a hostess, I'd see a huge improvement in my savings.

I haven't told anyone I know that I'm in the industry. I'm also worried that if I quit the company out of nowhere, I'll leave a mess behind me.

But I feel like I'm finally doing the work I want to be doing. I'd be so grateful if you have any advice on how to help those closest to me to understand my position and how to quit my day job on good terms.

Thanks for your help!

—Dubious Doggy

Atsuya snorted. "Oh, great. Can you believe this shit? *This* is the last letter we've got to respond to?"

"She's in for it," said Shota smugly. "She'll learn. There's always gonna be girls who go in for that kind of work, thinking it's going to be glamorous."

"I bet she's really pretty," deemed Kohei. "She got scouted on the street, and it only took her two months to make a solid living."

"Sounds like she's got a new admirer. Snap out of it. Hey, Shota, write her back."

"What should I say?" He readied the pen.

"You know, talk some sense into her. Rough her up. Get her head out of the clouds."

He puckered his face. "Does it have to be rough? This girl's only nineteen."

"For a dummy like her, you need to be a little harsh, or it won't sink in."

"I know what you're saying, but let's maybe take a softer approach." Atsuya clucked. "Grow a pair."

"If we're too harsh on her, she'll snap. Something I think *you* can personally relate to."

Here's what Shota came up with:

Dear Dubious Doggy,

Thanks for the letter.

I'll be blunt. You should quit the club. That's no life for you.

Yeah, yeah, I can understand the appeal of making way more money than you would working at some office job, and more easily, at that.

You've made it into a world of luxury, and it's only natural that you'd want to stay.

But it won't always be this easy. You're still so young. It's been a good two months, but that isn't long enough to comprehend how hard it's going to be. You'll have all kinds of men for customers, and no shortage of them will drool all over you. You think you'll be able to brush them off? Or will you just give up and let them all do what they want? That's no way to treat your body.

How long do you plan to do this hostess thing full-time? Until you're how old? You say you want to be an independent woman, but once you reach a certain age, no one's going to want to hire you.

What comes after that? Are you hoping to open your own club? In that case, best of luck. But don't expect running your own business to be a breeze.

Don't you want to marry someone someday and start a family? If you do, then listen up and quit while you're ahead.

If you keep on working as a hostess, who do you suppose you'll marry? One of your customers? Just what percent of your customers do you suppose are single?

Let's not forget your parents. I doubt they raised you and put you through school only for you to enter this line of work.

What's wrong with being a throwaway employee? You're part of the company, you get paid without doing much of anything, and you can't walk into a room without everybody noticing. And once you marry some guy from the company, you never have to work again.

What's wrong with any of that? It sounds awesome.

In case you weren't aware, Ms. Dubious Doggy, there are tons of guys out there who can't find work and don't know what to do. Those guys would gladly make tea or whatever else for half the wages that they're paying girls right out of high school.

I'm not writing this to bust your chops, okay? This is for your own good. Take my word for it. I'd listen to me if I were you.

—Namiya General Store

"Yeah, this seems like the right tone to take." Atsuya nodded approvingly at the letter. Of course, if it were him, he would have given her an earful.

Her folks put her through school, she finally finds a decent job, and then what? She becomes a hostess. What was she thinking?

Shota went out to drop their answer in the milk bin. He came back in and shut the door behind him. There was a faint rattle at the shutter. "I'll get it," he said and ran out into the shop.

He came back grinning. "Got it!" He flapped the envelope in the air.

To the Namiya General Store,

Thank you very much for your timely response. I was relieved, since I was worried I might not hear from you.

But when I read your letter, I knew I had made a few mistakes. I think we've had some miscommunication between us. Perhaps I should have been more forthcoming about the particulars of my position.

I'll have you know that I did not decide to devote my time to working as a hostess to fuel some decadent lifestyle. What I want is financial independence. That means having the resources to live life on no one's terms but my own. I don't think I'd ever get there if I stayed on at that company.

Second, I have no plans to marry. I'm sure having children and becoming a housewife offers its own kind of happiness, but that's not the life for me.

And I think I have a pretty good idea of how hard life in this industry can be. Looking around at my coworkers, it's easy to imagine the hardship that awaits me in the years to come. I took this route aware of that. And yes, I'm hoping to have my own club someday.

I believe in myself. I've only been at it for two months, and I already have a bunch of customers who favor me. But there's only so much I can do for them. The main reason is that I'm still working my day job. I can't get to the club until the early evening, which leaves no time to join them for dinner. That's another part of why I want to quit.

Let's clear something up, though. This seems to be bothering you, the idea that I'm sleeping with these men. Well, I haven't. Not even once. I'm not saying I haven't been propositioned, but I know how to ward them off. I'm old enough to handle that.

My legal guardians will be concerned when they find out. But in the long run, I'm doing this for them so that I can pay them back for all they've done

I wonder if you still find me so naive.

—Dubious Doggy

PS. I was asking for advice on how to explain my work life to my friends and family. I have no plans to leave the industry. If you don't agree with my lifestyle, please disregard this letter.

"Let's ignore it," suggested Atsuya. He held up the letter. "What's this crap about believing in herself? She better get ready for the real world."

Kohei was despondent as ever. "Yeah, I guess you're right."

"Wait, though," Shota said. "What this girl's saying isn't so far off. If a woman wants financial independence, working at a club will get her there, and fast. She knows the deal. Money is everything. Without it, you're nowhere."

"I don't need you to tell me that," Atsuya spat. "You're right, but things aren't gonna go the way she wants them to."

"And why is that, exactly?" Shota asked. "How do you know things won't work out for her?"

"Because things don't work out for most people," he explained. "Sure, she's hot shit now and could probably open up her own club, no problem, but plenty of shops close six months after opening. A business isn't easy to get going. It's hard building that momentum. You need money to start, but money isn't enough. It's easy for her to write to us and say she's gonna do it, but words are words, and she's just a little girl who doesn't understand the world yet. Once she's neck-deep in this lifestyle, she'll give up on all of this. But when she comes to her senses, it'll be too late to catch up. She'll have missed her chance to marry, and she'll have aged twice as fast from working as a hostess. By then it won't do any good to wish she'd done things differently."

"Yeah, but she's only nineteen. She doesn't have to worry that far ahead."

"That's exactly *why* she has to worry." Atsuya raised his voice. "Because she's young. Write her back and tell her to cut the shit. She's gotta quit the club and find some eligible bachelor at the company."

Shota stared down for a few seconds at the stationery on the tabletop and began to shake his head. "No, I want to encourage her. This girl didn't ask us for advice for kicks."

"It's not about how serious she is. It's about living in the real world."

"I think she's being pretty realistic."

"Think so? Let's make a bet. On whether she succeeds as an entrepreneur. I'll bet that working as a hostess, she'll get tangled up with some shitty dude and wind up as a single mom and an all-around pain in the ass."

Shota gulped his next words down. His head hung heavier than ever.

A leaden silence fell over the room. Even Atsuya's eyes were on the floor.

"Hey," started Kohei. "How about we ask her?"

"Ask her what?" Atsuya replied.

"To explain. I don't think either of you is wrong, based on this conversation. Let's ask her how serious she is about her plan and go from there."

"Of course she's gonna say she means it. She takes herself so seriously."

"We could ask her for some details," Shota offered. "Like if there's a reason she wants to be financially independent, and how come she thinks marriage wouldn't make her happy. Oh, and we could ask about her specific plans for starting up her business. Like Atsuya said, it isn't easy. If we ask her and she can't come up with decent answers, then I'll agree that her dream is unrealistic, and we can tell her she should give up working as a hostess. Deal?"

Atsuya sniffled and nodded. "I don't see what good it's gonna do, but sure, go ahead."

"Here I go," said Shota, and he took up the pen.

As Shota filled the lines with text and paused to think before starting each new sentence, Atsuya watched and meditated on the last thing he'd said: *Working as a hostess, she'll get tangled up with some shitty dude and wind up as a single mom and an all-around pain in the ass.* That was what happened to his own mother. Shota and Kohei had held their tongues because they knew that things were getting personal.

Atsuya's mother had him when she was twenty-two. His father was a younger guy who worked at the same club as a bartender. Right before she gave birth, he left without a trace.

Stranded with a nursing baby, Atsuya's mother continued working as a hostess. She probably had no other prospects.

In a few of his earlier memories, his mother had a man around. But Atsuya didn't see him as a father. Eventually, he disappeared, and not long after, another man was staying in their apartment. His mother gave the man money, since he wasn't employed. As time passed, he vanished, too, and another man came in. They came and went in cycles. Then came the worst of the lot.

This one beat up Atsuya for no reason. Well, maybe he had his reasons, but none that Atsuya could comprehend. Once, Atsuya got punched in the face because the man said he didn't like the way it looked. That was when he was in the first grade. His mother didn't speak up. She seemed to think he deserved it for getting on her man's nerves.

Atsuya always had a bruise somewhere, but he tried to cover up. If they'd found out at school, it would cause a commotion. And he was sure that would only make things worse for him at home.

That man was arrested for gambling when Atsuya was in the second grade. A gang of detectives came to see them at home. When they showed up, Atsuya was in a tank top, and one of the detectives saw the bruises on his body. They pressed his mother for an explanation, but the excuse she gave was so weak they caught her in the lie almost instantly.

The precinct contacted Juvenile Affairs, who sent over a case agent.

When the agent came by to ask him a few questions, his mother insisted she could raise him on her own. To this day, Atsuya didn't understand why she'd said that. He'd heard her lamenting over the phone about how much she hated being a parent, how she wished she had never had a kid, over and over again.

The agent left. Now it was just Atsuya and his mom. *No more getting beat up at home*, he thought. But while that was true, there was frequently no one home at all. More often than not, his mother didn't come home at night. But it wasn't as if she prepped his meals or left him money for food. Before he knew it, school lunches were the only thing keeping him alive. Atsuya told no one of his miserable existence. He wasn't sure what was holding him back. Maybe he didn't want their sympathy.

The season changed to winter, and Atsuya spent Christmas alone. It was winter vacation, and school was closed. His mother hadn't been home in over two weeks. There was nothing left in the refrigerator.

On December 28, Atsuya was caught stealing a chicken skewer from a street stand. He was famished. He had no memory of how he'd been eating since the start of winter break. Honestly, he didn't even really remember stealing the skewer. They had caught him in the act. He was apprehended swiftly, since he'd collapsed as he was about to make his escape. Anemic shock.

Three months later, Atsuya entered Marumitsuen.

3

Dear Dubious Doggy,

Thank you for your second letter.

It's clear to me you aren't working as a hostess just so you can live a life of luxury.

Your ambition to own your own business is commendable.

Still, I can't help but suspect that after two good months of working as a hostess, you're a little tipsy on the glamour and easy money.

How are you going to go about saving the money to start a business? Do you have a timeline for your savings? And how will you proceed from there? To run a club, you'll need to hire a lot of people. Where will you get the experience you need to manage everything? Do you think you'll figure it out just from working as a hostess?

Are you confident that your plan will be enough for you to succeed? If so, what are you basing that on?

I think it's admirable that you want to have financial independence. But don't you think it's just as admirable to marry someone with money and win yourself some security and stability? Even when a woman doesn't have a job, providing support for her husband gives her a certain kind of independent status.

You mentioned wanting to do something to show your gratitude toward your parents, but money isn't enough to pay them back. You need to make yourself happy, comfortable. You know, settle down. Once you do, your parents will be satisfied, and I think they'll feel gratified, too.

You said I could ignore your letter if I disagreed with your lifestyle, but I couldn't overlook your situation. I had to write back. Please share your honest thoughts.

—Namiya General Store

"Looks good to me," agreed Atsuya. He handed the letter to Shota.

"Now it all depends on what she says. Whether she writes back with a solid plan."

He shook his head at Shota. "I'm not banking on it."

"Why not? If you're gonna be dismissive, at least back it up."

"Even if she has a plan or whatever, I wouldn't expect it to be more than a daydream. Like getting some celebrity or baseball player to be her sugar daddy."

"Hey, that could work." Kohei piped up with an endorsement.

"Shut it, numbskull. That's never gonna happen."

"Anyway, I'll be right back." Shota slipped the letter in an envelope and stood.

They watched Shota exit through the back door and listened to him opening the lid of the milk bin and letting it slam shut. Atsuya wondered how many times they'd heard that exact sequence of sounds that night.

Shota came back inside and shut the door behind him. A second later, they heard the shutter rattling. "I'll get it," Kohei volunteered, and he ambled into the storefront.

Atsuya looked at Shota. Their eyes met.

"What's next?" he asked.

"Dunno." Shota shrugged.

Kohei came with another envelope. "Can I read it first?"

"Go ahead," Shota and Atsuya both told him.

Kohei began to read the letter. At first, he seemed to be amused, but gradually, his expression shifted into something ominous. He started chewing his thumbnail. Atsuya gave Shota a look. Kohei had a habit of doing that when he was panicking.

There were more pages than last time. When Kohei was done, Atsuya snatched the letter from him.

To the Namiya General Store,

Your second letter made me feel the same dissonance again.

Frankly, I was insulted by your suspicion that I'm merely drunk on what you call "the glamour and easy money." Who in their right mind would do this job for fun?

But when I cooled down, I realized your choice of words was sensible. It's to be expected that you'd be skeptical about a nineteen-year-old girl who writes to tell you she wants to start a business.

I decided I wasn't helping anyone by being secretive. I figure I might as well clue you in on everything now.

As I've mentioned again and again, I want to be a financially independent person. And I'm not talking about making a modest living. I want to make the big bucks. But I don't want to make it for myself.

To tell you the truth, I lost both my parents when I was very young and spent six years, up through elementary school, living in a children's home. A place called Marumitsuen.

But I was one of the lucky ones. Just when I graduated elementary school, some relatives were able to take me in. It's thanks to them that I made it as far as high school. In the children's home, there were all too many kids who had been abused by their parents. There were kids taken in by foster parents who pocketed the child support and fed them close to nothing. After seeing their misfortune, I was able to understand how blessed I was.

Which is all the more reason that I want to do something to repay my guardians, as soon as I can. I'm running out of time. They're elderly, and since they aren't working anymore, they're scraping by on their meager savings. They don't have anyone but me to help them. And I can't earn enough money making tea and copies all day long.

And by the way, I do have a plan for starting my own club. Saving up is a major part of it, but I also have an adviser who will help me get things started. He's one of our customers, but he has a hand in a bunch of other businesses in the food industry and owns a spot himself. He told me that when I decide to go off on my own, he'll help me cover all the bases.

But I bet you think my plan is dubious at best. Why can I be so sure that this guy will help me out?

This part I need to confess. Lately, this man has been asking me to be his lover. If I say yes, he'll give me a monthly allowance. And I don't mean pocket money. I'm seriously considering this. He's not a bad guy, and I don't dislike him.

That should answer all your questions. I hope I've made it abundantly clear that I am not working as a hostess for the heck of it. Or did you find this letter lacking in direction, too? You'll probably call it all a fairy tale, la-la land, a little girl's misunderstanding of the big wide world. If that's the case, please point out whatever it is I'm missing. I would appreciate the guidance.

—Dubious Doggy

4

"I'm heading up to the shops by the station," Harumi told Hideo, her great-aunt. She was at the stove, her back to Harumi. The air was fragrant with the smell of bonito flakes.

"All right." Hideo nodded her good-bye over her shoulder. She had just scooped some broth into a dish and was giving it a taste.

Harumi stepped out and hopped onto the bicycle parked by the gate. She started pedaling nice and easy. This was only the third time that summer that she'd gone out early in the morning. Hideo must have known something was going on, but she didn't pry because she trusted Harumi.

She rode the familiar route at a familiar pace. Before long, she was at her destination.

The Namiya General Store was surrounded by a light mist, the aftermath of last night's rain. She made sure no one was around and walked down the alley alongside the house. The first time, she'd been really nervous, but she had since gotten used to the system.

Around back was a second entrance, and bolted to its wall was a beat-up milk crate. She inhaled deeply, exhaled, and lifted the lid. Inside, like all the other times, she found an envelope.

She let out a long exhale in relief.

Out from the alley, she hopped back on her bike and headed home. What would the third letter have to say? She pedaled hard; she wanted to be home as soon as possible, to open it and see for herself.

Harumi Muto had come back home on the second Saturday in August. She had lucked out that her day job and her side gig at the club in Shinjuku had set their Bon break for the same week. If the two breaks had not perfectly overlapped, she may not have been able to make the trip.

At the company, she couldn't expect to get time off before or after Bon. They would probably deny her request. The club, on the other hand, had no problem with her taking extra days, as long as she gave them enough notice. But Harumi didn't want to take any days off; she wanted to work every day she could.

To call this place her home wouldn't tell the whole story. This wasn't where she was born. The family placard on the front gate read TAMURA.

When she was five, Harumi lost her parents in a car crash. It was an uncanny collision; a truck crossed over the median into their lane. Harumi was in preschool, rehearsing for a school play. She had no recollection of when she heard the news. She was sure she'd been overwhelmed with sadness, but the memory had slipped free in one clean piece. The same goes for the six months she supposedly went without speaking to anyone. She knew about this only from what she had been told after the fact.

It wasn't that she had no relatives, but she barely ever saw them. She wouldn't have expected anyone to rush to take her in, but that was when the Tamuras held out their hands and welcomed her in.

Hideo Tamura was the sister of her maternal grandmother, which made her Harumi's great-aunt. Harumi's grandfather had died during the war, and her grandmother had fallen ill and passed away soon after. Like an angel sent from heaven, Hideo rescued Harumi and treated her as her own when there was no one else to count on. Harumi's great-uncle was just as kind and good.

But those happy days would not last for long. The Tamuras had only one daughter, but she showed up unannounced with her husband and their children one day to live at home. Later, she heard that the husband had lost everything in a business venture and accumulated an exorbitant amount of debt, and they lost the house they lived in.

Just before entering elementary school, Harumi was given over to the children's home. "I'll come and get you soon." That's what her great-aunt said the day she dropped her off.

Six years later, she came as promised. Her daughter's family had finally moved on. On her first day back, Harumi saw her great-aunt kneeling before the family altar and praying.

"It feels like a huge weight has been taken from my shoulders. I can finally face you again," she whispered to a picture of her sister.

Diagonally across from their house lived the Kitazawas. They had a daughter, Shizuko, who was three years older than Harumi.

When Harumi had lived here previously, Shizuko had played with her fairly often. Now that she was back, ready to go to middle school, Shizuko was entering high school. When Harumi saw her for the first time in ages, Shizuko had something mature about her that Harumi didn't have yet.

From that day on, the two of them were practically inseparable. Shizuko doted on Harumi like a little sister, and Harumi thought of her as the older sister she never had. With their houses so close, they could hang out anytime they liked.

Even now, she was looking forward to seeing Shizuko when she came home.

Shizuko was a fourth-year student at a college specializing in physical education. She had been fencing since high school and became strong enough to vie for a position on the Olympic team. Most of the time, she commuted to college from home, but once she became an elite athlete, her practice regimen went into overdrive; it wasn't odd for her to be away from home for weeks on end with frequent travel overseas.

But this summer, Shizuko was just hanging around the house. The Moscow Olympics had finally been boycotted by the Japanese government. When Harumi heard the news, she worried Shizuko would be devastated, but it turned out that her worry had been groundless.

Shizuko was in good spirits when Harumi saw her during Bon. There was no avoiding the topic of the Olympics, and Shizuko didn't try to change the subject. She told Harumi she had failed to make the final cut for the Olympic team, but she was lighthearted about it all. "I feel sorry for the athletes who did get picked," Shizuko said in a lowered voice. She had always been kind.

It had been about two years since Harumi had last seen Shizuko. Once slender and svelte, her friend had bulked out considerably and exuded the latent energy of an athlete. Her shoulders were broad, and her biceps were more developed than most of the rail-thin guys around town. *To qualify for the Olympics*, thought Harumi, *you have to have a special kind of body.*

"My mother's always saying the room gets cramped when I walk in," joked Shizuko. She squinted a little, making a wrinkle just above her nose. She was always doing that.

Harumi first heard about the Namiya General Store one night when they were walking home from a Bon dance in town, dressed in festive *yukata* robes. They were talking about their dreams for the future and marriage, when Harumi asked Shizuko, "Hey, if you had to pick one, which would it be—fencing or romance?" She had meant to get a rise out of her. It worked.

Shizuko stopped dead and looked Harumi straight in the eye. The light in her eyes was full of sincerity. She began to weep.

"Hey, wait, what's wrong? Did I say something to upset you? I'm sorry. I didn't mean to make you feel bad," she apologized hastily.

But Shizuko shook her head and wiped her tears on the floral sleeve of her *yukata*. "It's fine. I'm sorry I scared you. It's fine. I'm fine." She shook her head and started walking.

They were quiet after that. The walk started to feel very long.

Then Shizuko stopped short again.

"Hey, Harumi, want to take the long way home?"

"The long way? Sure. But where're we going?"

"You'll see when we're there. Don't worry; it isn't far."

Shizuko led Harumi up a few streets to a small, old shop. They stood outside. The sign read NAMIYA GENERAL STORE. The shutter was down, but it was hard to say if the store was closed for the night or closed for good.

"Do you know about this place?" asked Shizuko.

"Namiya... I feel like I must've heard that name before somewhere."

"'Let me answer your questions! Namiya!'" Shizuko sang.

"Oh, right, Namiya!" she cried. "Yeah, I remember people saying that in school. So this is where it came from..."

She'd first heard rumors in middle school, but she'd never been by until now.

"The store itself went out of business, but they're still doing the advice thing."

"Whoa, really?"

Shizuko nodded. "I mean, just the other day, I got some good advice."

Harumi looked at her wide-eyed. "No way."

"I haven't told this to anyone else, but I know I can tell you. I mean, you've already seen me cry tonight."

When she said it, her eyes teared up again.

Shizuko's story caught Harumi off guard. She was surprised enough to hear her friend had fallen in love with her former fencing coach and was considering marriage, but what shocked her most of all was hearing that the man was no longer alive, and that Shizuko had trained for the Olympics knowing he was about to die.

"There is no way I could have done that," Harumi admitted. "I mean, when the man you love is dying, I don't see how you can spend all your time on sports."

"That's because you don't know how things were with us," Shizuko said. Her face and tone were at peace. "He knew his life was almost over, but that made him want to spend what little time was left on prayer. Praying that my dream, his dream, would come true. Once I understood that, I didn't worry anymore."

Shizuko said her worry had gone away thanks to the Namiya General Store.

"He's an amazing guy. No tricks, no bullshit. I mean, when I told him about my problem, he practically bopped me on the head. But he forced me to figure things out and see that I was getting in my own way. He's the reason why I was finally able to stop worrying and throw myself into the training."

"Really..."

Perusing the battered shutter of the store, Harumi was overtaken by a curious observation. It didn't look as though someone could have possibly been living here.

"I know what you're thinking," said Shizuko, "but it is real. I don't think anyone is here most of the time. He must come by at night to collect the letters. Once he has his answer, he leaves it in the milk crate. It's there by morning."

"Unreal." *Why would anyone go to all the trouble?* she wondered. But this was coming from Shizuko. It must be true.

That night, she couldn't rid the Namiya General Store from her mind, and for good reason. Harumi had a big problem, and she didn't have anyone who could give her advice.

In a word, her problem was financial.

Though Hideo had never mentioned it directly, the finances of the Tamura family were in rough shape. If their household were a boat, it would be minutes from slipping under. By bailing bucket after bucket from the cabin, they had somehow stayed afloat, but they couldn't keep up the bucket brigade forever.

Once upon a time, the Tamuras had been a family of substantial means, owning a great deal of property in the area, but over the years, most of the land was sold off to clear their daughter's liabilities. Once they paid everything off, their daughter moved on, and they were able to welcome Harumi back into their home.

But that was not the end of the hard times for the Tamuras. The previous year, Harumi's great-uncle had a stroke and fell. He could barely move the right side of his body.

This was what compelled Harumi to move to Tokyo to start

working. She felt a duty to support her guardians in their old age, but with almost all her salary eaten up by living expenses, the thought of being any sort of aid to the Tamuras was a pipe dream.

She had her first encounter with the nightlife industry during this period of emotional crisis. If the offer had come at any other time, she wouldn't have ceded. To be honest, she thought working as a hostess was beneath her.

But things changed. She now thought she should quit her job and hostess full-time so she could give back to the Tamuras in their time of need.

Can I really ask for advice about this? Won't it be an annoying problem to have to respond to? Harumi sat at the desk she'd used since middle school and thought it over.

But then again, Shizuko's problem had been quite difficult as well, and the Namiya General Store had solved her conundrum brilliantly. She should expect to get some kind of advice on her dilemma.

There's no use worrying about this. Just write it. With that, Harumi began her correspondence with the Namiya General Store.

But when she showed up at the store to put her letter in the mail slot, she hesitated. Would she really get a response? Shizuko said she conducted her exchange the year before. What would happen if the house had been abandoned, and Harumi's letter was left sitting on the floor?

Ah, what the hell, she thought, and she slipped the letter in the mail slot anyway. It didn't have her name on it. Not her real name anyway. If someone found it and read it, it wasn't as if they could trace it back to her.

But the next morning, she went back to check the milk bin and found an envelope inside. Of course she didn't want it to be empty, but it felt bizarre to hold this letter in her hands.

When she read the message, she realized Shizuko wasn't kidding. The Namiya General Store didn't sugarcoat a thing. This was straight talk. Unreserved, insensitive. It almost felt as if he was intentionally trying to piss her off.

"That's how Mr. Namiya gets the job done," Shizuko had told her. "He gets you to speak your mind and encourages you to discover the right path on your own."

Even so, Harumi found the response a little too rude. Mr. Namiya had already decided that she was so eager to consider this avenue because she had lost her senses to the allure of being a hostess. Nothing more.

She wrote back with a rebuttal straightaway, saying she wasn't going to quit her job and go full-time as a hostess just so she could have a decadent lifestyle; she had a dream to start her own club someday.

But the letter she got from the Namiya General Store in return infuriated her even more. Unbelievably, he had dared to question her level of commitment. If she really wanted to repay her guardians for their kindness, why not get married and raise a family? The letter had really gone off the deep end.

Harumi felt that this miscommunication was on her. By leaving out the vital details, she had failed to get her point across.

For her third letter, she made an effort to open up a little. She clarified the details of her upbringing, the dire circumstances of her guardians. She delved deeper into her plans.

How would the Namiya General Store react? Half eager to hear, half scared to know, she pushed the letter through the mail slot.

Back home, breakfast was long since ready. She sat on the tatami at the low table and ate her meal. Her great-uncle was lying down in the next room. Hideo was feeding him rice porridge from a spoon and having him sip cold tea from a feeding cup. As Harumi observed them, she felt her sense of urgency all over again. She had to help them; she had to do something.

After breakfast, she went upstairs to her old room. She took the letter from her pocket and sat in the chair at her desk. Unfolding the pages, she saw the usual chicken scratches.

But the letter itself was utterly different from everything she'd seen so far.

Dear Dubious Doggy,

I've gone through your third letter. It's clear you're in a very difficult situation, and you're determined to get to a point where you can give back to those who've helped you. In that vein, I have a few more questions.

- *Are you sure you can trust the person who wants you to be his lover? You've said this man had a hand in setting up a bunch of businesses, but have you asked him what they're called, and how exactly he was involved? If you can get him to take you to one of them to visit, go outside regular business hours and ask the staff about their experience with him.*

- *Do you have any sort of written guarantee that this man will help you start your club, no matter what? Would he keep his promise even if his wife found out about the affair?*

- *Do you plan to keep on with this man indefinitely? What will you do if you fall in love with someone else?*

- *You've said you're working as a hostess to build up financial resources so that someday you can open your own club. Would you consider making money some other way? Or is there a reason you need to do it as a hostess?*

- *What if I told you there was a way you could make all the money you wanted without working as a hostess? Would you be willing to do what I say? There's a chance I may advise you to quit working as a hostess and stop dating creepy dudes.*

Please write back one more time with your answers to these questions. Once I have your answers, I'll see if I can help you make your dreams come true.

I bet you're finding this pretty hard to swallow. But I promise I'm not trying to deceive you. Remember, even if I were to deceive you, I would get nothing out of it. You can trust me.

But a word of caution.

I can only go back and forth with you until September 13. After that, it will no longer be possible to reach me.

—*Namiya General Store*

5

Once Harumi had seen the third group of customers to the door, Maya pulled her into the staff-only powder room. Maya was four years older.

She shut the door behind them and grabbed Harumi's hair by the roots. "You think because you're young you get a free pass?"

Harumi's face was tight with pain. "What do you mean?"

"What do I mean? I saw you making eyes at my man." Maya bared her teeth. Her lips were glossy with red lipstick.

"At who? I wasn't doing anything."

"Don't play dumb. I saw you cuddling up with Mr. Sato. I'm the one who brought that geezer here from my last job."

Mr. Sato? Harumi couldn't believe this. *Make eyes at that old fat-ass? Please.*

"He came over and said hi," she explained. "I was just being polite."

"You liar. You were getting all cute with him and shit."

"We're hostesses. It's our job to be friendly."

"Stuff it." Maya let go of her scalp and shoved Harumi in the chest. Harumi's back slammed against the wall. "Next time I won't be so nice. Hear me?"

Maya laughed at her and left the powder room.

Harumi looked at herself in the mirror. Her hair was a mess. She combed it back into place with her fingers and made a conscious effort to relax the muscles of her face. She couldn't let this kind of thing unsettle her.

Outside the powder room, she was asked to sit at a table with three men who looked well-off.

"Why, hello, here's another young one." The man addressing her had a lecherous laugh and a gleaming scalp. He looked Harumi up and down.

"Good evening," she responded, looking the man in the eye. "I'm Miharu. It's a pleasure." She sat beside him.

One of her older coworkers who was already seated at the table made a fake laugh and gave Harumi a cold stare. This girl had chided Harumi before, too, telling her to stop making herself stand out so much.

Yeah, whatever, she thought. *If you can't get a customer's attention at this job, what's the point?*

A little while later, Shinji Tomioka showed up alone. He was wearing a gray suit with a red tie. Fit, and with no hint of a beer belly, he hardly looked like he was forty-six.

As expected, Harumi was called over to sit with him.

"There's a classy bar in Akasaka," Tomioka whispered. He took a sip of his whiskey and water and lowered his voice even further. "They're open till five, and they have wines from all over the world. They just got in some choice caviar and asked me to come try it. Care to join me later?"

Harumi was intrigued, but she pressed her palms together and made a cutesy bow. "I'm so sorry. I can't be late tomorrow."

He made a dour expression and sighed loudly. "That's exactly why you need to quit that job. What do they do again?"

"We're a stationery manufacturer."

"What do *you* do? Just desk work, right?"

Harumi nodded, though it technically wasn't even that. More like grunt work.

"How are you going to get ahead, stuck making minimum wage? You're only young once. You need to make the best of these years if you want your dreams to come true."

She nodded again and looked straight at Tomioka. "By the way, if I recall correctly, you said you'd take me to that dinner club in Ginza. The one you said you helped get off the ground."

"Ah, that's right. Sure, whenever you like. When works?"

"If possible, I'd like to visit outside business hours."

"Why?"

"For future reference. I want to ask the staff about their experiences and see what things are like behind the scenes."

Tomioka's face clouded. "Not sure that's gonna fly."

"What's wrong?"

"I like to draw a line between work and play. And being close with the owner doesn't give me the right to barge in with someone who's unaffiliated with the restaurant. It might upset the staff."

"Ah… That makes sense. I didn't mean to impose. I'm sorry." Harumi looked down.

"But there's no reason we can't go as regular customers. Let's go sometime soon." The life returned to his face.

That night, Harumi made it to her apartment in Koenji a little after three. Tomioka saw her home in a taxi.

"I'm not going to invite myself upstairs." This was his favorite line. "Think over what I proposed."

The romantic agreement. Harumi laughed in lieu of giving an answer.

Upstairs, the first thing she did was drink a cup of water. She went to the club four nights a week. On nights she worked, this was around the time when she got home. That left only three days when she was home in time to visit the bathhouse.

She removed her makeup, washed her face, and sat down to have a look at her planner. There was a big meeting in the morning, and she had to arrive half an hour earlier than usual. This left a mere four hours for sleep.

Harumi dropped her planner in her bag and pulled out an envelope. She unfolded the pages and sighed. She'd read the letter so many times she had it essentially memorized. But she still read it once a day. This was the third letter she had received from the Namiya General Store.

Are you sure you can trust the person who wants you to be his lover?

Harumi had been harboring the same doubts, but she pushed it from her mind. She would rather not dwell on it. If Tomioka was all talk, it would put her even further from realizing her ambitions.

The Namiya General Store was right to be skeptical. If she became romantically involved with Tomioka and his wife found out, could she really expect him to offer her assistance? Unlikely. Who would expect otherwise?

His behavior that evening had been suspect. On its own, it isn't strange to say you like to draw a line between work and play, but Tomioka was the one who had proposed the visit to the dinner club to show off his accomplishments in the first place.

Maybe she couldn't rely on him after all. But in that case, what was she supposed to do about the future?

She read through the letter yet again. One part said: *What if I told you there was a way you could make all the money you wanted without working as a hostess? Would you be willing to do what I say?* It went on to say: *Once I have your answers, I'll see if I can help you make your dreams come true.*

What was going on here? How could he expect her to believe a word of this? It made him sound like a con man with a get-rich-quick scheme. Under any other circumstance, she would have tossed the letter in the trash.

But this was a letter from the Namiya General Store. Mr. Namiya had solved Shizuko's predicament, and even if he hadn't, he would have earned her trust based on how he had conducted their exchange thus far. He didn't mince words or fuss over her reactions. His direct style came right at you, clumsy but genuine.

This letter was clear on one thing: He had nothing to gain by tricking Harumi. All the same, she still found the whole idea hard to believe. If making money were so easy, no one would need to struggle. And more importantly, Mr. Namiya would be a millionaire himself.

Harumi's trip home had come to an end before she had time to respond. She was back in Tokyo, back to working as a hostess and at the office. Back to living two lives out of one body. And that body was taking a beating. Once every couple of days at the office, she would tell herself, "That's it—I'm done."

Harumi checked the calendar on the table. Another thing was on her mind. Today was Wednesday, September 10.

The last letter had mentioned they could correspond only until September 13. After that, she would have no way of reaching him. The thirteenth was this Saturday. What was so special about that day? Was he retiring from giving out advice?

She figured she may as well answer his questions. She wanted to hear what he had to say, for one thing, and she could decide whether to follow through afterwards. Even if she made a promise, it didn't mean she had to keep it. If she broke her promise and kept on working as a hostess, he would have no way of knowing.

Before bed, she peeked into the mirror and found a pimple by her lip. It had been far too long since she'd had a proper night's sleep. If she quit her day job, she thought, she could sleep past noon.

*   *   *

When she got off work on Friday, September 12, Harumi headed to the Tamura house. She took the night off at the club.

Harumi showing up at home less than a month after the break came as a surprise to the Tamuras, but they were thrilled. On her last visit, she and her great-uncle hadn't had much of a chance to talk. That night at dinner, she caught him up on things. Needless to say, she told neither of them about working as a hostess.

"Any trouble making rent, utilities? If you come up short, do-don't hesitate tuh…to ask." He had to fight to get his words out. He let Hideo handle all their finances, meaning he had no idea what dire circumstances they were in.

"I'll be fine, as long as I budget," she assured him. "The good news is I've been so busy lately that I've had no time to relax, which makes it hard to spend anything."

No time to relax—that was the truth.

After dinner, she took a bath. Through the screened windows of the bathroom, she looked up into the night sky. The moon was full and high, predicting that the next day would be a sunny one.

What would she learn from the next letter?

On her way home to the Tamura house, Harumi had stopped by the Namiya General Store. She left a letter in the mail slot saying she couldn't care less about being a hostess, and if he knew some other way she might attain financial independence, she would turn down the proposed affair and quit working at the club and do whatever else he said.

The next day was the thirteenth. Regardless of what he had to say, she would have no chance to question it: This was the end of their exchange. She'd have to make her plans based on whatever the last letter said.

The next morning, it was before seven when she woke—or, more aptly put, when she got sick of tossing and turning between bouts of shallow sleep and kicked herself out of bed.

Her great-aunt was already up fixing breakfast. A stench wafted over from the tatami room. Hideo must have been assisting her great-uncle with cleaning his nether regions; he couldn't go to the bathroom on his own.

Harumi told Hideo she was off to get some fresh air and left the house. She hopped on her bike and pedaled the route she'd come to know so well that summer.

Before long, she was in front of the Namiya General Store. A holdout from another era. The storefront looked as if it had been waiting for her to come. She went down the alley alongside the building.

Inside the wooden box, she found the envelope. Her heart was besieged by hope and distress, suspicion and curiosity. When she reached inside the bin to grab the letter, the surge of feelings made her hand throb.

The ride home tested her patience. Passing a park, she slammed on the brakes, looked around to make sure she was alone, and read the letter without even climbing off her bike.

Dear Dubious Doggy,

Thank you for your letter. I'm glad you're willing to trust me.

Of course, I have no way of confirming that you mean what you say. There's a chance you only want to see what my mysterious advice is. But at this point, it doesn't matter. I'll have to take your word for it.

So, how will you fulfill this dream of yours?

Two things: study and save.

For the next five years, learn everything you can about economics and finance. In particular, focus on securities and real estate. To do this justice, you'll need to quit your day job. In the meantime, you may as well keep working as a hostess.

You're going to save up to purchase property. The closer to Tokyo, the better. Land, apartments, houses, anything is fair game. It's okay if it's on the smaller side or old and dingy. Just make sure you've purchased something by 1985. This isn't for you to live in.

In 1986, Japan is going to enter a period of unprecedented economic growth. Real estate will skyrocket across the board. Sell what you've bought and use the profit to buy something more expensive. This, too, will increase in value. Do this over and over and invest the money in stocks. Here's where your education in securities comes in. Between 1986 and 1989, you can't go wrong with any of the major brands.

Equity memberships for golf courses are another promising investment. The sooner you buy in, the better.

There's just one catch: You will only see good returns from these investments until 1988 or 1989. Things are going to change dramatically in 1990. Even if it looks like prices are still rising, you must liquidate everything. It's like the card game Old Maid. Timing makes all the difference between success and failure. Just believe me and do it.

After that, the Japanese economy is going to tank. Whatever you do, get out of investing. Nothing good with come of it. Use the money you've made to start some kind of business.

By now, you must be pretty skeptical. How can I be so certain about what's going to happen in the years ahead? Does this guy think he can predict the course of the Japanese economy?

Yes. Unfortunately, I can't explain why. You probably wouldn't believe me even if I did. Think of me as a very good fortune-teller. Whatever floats your boat.

With that, allow me to predict some things a little further down the line.

I mentioned the Japanese economy will fall apart, but that doesn't mean there'll be no room for hopes and dreams. The 1990s will offer you a chance to make it big on a different kind of business.

All over the world, computers are going to become a necessity of life. Pretty soon, every household, then every person, is going to have one. These computers will be connected over a huge network, and people all over the planet will be able to share information instantly. Everyone will have portable telephones, and before long, all these phones will be connected to this network of computers.

You must get involved as soon as possible in an industry that capitalizes on this network. This will be essential to your success. You could use the network to advertise for companies or stores, or to sell products directly. The possibilities are endless.

It's your choice whether to believe me. But don't forget what I said in the beginning. I don't have a single thing to gain from tricking you. I sat down and thought seriously about how I could help you live the life you want to live. This is the best I could come up with.

I wish there was more I could do. But we're already out of time. This will be our last correspondence. I won't be able to receive another letter.

It's up to you whether to believe me. But I want you to believe. I'm praying from the bottom of my heart that you'll believe me.

—Namiya General Store

Harumi was dumbstruck. The letter was more than she had bargained for.

This was a prophesy. And it was brimming with certainty.

From where she stood in 1980, the Japanese economy was nowhere near an upswing. The damage from the oil shock had yet to run its course, and even college graduates were struggling to find work.

But according to this letter, the country was due for unprecedented economic growth in just a matter of years.

She simply couldn't believe it. He had to be pulling her leg.

But there was truth to what he had written before. There was no way lying about all of this could benefit Mr. Namiya.

This letter didn't stop at prognosticating the economy. It made all sorts of suppositions about the future of technology. No, *supposition* made it sound as if these were theories. The letter read like a list of cold, hard facts.

Computer networks and portable telephones—this was not the world she knew. True, they were only twenty years shy of the twenty-first century. She would probably see all kinds of technologies become an everyday reality, even innovations she'd previously only dreamed of. But the letter sounded like something from an anime or a sci-fi novel.

Harumi fretted the whole day. By night, she had fretted herself out and sat down at her desk. She pulled out some stationery and wrote another letter. It went without saying that she was writing to the Namiya General Store. She knew she wasn't supposed to be able to reach him, but it was still September 13. As long as she got there before midnight, maybe she would have a chance.

The letter said she wanted to know what he was basing his predictions on. Even if it was going to be hard to believe, she wanted to know. Once she did, she could decide what to do next.

A little before eleven, she tiptoed out of the house and pedaled through the night to the store.

When she arrived out front, she checked her watch. It was only five minutes past eleven. She was safe.

But she was barely a few steps off her bike when she got a good look at the building and stopped dead.

She knew, right then and there, that it was all over.

The otherworldly aura that previously enveloped the store had dissolved into the night. Before her was nothing more than a general store, out of business and unremarkable. Harumi couldn't explain why she was so certain. But her confidence was unshakable.

This letter was not going in the mail slot. She climbed onto her bike and rode home.

About four months later, she confirmed that she had made the right decision. Home for New Year's, Harumi had gone with Shizuko to a neighborhood shrine for her first visit of the year. Shizuko had found a job, starting in the spring at the corporate headquarters of a big-name supermarket. Which meant fencing would not be among her responsibilities. She said she was done competing.

"But you worked so hard," Harumi lamented. Shizuko shook her head and smiled.

"I took fencing as far as it would go for me. When I was training for Moscow, I gave it everything I could. I think that up in heaven, he understands that." Shizuko looked up at the sky. "It's time for me to start thinking about the future. I want to make a good impression at the company, but once I'm settled in, I'll find myself a good man."

"A man?"

"Yep. I'm ready to get married and have a healthy baby." Shizuko laughed mischievously and made that signature wrinkle above her nose. Her smile showed no trace of the sadness of losing a lover in the past year.

What a strong woman. Harumi was impressed.

On their way home from the shrine, Shizuko exclaimed "Oh yeah," as if she'd just remembered something. "Do you remember last summer how I said there was this funny little store that gave out free advice?"

"Sure," Harumi responded nervously. "Namiya, right?" She hadn't mentioned their exchange to anyone, not even Shizuko.

"Yeah. Well, they closed for good. Its elderly owner passed away. I saw a guy taking pictures out front and asked what happened. He said he was the old man's son."

"Wow. When was that?"

"October. He said his dad had died the month before."

Harumi gulped. "So, September?"

"I guess so, yeah."

"What day?"

"He didn't say. Why?"

"Oh. Just asking."

"The store itself closed down when he got sick, but he kept on giving out advice. What's crazy is I think I must've been the last one. The thought of it makes me get kind of emotional."

No, it was me; I was the last one. As much as Harumi wanted to say it aloud, she held back. It occurred to her the old man had probably died the night of September 13. He must have said that was the last day he could communicate with her because he knew that would be the last day of his life.

If this was true, and the old man had predicted his own death, it meant his powers of clairvoyance were not to be discounted.

But that would mean...

She felt her imagination dilate and expand.

What if the last letter was all true?

6

December 1988.

Harumi was sitting in a room decked out with oil paintings, ready to sign a bill of sale for a certain property. The past few years, she'd been through this rigmarole countless times. Six-figure purchases barely fazed her anymore. This particular property wasn't even that expensive. Nevertheless, she felt a nervousness she was not prepared for. She'd never been so emotionally invested in purchasing a piece of real estate before.

Wearing a two-piece suit from Dunhill that would have been a steal at two hundred thousand yen, the agent turned to face Harumi. His skin was the color of whole wheat; she figured he must frequent tanning salons.

"As long as there are no objections, please sign here and stamp your seal on this line."

They had borrowed a room at the Shinjuku branch of a major bank, one that her company used to take out its loans. Apart from the man in Dunhill, who served as mediator, she was joined by Hideo Tamura and Kimiko Kozuka, the sellers of the property, along with Kimiko's husband, Shigekazu. Kimiko had turned fifty the year before. Her hair was showing streaks of white.

Harumi looked at each of the sellers. Both Hideo and Kimiko hung their heads. Shigekazu, disconsolate, refused to look at anyone. *What a sorry excuse for a man*, thought Harumi. *If you have a problem, at least have the balls to glare at me.*

She took a pen from her bag. "No objections." She signed and stamped the form.

"Thank you very much for your time," said the Dunhill man. "That just about wraps things up. Congratulations." He gathered up the documents, looking quite satisfied with himself. And why shouldn't he be? It was a quick job, but it earned him a tall fee.

Both sides took their copies of the forms. Shigekazu scooted back his chair and stood. Kimiko was staring down at the table. Harumi extended her hand. Kimiko was taken aback.

"We're finished. Let's shake on it."

"Oh, okay." Kimiko squeezed her hand. "Uh, I'm sorry."

"For what?" laughed Harumi. "There's no need to apologize. Everyone benefits from this."

"I guess. I mean, that's true, but..." Kimiko wouldn't look her in the eye, either.

"Hey," barked Shigekazu, "come on. Let's get out of here."

"All right." Kimiko nodded and turned to her mother. Her eyes were lost.

"Don't worry about Auntie," Harumi said. Even though Hideo was her great-aunt, she'd always called her that. "I'll take her home."

"Really? I might just take you up on that. Is that okay with you?"

"I don't mind either way," said Hideo quietly.

"Okay, then. Take care, Harumi."

Before she could say "You too," Shigekazu was out the door. Kimiko, a little penitent, nodded once and followed after him.

Outside the bank, Harumi walked Hideo to her BMW, parked in a nearby lot, and drove her home. But strictly speaking, the house was no longer Hideo's. The Tamura family residence was now Harumi's property. The contract they just signed made it official.

Her great-uncle had died of old age that spring, leaving this world on a futon soaked with urine. Hideo's extended tenure as his caregiver was finally over.

The question had been on Harumi's mind since she first heard that he hadn't had much time to live. What would happen to the house?

The Tamuras had once possessed a number of assets, but the house was the only one they had left.

Real estate prices had been rising in Japan for three years straight. Located two hours from Tokyo, the Tamura house was a bit out of the way, but the property was plenty valuable. Which meant Kimiko and especially Shigekazu had their eyes on it. Those two had fallen back into some shady dealings, but it didn't look like things were going well.

It was the day after they participated in another Buddhist service for her great-uncle, forty-nine days after his death. Kimiko called her mother, as if on cue. She was hoping to discuss the inheritance.

Kimiko proposed that since the house had been her father's only asset, they could split it down the middle. Since they couldn't cut a building in half, they'd transfer the deed to Kimiko, who would have an expert appraise the property and pay Hideo for her half. Hideo could, of course, continue living there, but she would need to pay rent. To make things easy, Kimiko could deduct the rent from what she owed Hideo. Everything would even out.

The deal was legally sound and at first glance even sounded fair, but when Harumi heard Hideo explain it, she smelled something fishy. The end result would be Kimiko seizing total control of the property without paying a thing to Hideo. And Kimiko could sell it out from under her anytime. This wasn't some random tenant. It was her own mother. There were plenty of ways to get her out of the house. If she took that route, she would be obligated to pay Hideo for her portion of the property, but she must have known that her mother wouldn't take her to court if she tried to pay it off piecemeal.

Harumi didn't want to think that this wicked plan had been hatched by Hideo's own daughter. Shigekazu must have been behind it.

Harumi proposed Hideo and Kimiko become co-owners of the property, which she would buy from both of them. They would split the money down the middle, and Harumi would let Hideo go on living in the house as usual.

When Harumi explained her plan to Kimiko, Shigekazu remonstrated, as expected. "What's wrong with what we proposed?" he asked.

But Hideo had this to say: "I think it's best for everyone if Harumi buys the house. I hope you can excuse me for being so selfish."

Shigekazu had no rebuttal. He hadn't had any right to speak in the first place.

Once Harumi had driven Hideo back to their house, she opted to spend the night. She would need to head out early in the morning. Her company was closed on Saturdays, but she had to focus on executing a big project. She was presiding over a party cruise around Tokyo Bay. Some holiday revelry for Christmas Eve. The two hundred tickets for it had sold out almost instantly.

Lying on her futon, Harumi gazed up at the familiar markings on her ceiling and lost herself in reverie. She still couldn't believe that this house was hers now. It was a different feeling from what she felt when she purchased her apartment.

This purchase was not intended as a real estate investment. When Hideo passed away, she would hold on to it in one form or another. Maybe she'd use it as her second home.

Everything was going splendidly. So much so that it was frightening. It almost felt as if someone was protecting her.

Well, it had all started with that letter.

She closed her eyes, and those unique words appeared before her. That last mysterious letter from the Namiya General Store.

The letter was too much to handle all at once, but after much deliberation, Harumi had resolved to follow its advice. No other plan of action came to mind. She had realized she couldn't bet her livelihood one the likes of Tomioka, and no harm could come from studying economics.

She quit her day job and started taking classes at a technical college. During any extra time she had, she studied stocks and real estate and obtained a handful of certifications.

At night, she worked harder than ever as a hostess, but she resolved to be out of the industry in seven years. By giving herself a self-imposed expiration date, she became more focused than ever.

There was an almost comically proportionate return on how much effort she put in at the club. In no time, she had more regulars than any of the other girls and registered an all-time high in sales. Tomioka stopped coming after she rejected him, but she easily accounted for the loss. Later, she found that his claim to have had a hand in setting up a number of businesses was hyperbole at best. A few people had asked for his opinion, and that was the extent of his contributions.

In July 1985, Harumi threw her hat into the ring. Over the course of a few years, she'd amassed over thirty million yen in savings and finally coughed up the cash to purchase an apartment. It was an old building in Yotsuya. There was no way it was going to go for any cheaper, and she made the purchase knowing she'd face no major financial losses.

A few months later, economies the world over suffered seismic upheaval. Because of the Plaza Accord, the yen appreciated, and the dollar took a nosedive. Harumi had goosebumps. The Japanese economy depended on its export industries. If the yen continued to skyrocket, the country could plummet into a depression.

By now, Harumi was dabbling in stocks. She knew if the market slumped, the value of her stocks would fall. How could this be happening? It was the complete opposite of what the Namiya General Store had predicted.

But things did not take a turn for the worse. Facing a slump, the Japanese government issued an easy money policy and pledged to increase its investment in public enterprises.

Then in the summer of 1986, she got a call. It was the real estate office who had brokered her first apartment. "It appears you haven't moved in yet," they noted, "but we're just calling to see if you have any plans to do so anytime soon."

Harumi responded vaguely. The agent said that if she was interested in selling, they would like to buy it back.

It was happening. The real estate market was on the rise.

She said she wasn't interested and hung up. Instead, she went straight to the bank. She wanted to see how much she could borrow with her apartment as collateral. Later that week, when they called her in to talk about the numbers, she was flabbergasted. The property was worth 50 percent more than what she paid for it.

She applied for a loan and started browsing other properties. She found a modest building near Waseda and bought it with the money from the bank. In a short time, that value shot up, too. Prices were going up so fast that the interest rates were barely a concern.

Now she borrowed again, using the second property as collateral. At this point, the loan officer suggested that she start a company. It would be easier to manage her finances that way. This was the birth of "Office Little Dog."

Harumi was convinced. The Namiya General Store's prediction had come true.

Through the fall of 1987, Harumi flipped apartment buildings. In some cases, property values tripled in a year.

As her stocks increased in price, her portfolio of assets began to swell and expand. She bid farewell to working at the club, but she cashed in on the contacts she had made there and turned her focus to event planning. She came up with ideas for events and dispatched party hostesses. The world was bubbling with prosperity, and somewhere every day someone was hosting an ostentatious soiree. She had no shortage of work.

In 1988, she assessed her holdings. She had buildings, stocks, equity memberships. The prices were hovering at what seemed to be a ceiling. The conditions were still favorable, but she had better play it safe. Harumi trusted Mr. Namiya's word. He was spot-on with his comparison between investing and Old Maid. It would be far stranger if the boom went on forever.

There were only a few months left in 1988. What would the new year bring? Wondering endlessly, Harumi fell asleep.

7

The Christmas cruise turned out to be a huge success. Harumi toasted with the staff till morning, popping open more bottles of Dom Pérignon Rosé than she could count. The next morning, when she woke up at her place in Aoyama, she had to admit she could feel the wisps of a lingering headache.

She crawled out of bed and turned on the TV. The news was finishing a story. A building had caught fire. She had been watching in a daze, but when she saw the letters run across the bottom of the screen, her eyes went wide. "Flames Cripple Children's Home Marumitsuen," it said.

Startled, she listened closely, but the segment was over. She changed the channel, but no one else was running the story.

She dressed in a hurry to go down and get the paper. The automatic locks of her building added an extra layer of security, but they meant she had to go down to the ground floor herself to fetch the newspaper.

It was Sunday; the paper was thick. Thicker with the flyers. Almost all for real estate.

She looked through every article, but there was nothing on the fire at Marumitsuen. Maybe because it had happened outside the city.

She called Hideo to see if she had heard anything, assuming it would at least have made the local paper. She was right. Hideo said there was an article in the Local News section.

The fire broke out on the evening of December 24. One fatality, ten wounded. The deceased wasn't someone from the building but an amateur musician who had been hired to play at their Christmas party.

She wanted to drop everything and go, but she held off, unsure how things would be there. If she barged in on an already chaotic scene, it would only make things worse.

Harumi had moved out of Marumitsuen when she graduated elementary school, but she'd been back to visit several times. She went to say a few words when she entered high school and after she had graduated and found a job. But ever since starting as a hostess, she had kept her distance. Something about her, some look or tone, might have betrayed her involvement in the industry.

The next day at the office, Harumi got a call from Hideo. The morning paper had more to say about the fire. The staff and children had taken refuge in the gymnasium of the nearby elementary school.

Living out of a gymnasium in late December… The very thought of it sent shivers down her spine.

She quit work early and drove her BMW to the scene. Along the way, she stopped at a pharmacy and bought a box of disposable hand warmers and some bottles of cold medicine. The kids were probably getting sick. There was a supermarket in the same lot, where she bought armfuls of prepared meals. The staff must have been stressed out trying to keep all of those kids fed with no kitchen.

She packed her shopping bags into the trunk and drove off. "Everyone's Song [*Minna no uta*]" by Southern All Stars was playing on the radio. The chorus was supposed to be uplifting, but it wasn't working. This had been a year of almost entirely good things, one after the other, only for this to happen at the very end.

The trip out to the building took her about two hours. The white walls of her childhood home had been reduced to blackened rubble. The police and fire departments were still conducting their investigations, preventing her from getting any closer, but from a distance, she could smell the reek of quenched flames and soot.

The gym was about half a mile away. The director, Yoshikazu Minazuki, was startled and effusively appreciative of her visit.

"Thanks for coming all the way out to see us. I never would have expected to see you today. You've grown into a fine young woman." Mr. Minazuki kept looking at the business card Harumi had given him. "A self-made woman, at that."

Mr. Minazuki looked much skinnier than she remembered. The fire must have taken its toll. By now, he had to be somewhere in his seventies. Last time they met, his white hair had been fluffy, but it had thinned out.

He gladly accepted the hand warmers, medicine, and food. She had guessed right about their being in need.

"If there's anything else I can do, please let me know. I want to do everything I can to help."

"Thank you. It's reassuring to hear that." His eyes were moist.

"Please don't hesitate to ask. I want to take this opportunity to give back for all you've done for me."

"Thank you," he repeated.

On her way out, Harumi ran into someone from her past: Hiroshi Fujikawa. He had been at the home the same time as she had been, but he was four years older and left right after graduating middle school. He was the one who made her the carved wooden dog she carried everywhere as a good-luck charm. The namesake of Office Little Dog.

Hiroshi had become a professional woodworker. He said he heard about the fire and rushed over, just like Harumi. He was just as she remembered him, still reticent as ever.

After saying good-bye, she realized there were probably lots of people like them who had heard the news with great concern.

In the first days of the new year, the emperor crossed the great divide, ushering in a new imperial generation—the Heisei era. The days that followed were far from normal: The usual programming was suspended from television, and the first sumo match of the year was delayed by a whole day.

Once things settled down, Harumi took another trip to Marumitsuen. Outside the gym, they had set up an office, where she met with Mr. Minazuki. The children were still living in the gym, but a temporary dormitory was under construction, and once it was done, the kids would move in while a proper structure was being rebuilt on the ruins of the old one.

The police and fire department had determined the cause of the fire: a gas leak from an antiquated pipe in the cafeteria. They assessed that the air was so dry that static electricity could have sparked the flame.

"We should have renovated before this ever happened," said Mr. Minazuki ruefully.

He seemed particularly grieved by the death of the musician. He had gone back in after one of the children, but the rescue was a beat too late for him to escape himself.

"It's a shame that man had to die," she tried to console him, "but with everything that happened, it's fortunate that all the children came out safe."

"I suppose you're right," Mr. Minazuki agreed, nodding. "Since it happened during the night, most of the kids were asleep when the fire started. One misstep, and it could have been catastrophic. That's why I was saying to the staff, I think our old director was watching over us."

"I think I remember her. It was a woman, right?"

Harumi vaguely recalled the former director, a petite old woman with a tranquil smile. At some point, she disappeared, and Mr. Minazuki took over.

"She was my older sister. She's the one who started Marumitsuen, you know."

Harumi looked at the wrinkles on his face. "I didn't realize."

"Really? I guess you were pretty little when you came to live with us."

"This is the first I've heard of it. Why did she start a children's home?"

"Long story short, she wanted to give back."

"She did?"

"I don't mean to brag, but factually speaking, our family used to have a lot of land and some decent assets. When our parents died, my sister and I inherited everything. I invested my portion in a company I started, but my sister used hers to create a space for kids who weren't so fortunate. She had been a teacher during the war, and it hurt her to see all those children lose their parents."

"When did you lose your sister?"

"Nineteen...no, I guess it would be twenty years ago now. She was born with a weak heart. Everyone was with her in the end. When she died, it was like she just fell asleep."

Harumi nodded. "I'm sorry. I had no idea."

"That doesn't surprise me. In her will, she asked us not to tell the children. We announced that she had gotten sick and was recuperating. I had my son take over my company, and I took over for my sister. For a while, we changed my title to interim director."

"What did you mean about your sister watching over you?"

"Before she died, she turned to me and whispered something. 'Don't worry,' she said. 'I'll pull some strings up there and make sure you're taken care of.' When the fire happened, those words came back to me." Mr. Minazuki gave her a bashful smile. "Maybe I'm just being superstitious."

"No, I think it's a wonderful story."

"I appreciate that."

"Did your sister have any family?"

He sighed and shook his head. "She never married, single her whole life. You might say she devoted her existence to the cause."

"Wow. What a strong woman."

"If she heard you up in heaven, I think she'd disagree. She saw it as living life on her own terms. And how about you? Do you have any plans to marry? You seeing anybody?"

Harumi faltered when he turned the conversation to her. "No, I don't have anyone like that." She waved her hand at the idea, totally dismissing it.

"Is that so? If a woman focuses too much on work, she'll miss her chance at marriage. Running your own business is all well and good, but you ought to try to find a decent man."

"I'm afraid I might wind up like your sister. I'm living life on my own terms."

Mr. Minazuki laughed. "Sounds like you're the strong one. But prioritizing work wasn't the reason why she didn't marry anyone. You know, in fact, when she was very young, she was involved with a man, and they almost eloped."

"Really?"

Things were getting interesting. Harumi scooched forward in her chair.

"The man was ten years older than her and worked at a small factory in town. They met when he fixed her bicycle for her, the story goes. They must have sneaked off together on his lunch breaks from the factory. Back then, the mere sight of a man and woman in public together was enough to set the rumor mill in motion."

"Were they trying to elope because your parents didn't approve?"

He nodded. "There were two main reasons. First off, my sister was still in high school. That wasn't so terrible, since time would have solved that problem. The other reason was the big one. As I mentioned earlier, we came from a family of considerable means. Once you have money, the next thing you want is respect. My father wanted her to marry into a good family. He wasn't about to pawn her off on some nobody mechanic."

Harumi's expression tensed. She drew in her chin. Back then, over sixty years ago, this sort of thing was probably not such a rare occurrence.

"So what happened when they ran away?"

Mr. Minazuki shrugged. "It didn't go so well. Her plan was to stop by the shrine on her way home from school and change out of her school clothes."

"Change into what?"

"There were a number of maids working at the house. One of them was almost the same age as my sister, and they were good friends. She asked the maid to bring a change of clothes over to the shrine. One of the maid's kimonos, since her fancy school clothes would attract too much attention. The mechanic was waiting at the station, in his best attempt at a disguise. If she had made it to him, they would have hopped aboard that steam engine and made a grand escape. Their strategy was pretty well thought out."

"So what went wrong?"

"It was awful. When my sister made it as far as the shrine, she didn't find the maid, but two men my father had hired to catch her. The maid had originally agreed to help my sister, but she got scared and asked an older maid for advice. You can imagine what happened next."

Harumi could see where the maid was coming from. Considering the time, you really couldn't blame her for spilling the beans.

"What happened to her boyfriend, the mechanic?"

"My father had a messenger take a letter from her to the station. The letter said: 'Forget I ever existed.' It was signed in her name."

"He had somebody forge her handwriting?"

"No, she had to write it herself. She didn't have a choice. My father had decided to let the man run, but he had an in with the police. If he had wanted to, he could have had him thrown in jail."

"What did the man do when he read the letter?"

Mr. Minazuki cocked his neck to the side.

"All I know for sure is that he left town. He wasn't local, you see. People said he went back to wherever it was he came from, but there's no way of knowing if that's true. But I did see him one more time."

"Really? What happened?"

"It was three years later. I was still a student. I left the house to go to school, and I'm walking along, when someone calls me from behind. I turn around, and there's this man, looks like he's maybe thirty. I had never seen the mechanic, only heard about him, so I had no idea who this guy was. But he holds out a letter and says, 'I want you to give this to Akiko.' That's my sister's name. Akiko."

"Did he know you were her younger brother?"

"I don't think he could have known for sure. I guess he followed me from the house. I hesitated, and he said, 'If you have any suspicions about its contents, by all means read it first, or show your parents, as long as you deliver this to her.' So I took it. To be honest, I wanted to see what it said."

"Did you read it?"

"Of course! It wasn't even sealed. I read it on the walk to school."

"What did it say?"

"Well…" He looked at Harumi. He appeared to be deciding something. He slapped his knee. "Know what? I'll let you see for yourself."

"You still have it?"

"Should be somewhere. Just a minute." Mr. Minazuki opened one of the boxes in the pile next to him and started rifling around. The box had *Director's Office* written on the side of it in black marker.

"My office was a fair distance from the kitchen, so there was hardly any damage from the fire. I had them bring all my files down here, and now that I have a little time on my hands, I'm going to try to get myself organized. A lot of this stuff was left to me. By my sister. Ah, found it. Here it is."

Mr. Minazuki pulled a square tin from the box. He opened it in front of her so she could see inside.

There were several notebooks with photographs scattered among them. From the pile, he extracted an envelope and put it down in front of Harumi. It was addressed to "Ms. Akiko Minazuki."

"Are you sure?"

"Absolutely. He wrote it knowing she wouldn't be the only one who read it."

"Okay, let's have a look, then."

Inside the envelope were several folded sheets of ivory stationery. Harumi smoothed them flat on the desk. The handwriting was exact and fluid. The product of a fountain pen. Not the script she was expecting from a mechanic.

> *Salutations.*
>
> *Please allow me to begin with an apology for my intrusive method of delivery. I was afraid that if I sent the letter via the mail, it would be thrown away upon arrival without ever being read.*
>
> *Akiko, I wonder how you are. This is Yuji. The Yuji who used to work at Kusunoki Machinery. Perhaps you've forgotten me already, but I would be grateful if you would read this letter to the end.*
>
> *I'm writing to you for one reason alone: to extend an apology. I've tried to do this several times before, but I'm afraid I'm skittish by nature, and I couldn't get myself to do it until now. I'm so sorry for everything that happened. I know it's too late now, but I need you to know how deeply I regret the stupidity of my own actions.*

You were still in high school, and I led you astray. When I look back now, I can see I was wholly in the wrong. What was I thinking, encouraging a girl like you to leave her family behind? There's simply no excuse.

You were right to call things off. I've often wondered if maybe your parents pressured you to do it, but if they did, I owe them my sincerest gratitude. You stopped me one step shy of a grave, unforgivable error.

I've moved back to my hometown, where I'm working in the fields. Not a day passes when I don't think of you. Our days together were few, but they were the best times of my entire life. And not a day passes when I don't feel regret. When I think about how that episode must have scarred your young heart, it's hard for me to sleep at night.

Akiko, I wish you a happy life. That's the only thing I can ask of you. I'm praying that you meet someone deserving of the person you are.

—Yuji Namiya

Harumi looked up and met eyes with Mr. Minazuki.

"What do you think?" he asked.

"He sounds like a good man."

He nodded in agreement.

"I think so, too. I'm sure that when things fell apart, all kinds of thoughts went through his head. He probably despised my parents and felt disillusioned by my sister's betrayal. Looking back, after three years, he could see that things had gone the way they needed to go. But he knew that realization wasn't enough. If he never apologized, my sister's heart would never be able to heal. He couldn't be sure she hadn't taken all the blame upon herself for double-crossing him, the man she loved. So he finally wrote this letter. When I read it, I understood where he was coming from and gave it to my sister. We had no reason to tell our parents."

Harumi returned the letter to its envelope. "And your sister kept this with her."

"Seems that way. When I found this in her desk after she died, my heart skipped a beat. I realized she had been single all her life because her bond to him was never truly severed. She never loved another man. Instead, she devoted everything to Marumitsuen. But why do you think she built the building here? My family had no connection to this place. My sister never told me, but my theory is that it's close to his hometown. It's not like I know his exact address, but based on conversations I've had, I've narrowed it down to this area."

Harumi nodded solemnly and sighed with admiration. She thought it was a shame they couldn't have wound up together, but she was envious of Akiko for being able to love one man so endlessly.

"She promised me she'd pull some strings up in the sky and make sure we were taken care of. I wonder if she's watching over him, too. Mind you, if he's still alive." His face was serious.

"Yeah, I wonder," Harumi said, being polite.

There was one thing she was stuck on. The man's name. Yuji Namiya. How many Namiyas could there be?

In her correspondence with Mr. Namiya, she had never learned his first name. But according to Shizuko, he was pretty far along in years by 1980. It wasn't out of the question that he was the same age as the man in Mr. Minazuki's story.

"Something the matter?" he asked her.

"No, no, I'm fine. Thanks." Harumi waved her hand in front of her face.

"So anyway, I figured, hey, my sister put her heart and soul into this place to keep it going; the least we can do is rebuild it," he concluded.

"I think that's a noble mission. You have my full support." Harumi gave him back the letter.

She saw the script on the envelope again. *Ms. Akiko Minazuki.* The hand was conspicuously different from what she had seen in the letters she received from the Namiya General Store.

It must have been a bizarre coincidence.

Harumi decided not to ruminate on it anymore.

8

Seconds after Harumi woke up, she sneezed magnificently. Shivering, she yanked the terry-cloth blanket up over her shoulders. The air-conditioning was on full blast. The night before had been so hot that she had clicked it down a few degrees colder than usual, but she forgot to turn it back before going to sleep. Her most recent read was abandoned by her pillow. Her lamp was still on from the night before.

Her clock said it was a few minutes before seven. Her alarm was set to ring then, but she almost never let it. Most days, she woke before it and switched it off.

Today was no different. She reached to click it off and rolled out of bed in a smooth motion. Rays from the summer sun sliced through her curtains. It was going to be a hot one.

She used the bathroom and went to the sink to wash up. She stood in front of the large mirror, surprised by her own reflection. She'd felt a certain lightness in her body that made her feel as if she were back in her twenties, but the face she saw in the mirror belonged to a woman at fifty-one.

Harumi looked quizzically at her reflection. She figured it had been the dream that made her body feel this way. She had a gauzy, evanescent recollection of having dreamed of being young again. And Mr. Minazuki, the director of Marumitsuen, was in the dream, too.

Since she had an inkling of what had inspired that dream, it wasn't really that bizarre. What was unfortunate was that she couldn't remember it in detail.

She looked at her face and nodded. The modest wrinkles and the slackness of her skin were a matter of course. Proof she'd seized the reins in life. Nothing to be ashamed of.

She washed her face and did her makeup, then checked a few things on her tablet over breakfast. She had bought herself a sandwich and a vegetable juice the night before. She couldn't remember the last time she cooked. Evenings, she generally ate out.

Once she was ready, she left for work, same time as always. Her car was a domestic hybrid, compact and manageable. She was sick of foreign luxury cars, which she found unnecessarily big. She drove herself to the office in Roppongi, arriving a little after half past eight.

She parked her car in the garage of the ten-story building of her office and headed toward the elevator.

"Ms. Muto, Ms. Muto!" a man's voice wailed.

She turned and saw a chubby man in a gray polo waddling after her. His face was familiar, but she couldn't place him.

"Ms. Muto, please, I beg of you, give us one more chance at the Sweets Pavilion."

"Sweets? …Oh." This man was the president of a confectionary company specializing in *manju*, a floury Japanese bun filled with bean paste.

"Give us another month. Is that in any way possible? We'll prove we have what it takes." He bowed too deeply. His thin hair was plastered across his scalp in black bands like a barcode. His head had a sheen not unlike the confectionary glimmer of one of his company's chestnut *manju*.

"Are you forgetting our agreement? If a shop ranks lowest in the polls for two consecutive months, we reserve the right to ask them to leave. It's in the contract."

"I understand that. That's why I'm here, begging you, to hold off for just one month."

"That won't be possible," retorted Harumi. "We've already secured another vendor."

She sauntered off.

"But maybe you could…" He would not relent. "We'll show you we can do it. I'm confident we can. Give us a chance. If we pull out now, our business is done for. Just give us one more chance."

Alerted to the disturbance, a security guard came over. "What seems to be the trouble?"

"This man has no business here. Kick him out."

The color of the guard's face changed. "Understood."

"No, wait, I have business here. We're business partners! Ms. Muto, wait, Ms. Muto!"

She could hear him whining until she entered the elevator lobby, and the doors closed.

The offices of Little Dog Inc. occupied the fifth and sixth floors of the building. The company had moved here nine years ago from their old office in Shinjuku. Her office was on the sixth floor.

She checked a few more things on her computer and settled in for the day. Her in-box was full of useless messages. Her spam filter was supposed to automatically sift out the trash, but there were still plenty of emails that were essentially pointless.

Responding to a handful of messages took her until past nine. She picked up the receiver and dialed an extension. The person on the other line picked up right away.

"Good morning." It was Mr. Sotojima, the executive director.

"Could you come up for a moment?"

"Absolutely."

Sotojima was there a minute later. He was wearing a short-sleeve button-up. Just like last year, they were cutting back on the air-conditioning.

Harumi told him about her encounter in the parking lot.

"That old guy? The rep was saying he talked her ear off, too. I didn't think he'd try to appeal directly to you."

"What do you mean? You told me you talked it over with them and they agreed to pack up."

"I was under that impression, too, but I guess he can't let go. It sounds like their main location isn't doing well. Things are looking pretty bad for them."

"I'm sorry to hear that, but we're a business, too."

"You're absolutely right. It's none of our concern," Sotojima replied coolly.

Two years back, a developer who was renovating a shopping mall on the coast contacted Harumi's company with a project. They had an event space and wanted to make better use of it. The original idea had been to use it for small concerts and the like, but it wasn't being used effectively.

They did some research and analysis, and they proposed turning the space into a mecca of sorts for confectionary companies. All the sweets shops and cafés scattered throughout the mall would centralize, and the rest of the space would be filled out with satellite shops of vendors from throughout Japan. This was the idea behind the Sweets Pavilion. To date, there were thirty shops and counting.

Thanks to an aggressive campaign of ads in women's magazines and television commercials, the project had been a great success. Any shop who gained a reputation here could expect to experience a huge boost in sales at its original location.

But they couldn't just set things up and walk away. If you don't change it up, people get bored. The most important thing is to garner repeat customers. Which is why they periodically changed the lineup of shops. They polled visitors at the food court and warned shops if their results were consistently unfavorable. On occasion, they asked a business to leave. This kept everyone on edge month to month. Every neighboring store was a rival.

That president of the *manju* store had his main shop in her hometown. When they were putting Sweets Pavilion together, she invited him to join on the belief that "home comes first." They were thrilled to participate. But their bestselling product was a fairly nondescript chestnut *manju*, a knob of sweet dough with a sweeter center. It wasn't good enough. In recent surveys, their shop had consistently come in last place. They were setting a poor standard for the other shops. Pity wasn't part of the equation. That was what made this business hard.

"And what about that 3-D anime?" Harumi asked. "Can we use it?"

Sotojima grimaced.

"I saw the demo reel. At a tech level, it's not there yet. It won't look good on a tiny smartphone. They said they're going to make a beta version. I'd wait till then to see it."

"That's fine; I was only curious." Harumi smiled. "Thanks. That should be good for today. Do you have any updates?"

"No, I've already emailed you about anything pressing. There was one other thing, though." Sotojima gave her a meaningful look. "About that children's home."

"That's an independent venture. It has nothing to do with the company."

"I know, but that's because I work for you. From the outside, it won't necessarily look that way."

"Did something come up?"

Sotojima worked his lips. "It appears someone contacted us about it, asking what our company plans to do with the building."

Harumi frowned and scratched the roots of her bangs.

"Crap. How'd it come to this?"

"Being president makes you an easy target. Even when you're doing something normal, it won't look that way. Please keep that in mind."

"Is that some kind of snide remark?"

"Not at all. I'm being realistic," said Sotojima with aplomb.

"Okay. That's all."

"Excuse me." With that, he left the room.

Harumi got up and stood by the window. They were only on the sixth floor. It wasn't so high up. They'd had the option to move into a higher set of units, but Harumi passed. She didn't want to get overly self-confident. But when she looked outside at the cityscape, it still reminded her how far she'd come.

The events of the past twenty years washed over her. She knew that it was more important than ever for a business to keep up with the times. Sometimes that meant the whole world had to be turned upside down.

In March 1990, to pull down absurd real estate costs, the Ministry of Finance imposed restrictions on loans for all financial institutions. This was a hard line, and it was unavoidable. Land had become so expensive that the average family man had given up on owning his own home.

Harumi was not alone in doubting whether such a stratagem would actually pull down the price of land. The media had unanimously declared the directive "a drop in the bucket," saying nothing would make prices drop overnight.

But these restrictions dealt a body blow to the economy.

The value of stocks in the Japanese market took a downward turn. Then in August, Iraq's invasion of Kuwait caused oil prices to shoot up and spurred a recession.

And eventually, the price of property did begin to fall.

There were still a few pots of gold scattered around. One-off real estate miracles. A lot of people maintained that things would turn around. It wasn't until 1992 that everyone accepted that the carnival was over.

Harumi had been briefed by her letter from Mr. Namiya and made it out in time. She knew ahead of the game that the era for flipping real estate was over, and she divested from all her investments by 1989—stocks, equity memberships, everything. She had won at Old Maid. Over the course of the Japanese asset price bubble, she had turned a profit of several hundred million yen.

By the time the world had wised up, Harumi was already putting out new feelers. The Namiya General Store had predicted the advent of an information network that would connect personal computers with portable telephones. A cellular phone in every pocket, and a computer in every home. If he was right about this, too, she could not afford to miss out.

Harumi expected that increasing computer connectivity would usher in an era the world had only dreamed of. She did her best to stay informed and up-to-date.

In 1995, as the Internet was beginning to become a fixture of their lives, Harumi hired a handful of tech majors to work for her. She set each of them up with a computer and tasked them with figuring out ways to utilize the Internet. These innovators spent entire days in front of their computers.

Office Little Dog made its first foray into web-related business designing home pages. For starters, they created a website for themselves to advertise their services. The newspaper picked them up for a feature story, and the response was superb: a steady stream of queries from companies and individuals alike who wanted to have their own home pages. This was years before the Internet was universally and constantly accessible, but the recession gave people high hopes for new modes of advertising. Jobs kept rolling in.

In the ensuing years, Office Little Dog was conspicuously successful. Web-based advertising, sales, game distribution, you name it. Everything they touched turned to gold.

At the dawn of the new millennium, Harumi began to think about branching into other areas and founded a consulting department. What motivated her was a message from an acquaintance who ran a restaurant that was unable to turn a profit, barely scraping by.

Harumi was already a federally certified small business management consultant. She assigned dedicated staff to the project and conducted a thorough analysis. Their conclusion was that advertising on its own would not suffice; the business would have to be overhauled and rebuilt on a stronger foundation. This meant a whole new menu and interior.

When the restaurant implemented their suggestions and reopened for business, it experienced unprecedented success. Three months following their reopening, it was hard to even book a table.

Harumi was convinced there was good money in consulting, but she needed to take it all the way. It was easy to pick apart the root cause of poor performance. But to make the business viable, they would need to demonstrate an ability to take drastic measures and yield results. Harumi headhunted talent. At times her team played a proactive role in product development for clients, and at times they recommended heartless layoffs.

Propped up by the twin pillars of their IT and consulting departments, the newly dubbed Little Dog Inc. continued to grow. In retrospect, her success was preternatural. Harumi became renowned as an "industry visionary." This was true to a degree, but without that letter from the Namiya General Store, things never would have gone so well. Which is why she wanted to give back, if she ever had the chance.

And along those lines, she couldn't forget everything Marumitsuen had done for her.

She heard rumors that their management had fallen into disarray that year. The rumors turned out to be true. In 2003, when Mr. Minazuki died, his eldest son kept the home running on the side, but when his transportation business fell into the red, there was little room for keeping Marumitsuen afloat.

Harumi contacted them as soon as she heard the news. As it turned out, Mr. Minazuki's eldest son was the director in name only; his vice-director, Mr. Kariya, was the real one running the show. Harumi told him to let her know if there was anything she could do and even offered to invest if necessary.

But he was not enthused. He even made a point of telling her that he preferred not to rely on others.

Frustrated, Harumi tried asking the Minazuki family directly if they would let her take over managing the home, but she got the same dismissive reaction: "Kariya is already taking care of it."

Harumi did some research on Marumitsuen and discovered that in recent years the number of full-time staff had been halved. In turn, the number of temporary employees with dubious titles was concerningly high. To make matters worse, she found no evidence that any of these people had actually worked there.

She put it all together. Following Mr. Minazuki's death, the children's home had·become involved in fraudulent activity, most likely false claims for subsidies. She suspected Kariya was the principal offender. No doubt he had refused her offer to help manage the building to keep the truth from coming out.

It became increasingly difficult to look away. She had to do something about what was happening. Harumi began to see herself as the only one who could save Marumitsuen.

9

Harumi acquired this information almost by accident. Punching a search into her newly upgraded smartphone, she stumbled upon a result that said "the Namiya General Store—One-Night Special."

The Namiya General Store... These were words Harumi would never—*could* never forget. When she clicked on the result, she was routed to a proper website. The site announced that with September 13 marking the start of the thirty-third year after his death, they were hosting a memorial service for the old owner with hopes that people who had written to him for advice would write again and tell them whether it had made a difference in their lives. They asked for people to leave their letters in the mail slot out front, between midnight and sunrise.

This was unbelievable. After so many years, she was not expecting to see that name today. And what was this about a "One-Night Special"? The site was apparently being managed by someone in his family, but beyond saying the event was being held to coincide with the old man's memorial service, it gave no other details.

At first, she suspected it must be a prank. But why would anyone bother? What payoff could there be in fooling people? How many people would even read the post?

What moved Harumi most profoundly was discovering that September 13 was the date of the old man's death. On September 13, it would be precisely thirty-two years since her contact with the Namiya General Store had been suspended.

This couldn't be a prank. She was certain the event was real. And if it was, she couldn't sit back on the sidelines. She, of all people, had to write one of these letters. It would of course be a letter of thanks.

But there was something she would have to check first. Was the Namiya General Store really still around? Was it still there? Harumi went back to the Tamuras' old house a few times a year, but she had never ventured as far as the shop.

She had an errand to run at Marumitsuen that day anyway. A meeting about transferring over the building. She could stop by the store on her way back.

The meeting, as before, was with the vice-director, Mr. Kariya.

"The Minazukis have given me full authority on this matter. As you know, it's been their policy to stay out of managing the home." His thin eyebrows twitched as he spoke.

"In that case, you might apprise them of the fiscal standing of their property. It may well change their way of thinking."

"They're regularly informed, thank you very much. That was part of our agreement when I took over."

"I see. Would you mind sharing the same information with me?"

"I'm afraid that won't be possible. It's none of your concern."

"Mr. Kariya, I need you to listen to me. As it stands, this building is going to go under."

"That's not for you to worry about. We'll get by one way or another. Safe trip home." Kariya bowed his head of slicked-back hair.

Harumi decided that was enough for today, but she had no intention of giving up. She would just have to figure out a way to persuade the Minazukis.

In the parking lot, she found her car covered with clots of mud. She spun around to see a posse of kids was peeking over a fence. They ducked down to hide their faces.

Oh dear, she sighed. *They must think I'm a bad guy.* No doubt Kariya had told them some tall tale.

She drove away without cleaning off the car. Through the rearview mirror, she saw the kids had spilled into the street, shouting "Don't come back"—or something like it.

Despite this unpleasant distraction, she had not forgotten her intention to stop by the Namiya General Store. Harumi turned the wheel, relying solely on a fading memory.

Soon she was back in a familiar scene. In those thirty some odd years, it had barely changed.

The store was just as it had been when she came by with her letters. Its sign was all but indecipherable, and the rust scabbing its shutter was painfully thick, but the structure was swathed in the warmth of an old man waiting for his granddaughter.

Harumi came to a stop, rolled down the passenger-side window, and looked out at the building. When she drove off, she drove off slowly. She thought she may as well have a look at the Tamura house, too.

After finishing work on September 12, Harumi stopped home and cracked open her laptop to draft her letter. She had meant to start sooner, but the last few days had been crazy, and she couldn't find the time. That night, she was supposed to have dinner with a client, but she told them she needed to deal with an urgent matter and asked the most trusted member of her staff to go in her stead.

Rereading and rewriting the letter again and again, she didn't finish until after nine. After that, she wrote out the text on stationery. She had a personal rule about handwriting all correspondence to important contacts.

She had a look over the final copy, checking for mistakes, and folded it into an envelope. She had purchased the stationery and the envelope especially for this occasion.

Packing took some time. It was getting to be ten when she left the house. Mindful of the speed limit, she kept her foot on the gas.

It took her just under two hours to reach the vicinity of the shop. Her plan had been to go straight there, but she had a little time left before midnight and decided to drop her bags off at the Tamura house, where she was going to spend the night.

After purchasing the house, Harumi had made good on her promise to let Hideo carry on with her life there, but Hideo hadn't lived to see the start of the twenty-first century. With the passing of her Auntie, Harumi touched up a few things and began using the house as a suburban getaway. This was the closest she had to a childhood home. She loved how green it was around there.

The last few years, she had been going only once every month or two. The refrigerator was empty, save for condiments and whatever was in the freezer.

The area around the house had only a smattering of streetlights. It was usually too dark to see beyond the headlights of her car this late into the night. But in the moonlight, she spotted her old house from a distance.

There was nobody in sight. They had a garage, but she parked on the street. Shouldering a tote bag with her change of clothes and makeup, she stepped out into the night. The big round moon was beaming in the sky.

She walked under the gate and unlocked the front door, opening it to the smell of an air freshener. The fragrant pod was sitting on the shoe cabinet. She had put it there herself last time she came by. She set her keys beside it.

She felt her way along the wall until she found the light switch, then took off her shoes and stepped up into the house. There were slippers, but she rarely bothered wearing them. She went down the hall to the door at the end, leading into the bedroom.

She opened the door to the bedroom and again felt the wall for the switch, but she stopped before she found it. Something was out of place. No, it was more as if she smelled something out of place. A faint but foreign smell that did not belong in her bedroom.

Sensing danger, she motioned to turn, but something grabbed her hand before she could flick the lights on. It tugged her arm and pressed something over her mouth. She didn't even have a chance to scream.

"Easy, now. Keep quiet, and we won't hurt you." The man was behind her. She couldn't see his face.

Harumi's mind went blank. Why was this man in her house? What was he doing here? Why did this have to happen to her? A flurry of questions spun around her.

She felt compelled to resist, but her body wouldn't move. It was as if her nerves were paralyzed.

"Hey, I saw some towels in the bathroom. Grab me a few." The man was yelling, but nobody responded. He repeated himself, clearly vexed. "I need those towels! Stat!"

She sensed another shadow tripping through the darkness. Someone else was here.

Harumi breathed fiercely through her nose. Her heartbeat was still violent, but gradually, her decision-making skills were returning. She realized what was pressed over her mouth was a hand in a latex glove.

"Aw, come on," whispered yet another man, off to the side behind her.

"Too late now," barked the man restraining her. "Come on, look through that bag. There's probably a wallet in there or something."

The bag was pulled away from her. She heard someone fishing through her things. "Got it," a voice finally confirmed.

"How much?"

"Only twenty, thirty thousand, and a bunch of random point cards."

The man sighed by Harumi's ear. "That's it? Whatever. Just pull out the cash. Those cards aren't good for anything."

"What about the wallet? It's from a good brand."

"It's no good if it's broken in. The bag's pretty new; it'll come with us."

Footsteps approached them. "Are these okay?" The voice was young, like the others.

"All right. Use one as a blindfold. Tie it tight behind her head so that it won't come loose."

She felt him hesitate for an instant, but a second later, true to his word, a towel was pulled tight over her eyes. It smelled a little bit like laundry detergent. The one she always used.

The towel was tied tight at her neck. This was not a knot you could wiggle out of.

Next, they made her sit down at the dining room table and tied both of her wrists behind her to the backrest and bound her ankles to the legs of the chair. All the while, the gloved hand remained pressed into her face.

"We'd like to have a little talk with you," said the leader, the one with his hand over her mouth. "I'm going to take my hand away, but you'd better not make a racket. Trust me, you don't want to see our weapons. If you start yelling, we'll kill you. But we don't want it to come to that. Talk nice in a quiet voice, and you won't be harmed. Nod if you promise you'll behave."

Having no reason to disobey, Harumi nodded. The hand let go of her face.

"So, as you have probably already guessed, we're burglars. We thought the house was empty. We weren't planning on you showing up, and we weren't planning on tying you up like this, either. No hard feelings."

Speechless, Harumi sighed. This late in the game, saying "no hard feelings" was an empty pleasantry. Meaningless.

And yet, she found it in her heart to see where they were coming from. Instinctively, she knew these guys weren't true villains.

"Once we've gotten what we came for, we're out. But we're not ready to leave yet, 'cause we haven't found anything worth taking. Which brings us here. We need your valuables. Where do you keep them? We're not picky. Trinkets, honestly anything. Speak up."

Harumi was catching her breath. "There's nothing...here."

She heard him snort.

"Yeah, right. We looked you up. Don't try to fool us."

"I mean it." Harumi shook her head. "If you looked me up, you'd know that. I don't stay here often. That's why there's no money, nothing valuable around."

"You can say that, but there's gotta be something." His voice was strained. "Think harder. You'll come up with something. We can wait until you do. You wouldn't like that, would you?"

He got that right, but Harumi had nothing to tell him. There was nothing valuable in the whole house. The few heirlooms she inherited from Hideo were at her apartment in the city.

"There's an alcove in the next room, the room with the tatami. The bowl set up there came from a famous studio."

"We got the bowl. And the calligraphy scroll on the wall behind it. What else you got?"

Hideo had told her the bowl was real, but the scroll was screen printed, a fake. Harumi figured she had better not tell them.

"Did you see the bedroom upstairs? The smaller one."

"We poked around, didn't see anything good."

"Did you check the drawers in the dresser? The second one down has a false bottom, and the lower half is full of jewelry. Did you see that?"

The man didn't answer her. He seemed to be gesturing to his friends.

"Go check," he ordered. One of them ambled upstairs.

The dresser had belonged to Hideo, and its antique design had made it hard to part with. It was true that there was jewelry in the secret drawer, but it wasn't Harumi's. They were accessories that Hideo's daughter, Kimiko, had bought herself when she was single. Harumi had never properly gone through them, but she suspected there was nothing valuable. If there had been, Kimiko would have taken it when she got married.

"Why did you pick me…my house to rob?" Harumi asked them.

The leader seemed to shrug. "Worked out that way."

"Then why'd you bother to look me up? You must have had a reason."

"Shut the hell up. It doesn't matter."

"It matters to me."

"No, it doesn't. Zip it."

Harumi listened to him. She knew not to provoke an adversary.

The awkward silence was finally broken by the words "Do you mind if I ask a question?" It wasn't the leader who said it. She was not expecting something so polite.

"Dude," spat the leader. "What are you saying?"

"Come on, man. I really want to see what she says."

"Forget it."

"What is it?" Harumi said. "Ask me anything."

Someone clucked melodramatically. It sounded like the leader.

"Are you really gonna make it a hotel?"

"Make what?"

"I heard you're going to tear down Marumitsuen and put up a love hotel."

That was a name she wasn't expecting to hear. She felt caught. Kariya must have sent them.

"I'll do nothing of the sort. I'm hoping to renovate the building and take it over, as a children's home."

"Everybody knows that's just a front," the leader interrupted. "Your company makes its money by giving makeovers to dying businesses. Like the business hotel you turned into a love hotel."

"We took that job, true, but it has nothing to do with this. I'm funding the Marumitsuen project myself."

"Liar."

"I'm not lying. I hesitate to add this, but I would never build a love hotel out there anyway. No one would come. I'm no idiot. Trust me. I'm a friend of the voiceless, the powerless."

"Really?"

"Dude, she's obviously lying. Don't listen to her. Friend of the voiceless? Listen to that shit. She'd part with anything that doesn't turn a profit."

Footsteps thumped down the stairs.

"What took you so long? What were you doing up there?"

"I couldn't figure out the false bottom. But then I got it. Look at all this stuff."

The costume jewelry jingled. He'd apparently brought down the entire drawer.

The other two were quiet. They were probably calculating how much the hoard of trifles could possibly be worth. Not that they knew any better.

"All right, take it," someone ordered. "It's better than nothing. Let's put it in the bag and scram."

Harumi heard fabric against fabric and a zipper pulled open and shut. They were adding the accessories to the rest of their loot.

"What should we do about her?" asked the man who broached the question about Marumitsuen.

After a beat, the leader said, "Get the duct tape. We don't want her causing a ruckus."

She heard tape tearing, then felt it strapped across her face.

"We can't just leave her like this. If no one comes and finds her, she'll starve to death."

There was another beat. The leader generally got the last word.

"Once we're a safe distance away, we'll call her company and say their president is bound and gagged. That solves things."

"What if she has to go?"

"She can hold it."

"Do you think you can hold it?" They were asking Harumi.

She nodded. As a matter of fact, she didn't have to go yet. But even if they'd offered to bring her to the bathroom, she would have refused, if it meant having them out a second sooner.

"All right, let's get out of here," he commanded. "Don't forget anything."

She felt the three of them leave the room. Their footsteps plodded down the hall and out the front door.

A little later, she heard their voices again. She made out the words *car keys*.

Harumi remembered she'd left them on the shoe cabinet.

"Shit," she mouthed through the tape and bit her lip. Her handbag was on the front seat of the car parked in the street. She'd pulled it from her tote bag on her way out of the car.

The wallet inside her tote bag was her backup. Her actual wallet was in her handbag. It had at least two hundred thousand yen in cash, not to mention all her credit cards and debit cards.

Thing is, the wallet wasn't what was bothering her. She'd be happy if that was all they took. But she doubted they'd be so focused. They were in a rush and would probably make off with the handbag without even looking inside.

If they had, they would have found her letter to the Namiya General Store. This she could not let them take.

But what difference would it make? Even if they left behind the letter, she would still be stuck, until morning at the earliest. And the "One-Night Special" at the shop would be over at the crack of dawn.

She had only wanted to say thank you. To tell him that thanks to him, she had become a person of consequence, and that she planned to use her high position to make a difference in the world. The letter was her chance to say so.

But then this had to happen. Why her? What did she ever do wrong? She hardly felt like she deserved it. All she'd done was take this as far as she could, and in good conscience.

The leader's words came back to her.

Friend of the voiceless? Listen to that shit. She'd part with anything that doesn't turn a profit.

That had been a blow. When had she ever done anything like that?

But then she remembered the bawling face of the president of the *manju* company.

Harumi blew air through her nose. Blindfolded and bound to the chair as she was, she smiled ruefully.

She had tried so hard and gotten so far, but maybe she had been a little too pragmatic. This wasn't comeuppance. No, it was a warning that she'd do well to open up her heart a little.

Maybe she would save the *manju*-head after all.

10

There was no way to tell, but dawn seemed to be getting close. Atsuya looked down at a blank sheet of stationery.

"You think it's really possible?"

"What? Think what's possible?" asked Shota.

"You know," he huffed. "That this house could be connected to the past, and these letters could somehow make it here. And if we put a letter in the milk crate, it winds up traveling across time."

"Did this only now occur to you?" Shota looked puzzled. "Yeah, it's really happening. How else would we have gone back and forth with all these people?"

"It's definitely weird, though," concurred Kohei. "It's gotta have something to do with the 'One-Night Special' being tonight."

"Be right back." Atsuya got up with the paper in his hand.

"Where are you going?" Shota called out.

"To check. I'm gonna try it out."

Atsuya went out through the back door and closed it tight behind him. He proceeded down the alley and around to the front of the shop, whereupon he folded up the paper and slipped it through the mail slot. He came around back again and went through the house out into the storefront and looked into the cardboard box set up against the shutter. The piece of folded stationery wasn't there.

"Just as I thought," said Shota triumphantly. "If you put something in the mail slot now, it lands in the shop thirty-two years back. That's what's behind the 'One-Night Special.' All this time, we've been on the other side of it."

"And once it's morning here, thirty-two years back...?" asked Atsuya.

"The old man dies. The guy who used to own the store."

"That's gotta be it." Atsuya let out a long, belabored breath. It was truly bizarre, but there was no other explanation.

"What happened to that kid?" wondered Kohei. Atsuya and Shota both looked at him. He flinched. "You know, Dubious Doggy. I wonder if our letter helped her."

"Who knows?" said Atsuya. "She probably didn't believe us."

"It must have sounded shady, any way you slice it." Shota scratched his head.

When the three guys read the third letter from her, they had to act—fast. Some dodgy guy was tricking her, trying to use her. And then they found out she had lived at Marumitsuen! They had to do something to save her—no, not just save her; they had to do something that would make her successful.

The three of them decided they would tip her off on the future. The Japanese price asset bubble was just around the corner, at the end of the '80s. They could advise her on how to capitalize on what was coming.

They looked it up on their smartphones and crafted their letter to Dubious Doggy, making it like a prediction. They threw in a few hints on what to do after the bubble burst. It was hard not using the word *Internet*.

It was even harder deciding whether to warn her about accidents and disasters. There were some big ones coming—the Kobe earthquake in 1995 and the Tohoku earthquake in 2011.

But ultimately, they decided not mention them. Just like how they decided not to tell Floundering Musician about the fire. They knew better than to mess with matters of life and death.

"It's so weird that there's all these connections to Marumitsuen," Shota commented. "What's that all about? Could it be just a coincidence?"

Atsuya had been wondering about that, too. That would be a hell of a coincidence. After all, Marumitsuen was why the three of them were here tonight.

Shota was the one who broke the news that their childhood home was in dire straits at the beginning of last month. As usual, Shota and Atsuya and Kohei were sharing a few drinks, but not at the pub or anything. They bought cans of beer and *chuhai*, a mix of *shochu* and carbonated water, at the discount liquor store and cracked them open in the park.

"I heard some lady CEO is really gouging them. She says she's gonna renovate it. I bet she's full of shit."

Shota had been laid off by a big-box electronics retailer, currently getting by with shifts at a convenience store. It wasn't far from Marumitsuen, and he still went by to visit from time to time. As a side note, he lost his job only because of mass layoffs at the company.

"Shit, man, I was hoping if I wound up homeless, I could live there," Kohei whined.

He was unemployed. His job as an auto mechanic fell through

when the company went bankrupt. He was living in a company dorm, but he could be kicked out any day.

Atsuya was in between jobs, too. Up until a couple of months ago, he had been working at a parts factory. During his time there, they got an order for a new part from a new company. The dimensions were totally different from any other orders in the past. He checked and double-checked, but that was what it said, so he went along with the design. As it turned out, it was a mistake. Their contact, a new hire at the new company, had mixed up his units. The result was a useless batch of rejects, but somehow, they held Atsuya responsible. They said he didn't check hard enough.

This sort of thing happened to them all the time: Their company can't talk back to the parent company. Their boss doesn't stick up for them. Whenever there's trouble, the blame falls to the bottom of the ranks and lands on people like Atsuya.

He'd lost his temper. "I'm done," he announced and turned his back on the job and the factory.

He had almost no savings. When he checked his balance, it was worse than he thought. He was already two months behind on rent.

No matter how much these three guys cared about Marumitsuen, they were in no position to help. The most they could do was bad-mouth and curse at the woman trying to buy the building.

Atsuya couldn't remember whose idea it had been. Maybe it was his.

At the very least, he remembered clenching his fists, proclaiming, "Let's get her. Even Mother Mary would forgive us for stealing money from that bitch."

Shota and Kohei thrust their fists in the air. They were pumped.

They were all the same age, always together through middle school and high school. As students, they had done a whole slew of bad things. They'd shoplifted, stolen handbags, and broken into vending machines. They favored nonviolent acts of theft. They still thought it was a miracle that they were almost never caught. They had their theories—never hit the same spot twice, always change up your technique—and they didn't do anything taboo.

Just once, they robbed somebody's house while the owners were out of town. It was their third year of high school. They'd put a pause on their job hunt, but they really wanted new clothes. Their target was the richest kid in their school. They figured out the day that he was leaving with his family on vacation, thoroughly checked for security devices, and made their move. No part of them considered what would happen if they failed. They came out with about thirty thousand yen, just sitting in a random drawer. They were satisfied and split. The best part was that no one seemed to notice. This game was pretty fun.

They stopped messing around once they were out of high school and turned over a new leaf. In the eyes of the law, they were adults. If they got arrested, their names would wind up in the paper.

But this was different. No one spoke out against the plan. All of them were sick and tired of their circumstances and wanted to take it out on someone. To be honest, Atsuya wasn't shaken up about what was happening to Marumitsuen. The old director was a good man, but this Kariya guy was an asshole. Once he took over, the whole operation went to shit.

Shota was the one who scouted out the house.

When they met up a few days after their first discussion, he started off with "Good news." He had a twinkle in his eye. "I found the second home of the CEO. After I heard she was coming to Marumitsuen, I staked out nearby on my scooter. I followed her back and figured out the address of her house. It's only, like, twenty minutes from the children's home. It's just a little cottage, a sitting duck. Should be simple getting in. According to her neighbors, she's only there, like, once a month. Oh, don't worry; it's not like I actually asked someone in the neighborhood face-to-face."

As long as Shota was right, this was great news. The only problem was whether there was anything worth stealing.

"There's gotta be," Shota argued. "This lady wears designer goods from head to toe. That second home is probably where she keeps her gems. I bet it's full of expensive vases and paintings."

"Damn right," said Atsuya and Kohei.

In actuality, they had no clue what rich people had in their houses. They were going off the mansions of impossible millionaires in anime and dramas. All conjecture.

They planned to do the job on September 12. The date had no significance. Shota was off that day, but he had plenty of days off. It was just a coincidence.

Kohei had procured the getaway car. He used some tricks from his time as a mechanic, but he was embarrassed that he only knew how to steal the old ones.

A little past eleven, the three men made their entry. They busted the glass door on the garden side and spun open the latch, a classic move, although they first made a big star on the glass with duct tape to keep the breaking glass from shattering and going everywhere. Or worse, making a clamor.

As predicted, there was no one home, and the whole house was theirs for the taking. They were amped up and ready to grab anything and everything. But there was nothing to lay their hands on. They had swung—and missed.

They searched every corner of the house; no dice. For the second home of a CEO who supposedly decked herself out in designer goods, it was surprisingly plebian. *That's weird*, thought Shota, cocking his head. *There has to be something somewhere.*

But there wasn't.

That was when they heard a car stop right outside the house.

They switched off their flashlights in a start. Then they heard the key turn at the front door. Atsuya's balls ducked up into his stomach. That lady CEO, of all the nights she could have come. He was going to tell Shota that this wasn't what he promised, but it was too late to complain.

Lights went on at the entrance and the front hall. Footsteps were coming closer. Atsuya braced himself.

11

"Hey, Shota," said Atsuya. "How'd you find this dump anyway? You said you stumbled on it when you came to check things out. What were you doing all the way out here?"

"Yeah, well, it wasn't exactly an accident."

"It wasn't, huh? Then what was it?"

"Stop glaring at me. It wasn't anything, okay? Remember how I said I followed her home on my scooter? On the way, she came and stopped out front of the store."

"Stopped? For what?"

"How should I know? For some reason, she was staring up at the sign. She got me wondering, so after I followed her home, I swung back here to see for myself. I figured it would come in handy if we had to hide, so I made a mental note of where it was."

"But your perfect hideout turned out to be a frigging time machine."

Shota shrugged. "That pretty much sums it up."

Atsuya crossed his arms and groaned. He turned his eyes on the bag against the wall.

"What's up with that lady CEO? What's her name again?"

"Something Muto. Haruko? Haruko Muto?" Shota couldn't remember, either.

Atsuya reached for the bag, undid the zipper, and pulled out a handbag. If he hadn't noticed the car key left on the shoe cabinet by the front door, they would have missed it. When he opened up the passenger-side door and saw the handbag sitting on the seat, he'd stuffed it in the duffel, without another thought.

He opened it. Just under the clasp was a slender navy wallet. At least two hundred thousand yen in cash. That alone redeemed the burglary. He couldn't care less about the credit and debit cards.

He found her driver's license, which said *Harumi Muto*. Based on her picture, she was pretty hot. Shota had said she was over fifty, but she certainly didn't look it.

Now Shota was staring at Atsuya. His eyes were a little bloodshot, probably from lack of sleep.

"What's wrong?" asked Atsuya.

"This… This was in the handbag."

Shota was holding out an envelope.

"What's that? What's wrong?"

He showed Atsuya the face of the envelope. When Atsuya saw what it said, he looked like his heart was about to jump from his mouth.

To the Namiya General Store, it said.

To the Namiya General Store,

> *When I heard about your "One-Night Special" on the Internet, I asked myself if this was really happening. But I'm writing you this letter because I'm going to believe that it's true.*

> *I wonder if you remember me. I wrote you a letter in the summer of '80 as "Dubious Doggy." At the time, I was barely out of high*

school, a real neophyte. In my letter to you, I declared I was going to make a living as a hostess but didn't know how to tell my friends and family. You put me in my place. You slapped me silly.

But I was young and disagreed with your advice. I described my upbringing and my circumstances, and I insisted that to give back, this was the only way. It must have been exhausting to put up with such a stubborn little girl.

You could have easily brushed me off and told me to do as I pleased, but instead you gave me valuable advice and steered me in the right direction. And not in some general direction, but on a very specific trajectory. You told me what to learn and when to know it by. The games to play, and which cards I should toss or hold. This was no usual advice. It was a prophesy.

I did what you instructed me to do. To be honest, I had my doubts at first, but once I saw the world begin to change in accordance to your predictions, I let go of my misgivings.

I can't help wondering where it came from. How did you predict the Japanese asset price bubble and its demise? How did you foresee the coming of the Internet?

But maybe there's no sense in asking all that now. An answer wouldn't change the way things played out.

I guess my message for you is pretty simple.

Thank you, Mr. Namiya.

I thank you from the bottom of my heart. If I had never received your advice, I would never have made it to where I am today. In a worst-case scenario, I could even have wound up in the gutter. I will remain indebted to you for as long as I live. I'm frustrated at having no way to return your kindness, but I hope you can accept this mod-

est letter as a substitute. I am going to pay it forward as best I can and help others however I am able.

According to the website, this coincides with your thirty-third memorial service. It's been thirty-two years since I wrote you for advice. It makes me emotional to consider that I may have been your last. I believe it was fate.

May you rest in peace, Mr. Namiya.

—*Doubtless Doggy*

Atsuya held his head in his hands. He felt as if his brains were curdling. He wanted to tell the others how he felt. No words would come out of his mouth.

The other two hugged their knees, equally perplexed. Shota was staring off into space.

How could this be? It was only a little while ago that they had steered the aspiring hostess on a different route, tipping her off on the future. By all accounts, she was successful. But thirty-two years after the fact, Atsuya and his friends busted into her house...

"Something's up," muttered Atsuya.

Shota looked up. "Up with what?"

"I mean…like, look. Something must be linking Marumitsuen to the Namiya General Store. An invisible thread, or something. It's like someone in the sky is tugging on the strings."

Shota looked at the ceiling. "Maybe, yeah."

"Ack!" Kohei was looking at the back door.

The door was ajar. Morning light was filtering in. The night was over.

"Looks like this letter's never gonna make it to the Namiya General Store."

"That's all right. I mean, this one's for us. Right, Atsuya?" said

Shota. "We're the ones she's thanking. She tells us she's grateful to us. *Us*, of all people. This crew of scumbags."

Atsuya looked into his eyes, rimmed red with tears.

"I believe her. You know? When I asked, 'You gonna turn the building into a love hotel?' She said no way. She wasn't lying. Dubious Doggy would never lie to us."

Atsuya felt the same. He nodded.

"So whatta we do now?" asked Kohei.

"We're going back." Atsuya stood up. "Back to her house. To put back what we stole."

"We gotta untie her," Shota continued. "And take off the blindfold, and the duct tape."

"Yeah."

"Then what? Run?" Kohei asked.

Atsuya shook his head. "We won't run. We'll wait for the police."

Shota and Kohei showed no signs of protest.

Kohei muttered "We're going to jail" and drooped his shoulders.

"Maybe they'll give us parole for turning ourselves in," said Shota, before turning to Atsuya. "But that's only the beginning of it. You think it's hard to find work now? Just wait. What'll we do?"

Atsuya shook his head again. "I dunno. But I do know one thing. I'm done messing with other people's stuff."

Shota and Kohei nodded in silence.

They got their things together and went out the back door. The sun was bright. They could hear sparrows chirping.

The milk crate caught Atsuya's eye. How many times had they opened and shut that thing that night? It made him sad to think he'd never handle it again.

He popped the lid open one more time. Inside, he found a letter.

Shota and Kohei were halfway down the alley.

"Hey! Look what I found," he yelled, waving the letter.

The front of the letter said *To John/Jane Doe* in fountain pen. The handwriting was beautiful.

He opened the envelope and pulled out the pages inside.

> *What follows is an answer to whoever sent me the blank letter. If this does not concern you, please put it back where you found it.*

Atsuya gulped. He had been the one who slipped the blank sheet of paper through the mail slot. This letter was for him. An answer. Written by none other than the real Mr. Namiya.

Here's what it said:

Dear John/Jane Doe,

It took all my brainpower to understand why you would bother to send me a blank sheet of paper. I'm an old man, after all. But I knew this had to be something extraordinary. I could spare no effort in crafting my response.

My mind isn't what it used to be, but I whipped it into shape, and I think I have finally managed to parse things out. This blank sheet symbolizes the absence of a map.

Compare the people who write to me as lost, astray. In most cases, they have a map but just won't look at it, or don't know how to find their own location.

But my guess is neither applies to you. Your map has yet to be drawn. Which makes it impossible to decide where you're going, much less how you're going to get there.

Faced with a blank map, who wouldn't feel lost? It would puzzle anyone.

But try this on for size. A blank map means you can fill it in however you like. It's entirely up to you. Everything is open; the possibilities are limitless. It's a beautiful thing. I can only hope this helps you find a way to start believing in yourself, and to move through life with no regrets.

I thought I would never get to answer another letter. It gives me great pleasure to end on such a thorny riddle.

—Namiya General Store

Atsuya looked up from the page of paper. He met the gazes of the other two. Their eyes were twinkling.

He was certain his eyes were twinkling, too.